TERROR TALES OF NORTHWEST ENGLAND

TERROR TALES OF NORTHWEST ENGLAND

Edited by

PAUL FINCH

First published in 2019 by Telos Publishing,
139 Whitstable Road, Canterbury, Kent CT2 8EQ,
United Kingdom.

www.telos.co.uk

ISBN: 978-1-84583-133-2

Telos Publishing Ltd values feedback. Please e-mail any comments you might have about this book to:
feedback@telos.co.uk

Cover: Neil Williams

British Library Cataloguing in Publication Data.
A catalogue record for this book is available from the British Library.

TABLE OF CONTENTS

COPYRIGHT INFORMATION

NORMAL BONES
Jason Gould

Have you heard the one about the man who walked into a theatre with all the wrong bones? Stop me if you've heard it. No? It doesn't sound familiar? All right, let me tell it to you now.

First, I should explain that phrase – the wrong bones. You see, to make people laugh, you need funny bones. At least, that's what they say. And if you're not one of those people – if you have dull, boring, humourless bones – then you're never going to have them rolling in the aisles. It's another way of saying you need to be made from the right stuff.

Most hopefuls nowadays tend to be made from normal stuff, normal bones. Yet they believe otherwise. They walk out on stage, they grip the microphone, they race through their set – the gags, the witty observations, the putdowns – and at the end they take their bow, despite the grim absence of laughter. And they put themselves through it the next night and the next. And each night they fail to realise that the feet they're standing on, shaking and trembling in the spotlight, and the knees that feel like water, and the white-knuckles wrapped around that microphone – they fail to realise how all these bones, these many bones of which they are made, they are each of the incorrect type.

Every year I see normal bones get up on stage in bars and theatres and on the wind-swept piers of this town.

Take Jerry Van Day, for example – the man I'd like to tell you about. And the time he walked into a theatre with all the wrong bones ...

'Why would I put you on my stage?' said the big man in the big chair. 'Why would I take that risk?'

It had taken Jerry less than five minutes to realise that

Butterfield hadn't changed. He still dressed like a banker in that three-piece pinstripe suit, still slouched in his chair with his eyelids half-closed, as if he'd spent the morning negotiating deals with promoters and agents, followed by a wine-soaked lunch rubbing shoulders with local dignitaries. Jerry knew from bitter experience that Butterfield slid down in his seat because it was the perfect position from which to destroy the dream. And it wasn't just Butterfield who looked down his nose at Jerry. Every theatre, nightclub and live-space promoter Jerry had ever met had exhibited some kind of tell-tale body language the moment Jerry entered the room. Business types seldom understood people of creativity and vision.

Jerry grew more despondent as the conversation played out, as it had played out at each of Butterfield's former clubs. The difference was that the scene of Jerry's humiliation today did not look out over the wine bars, music venues and live art establishments of gentrified Manchester. From the window behind Butterfield you did not look down upon lampposts and bus shelters covered in flyers for bands nobody had heard of, DJs the popularity of which would rise and fall within a single weekend, and, worst of all to Jerry, the endless supply of avant-garde comedians who would bring down the house with tales of loss, inequality and existentialist angst, all without delivering a single joke or punchline. Instead, the office into which Jerry had been summoned, after being made to wait two hours in the cold foyer downstairs, looked through its second-storey window onto the disembodied head of a clown, nodding gently on the breeze behind Butterfield's left shoulder.

Despite its bulbous cheeks, wide grin and tiny bowler hat, the fibre-glass clown gave off an odd sense of melancholia. Like the other illuminations the clown outside Butterfield's window would not be switched on until dusk. Perhaps it was that absence of technicolour that made it seem sad, hanging against the grey Blackpool sky as gulls wheeled and screamed and spray blew in across the promenade from the wild Irish sea. Once they flicked the switch the face outside would be animated and happy. Entertainers always lacked life before the curtain.

And this town, Jerry believed, was the spiritual home to all entertainers. Great comedic talent had gravitated toward this town since the days of music hall. You could see it everywhere: the absurdity of life caught in the gaze of Laurel and Hardy at the entrance to the wax museum; handprints of the famous sunk into the pavement along the Golden Mile; and in theatres all over town, in foyers and auditoriums in gilded, ornate frames, the black and white portraits of dead comedians keeping watch from the grave, laughing, forever laughing ...

'Renovation isn't cheap,' said Butterfield. 'Especially in Blackpool. You'll see an abandoned theatre on every corner.'

'You've saved this place,' said Jerry, hoping to play the other man's ego. 'It looks fantastic.'

'At a cost.' Butterfield raised himself up into a more business-like position at the mention of money. 'Some people would like nothing more than to see this place fail.'

Butterfield stopped, distressed, it would seem, at the thought of potential ruin. He looked Jerry up and down, as if attempting to judge whether the man before him was a funny man, or simply a man.

'I've booked a New Talent night once a month,' said Butterfield. 'It won't make much but it's better than the place standing empty on a Wednesday. Ask Josie to book you in.'

'I was hoping –'

'And ask her to show you round. See what we've done with the place.'

'I was hoping for a show,' said Jerry. 'Maybe a run.'

'Just make them laugh,' said Butterfield. 'Show me you've got what it takes.'

While Josie input his details into the computer, Jerry stood outside Butterfield's office and called Collette. The phone rang and rang. He'd got the gig – the sole reason he'd driven from Manchester to Blackpool that morning – and now he needed to speak urgently with his assistant.

The phone continued to ring and Jerry wandered with it

pressed against his ear. He pushed through several heavy wooden doors, each fitted with padded kick-boards and leatherette finger-pads to preserve the wood. He strolled deeper into the heart of the refurbished building, increasingly agitated at Collette's inability - or reluctance - to pick up.

Soon, Jerry was lost, his only means of orientation the auditorium below, and the sound of the audience laughing at the matinee.

Planning not if but when his assistant would be dismissed, Jerry disconnected Collette's number and immediately called it again. As the device dialled he looked around.

He found himself in a long dimly lit corridor somewhere in the labyrinth of corridors at the top of the theatre. The embossed wallpaper depicted a garden scene: violet flowers that seemed to lure the light and trap it inside their fat drooping heads. The air smelt old, as if the final door he'd passed through had swung shut years before and not been re-opened.

Entering the previously undisturbed atmosphere hit him like an act of trespass. It reminded Jerry of the first time he'd walked on stage. Suddenly - like then - he felt he did not belong, as if he was about to be unmasked as some kind of charlatan.

Along each wall hung black and white portrait photographs of singers, comedians and veterans of music hall and variety. They had each, Jerry assumed, earned their place on these walls by bringing down the house, before the curtain had fallen on the theatre's golden age and the rats and the pigeons moved in.

Slowly he walked between the famous faces. Some he recognised - Stanley Baxter, George Formby, Hilda Baker - but others he was unable to name. Jerry knew show business history the way Butterfield knew how to make cash, but most of these faces did not look familiar. They would have had their fifteen minutes then walked off stage and into oblivion. Except up here they could always stay famous.

One photograph in particular caused Jerry to stop. At first he had no idea why he had been attracted by this picture. It was nothing but the face of an old comedian hanging on the wall of an old theatre.

The other performers all appeared intense and somewhat serious in their art, not just the singers and actors but the comedians too. The chap in the photograph, however, looked different.

He was funny. It was simple as that. He possessed that innate, indefinable quality that made you want to laugh. Jerry imagined this fellow standing centre-stage in absolute silence, staring at the audience, simply staring, saying nothing, not a single word, moving not a muscle (apart perhaps for an eyebrow), and yet reducing the audience to tears.

It was odd that Jerry could not put a name to the face. Fortunately, the picture carried an inscription:

Arthur Beckett
1893 - 1955
'The King of Blackpool'
I Can See You!

The portrait had faded as if it had hung for decades in direct sunlight. Perhaps it had been the centrepiece in the foyer downstairs, at the foot of the grand staircase, caught by the sun as it sank into the sea in the evening. Too much exposure had made everything in the photograph part of everything else. The wide smile on the dead comedian's face, the hand-rolled cheroot in the corner of his mouth, the Brylcreem in the fine, neatly parted hair - all of it had bled into the dressing room mirror before which Arthur Beckett had been seated for his moment of posterity.

Mesmerised, Jerry stared through the glass at Arthur Beckett (or did Arthur Beckett stare through the glass at Jerry?). He wondered if Arthur had been the star of the Golden Mile. Had he made them roll in the aisles? Had he delivered his catchphrase, which Jerry assumed to be '*I can see you!*' until they stamped their feet and demanded an encore?

In short, had Arthur Beckett had it in him? Looking at Arthur's dark deep eyes and delicately raised eyebrow, Jerry thought the comedian behind the glass might be asking the same question of the comedian in front of it.

'What do you want, Jerry?'

The voice was cracked, faraway, as if the speaker had been disturbed from sleep.

He realised it was Collette.

'At last,' he said, turning away from the framed photograph. 'Where have you been?'

'I was sleeping.'

'You won't believe it, but I got the show.'

'Oh,' she said. 'Good.'

'You don't sound pleased.'

'I'm pleased. You got what you wanted.'

'You should see this place, Collette. It's amazing.'

'*The Palace*?'

'Not just the theatre, the town. Blackpool. It's incredible. It's like ... nowhere on Earth.'

'I know.'

He detected an unhappy note in her voice.

'Are you okay?'

'I was sleeping when you called. I didn't feel too good.'

'What's wrong?'

'I was worried,' she said. 'About you.'

'Why?'

'I was sitting here, in my flat, thinking about Blackpool. And suddenly I felt worried.'

'Have you taken your medication?'

The phone went quiet.

'Your medication,' he said. 'Have you taken it?'

'I don't remember.'

'I want you on the next train to Blackpool.'

'I can't come to Blackpool.'

'Why?'

'I told you, I had a bad feeling about the place. Still have. In fact, it's worse now you've called.'

'I'm on stage in two days. I need material.'

'You can't expect me to write a new routine in two days.'

'Five minutes, that's all I need. Ten if they like me.'

She was silent. He knew her silence to be a sign she was not up for the challenge. He wondered if Arthur Beckett had experienced similar problems with whoever had written his jokes.

'Look, Collette, it's easy. Find some funny words. String those funny words into a funny sentence. And repeat, until I have an act.'

She did not reply.

In the auditorium below, the performance began to peak. For a pre-season weekday the atmosphere sounded electric.

'What name should I put on the booking form?' she said.

'What?'

'After Manchester you said you wouldn't use Jerry Van Day.'

She was right. He had said that. He had been punching the wall backstage at the time, the heckling still loud in his ears.

'Don't put Jerry Van Day,' he said. 'Whatever you do, do not put Jerry Van Day.'

'So who do you want to be?'

Jerry turned back to the framed photograph of Arthur Beckett, and reread the inscription.

'The King of Blackpool. Tell them to put me on the bill as The King of Blackpool.'

Downstairs, the house erupted.

The computer in Josie's office refused to accept Jerry's booking. She hammered at the keyboard but gave up and handed Jerry a pen and paper. He filled in the form but when he arrived at the box entitled STAGE NAME, the pen refused to write. He shook it - and again, more vigorously - but the ink did not want to flow.

'I shouldn't worry about it,' said Josie, handing him a replacement pen. 'Strange things happen here all the time. If you ask me the place didn't want to be re-opened.'

'Seems popular,' said Jerry. 'Whoever was on stage this afternoon brought down the house.'

Butterfield's assistant looked confused.

'The matinee,' said Jerry. 'I heard it from upstairs.'
'Matinee? We don't do a matinee.'

If this story was a joke, if I was telling it on stage - and I've told many jokes on stage - the part you have already heard would have been the setup. It's what we in the trade refer to as, the '*in*'. It's the part at the beginning of the gag, before the middle section and punchline. In the good old days, I was master of the setup. I could find an '*in*' to anything - any subject, any crowd. Even the harshest critic at the *Evening Standard* had to admit I had the best opening lines.

Now, it's not for me to go around shattering illusions - though I don't have much else to do nowadays - but talent does not come easy to everyone. The newcomer, the fame-hungry, the yearning, bright-eyed hopeful desperate to put a grin on every face in the audience - he or she will tell you that wit and humour and rib-tickling funniness can all be learned, the way you might learn how to build a wall.

Sorry to be the bearer of bad news, ladies and gentlemen, but that is not true. The thing about comedy is that it's mostly art and not much craft. It's either inside you, or it is not.

And if it's not inside you, please do not attempt to put it there.

The night before the show Jerry stayed out late, dreaming of when he would be king of this town. He loitered outside *The Palace* most of the evening, waiting for its audience to empty. Not much live entertainment played this time of year, and he reckoned certain members of the crowd might return the next evening, desperate to get through their miserable out-of-season holiday. If he sized them up he figured he might be better prepared.

He watched the main doors, above which he dared to imagine his new stage name might one day be announced in neon. A few punters trickled out early, turned up their collars and hurried away into the wet and the wind. Regardless of who had been on stage tonight, it was not a good omen to see members of an audience depart their seats before the final curtain.

Fifteen minutes later the main body of theatre-goers emerged. Jerry scanned their faces. They did not look happy. In fact, they looked positively annoyed that the show they'd endured had been sold as entertainment. An air of regret suffused the crowd as it milled around in the foyer and then dispersed - regret, presumably, that they hadn't spent the evening walking in the drizzle on the seafront, or playing bingo in the damp, deserted amusement arcades that flashed and jingled all along the Golden Mile.

The thought of a tough crowd - up for a good fight more than a good laugh - flattened yesterday's exhilaration. It was more than first-night nerves. It dug deeper. It was the fear of the charlatan, back again, the sense that he did not deserve his moment in the limelight, and that he would be unmasked with an almost justified inevitability.

How could he face his public, he thought, when all he had was a dream and a stolen stage name?

Jerry lost track of time and realised he should catch a tram to his bed and breakfast. At the tram stop he glanced back at *The Palace.* Behind its elegant windows hung nothing but darkness, while downstairs a caretaker dragged a mop over the foyer floor, and prepared to lock up.

Down the side of the theatre Jerry noticed the stage door open and close, as if on a breeze. He did not, however, notice the man who hurried out through the stage door as if late for an appointment.

Nobody would have noticed that man, for that matter, apart perhaps from someone like Collette. She was sensitive to such things. She picked up on things that fell in and out of view. And she saw, and felt, those things more often, with greater clarity and depth of feeling, if she was behind on her medication, as she was at present.

Had Collette been outside *The Palace* that night - had Jerry not locked her in her room at the bed and breakfast, under orders to write something funny - she might have detected a few things about the man who slipped out through the stage door. She might, for example, have wrinkled her nose as he bustled past her, turned it up at the acrid aroma of the hand-rolled cheroot he had clenched between his lips, the smoke saturated into the fabric of his double-breasted jacket, tailor-made decades earlier. She might have heard him shout his catchphrase – '*I can see you!*' – as he ran across the tram tracks. And she might have felt the anger he radiated, rising off him like steam in the cold Blackpool night, as he stood in front of Jerry – invisible to Jerry and everyone else in the tram queue – and stared him square in the face, toe to toe, like a jealous father.

The tram Jerry boarded rolled past the Tower Ballroom and North Pier. He'd rented a room, and a room for Collette, north of Talbot Square, toward Bispham. It was the less boisterous end of Blackpool. If you opened your bedroom window at night it was not the fun fairs, video games and stag and hen parties that you heard, but simply the tide, as it curled and uncurled against the harbour wall.

The tram approached the stop nearest Jerry's guesthouse. He was about to pull the cord when somebody else on the tram pulled it for him. Whoever it was had to be riding in the upper saloon, given that the lower saloon was empty apart from Jerry and the conductor who'd issued his ticket.

The brakes made a noise that suggested the tram travelled not on wheels but knives that clashed together when it slowed. Jerry moved along the aisle, between the beige and green upholstered seats, each fitted with a mechanism that meant it could be flipped to face whichever way along the seafront the tram was headed.

The vehicle stopped. Jerry stepped down to the pavement. The conductor rang the bell twice and the tram pulled away, its big iron wheels vibrating the ground.

He looked around for whoever had pulled the cord to alight at this stop, but the pavement was empty. He presumed the other passenger had decided to stay on until further down the line.

The tram, however, had not travelled far before the driver

switched off the lights in each saloon, upper and lower, and the conductor cranked the hand-operated destination scroll through NORTH PIER, TOWER BALLROOM and PLEASURE BEACH, until it read NOT IN SERVICE. Then the tram switched to the tracks that would take it back to the shed, and rumbled away down the dark promenade.

Jerry crossed the tramlines in the direction of his guesthouse. Behind the patterned glass of the front door the hallway light was subdued. The key he'd been given by the landlady seemed too small when he slipped it in the lock, but after some trial and error it was gripped by the mechanism.

He stepped into the kind of silence that settles in seaside guesthouses at night: immersive and deep, yet blown away by the tiniest sound. The glass panels rattled in the door as he closed it. On the parquet floor the heels of his shoes echoed and scratched. And the staircase, from the first step up through each flight, creaked and clicked and everyone in the house heard it.

On the third floor Jerry turned right and right again. He walked past his room and knocked gently on Collette's door. He was ready to knock again, louder, when Collette said something from inside. It was mumbled but Jerry took it to mean he might enter. He pulled the key from his pocket and unlocked her door.

Inside, he found Collette sitting in the cold at an open sash window. When he first walked in he thought a third person was in the room, crouched on the floor in front of the window, shaped like a hunchback dressed in white. But it was only the net curtain, lifted by the breeze.

Collette was sitting at an oval table with her hands hiding her face. On the table was a notebook folded open at the first page. Apart from some crosshatching in the upper right-hand corner, the page was blank.

Jerry walked over and looked down at the notebook. He did not need to flick through the other pages to know they were empty.

Collette had not written a single word.

Neither comedian nor writer said anything. He felt she could feel him standing behind her. If it made her uncomfortable, he did not care.

At last, he said, 'I don't understand. You said you had ideas.'

Collette did not reply.

He said her name, and from behind her hands she said, 'What?'

'You said you had ideas.'

'I do.'

'So where are they?'

She shrugged. 'Sometimes they won't come.'

'Make them,' he said. 'How hard can it be?'

She began to stutter a reply but didn't finish. For the first time since he'd entered the room, Collette altered her posture. Her movements were slow, tired, as if, since he'd gone out and locked her in, she had been engaged in hard labour, striving to make something happen that did not want to. She kept her hands over her face but spread her fingers and looked out the open window. A storm was preparing to move in from above the sea. Rain clapped the pavement. Fat droplets rolled off the chin of an illuminated fibre-glass frog that hung from armoured cabling strung between two lampposts. Its tongue - pink and extended to an impossible length - had stuck to its tip an enormous bluebottle. On its lumpy head the frog wore a tiny crown at an oblique angle.

Collette turned her gaze from the grotesque decoration. 'I hate this place,' she said. 'Why did it have to be here?'

'It's the spiritual home of comedy.'

'Maybe at one time. But that's the trouble with Blackpool. It tries too hard to be something it's not.'

It was the eve of Jerry's big break and he felt less like the King of Blackpool and more like the fool. He was on stage in less than twenty-four hours and he did not have an act.

He lay in bed and tried not to think of fleeing like a coward. It was tempting. He could get in his car and drive far from this mess. If he put his foot down, he could be at the other side of the country by dawn. Then he could vanish into a place where nothing was expected of him. More importantly, a place where he expected nothing of himself. But it would be over, if he ran away. Word would spread through the comedy circuit and he would never be trusted to perform again.

Despite feeling cornered and alone, he began to doze. At the edge of Jerry's dozing mind skulked an unwelcome but familiar dream, the one in which he was on stage but afraid to speak. In the dream he had his tongue, his vocal cords and his lungs, but he lacked whatever it was that turned humdrum thoughts into wit, as if when he'd been born something had been left out. It was a dream he despised.

He was saved from the dream only by the sound of another guest moving about somewhere in the house. He half-opened his eyes. It was difficult to tell where the other guest might be, on which floor, or in which room. The groan of old wood, and the interval between each sound, suggested whoever it was had been moving up the stairs.

His eyelids came down again. And as they did, Jerry noticed - or thought he noticed - the thin strip of light beneath his door dim slightly, as if someone had paused outside his room, thought better of it, and walked on, although not before they'd left behind the smell of rough, hand-rolled tobacco.

It wasn't until he woke in the morning that he realised he'd forgotten to lock Collette's door.

Thunder off the Blackpool coastline stirred Collette. She lifted her head from the writing table. She felt drained. She had no clue how long she'd been asleep. Everywhere in her body ached for the medication she'd left behind in Manchester. It opened inside her an awful sense of vulnerability, of emptiness, as if any germ or virus might find its way in. She looked down. She blinked. And although Collette blinked, the writing that filled the first page of her note book did not disappear. The cursive style sloped this way and that. Sometimes a word had not been finished before the next had begun. Sentences had been written over each other. And yet it was readable.

It was a comedy routine, or the beginning of one.

She began to read the text but realised that her right hand hurt. She flexed the fingers. They tingled. They did not feel right. And she knew, then, that something had its hand inside hers.

Less than an hour before he was due on stage, Jerry collapsed in the dressing room. He'd been practicing his routine, speaking it aloud in the mirror, when without warning the room spun on its axis. Around the edge of the mirror the filament in each lightbulb burned red, but did not blow, and the glass in each bulb hummed, but did not shatter. And Jerry was swept up in that unannounced arrival of blinding light and high-pitched whistling - swept up and shaken and thrown to the floor. It was over in an instant.

He was not out long. He came to, groggy and crumpled in front of the dressing table.

It was nerves, he told himself. He had never fainted before a show, but he had never played Blackpool. He would give himself a moment, then continue to learn his lines. The routine was short (and perfect for a Blackpool audience) but Collette had pushed the handwritten pages under his door only that morning, and while he'd rehearsed the material throughout the day he still felt paranoid that the success of the set rested entirely upon his skill to master its timing.

Gripping the edge of the dressing table, Jerry pulled himself to his knees and then his feet. He picked up the chair that had tipped over as he'd fallen. He sat down. And he realised then that the dizzy spell had affected his senses more than he'd thought.

Looking at Jerry and smiling, in the dressing room mirror, was the dead comedian Arthur Beckett.

Jerry turned aside and closed his eyes, but when he opened them, expecting the hallucination to have returned to the anxiety-addled corner of his brain that had conjured it, he could tell the other man was still there, present at the edge of his vision.

Slowly, Jerry turned his head. For a moment he believed it might be the photograph of Beckett he'd seen upstairs, projected onto the surface of the mirror, for a laugh by Butterfield, perhaps, or to spook Jerry before he went on stage. But the theory of the photograph fell apart when the dead comedian moved.

First, Arthur smiled, even wider than before. Then he plucked the cheroot from his mouth and held it aside, between two fat fingers, while through pursed lips he blew smoke rings at Jerry, each of which dissolved - one, two, three - against Arthur's side of the mirror. As he inserted the cheroot back into its rightful place, Jerry noticed, hanging from Arthur's wrist, a gold-link bracelet engraved KING OF BLACKPOOL. Arthur winked. And after a pause - the timing of which was, of course, impeccable - he said, 'I apologise. I interrupted your rehearsal. Please, continue. In fact, take it from the top.'

'The top?'

'I insist. Let's hear it.'

As in the dream the previous night, Jerry choked - not on his words, but his confidence to deliver them.

Recognising that Jerry was in trouble, Arthur dimmed the lights his side of the mirror. 'Pretend I'm not here.'

It made no difference. Still, Jerry choked. Still he felt unable to launch his delivery, despite it being an audience of one, and a dead man at that. He could remember each line - they were queued up ready in his head. But he was certain they would come out wrong. They'd be in the wrong order. Or he'd say them too fast, or too slow. Worst of all was the fear he'd say the lines in the clumsy, parrot-like monotone of a person reciting a foreign language for which their mouth had not been made.

'Repeat after me,' said Arthur. 'You would not believe what happened to me today, ladies and gentlemen ...'

How Arthur could quote the opening line to his new routine was lost within Jerry's unprecedented sense of failure at not even having the talent to be walked through his repertoire by the *real* King of Blackpool. 'I can't ...' said Jerry, thinking again of running away. 'I can't do it.'

The dead comedian stared at the living comedian more

intently. Jerry couldn't tell if he was angry or disappointed.

On Arthur's side of the mirror the dressing room was cluttered with costumes and props and theatre paraphernalia of the day. Silver-studded leotards glinted on a rail beside tutus and dinner-jackets. On a separate rail hung the masks: comedy and tragedy, long-nosed Venetian death masks, a mask for Puck, another for Caliban, and further along wolf-masks and weasel-masks and masks for human-sized rabbits. In the corner stood an artificial toadstool. In the other corner the back end of a pantomime horse. On a table, the squeezed tubes and finger-smeared tubs of greasepaint, surrounded by applicators and brushes and trays of false eyebrows and exaggerated ears.

Leaning against the wall behind Arthur was a piece of wood the size and shape of a coffin-lid. Painted on it was the silhouette of a woman. Half a dozen daggers protruded from the wood, from where they'd been thrown during the act for which the prop had been made: one either side of the neck, two more to the left and right of the ribcage, one above the head, and the last between the legs. Arthur twisted round and yanked out the nearest dagger. He held the blade aloft, and the tip glinted. 'We need to do something about those bones of yours,' he said, leaning forward until he pushed through from his side of the mirror, and into Jerry's side. 'It won't hurt,' said the dead comedian. 'Although, you might feel a bit funny.'

They say, ladies and gentlemen, that talent should be played close to the chest. They say hold back, hang on, be patient. They say only when talent is truly polished should it be revealed to the world.

Believe me, I tried to resist. I told myself not to get involved. I said it was not my place to interfere, or to lend a hand.

But I felt obliged. He'd named himself after me. It would be my name – the King of Blackpool – that would be emblazoned across the night.

Here, ladies and gentlemen, we prefer to do things the way they're meant to be done.

Here, you don't get on stage unless you're made of the right stuff.

In the wings and the dressing rooms and the corridors backstage – in all the places in this town where we used to be magnificent – what else can we do but be true to our bones.

THE LOST LADS OF RIVINGTON

North Lancashire's moors are notoriously bleak and expansive, covering vast tracts of wilderness. But it is in the south of the county, amid swathes of post-industrial conurbation, where some of the wildest and most dangerous reaches of open country can be found.

The West Pennine Moors, for example, are at first glance idyllic. Situated roughly in the centre of a huge geographic triangle lying between the townships of Blackburn, Bolton and Wigan – three points on the Northwest map famous for their terraced houses, tall chimneys and smoky skies – they are a green haven in the heart of an urban landscape. Some 90 square miles of heather, rocks, woods and rolling, open grassland, they rise to 1,500 feet, and their summit, Winter Hill, from which almost the whole of Northwest England can be seen, is the habitat of kites, foxes, buzzards and deer. Even if the occasional marks of man can be found up here – the Victorian-era dams on the reservoirs of Anglezarke, Yarrow and Upper Rivington, and more modern blips of technology in the form of the Winter Hill TV Mast – the overall rural grandeur of this scene is breath-taking.

But while in spring and summer, the West Pennine Moors might be a paradise for walkers and nature-spotters, in autumn and winter it is a different story. Rivington Moor, for instance, stands so high above sea-level that it possesses a microclimate, the temperature often plunging much lower than on the Lancashire Plain, lying to the west. Thick fogs – as in literal peasoupers – are common throughout November, December, January and February, and once the snow and frost sets in, it will likely remain until April. As such, there have been many deaths on the West Pennine Moors, hikers underestimating the immensity of the space, the solitude and silence, becoming lost, disoriented, maybe suffering injury, and ultimately falling prey to the most vicious elements in the whole of Northwest England.

Unsurprisingly, these high, wild moors are also said to be haunted.

A headless cavalier, a sad relic of the terrible Civil War battles that raged so relentlessly in this part of Britain, is said to gallop nightly across the wilderness in a meandering, directionless charge. Inexplicable wailing cries have been reported, some of which have led to search parties being sent out, though in so many of these cases no casualties were ever found. Swarms of glowing orbs have been spotted floating above the moors. One snowy New Year's Eve, one such swarm was mistaken for Chinese lanterns, until the party-goers watching them from a distance were shocked to see them suddenly hurtle away at mind-boggling speed.

But perhaps the most frightening of all the paranormal stories connected with the West Pennine Moors is that of the Lost Lads of Rivington.

The Lost Lads ...

It is a commonly spoken phrase in this part of Lancashire. It comes to us from time immemorial, with so little factual basis that many folklorists refuse to acknowledge an explanation for the term, simply regarding it as a phrase that no longer has meaning. Others have suggested that it refers to so-called 'lead-stones', in other words boulders leading across the moor, painted white or yellow in order to provide markers for wanderers who might have lost their way in the fog or mist. There are no lead-stones now; perhaps they themselves became lost?

But the most chilling explanation dates from the early 1800s and holds that a trio of itinerants, perhaps laid-off cotton workers or soldiers newly returned from the Napoleonic wars, went looking for employment on the moors. They found billets and labour at a small farm near Rivington, under the shadow of the moors' isolated western watchtower, Rivington Pike. As with all seasonal workers, there would only be so much for the men to do before the farmer was forced to release them. But unfortunately, the autumn broke early that year, bringing terrific storms. There was still labour needed in the high pastures, but the farmer knew that soon there'd be snow as well and had all but given up on this far-flung portion of his land. Despite this, when the three men insisted on completing their tasks, he was unhappy. Not only was another furious rainstorm hammering the moors, the droplets driven like bullets on a freezing wind, but it was now the Sabbath – and back in those God-fearing days working on the Sabbath was a grievous sin. But the men wouldn't be told. They left their lodging that morning, cheerful and determined to do their master proud. Clearly, they were hardy types, undeterred by danger and discomfort. But by nightfall they had not returned, even though the tempest still raged so fiercely that it was impossible to go and look for them. Only two days later, when the deluge eased to a steady drizzle, was the farmer able to round up some additional labourers to help him scour the moorland. He was confident that he'd find three corpses. But there was no trace of the men, living or dead. Searches continued for the next few weeks, unsuccessfully, until the temperature fell, and the rain turned to snow. After that, the farmer gave up.

The question was asked had the men simply absconded, though this seemed unlikely as their belongings were still at the farm, along with satchels containing their pay.

And the mystery doesn't end there.

As recently as the early 21st century, usually during terrible rainstorms on the moors, walkers, or even motorists travelling the high, winding roads, have encountered three miserable, shivering lads in the deluge, who always ask directions to a farm that hasn't existed since the mid-19th century. When those they address are unable to assist, they move forlornly off into the murk. A few minutes later, there is no sign of them.

THE MUTE SWAN
Cate Gardner

Carys screamed.

Feathers rained from the costume, carpeting the floor with swan. Carys tore at the dress, at the bodice too tight for her expanding frame. The tips of the feathers pricked her arms, as if inking a message on skin, transforming it. The scream hitched against her throat. She coughed blood onto the bones of the dress. If she snapped the bodice, it would cover her front, her burgeoning chest, but little else. She stretched her neck. The scream would not stop.

They'd been on their way to the Cherry Tree shopping centre for a McDonald's, when Mother diverted and pulled Carys through the smoked-glass doors of the dance school on Wallasey Road. They'd discussed extra-curricular activities - well Mother had - with a firm no from Carys. A no scrawled in black marker on a well-thumbed notebook for Carys had no voice. Mute from birth, she was her mother's trial. Behind the door, a staircase stretched up to a darkened landing. Carys shook her head, tried to pull her mother towards the door, towards the street. Too thin. *Too puny.* She'd struggle to drag a doll if it insisted on staying put.

'It's just a dance class,' Mother said. 'A couple of hours on a Saturday morning, and then you can have all the fries you want. It will be good for you.'

Things requiring team participation were never good for her.

'Please, honey.'

A creak on the landing above. A door opened, offering light

and throwing the person who'd exited in shadow.

'Hello, down there. New recruits. Excellent. Come up, we always have space for new dancers.'

The voice was light, welcoming, a song. Still, Carys ached to run until she reached the river. She'd rather it had screamed, *go away*. She'd rather it chased. Mother pushed her up the stairs until she complied and climbed unaided. The figure had disappeared back through the door.

Compared to the dark of the staircase, the dance room blinded. Sunlight rippled, moving in waves as it caught the feet of the dancers who bounded about the room. No elegance here. A crispness to the air, as if entering had pushed June into January.

'All of them must be beginners,' Mother said, whispering.

Around the edges of the room, parents clapped. Mother would see the uselessness of this place and that she'd only learn to fall and stomp, to grow bruises; they'd go to McDonald's now.

The dance tutor, who'd not yet introduced herself, slapped her hands together. 'Right, right, all parents must go. We'll see you in two hours and not a second before.'

Mother hesitated.

'My classes are free. You can go, I will look after your daughter. I look after all the daughters.'

The tutor pirouetted towards where Mother stood frozen, her fingers stretching to grasp Carys' arm, to drag her out much as she'd dragged her in. The tutor sliced between them. A tremble caught in Carys' throat and it hurt, a sharp burst of air pressed against her vocal cords, bounded into her mouth. Beyond all expectation, she screamed. The girl who had never made a sound, not even a yelp, screamed and it was riotous.

It broke Mother's stupor. 'It's a …'

Do not say, miracle.

'… miracle.'

The tutor bent before Carys to consider her scream. 'They are all miracles here. I am Miss Penelope Cygnus. Miss Pen, for short. I promise your baby will be singing before lesson's end.'

'Yes,' Mother said.

Carys backed away from Miss Pen until her elbow hit the metal bar secured to the mirror. Throat calmed, the scream became a whimper. The other parents filed out, no concern for the screaming girl or that their daughters may catch the infection. Mother remained, transfixed by the memory of the scream.

Once again, Miss Pen pirouetted to inspect Carys. Carys balled her fists. Having no voice didn't mean she couldn't stand up for herself. She raised them. Boxing stance.

'This is dance, dear. We're not performing The Thug Swan.'

With Miss Pen's fingers at her wrist, again Carys found her scream. Throat swollen, ears throbbing, the blood vessels in her eyes threatened to burst. This scream would rip her inside out, transform her into a weeping monster. Miss Pen's grip tightened. She had to be unaware that she was the cause of the outburst. Eyes pecked at hers.

'Come on now, my foolish darling.'

Go away. Leave me be. I am not your darling.

Help arrived in the form of a short girl in a red tutu. The girl bit into Miss Pen's arm, causing Miss Pen to release her grip on Carys' arm. Teeth continued to bite. With a pinch to the girl's ear, Miss Pen was released.

'Anna-Elizabeth, explain yourself, my darling.'

Despite the ferocity of the bite, there wasn't a mark on Miss Pen's arm, as if Anna-Elizabeth had offered a toothless bite. *Baby teeth.* They stood together, Anna-Elizabeth and Carys, in this den of mutants. Despite the commotion, the other girls danced in the centre of the room, waving blue sheets between them, like waves on a barren sea. Anna-Elizabeth stood out more for her red costume. Anna-Elizabeth entwined her fingers with Carys', stilling the want to scream.

'I'm Anna-Elizabeth and I'm not seven. I'm thirteen and possibly related to the fairies in Vale Park.'

Carys fumbled in her pocket for her notebook. Releasing her fingers from Anna-Elizabeth's she wrote – *I'm Carys and despite my scream, I make no sound.*

'According to my parents, I'm obstinate in my refusal to grow up. Soon as I develop boobs they'll be calling for me to divorce them. My parents not my boobs. We're all whack-jobs here, until *she* forces the extraordinary from us, but we'll resist.'

They held hands again.

'Scream.'

It became the latest instruction. Her mother swerved the car towards oncoming traffic. They allowed her to watch *Insidious* and *The Babadook*. They filled her shelves with books by Stephen King and Shirley Jackson. They leapt from cupboards and locked her in rooms. They dug a hole in the garden and told her to climb in. None of these caused her to scream. They did, however, make her consider Anna-Elizabeth's route to divorcing her parents.

Her parents began to argue. Mother had imagined it. How do you imagine a scream that shakes windows, removes dust from lampshades, which offers pure terror?

Not wanting her parents to divorce, she practiced screaming until her throat tore. No sound emerged.

Blue sheets wafted between the girls. Carys and Anna-Elizabeth caught amongst them, spent most of the lesson tripping over fabric. There was to be a show. A group of incompetent, uncoordinated teens were to perform for parents and unspecified others, who were unlikely to be scouts from the English National Ballet or Sadler's Wells. An outdoor event, venue to be determined. Please not Cherry Tree Shopping Centre - school was already hell. *Sir, tell Carys to speak up, we can't hear her.* Miss Pen manipulated the girl's limbs, as if that would magic talent into their legs. She did not touch Carys. No one but Anna-Elizabeth did. Despite this, she still screamed, if sometimes only a whimper, whenever Miss Pen came within five feet of her. Dad should come to class.

'Girls, girls.' Miss Pen flapped her arms. 'All in a circle around

Carys, please. That means you, Anna-Elizabeth. Do stop chewing your fingernails, Ethel, or I'll bite off your fingers. We thought we had that problem solved. Your parents were so proud.'

'Sorry, Miss Pen,' Ethel said.

'That's okay dear, you are still one of my little feathers.'

Carys wished she could offer a groan. She hopped from foot to foot; the floor ice cold. The other girls, Anna-Elizabeth included, floated about her, swaying their fingers as if they were mini-trees rather than feathers. They represented a part of the central swan. Of Carys.

'Elegance, girls. Ethel lift those knees. What is with you today? Don't you want to be a feather?'

To Carys, it was obvious Ethel was trying hard. A confusion to the girl with each bite from Miss Pen. When they took a breather, Ethel stood in the corner plucking at her skin, itching. Miss Pen stalked her space, back and forth, looking as if she wanted to swipe at Ethel.

'They hurt, Miss Pen,' Ethel said. 'I can feel the feathers growing.'

'Nonsense. Back into your positions.'

Ethel's hands dropped to her side. With a flat, monotone voice she asked, 'Is Carys the dead swan, Miss Pen?'

Laughter spread amongst the other swans as they all turned to look at Carys. Her feet stuck to the dance floor, as if skin against ice.

She wants to kill me. Carys held her notebook out to her parents, pointing at each word. Then, she added, *Miss Pen.*

'Ridiculous,' Dad said, scraping his chair back and putting on the kettle.

Carys couldn't get warm. At dance class, the cold had seeped through her ballet slippers, crept up her legs, and now settled about her shoulders. Rubbing her fingers brought no warmth, nor did cupping them around the mug of tea.

Dead swan! She's going to drown me in the river.

The recital would be performed at Vale Park where it met the banks of the River Mersey. They'd crowd her until she couldn't breathe. They'd dunk her in the river and their feather arms would prove weights.

Dad laughed.

It's not funny.

'It's as funny as your scream, chicken,' Dad said.

He still didn't believe. Well he'd see and he'd hear and he'd drown trying to save her, because Miss Pen and the Feathers wouldn't allow her to surface. Carys thumped her fist against the table, then folded her arms.

'Uh-oh,' Dad said.

'We're for it now,' Mother said. 'Sweetheart, Miss Pen thinks you're talented. She wants you to be the star. That's marvellous. We could never have expected that much.'

Again, Carys pointed to her original comment.

'Why would your teacher want to kill you? Think about it. Hormones. Trust me, lately mine make me irrational too. I'm at the end while you, my love, are at the beginning. She found your voice, and we should be grateful for that. The doctors were right, there is sound in there. You will speak.'

I'll GARGLE when she drowns me.

'Enough,' Mother said, tearing the notebook from Carys' fingers.

Everyone knew not to do that, even the bullies at school. Carys' silence crept into all of them.

'Carys doubts she is accomplished enough to be the centrepiece of the show. She'd prefer a smaller role. A bit part,' Mother said.

Miss Pen raised an ice-white eyebrow. Carys and Anna-Elizabeth leant against the bar, mirrored-walls echoing the scene. Carys throat strained. She restrained the scream.

The feathered dress hung from Mother's hand, a listless, unwanted thing. A dead swan; drained of all purpose. The other girls' costumes were nude bodysuits and crowns of white flowers.

'That doesn't mean we're not proud of her, nor that we doubt her abilities. We are proud of our daughter.'

This was new.

'You brought your daughter here because she has *troubles*.'

'That doesn't mean we're not pr … proud. I'll take the dress. Darling, perhaps …'

Then, Mother was gone along with all the other parents.

'Darling!' Anna-Elizabeth said. 'I may puke on Miss Pen's ballet pumps.'

Whatever Miss Pen had done to fix the other girls, she'd struggle to make Anna-Elizabeth grow, to age her. Despite the scream, Carys didn't see how she could be fixed either. When Miss Pen clicked her long fingers, Carys slid across the floor to the centre of the group. Perhaps, she was breaking her after all. They should run, Carys and Anna-Elizabeth, sneak out of class and refuse to return. Sometimes, things aren't that easy. Especially when you are used to trying to please your parents because you feel you have failed them in other ways. The girls closed ranks around Carys, with Miss Pen on the outskirts.

This wasn't going to change unless she changed it.

I don't want to go to class anymore.

I'm scared.

I'll try to talk.

I'll scream.

Give me a chance. PLEASE. This will destroy me.

The others are puppets.

I don't want to be a puppet.

Mother fussed with the dishes. 'Just give it a little longer. Try the show. It'll be good for your confidence.'

It'll destroy it. Mother didn't see those words as she had her turned her back. So easy to end a conversation with the mute.

'The other children are so … well behaved.'

Dad said, 'From what I've heard, the other girls are so under the control of the teacher they're mute. You wanted her to go so that she'd be different. To me, it seems the other girls are becoming more like our Carys.'

Support. Dad didn't often speak up for her. It was the one thing her parents had determined they'd never do. An unspoken rule. If she wouldn't speak for herself then they wouldn't speak for her. At least the class had changed this one thing.

'Why don't we meet up with that friend of yours one evening? Have a picnic in Vale Park?'

They hadn't done that in ages. Since she was 11, perhaps.

Carys nodded.

Mother turned from the dishes, and from the window she'd been staring from. 'Excellent idea. They're doing the performance there. It may settle Carys' nerves.'

Or dash them.

As a group, Carys and Anna-Elizabeth's families, headed down the terraced street, which led to Vale Park. Cars parked on both sides of the road, straddled the pavement. With the sun out, and the lighter nights, it looked as if the park would be busy. They meandered through the fairy village, which was comprised of a weave of statues made from discarded branches, and toys, including plastic trolls with shocks of pink and blue hair, added by both committee and visiting children. Past the display of painted stones, one of which bore her name. She pointed it out to Anna-Elizabeth, who in turn pointed out her own stone. They were close. Almost in the same ring. Carys just outside Anna's.

'Look at the other names,' Anna said.

Except for Miss Pen, they matched the names of the girls in their dance class and some looked to have been excavated from their original site. Reading too much into it. After all, it was possible Miss Pen had organised it to go with the show.

After a feast of sandwiches, sausage rolls and lemon cake slices, Carys and Anna-Elizabeth ventured to the beach, which bordered the park. A light sea-fog obscured the other side of the River Mersey, with its collection of red dock cranes. A necessity for the revenue of the city of Liverpool (they'd covered Maritime History in school), if not for the view from the Wirral. Across the water, the fog horn blew.

'Maybe our performance will be fogged-out, and all they'll see is a twirl of white feathers and not figure out who is who.'

Only the parents will come.

'It's a public park. We're not that lucky.'

They stood on the wet sand.

'Think the tide will be out for a bit?'

They didn't have a clue.

Something splashed in the water. Obscured by the fog, they caught only hints of grey. Carys headed closer to the water's edge. They should get back but curiosity and all that. The fog surrounded them, not so much that it had thickened, but that it wanted to obscure the thing in the river from them or them from the thing in the river. Anna-Elizabeth grabbed her hand.

'What is it?' Anna-Elizabeth asked.

Carys shook her head.

Their parents' voices rang across the park. Anxious. Fretful.

How long had they been gone? It couldn't be home time yet. There was no school tomorrow only dance class. Carys wanted to tell Anna-Elizabeth that she thought Miss Pen a monster, but the air was too wet for her notebook, and besides, Anna-Elizabeth knew.

The fog shifted exposing the grey waters of the Mersey. Distorted ripples on the river, different to the surrounding movement of the water. Something disturbing the river. A surge of water. An uplifting, showering them. Something rising majestically. An orange beak with serrated edges like a row of jagged teeth, large enough to bite …

'Carys.'

Dad's hand at her shoulder, pulling her back from the monster. Anna-Elizabeth's dad doing the same. Did they see? A scream caught in Carys' belly. The thing, the thing, the thing. Her scream caused her dad to hug her tighter than he ever had before.

The fog lifted, dragging whatever monster had emerged with it, causing all to evaporate.

Anna-Elizabeth wasn't in class. A definite absence amongst this collection of mute swans. No one to discuss the monster of the previous night. If monster it was. Once her scream had calmed, pretty much by the time they'd stepped back onto the grass and headed through the fairy village, her dad had released her hand and looked at her as if she were a marvel. No telling off for this girl who screamed in a public place.

When Carys sat in the centre of the circle, refusing to dance, Miss Pen pushed the other girls aside and grabbed Carys' arm. All screamed out, Carys couldn't even whimper. The monster of the night before had stolen her scream.

'No little friend today, but you still have us. You'll become one of us now. Isn't that wonderful, Carys. Shush now, you don't have to sing. We'll sing for you.'

The other girls began a song, a monstrous hum.

'The unidentified body of a child, estimated to be aged seven or eight, has been pulled from the river.'

Dad turned the television off.

It wouldn't be Anna-Elizabeth as she was thirteen.

Couldn't be Anna-Elizabeth. Yet, she looked seven.

Anna-Elizabeth wouldn't be unclaimed, so that was the end of that speculation. She hoped. Where had Anna-Elizabeth been today? Had her parents finally listened to her cries to be removed from the class? It wasn't as if she was getting any taller. Miss Pen wasn't fixing her so-called faults. No more than she had fixed Carys'. Carys pressed her hand to her mouth. For all her desire to think otherwise, she knew the dead girl to be her friend.

This time she wrote, *Miss Pen killed Anna-Elizabeth. I'm next.* Then she scrubbed out 'I'm next' for it seemed a selfish thought. What Miss Pen planned for her didn't matter in that moment; only Anna-Elizabeth did.

Mother shook her head. Dad read the notepad, didn't comment.

Anna-Elizabeth is the unidentified body.

'For God's sake, speak,' Mother shouted.

'Audrey!' Dad said.

'Ed!'

Mother collapsed onto the leather sofa. She wiped sweat off her forehead, as if she'd been exercising not standing in the doorway watching the news. Then she cried, she cried harder than Carys had ever seen anyone do.

Between hitched sobs, mother said, 'You're not going back. Ed, she's not going back.'

So why didn't it feel like she'd finally won the battle?

When the house fell to silence, Carys slipped out of the house. They lived only a few streets from Vale Park and the river where the unidentified child, Anna-Elizabeth, had been found. Perhaps she'd find some trace, some hint. Better yet, maybe she'd find Anna-Elizabeth at the scene looking for her. With the recent spread of her hips and the budding growth of breasts, no one would confuse Carys for seven-years-old.

You are at the beginning. I am at the end. How many times her mother had said that lately.

As Anna-Elizabeth had proved, we never know when the end is. It shouldn't happen to girls who look seven. It shouldn't happen to thirteen-year-old girls at the beginning of everything.

Lights hung from the trees at Vale Park, killing the shadows that lurked behind trees and, at this hour, the monstrous growth of fairy and witch statues. At the end of the park, abandoned police tape flapped across the pathway to the beach. She didn't recognise the others at first. She thought them police or journalists, coroners or lifeguards, so she hid at the edge of the park, looking down towards the beach where people gathered.

They weren't people in the usual sense of the word; these weren't strangers. All dressed in their nude bodysuits, sans flowers, their arms covered in feathers, which in the dim light appeared to poke from skin. If this was a vigil for Anna-Elizabeth, why hadn't they invited her? She was the only one who was Anna-Elizabeth's friend.

She crept as close as she dared, her steps lighter than they used to be, ducking behind a litter bin attached to the railing that glistened wet with night and sea-spray. The water was coming in and the girls would be caught on the beach. They'd all drown; Miss Pen included. Her breath echoed, loud and thudding in her ears.

On the beach, the little swans turned as one, co-ordinated for once, to look towards where she crouched. Blood pounded through ears and chest. At least, she wasn't screaming. To run was the appropriate response yet she remained in situ, frozen, cold as January. Across the wash of water and sand, a creaking as Miss Pen stretched her neck to impossible lengths. The girls turned back towards their teacher and towards the water, where two nights before a monster had emerged.

A splashing from the river. Although she couldn't see much of the water from her position, the little swans obscuring her view, it sounded as if someone or something fought to emerge, as if saving itself from drowning. Anna-Elizabeth. She stood, knocking into the litter bin, causing a tinny ring to echo across the promenade.

Ice-cold breath at her neck. Please let it be the wind. She wouldn't scream. She mustn't scream. A hand at her elbow. Frozen fingers. In the water, a terrible, monstrous beauty emerged. A magnificent swan towered above the girls, its feathers six-feet across. It pecked at them, urging the girls to pluck the feathers from their arms and offer them to Miss Pen. In turn, Miss Pen jabbed the plumage into her arms.

'You could take the feathers,' a voice whispered at her ear. 'He recognises you.'

Carys wanted to turn, to see who whispered, thinking it couldn't be Anna-Elizabeth and yet there was a hint of her voice beneath its sharpness, but the thing kept her pinioned, kept her watching the waters. The swan strutted. The girls looked depleted; emptied things lying on the sand, scooped up and shaken in Miss Pen's emerging beak.

Breaking free of the alien grip, Carys wanted to scream *no* but of course, unused vocal cords didn't know how to form the word, they could only scream and scream and ... The male swan, the cob, turned towards Carys, while Miss Pen began to reform into their dance teacher, and the girls regained their feet, helping each other up.

Carys struggled to wake. She rolled to the side of the bed, dropped to the bedroom floor. Her legs had forgotten how to walk, how to hold her upright, let alone perform a routine on the uneven ground of sand or grass. It would be sand. Sand and water. That's what the plan was always meant to be. Her body felt wrong, mis-shaped, a thing changed overnight into someone or something she wasn't ready to be. Not for the first time, she wanted to be able to form the words *mum* and *dad*. She needed them. She could throw something, make a racket. That always got their attention.

Her image in the wardrobe mirror, what she could see of it below the hideous costume, beneath feathers and tulle, was more than misshapen. It was a naked stretch of wrong. It wasn't her. It couldn't be her.

Carys found her voice. Carys screamed.

Feathers rained from the dress, carpeting the floor with swan. Carys tore at the dress, at the bodice too tight for her expanding frame. The tips of the feathers pricked her arms, as if inking a message on skin, transforming it. The scream hitched against her throat. She coughed blood onto the bones of the dress. If she snapped the bodice, it would cover her front, her burgeoning chest, but little else. She stretched her neck. The scream would not stop, and feathers buried themselves within her new form.

THE RESURRECTION MEN

By the general standards of the early 19th century, the 1820s was not too difficult a period for those living in the United Kingdom. The country was still undergoing mass industrialisation, and associated ills like urban squalor, poor health, pollution and exploitation remained serious issues. But Britain had recently emerged victorious from the Napoleonic Wars – the terrible dual-spectre of Bonaparte and the guillotine was gone, the industrial and political strife of the previous decade was largely settled thanks to a systematic repealing of numerous harsh laws, London became one of the commercial capitals of the world, and The Times *newspaper was making great use of its brand new printing press, which was capable of producing thousands and thousands of pages an hour and for the first time ever sending out news to the entire nation.*

One grotesque story The Times *and other fledgling newspapers covered, which created horror and disbelief across the country, was that of body-snatchers Burke and Hare, who in Edinburgh in 1829 provided a local anatomist with a constant supply of fresh corpses by murdering tramps and drunkards. It created a national sensation and in purely criminal terms became one of the talking points of the era, completely overshadowing other macabre incidents - such as the city of Liverpool's own ghastly dalliance with the so-called 'resurrection men'.*

Despite all that, it is still surprising that this other event, which had occurred three years earlier in 1826, did not make a bigger impression, because it is a horrific tale by any standards.

On a dreary October day that year, a gang of stevedores was working at Liverpool's George's Dock, loading cargo onto a small boat bound for Edinburgh. Three particular items, supposedly kegs of salt-brine, gave off so foul an odour that the dock-gang refused to handle them, and the ship's master said that he wouldn't have allowed them on board anyway. The resulting argument was only resolved when the barrels were opened and discovered to be crammed with 11 corpses – the ruined and decaying relics of men, women and children.

The borough of Liverpool would not have an official police force in the modern sense for another ten years. However, the Dock Police and the Town Watch were in existence and were organised and efficient in the style of London's Bow Street Runners, and they took charge of the situation. A certain Detective Robert Boughey was tasked with investigating and tracked the delivery to a large house in Hope Street, where today the Everyman Theatre stands. The occupant was a certain Reverend McGowan, an apparently respectable gentleman who operated a school from the same premises. McGowan advised Boughey that he knew nothing about the kegs except that they had come from his cellar, which currently was rented by a Scot named John Henderson, a cooper from Greenock. But when Boughey asked if he could investigate the cellar, McGowan became obstructive, refusing to hand over the key and promising legal action if the detective used force. Boughey ignored him and shouldered the door down, descending the cellar steps into a scene of mind-numbing horror.

Rotting corpses lay everywhere. Some hung out of barrels, some were sacked and bound as though for delivery; others littered the filthy floor.

Some 22 human husks in total were found in that cellar. There was also a vat containing the semi-preserved remains of several babies. Various examinations followed, and it was finally determined that many of the decomposing figures, while they had all died from natural causes, had been retrieved from local graveyards, mainly the nearby cemetery at Cambridge Street, though it was also suspected that some of them were workhouse paupers who had never even seen the grave but had been sold on after death by corrupt officials of the parish. Another suggestion, though this was never proved, was that many more such sad remains had been procured at earlier dates from Ireland and had also been kept at the same Liverpool address, which clearly functioned as a kind of gruesome storage depot.

Despite the uproar in the city – the mere descriptions of the scene causing witnesses and jurors alike to vomit in court – the sentences handed down to the three members of the Hope Street gang convicted were relatively light: a year's imprisonment each. Detective Boughey was lionised for his breaking of the case, but in general terms there was dissatisfaction. It wasn't just the mysteriously short prison terms that raised hackles, but a clear implication that many others were involved who had evaded justice altogether.

FACTORY ROOK
Simon Kurt Unsworth

The sensors showed more movement.

Wood looked at the data now logged on his tablet. The various recordings showed as a series of jagged lines that indicated movement in the old Ragged School's structure, not much but certainly enough to need identifying and either eliminating or addressing. Wood would need to plot the movement against time and wider earth shifts to see if there were things that might account for the tremors that the lines represented. Some might be the ground shifting due to the passing of traffic, especially the denser blocks of shiver that showed around rush hour, but it wasn't anything he could be sure of without further work. He ran his fingers across the brickwork of the wall in front of him, cold against his fingertips, and thought instinctively that it was solid, but instinct wouldn't satisfy the development fund bankrolling the work nor Morgan, the project manager.

Behind Wood, as though summoned by his thinking of him like some bogey from a campfire tale, Morgan said, 'Well, that's fucked.'

Wood turned, assuming Morgan was looking at the readings from over his shoulder and ready to reassure him - not fucked, possibly *potentially* fucked, only *maybe* fucked - but found instead that Morgan was bending over the shoulder of a man in a blue utility company uniform who was sitting in front of a monitor perched precariously on a trestle.

'That's a problem,' the utility company man said.

'No shit,' said Morgan and Wood turned away, tuning him out. He'd find out what it was when they had a site meeting at the end of the day, it was guaranteed.

Even small problems were things to share for Morgan. Until then, he had more sensor data to download.

The Ragged School movement had started in southern England in the late eighteenth century, spread to Scotland and then crossed the rest of the country in an uneven wave, the charitable institutions providing free schooling and more for destitute children. Led by a series of individuals including the 'crippled cobbler' Reverend Doctor Thomas Guthrie and Lord Sainsbury, those early schools set the template for others that followed: education was provided to 'raggedly clothed' children, as well as meals, religious teachings and new, less ragged clothes. The first schools used existing free spaces but as the movement grew benefactors provided funds to create purpose-built institutions, often developing and expanding existing Mission buildings. By the middle of the 19th century, there were at least twenty of these schools in London.

Manchester's first and best-known Ragged School, *The Charter Street Ragged School and Working Girls Home*, opened in 1866. It was situated on the corner of Aspin Lane and Dantzig Street and was an extension of the Charter Street Mission. It was unusual in that it also provided free food to destitute men on Sundays and had an upper floor that was used to teach working girls the more socially acceptable skills of sewing, cooking and cleaning. Manchester's youngest poor and desperate were taught, helped to try to better themselves and looked after by servants who lived on the premises rather than in nearby lodgings, and were provided with laundry facilities, and good fresh food cooked on the premises. There were also cubicles where the children could gain some privacy and study in peace.

Following the Charter Street Mission's school, more Ragged Schools sprang up across the area: Minshull Street, in the city centre, provided teaching and work opportunities but did not cater for adults at the weekend; Hope Street provided education as a payment for listening to religious teachings, and allowed adults in on Sundays but did not provide anything but the most basic sustenance; and the Gaddum family ran a series of smaller houses, schools only in that they provided some basic education but whose main focus was to address the children's health, providing them with medicines and basic medical attention.

Unique amongst the Ragged Schools in Manchester was the institution built upon, and named for, Factory Rook in North Manchester, the Rook coming from the birds that had nested in the trees there until they had been felled in the name of industrial revolution. This school provided the usual educational opportunities but also functioned as an orphanage, taking in both state-sanctioned children whose parents had died or could not be found or who were sent by the courts following criminal behaviour, and foundlings. Factory Rook opened in 1855 in a building that had once been a small clog-manufacturers, its ground floors converted to teaching rooms, basements to the dormitories and nurseries and the upper floors to staff accommodation and offices, paid for by a consortium of local charities and individual businessmen with philanthropic notions. Such was its reputation that in its busiest periods, Factory Rook was supposed to house more than 400 orphans and to take in between ten and twenty foundlings from across the Northwest each month, children left in the night by desperate parents who knew that their offspring would be looked after or sent by a state which had few facilities for looking after the abandoned young of its chronically poor.

Factory Rook was open as a Ragged School for seventy-five years, becoming after that a state-run orphanage and school, then simply a school, before being closed in the early '60s, the building left to decay in an area all but abandoned economically, socially and politically. As the world moved on rain harried apart the slates on its roof, its red brick and cream terracotta walls and decorations fading, cracking and peeling and, in some cases, crumbling away. Windows were broken by winds and vandals, homeless men and women made camp in its empty halls and set fires, rain soaked the wood and buckled the floorboards around the broken panes, its ownership uncertain between the various trusts and boards that claimed interests in it. Eventually the

Council boarded it up, fenced it off and left it to die.

And then, after the boom and bust of the economy during which Factory Rook had stood resolutely unloved and unwanted, the area around it began to change. Money from Europe improved and increased housing stock, new roads allowed for the development of a commuter belt, out of town retail parks and leisure facilities sprang up, and efforts were made to finally unravel the tangled knot of legal strings that made Factory Rook's ownership so confusing. Despite various preservation orders and listings, Factory Rook was purchased, and plans put in place to upgrade it, improve it, make it a space fit to live in, if you could afford the high six-figure price tags the flats it would eventually become would command.

Which brought Wood to the party.

Leaving the room he had been in - one of the teaching rooms he thought – he crossed a corridor and through another door that led to what he thought might have been a dining room, throughout which his sensors were scattered. He went to each one and downloaded the data from it, finding in the process that two of the sensors had lost power at some point in the previous twenty-four hours so that he was missing whatever readings they might have taken. He put them into his bag and replaced them with spares. All the others seemed fine, so he reset them all and went upstairs where he had placed at least one sensor in each room, and two or three in the larger ones, covering all the internal and external walls. Downloading took a while and he had to step around architects making notes on tablets and pads, hard-hatted workmen carrying tools and equipment into place for when the work would commence and at one point a man who could only be the money: forward-facing suit and haircut still sharp despite the protective headgear and high visibility vest; pacing the room and saying, 'Yes, yes,' as he went.

After the ground and upper floors, Wood went to the basement.

The lower floor was reached by a narrow, dim staircase whose steps creaked and groaned under his weight, but which Morgan's initial survey team had assured everyone were safe. There were old wood handrails on either side of the staircase but set low, which made sense; the lower floor contained the orphans' sleeping quarters in two dormitories, one either side of a central corridor that led at its far end to a walk-in storage cupboard lined with splintered and broken wooden shelves.

Once at the bottom of the stairs, Wood found himself alone, the majority of the work happening above him on the ground and upper floors. He didn't like it down here. It always felt cold although the thermometers he'd set about the space told him it was only a degree or so lower than the upper floors, and it was quiet, the noises from upstairs muffled as though coming not just from a floor or two away but from a building or more away. Cobwebs hung from the ceiling and draped themselves down the walls, and the grime across the walls and floor looked thicker down here, darker and unhealthier. The air felt damp, as though a light mist hung in the atmosphere, and when he touched a wall it was clammy although not actually wet.

Wood made a note on his tablet to bring additional damp monitoring equipment in to check it out. The damp had already been checked and declared within reasonable limits but some of Manchester was built over tunnels dating from the Second World War or earlier which regularly flooded and where the levels of moisture could grow high, which might be the case at Factory Rook. He'd have to check the plans of the tunnels as well, to see if any were underneath the building or nearby, assuming the plans were accurate. He'd worked on a city centre store years ago that had a forgotten sub-basement leading to the tunnels. Forgotten, that was, until the damp of the continual subterranean flooding caused the shop's basement floor to collapse and hundreds of thousands of pounds worth of stock and two staff members to fall through into the water below.

It was dark in the two dormitories, stretching forlornly either side of the central access corridor. The rooms mirrored each other, with double entry doors and two sets of evenly spaced pillars onto which Wood had attached more sensors. There was no light down here yet, the strings of bulbs that ran across the ceilings in the two floors above him not yet webbing this space, and he had to use a helmet light to see by. There were no windows.

Wood entered Dormitory One and walked slowly from sensor to sensor, letting the light play ahead of him across the dusty floors, checking for breaks or weaknesses in the floorboards or for things he might trip over. It took him as long to collect the data from this one room as both the other floors had together. At the far end of the room he turned and looked back to the doorway, faintly outlined in glimmering streaks of pale light, and for a moment he thought he could see, or imagined, the shapes of metal cots crammed together and filling the room between the pillars and was struck with what an awful place this must have been to live, dark and mean and filled with odours and noise. How many children had been in here, he wondered, and remembered someone mentioning 200 ... in a room the size of little less than a modern sports field. It didn't seem possible, made him feel hemmed in, claustrophobic, and he left the room quickly and crossed to the second dormitory.

Dormitory Two smelled: a sharp aroma that reminded Wood of damp material, of sodden blankets left in lost piles and of animals burrowing through mud and earth. Despite the fact that he had been in here the previous day, and that the original safety crew had been working on the building for several weeks prior to Wood's and the others' arrival, entering the room was like opening the door to a long-forgotten folly, the air swirling and stagnant and dank, the dark seeming to have settled so that the shadows had weight, needing more than light to move them. Wood moved from sensor to sensor, linking each to his tablet and waiting for the data to sync, just him in the bubble of light created by his headlamp and tablet screen, feeling like a diver descending further and further towards the bottom of some depthless grey sea.

At the far end of the room Wood was kneeling by the final

pillar resetting the sensor mounted on it when his phone sounded an incoming text alert. It made him jump, as he'd assumed he'd be out of signal range here. He dug it out of his pocket, saw that he had only one bar of connection left, and then looked at the message, which was from Morgan: *Site mtg in 15 mins, B there.* He checked his tablet and made sure that all the data was saved as he'd be expected to give a preliminary view on it at the meeting and then, instead of going upstairs, he sat on the floor and leaned back against the rear wall, rummaging in his bag for his bottle of water. He took a long swig, savouring the taste and sensation of it, cold, cutting through the dryness of his mouth and the taste the dank air had left across his tongue. He wished he still smoked then, so that he could enjoy a slow, dragging cigarette, illuminating the air with its red tip, filling the place with the scent of the smoother tobaccos that he had always preferred. His fingers twitched, moving to his breast pocket where he had always kept his packet, then fell back to motionless. It had been five years since he had smoked but still the urge occasionally caught by surprise. He took another swallow of water and made do with that. He looked back along the room, imagined again the press of cots and the smells of the place and then of the luxury flats that were being planned. It seemed wrong somehow, money scabbing over the history of the place and sealing it below to dissipate unseen, to be slowly consumed by the passing of time

Wood shifted, uncomfortable. The wall was uneven against his back, with what felt like a ridge running vertically up from the floor or, he supposed, down from the ceiling. He shuffled forwards, taking another mouthful of water, and turned to look at the wall. In the light of his helmet he could see it now, a place where the boards that lined the wall at this edge had warped and formed a long, thin bulge. More evidence of damp, either now or at some point in the past? Had Factory Rook ever been flooded? Another thing to check, and he made another note on his tablet.

R you cmng? Where r u? Another text from Morgan, and Wood felt the swell of irritation inside him. Morgan was a grown man using childish text speak, presumably because he thought it reinforced his status of harried project manager, whereas to Wood's eye it simply made him look ridiculous. The man was anxiety in a suit, always stressed, always teetering on the edge of another furious rant, and it was exhausting to be around him. Still, he was the boss and he played the tune that Wood had to dance to. Sighing, he pushed himself to his feet, leaning against the wall to do so, and the wood panel bent under his hand. Surprised, he stood fully and then pushed against the panel. It bent again, giving several inches before coming up against something and he suddenly wondered why this wall was panelled, while all the others in the dormitories were simple painted brick. Running his hands along the panel, he found a seam, pressed one side to force it apart and then pushed his fingers into the gap he had created, trying not to think of spiders or rats or mice. Taking a grip, he pulled.

The panel came away easily, damp wood coming free from nails or tacks with a shriek like a child in pain. Wood cast the sheet aside and looked at the wall that he'd revealed. Only, it wasn't a wall; it was a door.

It was old, the brass lock plate scratched and dented, the wood of the panels and mouldings stained dark and thick with dust and some clinging grey mould. Wood tried to remember if there was anything beyond Dormitory Two on the plans he'd been working from but couldn't. He called up the scans of them on his tablet and scrolled through, finding no mention in any of the text descriptions or on the schematic describing a rear room. Another thing to note, which he duly did.

Wood turned and, trying not to think about lonely beds and the abandoned young and the sour smell of misery that must have filled the space about him, left the room and went to the meeting.

'So, the fucking main drain that runs under the building has suffered a partial collapse at some point and because there's not been water running through it it's now tangled with plant growth, and the fucking utility company say that because it's within the building's boundary line it's our job to fix,' said Morgan, face glum and glowering.

'That's maybe not so bad,' said Clarke, one of the site engineers. 'We were probably going to have to open up sections of the floor anyway. It just means going a little deeper to get to the blockage and clear it out, and then seal it over again.'

'Not so bad, just a little more expensive,' said Morgan.

'Of course,' said Clarke, ignoring Morgan's jibe. You had to, or you'd end up with the whining lecture about spiralling costs and how Morgan was responsible to the investors and how they'd crucify him and woe to it and woe to it and *woe*. They'd all learned to ignore it.

They'd already covered the problems with getting the crews into Factory Rook on time, the problems with the feeder roads, the shortage of scaffolding because another development had booked a lot of the city's available scaffolding and were refusing to release any of it to Morgan. The Factory Rook development was still on schedule, though, so no one around the table besides Morgan was too stressed.

'What about the subsidence?' he asked.

Wood, who had been thinking about the door and what might lie behind it, jerked around and said, 'It's fine.'

'Fine?' snapped Morgan. 'What the fuck does 'fine' mean?'

'Well,' said Wood, not rising to it, 'I've not had chance to model the data yet because I was still collecting it when you called the meeting, but my initial thoughts are that cracks in the outer walls are natural settling and only surface deep, rather than any indication of ongoing subsidence. They'll need filling and maybe reinforcing, to be sure, but I think the foundations are safe.'

'You think?'

'I think so, yes.' Still not taking the bait. 'But there are a couple of things I need to check about the area before I can be sure. I should have an answer by the end of tomorrow with luck, and I'll be able to show you the modelled data at tomorrow's meeting if you're interested?'

'Of course we're fucking interested,' said Morgan, and then turned to another of the people around the trestle table and demanded their report.

Wood could use programmes on his tablet to create real time models of the movement Factory Rook underwent over a twenty-four hour period, and then use these models to identify the type of movement he was observing. Although there were gaps because of the failed sensors he was able to see quickly that the vibrations being picked up were shuddering of the building because of the movement of traffic on the nearby ring road.

It made sense; the movement overnight was deeper but had distinct periods of activity and quiet, whilst during the day it was more constant but less heavy. More lorries transported cargo at night, when the roads were clearer, and the daytime was a constant welter of smaller cars.

That'll make Morgan happy, thought Wood, sending the man a quick email. Factory Rook would still need to be assessed by structural specialists to ensure that it could withstand the ongoing vibrations and to see how best to make good the cracks up the impressive front walls, but there would need to be little done at a foundation level. He could show them the line model of the building at the meeting tomorrow, show them the movement mapped against traffic data, show them the links, and that, he hoped, would be that.

The lowest floor was another matter, though.

There were readings from sensors in the two dormitories that Wood didn't recognise. Usually he could look at the vibration data, see the animated model, and know straight away what was causing the movement. Wood made sure before taking any readings that he understood the building, knew its construction materials, knew the surrounding areas, knew the earth beneath the construction, and all of this played into his knowledge and his expectation of the patterns he would see. Underground water created movements that were rhythmic but had several seconds between the upper peaks of the shifts. Traffic such as Factory

Rook was experiencing was sharper on the screen but the shifts smaller, the barks of a yipping dog rather than the ululating growl of a wolf. Subsidence was tiny, never ceasing, inexorable. These were the signatures that Wood knew and recognised.

The basement, though, was odd. Firstly, the vibrations occurred only on one or two sensors at a time rather than on all the sensors at once, and they did not progress from sensor to sensor as a person walking through the rooms would do. Rather, they jumped from one part of the room to another without apparently moving between the two points. Wood thought for a minute, leafing back through the rolodex of his mind, comparing the patterns to other odd signatures he had seen, but they resembled nothing he had investigated before. Watching them reminded him of the other notes he'd taken while in the basement, though, and he flicked into his browser and looked up the Manchester underground tunnels. Most were clustered around the city centre and none, or at least, none that had been mapped, stretched out far enough north to affect Factory Rook.

Something to do with the sewers, then? They'd already identified one problem with the sewer pipes, so was this another? And then there was the door that wasn't on the plans, and whatever lay beyond it. If there had been some kind of collapse behind the door, would that explain these odd readings? Or could it be some kind of burrowing creature in the earth below the building, fumbling in the dark, attracted by the remnants of the smell of bodies and flesh and sadness that had once suffused the room? *Mole people,* Wood thought and grinned and then stopped ginning because that's what the children in these rooms had been, really; mole people, forced to these dank spaces below the earth and clustered together in their misery. *Jesus,* he thought. *Jesus.*

Wood looked at the computer model of the movements: tiny delicate shivers as though the monitors had picked up the flapping of a bird's wing.

Ah, he thought, *maybe that was it. A bird was trapped in here and was flying around, up and down so only passing some of the sensors, creating a non-linear pattern.* But that wasn't an ideal explanation, not really. Wood had read bird movements on his sensors before many times, usually pigeons, sometimes sparrows and once a heron that had been trapped in a farm building he had been assessing for damage following a fire, and in each case the reading had been different to those he was seeing now. Bird movements tended to show as double pulses, an up- and then down-beat of their wings, and these were nothing like that. These grew quickly to a sharp peak as though the sensor, or the ground it was resting above, had been bumped which then dropped away again quickly, only to rise somewhere else.

A bat, then, coming not from below but above the sensors, swooping and darting? Wood yawned, tired, eyes aching from looking at the repeating animation of the Factory Rook's movement on the screen, and decided he'd investigate more the next day and only tell Morgan once he knew what he was dealing with. The movements he'd recorded weren't enough to cause a problem, and they certainly weren't subsidence, so there was no immediate need for concern. It was an anomaly, but one he'd put a solution to soon.

Yawning a second time, Wood flicked off the computer and went to bed where his sleep was deep and slow and dreamless.

Driving up to Factory Rook the next day, Wood thought again how he couldn't imagine anyone wanting to buy a flat in it once the building had been converted, no matter how nice they ended up being. The area around it wasn't a slum but it was poor, street after terraced street of small, featureless houses, little open land and less greenery, and shops that advertised things at heavily discounted prices and which were festooned with cheap plastic rubbish hanging above and in windows and standing on the pavements in tired piles. Contrary to the myth he'd heard about Manchester, it hadn't rained at all in the week he'd been working on Factory Rook and the streets had a worn, dusty look like an old dog lying in the sun. Sometimes it was possible to glimpse the modern city centre in the distance and it looked like another world, one that reached up to touch the sky rather than huddle, slouching, as the town around Factory Rook did.

The Rook itself was no better. It had survived the slum clearances of the '60s that had removed the buildings standing around it and now sat on a large concrete apron that was covered in the ghosts of painted lines delineating where sports courts had been during its time as a council-run school, and in places this apron had cracked and weeds choked the cracks, brown and sinewy and tangled. Over the years the building had gathered about itself a collar of old leaves and litter and it now formed a thick, unbroken band where the walls met the ground, as though the rot was trying to strangle the old Ragged School.

A chain link fence had been erected around the perimeter of Factory Rook, top bent out and crowned with rusting jags of barbed wire. Lower down, links had rusted into other links and leaves and other rubbish had caught in the chain, flapping in the frequent winds that swept over the exposed ground. Here and there the fence sagged, the columns it was attached bent and rusting, the chain hanging like old, torn sheeting. It was, Wood thought, a miserable place, drab and worn and tired.

At the main gate he found a new guard on duty who checked his identification with irritating slowness. 'Sorry, sir,' he said as he finally handed it back, 'but we can't be too careful.'

'Where's Eric?' Wood asked. He usually spoke a few words with the morning guard and his unexpected absence was unsettling.

'Gone, sir.'

'Gone? Where?'

'Just gone. Handed his notice in in the middle of the night and wouldn't stay. They had to bring me in from another site. Caused a bit of an upset.'

'Why did he quit?'

'I don't know, sir, I never met him.'

'But he'd been doing it for days now, weeks I think. Why suddenly quit?'

'Like I say, I didn't know him, but nights are funny when you're by yourself even when you're used to them, especially in a place like this.' His gesture took in not just Factory Rook but the surrounding areas. 'Sometimes, it just gets to you. It's too quiet, or not quiet enough, you know what I mean?'

Thinking of the dormitories, Wood said, 'Yes,' and drove into the site to do his work.

There had been more sensor drops overnight, including several places where the sensors had literally dropped, somehow coming loose from their mounts and falling to the floor. Most were undamaged, but one had landed on its edge and cracked open and its electronic guts had spilled out across the uneven boards. Wood remounted the fallen sensors, recalibrating them as he did so, and replaced the damaged one, and then downloaded the data from all of them on the ground and first floors. A quick check, even without the modelling he would do later, showed him the same readings as the previous day's: traffic, the twenty-first century's heartbeat and pulse. If he listened, he could hear its distant drone and whirr and almost match these sounds to the movements registering on his sensors. It was satisfying to know, and to be confident in this knowledge.

Only, he didn't know about the lowest floor yet, so he started to make his way to the basement. As he went he could hear Morgan holding forth with some new torrent of misery, this time about the cost of raw materials, and the answering raised voice of some contractor, the two men strident against a background clamour of feet and things being dropped and placed and picked up and moved. The peace of Dormitory One, when he reached it, was almost a welcome relief.

First, Wood downloaded the data from the sensors and then skimmed the information. There were more of those delicate, odd movements, feathering shivers of vibration or shifts, he still had no idea what they might be. This time, he spent longer in Dormitory One, using his helmet light to scan the floor carefully, looking for signs of birdlife, or flooding, but there was nothing; no white streaks of birdshit, no buckled boards or marks that would indicate any kind of water intrusion now or in the past. Nothing to explain the movement. He also checked the back wall of the room, but this was reassuringly solid, not panelled, and contained no hidden doors.

Dormitory Two was the same, no signs of flooding or animal incursion except for some old, chalky rat droppings that crumbled when he prodded them with the toe of his boot. The data from the sensors, most of which had survived the night with power and attached to the pillars, showed more of those irregular movements. He went from each sensor that had registered it trying to track some kind of path through the room, but it simply didn't make sense. It started here, suddenly appeared there, jerked back over to somewhere else, with no apparent movement between. If not an animal, which it didn't appear to be, it had to be something affecting the structure, but what?

Wood went to the rear wall and pulled away a couple more of the panels that lined it, fully exposing the door and the brickwork either side of it. He wasn't sure why he hadn't told Morgan about the door yet but rationalised it that he'd rather give the man a problem that he'd already solved than a problem he could moan about. Besides, there was something exciting about it, a mysterious room that shouldn't exist, being able to open it without interference. It was like one of the Boys' Own adventure stories he'd read as a child, the sort of thing his own son refused to read, favouring instead science fiction stories about aliens and rockets and wars between worlds, and Wood realised with a sad little jolt that he missed those stories, and missed thinking that one day he might be the hero of one of them.

The door was locked. No surprise, Wood thought, and pushed against it. There was no give in it, not even the normal movement he'd have expected in a locked door, the slight recoil from his touch until the lock itself stopped it. Over the years, he suspected the wood had swelled and fixed the door in place, so he took a step back and kicked at it. It shook and a puff of dust floated out. He kicked again, the sound of it a dull percussive *whump* and this time he felt movement. Another kick, the vibration of it rolling back up his leg, and then another and now the door snapped open and a thick, stale smell came out of the room beyond on a roll of air that was chilly and moist.

His helmet light didn't penetrate far into the gloom and he wished he'd thought to put another torch into his bag. No matter, he supposed, he'd just have to be careful. Stepping to the threshold, Wood looked down, so that he could see the expanse of floor just inside the door. The boards were bare and covered in undisturbed dust but seemed solid, and he placed one foot on them experimentally, pressing down. They held, and he entered the room.

It was an office and it smelled, not of damp but of something else, of age and mustiness and a lower, earthier scent like fruit that had turned in long-forgotten bowl or milk souring in a bottle. There was desk, furred with dust that almost obscured the old-fashioned blotter that sat upon it, a chair, and a series of wooden filing cabinets. Wood scrolled through the Factory Rook plans again on his tablet, the extra light from its screen filling the room with a shifted, dappling glimmer, but there was no office space to be found anywhere on the lower floor. A later addition, then, never added to the plans? Its proximity to the two dormitories made Wood wonder if it also doubled as a guard or night watchmen's office, someone to be close to the children during the darker hours.

To be close to the children to comfort them? Wood thought again about the dormitories filled with cots or bunks, about the children housed here and how cramped it would have been, and decided that no, comfort hadn't been part of the remit of anyone stationed in this office. Policing, maybe. Behavioural control, probably. This was not, he didn't think, a place where comfort lived, only austerity and charity as cold and hard as porcelain tiles.

He went to one of the filing cabinets and pulled on a drawer handle, not expecting it to open and was surprised when it did.

The cabinet, that drawer at least, didn't contain files. Instead, there was a pile of bound leather ledgers, the pile tilting unevenly, the top book stamped on its cover in gold foil with a crest of some sort and the words *Factory Rook Ragged School and Orphanage Accounts 1862.* The volume below was from 1863, the one below that from 1897. The bottom volume had bloated, and its paper pages disintegrated when Wood touched them leaving pale streaks across his fingers.

He shut the drawer and opened the next one down. More accounts, random years of bound finances, and when he opened the pages he saw simply column after column of transactions and donations, expenditure and cost and income along with, in the two right hand columns, a running tally of staff and resident numbers. The next drawer held similar, and the last in the cabinet yet more.

The next cabinet held folders, tied in string and labelled with years, containing invoices, receipts, paperwork, some faded to illegibility, some still clear. In 1865, in July, Factory Rook had taken delivery of '120 combes for the treatment of lice', whereas in 1894, in February, '100 woollen blankets (small)' had been bought. *Perhaps nits weren't a problem that year, just the cold,* he thought. A year later, he saw by flicking through the brittle pages, that the Rook had in one month bought half a hundredweight of small potatoes and half that weight of carrots but only two cuts of meat, both 'cheap and bony'. An appended menu listed 'meat stew' as being the main meal every day, although how much meat there could have been in it Wood didn't like to guess.

Wood discovered the foundling journal in the last drawer.

There were three ledgers in the drawer. The first of these was stamped not with the word 'Accounts' below the crest but 'Recipients', which he soon realised meant the children who attended Factory Rook. Each double page named a child and listed the numbers of meals they had had, the lessons they'd attended and whether they were an 'Orphan', 'Street Child' or 'Pauper's Child'. Where they were a pauper's child, the parent was also named. The second ledger was labelled 'Orphans' and seemed to list children delivered to Factory Rook by the state, often via the courts, giving details of their age and circumstances and parents, including on occasion what had killed these parents or what crime the child had committed that required their removal from their parents. In looking down the recorded fates of the parents, where it was known, Wood came across a depressing list of diseases including typhoid, cholera and scarlet fever, found murder and madness and once, the single phrase 'Died of lethargy'. *God,* he thought, *died of lethargy.* Did that mean some kind of wasting disease, or was the poor sod so exhausted with their poverty-stricken life that they had one day simply crawled under what blankets they had and stopped living?

The third ledger was labelled 'Foundlings'. It bulged oddly and when he opened it he discovered that some of the pages had strips of material attached to them, all at different points on the page to try to stop the ledger becoming impossible to close. His torch beam illuminated the pieces, various rough wools and blends, each a different pattern, most drab but one or two brighter, with yellows or red weaves running through the more usual greens and browns. He lifted one of the pieces carefully, reading what was written underneath. 'Child (F) left on church steps, St Clements, Martledge, sickly, approx. four days old. Cloth: possibly Gorton weave. N: Alice Gorton'. Another read: 'Child (M) two or three weeks, left at the school in the night, healthy but small. Cloth Kendal Green, travelling family? Salesman? N: Peter Kendal. Gone beyond, 23rd December 1884'.

Gorton weave? Kendal Green? He didn't understand for a minute, and then he did.

The poor fuckers couldn't write so they couldn't leave any details of their children, not names or where they were born or why they were being abandoned, so they left them for the church or the Ragged School to look after and they left a piece of local cloth to try and give the child a history. This child is from Gorton, this from Kendal, and the staff of Factory Rook knew nothing else about them so took them in and named them for their cloth. And what's 'gone beyond'? The child died, died here after being abandoned? In one of those underground dormitories, surrounded by other children who were strangers? Christ, Christ God, that's terrible.

Some of the entries didn't have cloths attached, but most did, and they were the saddest things Wood had ever seen, tiny little pieces of material that represented everything known about some of the children that had lived here. He dropped the ledger back in the drawer, slammed it shut with a bang of dust, and turned to leave the room. He'd had enough now, had enough of Factory Rook and its odd movement readings, and he wanted out. He'd pass this to Morgan, let him decide what to do. They were supposed to get in contact with the local historical society to let them take away and catalogue finds like this, but he suspected it would all be dumped in one of the skips that ringed the site, to be buried under wood and rubble. Historical societies took too long to investigate, and Morgan wouldn't want the delay. Whatever. Let it fall to him, he was project manager, he could read these entries and carry the burden of all those scraps of material to whatever fate he decreed for them, it wasn't Wood's responsibility.

As he moved to leave the room, Wood noticed the trapdoor for the first time. It was to the side of the open door and close to the wall which was why Wood hadn't seen it as he came in the room: a cut-away square of wood with a single recessed metal ring just above the centre. His light caught the metal, which gleamed dully in the yellow glow, years' worth of cobwebs and dust flattening the reflection of it to the milky glint of a cataracted eye.

If there was a trapdoor, then there was something below it. God *damn* it, and oh *fuck* it, now he'd have to see what was there because he couldn't leave it because it was his job, to understand the building's movements and to make recommendations on the kind of work that needed to be done before any restoration or rebuilding could start.

Wood used the tip of a screwdriver to clear the muck from around the handle and to lever it up, but even after wiping the metal clean using his sleeve it felt greasy in his hand. Pulling initially did no good, the trapdoor didn't move, but after he'd dragged the screwdriver around the edges of the wood, scoring into the caked dirt and breaking it apart, it only took several hard tugs to pull it open. Its hinges squealed furiously, cats in heat, and then the panel banged back, revealing the dark maw of an opening.

Even with the combined light of Wood's helmet and his tablet turned to torch mode, the darkness below the trapdoor was thick. A set of steps descended to a tunnel, he saw, the floor of which was rough and slightly curved as though the tunnel was circular rather than square. There weren't supposed to be tunnels here, not according to any of the sewer or building plans they'd obtained, so what were these? He leaned further down, head submerging into the gloom, sending his light all around. The tunnel seemed to stretch away in both directions, and there were openings off this main tunnel, if main tunnel it was. Some of the side tunnels headed back under Factory Rook, which might mean the ground under the building was riddled with tunnels, which might make it unsafe. *Fuck and damn,* Wood thought again. *Fuck and damn.*

Fuck and double damn. Morgan wouldn't accept 'I found a tunnel but didn't investigate except to stick my head in' as a report, so Wood sat on the edge of the opening and put his feet on the top step. Despite its age it held, creaking but not bending, so he balanced his tablet, torch mode still on, on the edge of the hole to illuminate his exit and took his phone from his pocket. He had no signal down here - there was too much stone between him and the rest of the crew, between him and Morgan – but it also had a torch mode which he turned on. He debated going back for better light but then decided against it. Do a preliminary scan of the area, maybe leave a few sensors, and then he could hand it over to Morgan to get it shored up safely, finally get lights down here and decide what to do about the cabinets and whatever might be in the desk. Five minutes, and he'd be done.

Wood went down the steps warily, testing each one, but they were all solid, and within a minute he was standing on the earthen floor of the tunnel. His initial impression had been right, it was curved, not a circle but a flattened oval. Closer inspection of the floor and walls showed a rippled surface, and the nearest side tunnel had the same design, if design it was. What were these, some kind of natural bore hole? Wood tried to remember what sort of rock lay under Factory Rook, what earth it was built on, but he was sure it was hard and not given to this kind of water erosion. Mole people, then?

'Real big mole people,' he said, looking around the tunnel and then he stopped speaking. His voice felt small and flat in the tunnel, and the joke didn't seem funny any more. There was something about the tunnels, something that made him uneasy. He took a single step into the nearest side tunnel, looking up at the ceiling. There were no cracks at least, but nowhere to attach a sensor either, just the ripples. Finally, Wood placed the sensor on the floor and turned it on. He could bring his tablet down later to properly calibrate it.

He placed another sensor a few metres further along the tunnel and then turned back. That was as far as he was going. He stepped back into the main tunnel, seeing the square of light that was his way into the office and the dormitory beyond and was glad of it. He hurried towards the light now, wanting to be away, put another sensor on the bottom step for good measure and had stepped above it when he stopped.

The tunnel walls reminded him of something.

What?

Wood didn't know, but something. *Something.* Something he'd seen, not in real life but what? On television? Yes, something on television, a documentary. But about what?

About tunnelling things, tunnelling creatures, about the tunnels they left.

That was ridiculous, these were tunnels through rock and earth and they were huge, but suddenly he saw some great blind worm drawn by the smell of all those cramped children, all the sweat and tears and misery and urine loosed in sleep, nosing up through the earth and criss-crossing beneath the Rook, questing, sniffing, drawing itself up to the boards above it. Would it bump against the underside of the floor, drop away, bump against the floor somewhere else? Looking for something, seeking what all animals sought, seeking food.

Feeding?

Wood could see it, not mole people, no, not mole people at all, but some great blind thing rising up through the earth to strike off the floor, heard the screams of the children above as it constantly banged against the wood, perhaps snuffling, perhaps silent, led by the stench of misery and loss and sweat and urine and tears.

But why the trapdoor? Why create an access to the creature?

To feed it, he answered himself, to stop its visits, the weakest ones being dropped down through the trapdoor to protect the larger group. He thought of the entry for Peter Kendal, so healthy yet with those words *Gone beyond* and the date just weeks after he'd arrived at the Rook, and was that it?

And if so, was it dead? Because there were still vibrations, still movements, weren't there? Weren't there?

Yes.

Wood turned, torch and phone sending a weak beam down the tunnel. How noisy had he been? How much did he smell, with his clean soaped skin and washed clothes and the cologne he used because Mary had bought it him even though he didn't really like it, and now his fear, this wash of terrible, stinking dreadful fear.

His light caught something in the tunnel, something glistening. Wood took a step back and up, a scream building in his throat because he could feel it now, feel the cold and the misery that was wafting up the tunnel, feel and smell the stench of a thing that fed on unhappiness and loneliness and loss and on salt tears and stinging, shameful bedtime urine, and took another step and the air was clammy against his puckering skin and his stomach turned, twisted and let loose a splash of hot, explosive vomit. He screamed then, but the sound never reached above the dormitories.

In the tunnels below Manchester, something surged towards Factory Rook.

NIGHT FALLS OVER PENDLE

There is still much debate about the extent and severity of the witch-hunting madness that swept through England in the 17th century, though remarkably little of it is well-informed.

For example, the perceived wisdom that witches were burned at the stake in England during a period stretching almost from the end of the Roman occupation right up until the early modern age is totally wrong. Witchcraft alone was never a capital offence. The medieval Catholic Church in England derided the mere notion of witchery, instructing its congregations to ignore it as superstitious folly. Even later, during the reign of James I (1603-1625), the first English monarch to truly fear the power of witches, most witchcraft offences were punishable by imprisonment; only witchcraft in the commission of murder was deemed worthy of the ultimate penalty, and execution in this case was by noose, not fire. And while written accounts list hundreds of unfortunates put to death on charges of witchcraft – about 500 is the current estimate – what the records don't tell us is how many more were acquitted. There were certainly many cases where magistrates not only rejected the evidence of prosecution witnesses but ridiculed them and turned them out of court.

That said, this legendary cold wind of madness did sweep England, and 500 is an appalling loss, especially under such spurious circumstances. One of the best examples of this, and yet one case with more than a few mysterious aspects, is that of the Lancashire Witches – or, as it is better known, the Pendle Witches.

After James I, a hard-line Protestant, passed his Witchcraft Act of 1604, England became a much more dangerous place for those with alternative beliefs. Religious dissenters had long been subject to accusations of heresy, but primarily these were intellectuals and thinkers, members of the upper and middle classes. Under the new 1604 laws, the threat extended right across society into remote villages where folklore was still a potent force. Moreover, superstitious fear in these primitive communities had been stoked by the Protestant Reformation. The protection against evil apparently offered by the Catholic Church with its arcane ceremonies and miraculous powers was gone. By comparison, the austere meeting-house was a distinctly non-magical place. Fearful peasants thus looked to their own defences, and this was especially the case in regions of the country where events beyond local control had caused horror and misery, where the concept of 'Merrie England', as born in the latter half of Elizabeth I's reign, already hung in tatters.

A good example of this was East Anglia, which during the 1640s suffered extensively from Civil War violence, and where the depredations of Matthew Hopkins would subsequently follow. But a better example yet would be Lancashire, where, by the turn of the 17th century, poor harvests and social upheaval had been tearing communities apart for decades.

In truth, Lancashire had never bought into the concept of Merrie England.

Throughout the Reformation, the county had been a Catholic hotbed, and in response to this, monarchs prior to James I – even Good Queen Bess herself – had suspected, interrogated and brutalised its occupants. The dissolution of the influential Whalley Abbey in the Ribble Valley in 1537, and the execution of its abbot by Henry VIII, caused terrible ructions among a vast range of native Lancastrians, who feared they were damned for not preventing it. This mass spiritual disorder didn't itself cause the terrible events at Pendle in 1612, but it laid the ground for them.

The disaster began unfolding properly on March 21 that year, when a pedlar was accosted on the road to Colne by a half-witted girl called Alizon Devize, who begged him for some pins. He refused, so she cursed him. A common enough event in the rural heartlands of England – except that this pedlar promptly had a seizure, which paralysed half his body. Though he later died, the pedlar remained conscious long enough to make an accusation, and Devize was arrested under King James' new legislation.

In her subsequent examination, during which no torture is recorded as having been used, the child freely explained that she was part of a local coven, the leader of which was her grandmother, Old Demdike, though she named a number of other women too, all of whom lived in villages around Pendle Forest. Follow-up arrests were made, there were more interrogations – again without the use of torture (according to the records) – and more names were named, and descriptions given of lurid rituals by which the accused claimed to have damaged local communities and taken the lives of their enemies. In due course, 11 women and one man were locked up in Lancaster Gaol. The lead investigator, the magistrate Roger Nowell, was even more convinced that he was doing the right thing when suspicious items like clay figurines and so-called 'witch bottles' – jars filled with urine, human hair, human fingernails etc – were found on some of the women's properties.

Could these damning clues have been planted by investigators? Yes, of course. But the accused never made that complaint. As before, several of those arrested later (though not all) willingly confessed to participation in witchcraft. Even by modern standards it would seem like a cut and dried case, though what was not being taken account of were the extenuating circumstances.

Most of these women were outcasts – old, ragged harridans, and probably nuisances in their neighbourhoods given the regular begging they indulged in, not to mention their frequent threats to pass hexes. Like Alizon Devize, many were described as half-witted, and quite possibly were so ignorant of King James' new laws that they thought they'd be empowered by claiming links to the Devil rather than endangered (minor forms of magic like healing and casting love-spells had been commonplace in village life for decades). In addition, there were factions among the accused. Old Demdike had a fierce rival in a certain Mother Chattox, the matriarch of a different clan and, allegedly, a separate coven. They disliked each other intensely, and it is probable that false allegations were made in both directions in the hope that enemies would get their just deserts. However, there is also a chance - much more so than during other trials of this period - that the accused were indeed practising witchcraft. Witness after witness came forward against Demdike and Chattox, claiming that local villagers had lived in fear of them for as long as 50 years. Even today, from the surviving testimonies, it appears that many of the accused believed they were sorceresses even if they actually weren't.

Either way, the outcome was predictable. The following August, nine women and one man were convicted of committing ten murders by witchcraft. Old Demdike, who was 80, had suffered so much from the harsh conditions inside the prison that she had already died. In that respect, she was lucky. On August 20, Chattox and the rest of the accused were led through a jeering crowd to a bleak hill outside Lancaster, where they were hanged on a public gallows, their bodies left there to rot - a terrible spectacle that would overshadow the district for centuries afterwards.

Even now, Pendle possesses a dark aura. Much of its mystique stems from the regular pilgrimages made there, usually around Halloween, by ghost hunters, sensation seekers, modern day pagan groups and even New Agers seeking a form of communion with the departed. But it is an eerie place in its own right, Pendle Forest an inhospitable realm of desolate moor and tangled wildwood, Pendle Hill a totem of grimness in a near-empty landscape. Visit it on a dreary autumn day, and it's quite easy to believe that eldritch powers still lie dormant in its ancient rocks and soil.

TIGHTS AND STRAW AND WIRE MESH

John Travis

Scarecrows don't bleed.

I have to keep reminding myself of this, even now. Tights and straw and wire mesh - that's all they are. Scarecrows don't bleed.

Only apparently, this one did.

It was a strange feeling, to be back in the country after twenty years. For myself, I still felt like a local - in the sense that I was a northerner if nothing else. But I soon realised that not everyone saw it like that: I had an 'accent' I was told, I 'sounded like an American'. People were friendly enough on the surface, but there was always something underneath; a vague distrust, a wariness perhaps, that somehow because I was now more confident and self-assured (and if living in America teaches you nothing else it's that anything is possible) that meant I wasn't a true Brit any more.

On top of all that was a nagging feeling from my childhood that I wasn't even considered a Lancastrian, despite moving there from Yorkshire when I was seven: to some I was born on the wrong side of the Pennines, simple as that - something that my peers made abundantly clear when I was at school. For a long time, my accent caused me problems - kids putting the letter 't' in front of everything I said when they wanted to get under my skin, for example - and I got into more than my fair share of tussles because of it. But it lost its rough edges and the vowel sounds got longer and I seemed to fit in a bit better. But even then, I was never sure it was enough. And as a result of flitting to the States in my early twenties my accent changed again, so when I came back I wasn't even thought of as a Tyke any more: now, I was a Yank. Luckily, I found it didn't rankle that much, the self-assured Yankee within me enabling me to put such nebulous prejudices aside and concentrate on my trip back home to see my mother.

Normally she came to stay with us in Iowa – Marge, the kids and me, every two years as regular as clockwork – but Mom's – sorry, Mum's – health had been on the wane since her last visit a couple of years back and this time she couldn't make it over, so it was decided that I'd come home (a strange expression, considering what was later to take place) and make the journey I'd been threatening to make for the past ten years or so. Initially the idea was for all of us to make the trip, but Marge couldn't get the time off work and Suse was due to go to summer camp around the same time and it wasn't fair to bring Dale over on his own, so we decided: next time, we'd all come. Which we have – but not for the reason any of us wanted.

I think when she visited me that day in the hospital Mum knew I wouldn't be coming back. Maybe it hastened her decline, I don't know. It was barely eight months after I got back to Marge and the kids that I got that awful phone call from Mum's neighbour saying that she'd died. So, we've all made the solemn trip over for the funeral and to stay on a few extra days, so the kids could see where Daddy and Grandma lived, knowing all the while that we'll also be going somewhere that Daddy really doesn't want to go.

And I mean *really.*

'You go, love – it'll do you good to get out, instead of staying round here all the time. And you did say you were looking forward to it.'

She was right, I was – because although Mum had mentioned them many times, scarecrow festivals were a new one on me. When the kids found out they made me promise to take lots of pictures, but the idea of going on my own took some of the sheen off my enthusiasm. I'd been shocked how much Mum had deteriorated since I'd last seen her, keeping the worst details of her illness from me in the lengthy emails she wrote, and it was obvious after a couple of days when we'd only managed to get as far as

Lancaster that she wouldn't be able to make it. Not that I minded – it was good to spend time with her regardless of location, and in truth I wasn't feeling that great myself – since I'd arrived I'd had several bad headaches, and the jetlag was really starting to kick in. But I had to admit that it wasn't going to be much of a visit if the furthest we could venture was ten minutes down the road.

'Are you sure? I'm pretty pooped myself. It's no great loss.'

'Look, you're going,' she told me, glaring out at me from under her untrimmed eyebrows. 'I watched you read that guidebook from cover to cover last night. What are you smiling at?'

I was smiling at her extra 'o's in 'loook' and 'guideboook' but I didn't think she'd understand. When I'd first met Marge, she used to tease me for talking like that myself. Somewhere along the line, I stopped.

'Okay, okay; I'll go. But just for a few hours.'

So, stepping out into an overcast August afternoon and a sky the colour of slate, I kissed her goodbye at the door and set out.

Leaving the town behind and heading north, the traffic and buildings began to thin and I cautiously navigated my way along narrow roads hemmed in by dry-stone walls, taking in the sight of the farmer's fields with their sheep and trees and farmhouses and grass of the same luminous hue as the peas we'd had with our pies the night before. Had the sun been shining it would've been pretty, but it hadn't put in an appearance since I'd got here, the sky always threatening rain. Suddenly I began to feel extremely weary – the jetlag again – when I saw a sign up ahead:

WELCOME TO THE
LUNE VALLEY

Soon after, the inevitable line of cars snaking off into the distance told me that I must be getting close to Wray Village. Falling in behind the last of the cars, I idled the engine and picked up the guidebook on the passenger seat.

Despite only being a short way up the road I'd never been to Wray before. I'd heard of the village of course and the famous flood of '67, but I'd never had any reason to go there. According to the guidebook, the scarecrow festival had begun around the time I left for the States. As well as the festival, the village was also famed for its maggot racing. And they say that Britain is an island of eccentrics. Sensing movement ahead, I put down the guide and edged forward a grand total of four feet.

After carrying on like this for the next twenty minutes or so I started with a headache, not helped by the muggy weather and the slate grey sky, low even by British standards (until I came back I'd forgotten how oppressive it could feel outdoors) and, hemmed in as I was by the dry stone walls, the sky started to remind me of the raised lid of a coffin. After a couple more minutes of this I was seriously thinking about forgetting it and going back home; but then I saw my first scarecrow, halfway up a tree.

At first, I'd thought it was a man climbing it, his hands reaching for the branches, until I saw the shapelessness of the hands themselves, gloves nailed to the trunk. Despite my headache, I laughed. Inching closer, I found myself impressed by the detail - the ragged old clothes, the straw for hair, even the way the shoes were fastened to the bottom of the trousers - whoever had made it had spent a lot of time getting it right.

After that the scarecrows began to appear with increasing regularity: one dressed in a suit sitting at a makeshift desk, tapping away at a painted cereal box-cum computer at the side of the road; then a vicar, complete with cardboard dog collar and dodgy woollen combover, standing outside the local village church with a collection plate; and, for some reason, an Egyptian Mummy and a retired army colonel complete with handlebar moustache, propped up against a bus stop. Each was very good, but my enjoyment was being increasingly spoiled by my headache, which was threatening to turn into a migraine. Hoping that it wasn't much further so I could park up and find somewhere that sold paracetamols, it was a relief when I saw what looked like a sign up ahead, presumably for the village; and, when three or four cars in front of me turned right up a side road leaving a considerable gap in the traffic, I put my foot down. I'd barely done so when a bolt of pain shot through my head, momentarily causing me to close my eyes. When I opened them, two things filled my windscreen: one was the sign, which in that panicked moment read *A WRY VILLAGE,* and the second was the rear of the estate car just ahead of it that I was about to smack into; thankfully just before I did, I spotted a narrow lane among the trees to the left. Gritting my teeth and spinning the wheel as hard as I could, I somehow managed to avoid a collision. Slowing down, I pulled onto the grass verge and stopped and tried to get my breath back.

As I did I wondered what to do. That was quite a jag of pain I'd just experienced - what if it happened again? Suddenly I wasn't sure if I was fit to drive any more. But at the same time, I didn't much fancy leaving the car abandoned in a narrow country lane and phoning for a taxi to take me home. Unable to make a decision, I started drumming on the steering wheel, and was just starting to get into a rhythm when I looked up and a possible solution presented itself in the form of a mud-smeared sign nailed to a tree ahead:

ECCLES SCARECROWS AHEAD
300 YARDS

I must admit the sign made me feel odd for a couple of reasons - mostly because I'd never heard of the place (it certainly wasn't mentioned in the guidebook) - but also because in some way I felt it confirmed others' beliefs about me being an outsider. But that was silly. Besides, it might be interesting - Mum had said that there were scarecrows all over the area, and in the most unlikely places. But the clincher was that it was close by and the road was clear. So, deciding to give it a try and see how I felt about driving later on, I trundled along at a steady twenty until I reached a farmer's field that acted as a car park and parked up next to a Portaloo, beside which was another scarecrow, its long, rubbery legs twisted around each other in agony as it waited to spend a penny. Then, after consoling myself that if nothing else I had at least remembered to drive on the left-hand side of the road, I took off my shoes, pulled on the wellies that Mum had warned me I'd need, and got out of the car.

Surprisingly, the headache had eased off slightly, but as I walked over to a man with mutton-chop whiskers squashed into a fold-up chair at a trestle table I wondered how long that would last; if anything, the mugginess outside was even worse than it had been in the car.

'What you blowin' at?' he asked me.

'Hot,' I told him.

'That's August for you. Tenner.' Before I had a chance to react, he tore a ticket off a roll and thrust it at me. Shrugging, I paid up.

Trudging back the way I'd come in, I took a closer look at the scarecrow outside the toilet, marvelling at the effort in its creation. It appeared to be made mostly from straw stuffed into old tights and bound in by discarded clothes and footwear, with thin bracelets of wire mesh around the wrists and ankles to stop everything spilling out. Sellotaped to the Portaloo was a piece of paper bearing the word *SCARECROWS*. Following the arrow beside it, I headed down a dense, wooded path to what was presumably Eccles village; but the little I could make out through the trees on the way made me think that 'village' was probably overstating it.

Apart from the half dozen or so scarecrows that were propped up against or sitting on dry stone walls, the whole place seemed to consist of little more than a newsagents/grocers, a pub and, amazingly, what looked like a working red telephone box. Outside it, a further scarecrow stood, holding a small black rectangle in its mitt, presumably representing a mobile.

Going into the grocers, I asked if they had any paracetamol.

'*'Parrots 'et 'em all'?*' a fat, red-faced man said, mangling my pronunciation from behind his Formica counter. 'If you mean headache tablets, then the answer is no.'

'Do you know where I could get s –'

'No. Try going for a walk. Best remedy for a headache I know.' Turning his back on me, he rummaged around among the few tins he had on his shelf. Staggered by the man's rudeness, I almost laughed: so much for customer service improving since I'd been away. But realising that he was probably right, I decided to get out into the fresh air and see what the place had to offer. But before I did I needed something to drink; and as heading back into the grocers for a bottle of water seemed like a bad idea, I went to the pub instead.

'*Tea?*' the barman said, widening his eyes.

'Well I'm driving, you know,' I said, trying to justify myself.

'Bully for you. The wife'll make you a cuppa if you want one.' He called back through a narrow door.

'Oh, sorry – I skipped lunch earlier. Could I get a sandwich too?'

This time I thought his eyes were going to pop out of his head. 'This is a *pub*,' he said as if to a child. 'And *this* is the twenty-first century,' I wanted to say but didn't. Instead, I waited uncomfortably for the tea to arrive, whilst doing my best to ignore the stares from the other patrons. Standing it for twenty minutes with no sign of any tea, I got off the stool and walked out.

Increasingly disheartened, I wandered up and down various dead-end lanes and back again, wishing that I'd stayed with Mum after all. I was tired, the headache was getting worse, and the air was as thick as treacle, with the sky shading towards the same colour. On top of that, the number of scarecrows seemed to be diminishing. So, reaching the next crossroads I decided I'd have a quick look around, turn back, take the pictures I'd promised to take and head back to the car.

Setting off up what was little more than a rutted dirt track, I found myself getting slightly out of breath with the rising of the road. At one point it became so steep that I could see nothing but the track ahead, the sky so low that I felt like I was about to walk up into it. Puffing like a carthorse and cursing myself for junking my diet in favour of fry-ups, it was with some relief when the road began to level out in front of me and I spotted a grey-brick farmhouse; and, slap-bang in the centre of a muddy field over to the left, a solitary scarecrow. I assumed the farmhouse was empty; if there'd been anyone inside, they'd have needed their lights on. But I gathered this wasn't unusual, as apparently most of the houses in Wray were empty while the festival was on, partly because it was August and holiday time, and partly because the locals didn't want sightseers staring into their gardens and through their windows for a fortnight. Still, it must've made the village eerie on an evening, the whole place being largely populated by scarecrows.

Looking across the table-flat landscape as I gasped at the humid air, I wondered whether to keep going.

On the long walk up, I hadn't seen any other scarecrows; also, this scarecrow was the only one I'd seen that was actually in a field - maybe it wasn't part of the festival at all but was actually there to scare crows. On the other hand, there was nothing to say I *couldn't* enter, so, following a well-worn trail of boot prints in the mud, I began slopping across the field towards the scarecrow, turning around every so often hoping to see somebody else walking up the hill, but no-one was. Besides the squelching of my boots in the mud, there was no sound. Not even the birds twittered, making me think that a storm was on the way.

It wasn't until I was a few feet away that I realised the scarecrow was probably part of the festival after all - unless the crows round here were frightened of schoolboys.

Stuck on its pole, the scarecrow was maybe five, maybe five-two tall and clad in what looked like a grubby school uniform, complete with blazer, black trousers, dirty white shirt and loosely knotted tie, the tongue of which was slung over the right shoulder. A pair of scuffed brown shoes completed the picture. But again, I wondered; something about its general demeanour, the sheer *grottiness* of it and the age of the clothing made me think that maybe it was just a bog-standard bird-scarer after all. But after looking at the head more closely I realised there was nothing bog-standard about it.

For a start there was the hair - or rather, the straw on its head, a thick, lustrous covering which although not combed into any particular style gave the impression that it was *supposed* to look as it did, stuck up all over the place like a blond chimney-sweep's brush. Then there were the stitched features of the face - the vicious, angular slits that served for eyes, the aggressive upturned arrow that was the nose - but most disturbing of all was the mouth, a pained, rictus grin at either end which became a swollen, bruised mess at the centre as a result of overstitching, and around which lashings of what looked like red marker pen had been applied. Finally, the whole thing, but the head especially, seemed to be waterlogged, with large drips of dirty water running down the pillowcase cheeks, threatening to blot the pen-work.

For some reason I couldn't quite place the overall effect but it disturbed me greatly, even more than it perhaps deserved – and made me glad that I'd made up my mind to go. But a promise is a promise, and I was sure the kids would love it, gruesome as it was, so I went to get my phone from my pocket and take a few snaps. But before I did, I took another look at the scarecrow and decided that something definitely wasn't right: the tie slung over the shoulder. Taking a step forward, I grabbed hold of it and at that instant a bolt of pain equal to the one I'd experienced on the way into the village shot through my head, followed by the sensation of being hit in the face by a wall of water, making me gasp and double up in pain; but just as soon as these sensations arrived they were gone, leaving my eyes stinging with tears and my mouth feeling like a huge bruise. Running my hand across it, it came away streaked bright red.

Wondering what the hell was happening to me, I remained bent over with my hands clamped to my knees as I tried to get my breath back, spitting blood into the earth, until I started to imagine unseen eyes watching me. Realising what I must look like if somebody was in the farmhouse, I looked round but saw no-one. Then a stupid thought popped into my head and I looked back at the scarecrow. Of course, its stitched eyes were staring straight ahead, because that's all they were – stitches. But then I found myself looking again at its mouth, bruised and red just like mine was, and its waterlogged head, which was how mine had felt seconds earlier.

Stumbling across the field, I spat repeatedly in the mud, trying to rid myself of the taste of blood along with something else that I couldn't place, and headed over towards the farmhouse on the off chance that somebody was in after all. If nothing else, I could apologise for damn near puking in their field, and perhaps they'd take pity on me, make me a cup of tea or something, even book me a taxi - because I knew now that I daren't drive home.

As I got closer I felt fairly certain the place was empty, but knocked on the door anyway, aware once more of the stillness around me. Amazingly it was now even darker than when I arrived, the sky almost black, and not only with clouds. I knocked harder, but to no avail. Strangely, the thing bothering me most at that point was the strange, almost chemical taste in my mouth - partly because it was so unpleasant and partly because I couldn't think what it reminded me of. Hawking another gob-full of it across the drive, I decided to look round for an outside tap - if nothing else, I could maybe swill some of the taste away. But before I'd taken a step the heavens opened, and a wall of water equal to the one I'd imagined seconds earlier bore down upon me. And as it did, suddenly, instinctively, I felt that I knew what that taste was; but I didn't have time to think about it, because at the same moment I saw a misshapen figure in a dirty school uniform lolloping across the mud towards me.

Despite the sickly chill that shuddered through me, a part of my rational brain tried to tell me that it must be a man - the farmer playing a trick, standing up there all day dressed as a scarecrow waiting for somebody to frighten - but God help me I knew that it wasn't. With nowhere to hide I ran down the track through the slanting rain, struggling to keep my balance on the steep gradient and slippery earth path, not daring to look back, knowing that it would only slow me down and stop me from seeing obstacles or potholes in the road; but mainly because I didn't want to see *it*.

So, I ran as fast as I dared, back towards the safety of the village and humanity. Nearly at the bottom, I could just make out the path ahead through the torrential rain, at the end of which was the junction. As I saw it, something caught my eye on the other side of the wall over to the right; running along at amazing speed down the churned-up field yet somehow keeping its balance, the scarecrow raced past me like a clothed bag of sticks before disappearing into the trees ahead.

Back on the flat now, it was too late for me to change course even if I'd had the energy to run back up to the farm. At the junction I scanned the trees on the other side of the wall, but it was too dark to see anything. So, forcing myself to look away, I kept running as hard as I could until, wonder of wonders, I saw a couple hitchhiking at the side of the road, a cardboard sign held between them, and slowed down.

'Help me!' I yelled out, my voice amplified in the darkness. '*Please!* There's a – he's behind me, and –'

I was virtually on top of them before I realised what they were, and that I'd seen them before, propped up against the wall. As one they turned to face me, the movement causing their sign to fall to the ground. Picking up speed again as I passed, one of them made a grab for me, a soft, soggy arm brushing against my face.

After that I passed six, seven more in quick succession; one posting a letter, two smaller ones, presumably children, sat on a wall, another halfway up a telegraph pole, each one coming to life as I approached, some reaching out to me. How long was it since I'd seen a human being? Remembering my earlier thought of what the village must be like at night populated only by scarecrows, I ignored the stitch in my side and ran. But when I saw warm, yellow lights up ahead, I slowed again, realising it must be the pub I'd been in earlier. But then I saw the figures sitting beside those lights at the windows and tables outside, with their pale, sagging, pillowcase features and unevenly stitched eyes, all looking in my direction. I kept moving, looking for somewhere to hide; and then I saw the grocery store. On instinct I shot towards it, and when I saw nobody on the other side of its lit-up glass door I could've cried. Nearly tripping in my eagerness to get across the threshold, I grabbed the handle, and as I did the man I'd seen inside earlier appeared at the glass. Only now he didn't look much like a man, his ruddy, meaty face a crumpled, off-white cream sack, his eyes thin stitches of thread, his cheeks half-filled with straw. Gulping in air, I turned back, ready to run once more: only to find the road ahead blocked by a small gaggle of grotesque, badly-dressed parodies of humanity, their features thankfully blurred by the torrential rain.

I had no option but to go straight at them. Taking several more breaths, I squeezed my hands into fists, lowered my head and charged, screaming as I ran, sending them skittling like bowling pins, their musty clothes brushing against me, their straw catching in my hair, a piece of wire from one of them dragging across the back of one of my hands, drawing blood. When I was sure I'd got through them all I raised my head only to see another one, the one standing outside the phone box. It was turned in my direction, but it didn't move. As I looked at it its fake cell phone dropped to the ground, the plastic case splitting open on the concrete; and when I cast a quick glance back towards the ones that I'd charged through, I found that most of them were now just piles of rain-soaked rags and straw on the road.

Then I felt it: something had changed.

Emboldened, I gave the phone box scarecrow a wide berth and walked back a little, close enough to see the pub. They were still there, sitting at the windows and outside at the tables, and they were all still facing in my direction, but none of them moved - there wasn't even a *suggestion* of life, as if their work was somehow done. I must've stood there for thirty seconds until a wave of nausea took hold of me and I was sick all over the pavement, hot bile stinging my lips. Wiping my mouth and taking as deep a breath as my scorched lungs would allow, I lurched back along the wooded lane towards the farmer's field.

The first thing I saw when I got there was the Portaloo. The scarecrow I'd seen earlier was still propped up beside it, legs crossed and still waiting to spend a penny. As I approached it, I spat a mixture of blood, bile and mucus in its general direction. Then before I knew what I was doing I had it by the throat and was ripping it to pieces, tearing its face open and removing handfuls of straw, punching it in the stomach and throwing it to the ground and stamping on it before finally coming to my senses. Suddenly worn out and not caring if I was fit to drive or not, I got the keys from my pocket, opened the car door and flopped down in the driver's seat. Turning on the ignition, I burst into tears.

Somehow that seemed to be the final indignity, the tough northern kid of old giving in to his emotions, and glad that nobody was around to see it. Tolerating it for a few seconds, I punched the steering wheel then revved up the car; and with tears still coursing down my cheeks I slammed into reverse, the car bobbing up and down as it went backwards up the muddy field. When I'd gone back far enough I ground the gears into first, pressed hard on the accelerator and headed for the exit; at which point a black-clothed arm wrapped itself around my throat and tried to choke me.

Looking in the rear-view mirror, I saw the blonde-haired, red-mouthed scarecrow I'd seen at the farmhouse. Tightening its grip, a piece of the wire mesh around its wrist dug into my neck. Grabbing at the arm, I tried to get it away from my throat, but despite its lightness I couldn't pry it free; and biting it didn't help, because there was nothing there to bite. As a last resort I took my other hand off the steering wheel, turning and punching it repeatedly in the face, which felt like a sack of wet oatmeal. Eventually the grip loosened, and the head came away from the body, spilling straw everywhere. Beneath me the tires were screaming, the car sliding dangerously in the mud; ahead, a dry stone wall glowed in the headlights; taking my foot off the accelerator and stamping on the brakes I yelled above the sound of the engine, knowing that it was already too late.

When I opened my eyes, groggy and disorientated, I was lying down and Mum was sitting at the end of my bed.

'So,' she said, trying to smile, 'you didn't get to Wray then.'

'No,' I said, sore all over. 'I ended up in Eccles instead.'

Mum frowned at me. 'Where?'

'Eccles. Next village along. That's where I crashed the car. In the farmer's field.'

She frowned again.

Turns out there's no such place as Eccles, at least not in

Lancashire. It also turned out that when they found me it wasn't amongst the rubble of a dry stone wall in a waterlogged muddy field; it was wrapped round a tree close to a sign for the village of Wray. Thankfully, I had just enough wits about me to stop me from mentioning anything else.

'I think he's a bit delirious,' Mum said to a passing nurse.

'Try and get some sleep.' She patted my hand. 'I'll come back later.'

When she did, I told her I didn't remember our earlier conversation and tried to reassure her that I was feeling better, but she didn't look convinced. So, when she asked me if I could remember what happened, I told her about how the jetlag had caused me to lose concentration and how I'd ploughed into the tree.

'So, you know that you didn't make it as far as Wray?' she said, looking at me anxiously. 'Because earlier you started coming out with such a tale –'

'No Mum. I know I didn't make it to Wray.' Relieved, she smiled.

No, I didn't make it to Wray.

But God knows I ended up somewhere.

Mum was right about there being no Eccles in Lancashire; a suburb of Salford bears that name, but the nearest village I found was in Kent. And judging by the pictures I saw of it online it looks nothing like the one I visited. It also looks nothing like Wray village either, which I also looked at online, just to make sure that I somehow hadn't made it there after all and forgotten all about it.

Eccles Village looked like nowhere I'd ever been before. Or would ever want to go to again.

The rest of my stay was subdued, to put it mildly. I didn't eat or sleep much and was sore from the crash, not to mention the rest of it. On top of that I was missing Marge and the kids. But a part of me didn't want to go back home, because I knew when I said goodbye to Mum outside the house - she was too weak to come with me to the airport – I probably wouldn't see her again. And I was right.

Then, on the last night, Mum said, 'Oh, I forgot to ask. Did you see the local rag earlier?'

'No. Why?'

'Something in it that might interest you.' Pointing at a particular article, she handed it over.

'Poor devil. I don't know – the things we do.'

Frowning, I took the paper off her. Reading the headline made me none the wiser – but when I saw the name on the third line my mind began to spool rapidly backwards through time. Reaching the end, I don't think I've ever felt as cold.

'SCHOOLBOY' WARLOCK IN LOCKED ROOM MYSTERY

A local man found badly beaten in a locked room claiming that his injuries were inflicted following an occult ritual is currently undergoing psychiatric evaluation.

Police were called to the address of Duncan Redfearn, 43, after neighbours complained about a disturbance at his house. Eventually gaining entry, police found Redfearn, described by locals as a loner, in an undersized school uniform, bleeding and semi-conscious on his living room floor, surrounded by broken furniture and occult paraphernalia. When later questioned about the incident, Redfearn, who claims to be a descendent of a local witch, said that he had been locked in a deadly struggle with one of his enemies who he had summoned by occult means, but refused to name them.

'As the property was securely locked both inside and out, the only plausible explanation is that Mr Redfearn caused the injuries himself,' a police spokesman said. A decision regarding Mr Redfearn's mental state is expected soon.

'"One of his enemies",' I said quietly, hoping Mum didn't hear the shock in my voice. 'I'd forgotten all about him.'

'I bet it took him a while to forget you. That was the third time I had to go into the headmaster's office because of your fighting.'

My heart thudding hard, suddenly I was back there, a schoolboy trying to justify his actions. 'I got sick of them all having a go at me all the time. I just defended myself.'

'Against the others I could understand, but not him - he was such a strange little boy, his hair stuck up like that the whole time. Sounds like he's got a lot stranger too. I couldn't believe it when Mr Norris said you'd split his lip.'

'I did that because he tried to push me into the swimming pool.'

As we were talking, the incident was playing in my head. He'd already pushed another couple of kids in by the time he got to me. But I was bigger than he was and stopped him. And that's when he called me my nickname.

'You did it because he called you a Yorkshire pudding,' Mum chided me. 'And then you called him - what was it?'

I winced at the memory. 'An Eccles cake.' At the time it'd been the best I could come up with. When everyone laughed at my feeble retort, I got angrier still and punched him in the mouth, knocking him into the pool. Suddenly I could taste blood and chlorine, like I had up at that farmhouse. 'Anyway,' I said, 'he never bothered me again after that. Isn't that what adults always tell children - to stand up to bullies?'

'Normally, yes, but after seeing him for myself I doubted that he was capable of hurting anyone. Apart from himself, by the sound of it.' Standing up, she tapped the newspaper. 'Right. I'm off to bed.' Leaning over, she kissed me on the cheek. 'Good night, love.'

'Good night.'

Later, turning the whole thing over in mind, I only managed to come to one solid conclusion. I wanted to go home.

So, when I did, it was a real joy to see Marge, Suse and Dale waiting for me at the airport. The kids rushed forward and hugged me, only stopping when they heard me groaning and remembered my accident. As I disentangled myself from them,

Marge stepped forward. Taking in my skinnier frame, haggard face and dry, unkempt hair she tried to smile. 'Martin, are you *sure* you're okay? You look –'

Trying to smile back, I finished her sentence for her. 'Like a scarecrow?'

So here I am back again, this time with Marge and the kids in tow.

It's been a bittersweet couple of days, what with the funeral and showing them round my old haunts. But it's been manageable, always keeping on the go and not having time to think. In keeping with that idea, and because the kids have been so well behaved, tomorrow we're doing something that they want to do.

Tomorrow, we're going to a scarecrow festival.

Not in Wray, but close by. Marge found it online. It'd give the kids something positive to remember their Grandma by. And, after hearing all Grandma's tales they've got their hearts set on it. Also, as Marge pointed out, I still hadn't been to one myself.

My arms and legs tingling with panic, I tried – and not for the first time – to tell her what happened, what *really* happened that day and why going to such a place might not be a great idea; but, as with the countless other times I've tried to broach the subject, the words just died in my mouth.

So, after taking a very deep breath, I reluctantly agreed, earning myself a kiss in the process.

When the headaches started two days ago, I told myself it was nothing. But then last night I had a dream, we're going to Wray village and when the sign appears it doesn't say *Wray,* or even *Awry*. Instead it says *Wary*. The next thing I see is a scarecrow in a field wearing a school tie.

If nothing else I've persuaded Marge to drive tomorrow.

And all the time I keep asking myself: *Does he really know that I'm home? If he does, it's more than I do.*

Is he incapable of hurting anyone, as Mum said? I can only hope that she was right. So, I keep telling myself: tights and straw and wire mesh, that's all they are. Tights and straw and wire mesh. Hopefully I'll believe it by the morning.

But if I don't, I have a plan. Earlier today after I bought my newspaper I went into the shop next door and picked up a few extras – paraffin spray and some stay-light matches – just in case. But I hope it won't come to that – it's not a side of me I want Marge or the kids to see.

A side that proves maybe I haven't changed *that* much after all.

THE LANCASHIRE BOGGARTS

It almost seems like a rude word, 'boggart'. Even folk in the know are amused by it, tending to picture such creatures as diminutive gnomes, cute little things that wouldn't be out of place in Enid Blyton's nursery books. Yet in former centuries, all across the North of England, in particular the Northwest - especially Lancashire - boggarts were no laughing matter.

To start with, the Lancashire version of a boggart is in some ways closer to a ghost than a goblin, and yet calling it a ghost would be too simplistic. The most unnerving aspect of this mythical entity, at least according to the gossips who first spread these tales, is that the boggart has never lived a normal life. This is not the soul of some deceased person or the spirit of an animal. It is far more mysterious and frightening than that, a sentient, shapeless something which hails from who knows where, is almost invariably attached to a particular land formation - a marsh, a hill, or a lonely tract of wood - and without exception is of malign disposition.

According to many stories, boggarts, in particular the boggarts of Lancashire, seemed to have no other purpose than to torment men, and this went much further than the mere plaiting of horses' tails or curdling of milk-churns.

Boggart hauntings were malicious, cruel and relentless, and could last for decades. There are stories of Lancashire families suffering at the hands of boggarts for generation after generation. For example, the famous Grizlehurst Boggart drove a farmer and his wife out of their minds by dancing noisily around their yard and across their roofs for night after night and leaving multiple cloven hoof-prints each morning. Proof of how seriously these evil beings were taken can be found in the way the Northwest has memorialised them in its place-names. Boggart Hole Clough is a municipal park in Blackley, Manchester, and allegedly was the domain of an especially dangerous entity, who, in the 19th century, was held responsible for a number of very real disappearances. Likewise, Boggart Bridge in Burnley was said to be subject to the whims of a 'gatekeeper boggart', who, if anyone crossing the bridge failed to make some kind of payment, would follow that person for months, maybe years, inflicting all kinds of misfortune on him.

This malevolent nature is reflected in the Lancashire belief that boggarts, like imps or demons, were very protective of their names. But whereas a priest performing an exorcism could bind a demon once he knew its name, the boggarts would simply lose what little control they already had and become mindless forces. When a boggart said to dwell in a small hazel wood near Moston in 18th century Manchester was named as Nut-Nan, it apparently went berserk, and could be heard shrieking incoherently among the trees for years afterwards – so much so that the nearby road was eventually abandoned.

Though the appearance of boggarts could vary, on the few occasions they permitted themselves to be seen, it was nearly always a physical imprint of their wicked nature. Some were said to be manlike and yet brutish, with animal features. The Boggart of Hackensall Hall was described as resembling a horrific, deformed horse.

Other boggarts were more subtly terrifying.

The Boggart of Longridge, whose period of activity was the mid-19th century, when coal-scuttle bonnets were the fashion for countrywomen, would roam the benighted rural lanes in one such disguise: dress, shawl and bonnet, carrying a basket. If it came across other night-time wanderers, it would join them, and only at the opportune moment reveal that there was no head inside its bonnet. If that didn't knock the innocent victims dead with shock, the thing would then open the basket to reveal its severed head, which would duly roar with laughter. The Boggart of the Brook, near Garstang, adopted similar tactics, appearing as a cloaked and hooded figure seeking a ride on any passing coach or cart. Once aboard, it would reveal rotting bones underneath, and shrieking ghoulishly, would hang onto the terrified driver with vicious claws until he either abandoned his vehicle or crashed – he knew that to take the thing home with him would be to invite it into his life forever

But perhaps the two most frightening boggart stories of all come from what is now the Fylde Coast, running north from Blackpool to the Furness hills, and from Dilworth, which again is close to Longridge Fell.

In the first case, a boggart known as the 'White Dobbie' was said to appear at dusk, tramping the coastal roads in the shape of a tired and very emaciated man, and dressed in curious white rags. It never spoke, but witnesses who attempted to entice the figure into conversation, having initially assumed it a troubled neighbour, described the thing suddenly turning and gazing at them with the most terrible bloodshot eyes they had ever seen – eyes that would induce appalling and very personal nightmares for weeks afterwards, if not months.

In the second case, a 19th century landowner took possession of a farm, in the yard of which lay a heavy stone, nine feet long and two feet thick, on which an engraving read:

Rauffe: Radcliffe: laid this: stone: to lye: for: ever A.D. 1655:

Dismissing the rumour that it had been laid to pin down a boggart, the new owner had it hauled away by a team of horses, intending to use it as a buttery stone. But that night, the house was stricken by amazingly violent poltergeist activity, pots, pans and other furnishings flying about in a blizzard of destruction. According to the story, the heavy stone – which can still be seen today, its inscription still legible – was promptly returned to its former position, and the ground around it sewn with holly as further protection against evil.

A WEEKEND BREAK
Edward Pearce

If you want to know about the haunting at Bethlehem Hall, I think I'd better tell you a bit about myself first, because whatever's there seems to pick up on your life and use it against you. You'll see what I mean by that later. So, if this seems a long introduction to a short story, it's all connected with what happened, and I hope you can find the patience to read it. If at the end you're disappointed and you feel you've sat through my life story for nothing, I'm sorry about that, but to understand what went on that night you need a bit of the background, well, mine at least, because I can't tell you much about the background to Bethlehem Hall.

I'm Eileen, from Ireland originally, and I'm a country girl with Romany blood. I can usually tell another Romany, though they don't often spot me, and it's not something I advertise. I'm not ashamed of my Romany family - far from it - but people have their prejudices, and mostly it's easier just not to mention it.

You often find in Irish and Romanies what people call the gift of second sight. Believe me, the combination of races is potent, and I grew up with some strange things in my life. I always knew our family were receptive, some of us more than others, but it was a while before I realised that not everybody is. As a child I'd take it for granted when sometimes there were footsteps in an empty house, or you'd know about things happening a long way off to someone you knew, sometimes before it happened. A shadow at the corner of the eye, an unexplained tap on the shoulder - those things don't bother me any more than, say, the noise of cats scrapping in the night. I'm not as strongly endowed as some with the sixth sense, for want of a better term, and it seems to have sort of jumped a generation, as my daughter has inherited more of it than I did. But I do have something of 'the gift'. It all feels natural to me, and it's difficult to explain in terms you'd understand. The nearest I can get is that it feels like a particularly strong intuition that comes out of nowhere.

Let me tell you about just one of the 'strange things' in my younger life. I was twelve, maybe thirteen. We'd moved to England and were living in Liverpool at the time. This particular day, I was away visiting at my Aunt Mary's out in the country, I forget where exactly, and I'd gone over to see Deirdre, a local girl of my own age. It was a fine and fairly mild day in November, and the evening crept up on us unawares. It was not more than a mile from Deirdre's house to Aunt Mary's, along a quiet green lane, and I decided to walk back in the dusk. Neither Deirdre's parents nor Aunt Mary had a phone, so there was no way of letting my aunt know I was walking back on my own, but I wasn't worried, and in any case, we didn't bother so much about that sort of thing in those days.

So, you should picture me walking, a daydreamer lost in my thoughts, along this winding and lonely country lane. It ran, so I was later told, past an old Quaker burial ground, though you wouldn't know that as the graves weren't marked, and in any case a high hedge, all neatly trimmed, was between it and the lane. I'd gone some distance and met nobody when a slight flickering of the shadows ahead, as if from a light at my back, made me stop and turn around. Behind me, maybe a hundred yards away, a light was bobbing about, held high on a pole on the other side of the hedge.

I stared at this light. It was plainly a lantern, an antiquated thing, swaying as it plodded towards me. Who could that be, I thought, and what were they doing out there at night in an open field? And how could they suddenly turn up like that without me noticing them? There was something not normal about that light. I was intensely curious about it, but I wasn't frightened. I knew straight off that it wasn't going to harm me, don't ask me how.

There was a faint gurgling sound, and I turned back round. What was that noise, and what - what on Earth - was that sheet of something looking like glass, or polythene, spread out in front of me? Dear God! It was the river, and I, all wrapped up in myself, had been about to walk straight into it. As I stood frozen with shock, I heard the gurgling again as cold, deep water sucked at the vertical bank immediately below me.

I looked again to see where the lantern was, but it had vanished. I just stood there for a moment, and then I ran back to my Aunt Mary's house as fast as I could. I didn't say anything about it then, because I was afraid she'd be angry at me for being so stupid as to nearly walk into the river. It was only many years later that I told her what I'd seen that evening, and she didn't seem all that surprised. It was then she told me about the Quaker burial ground. Perhaps one of the old Quakers was looking out for me that night. Who knows? It certainly seemed as though someone was.

Quite a number of other inexplicable things have happened to me, both before and since that little incident. The point I'm trying to make is that I'm not particularly afraid of the supernatural, because I'm used to it, and I know from experience that mostly it's neither terrifying nor threatening. It's just something different that's there. Sometimes you know about it, and sometimes you don't.

So that's not the kind of thing that bothers me. What I'm scared of is something quite different. I'm not talking about spiders, heights, stuff like that. It is death that frightens me, and what happens to your soul, if you have one. Do you know what I mean by the dark, dreadful terror of eternity, of yourself lost and spinning in an awful void for all time? That's not meant to sound Biblical, even if I am a Catholic (somewhat lapsed!). It's just my best way of putting it. I think most people have a glimpse of that sometime in their lives. What I hate is those spiteful reminders of mortality that sneak into your life every so often and won't let you forget what's awaiting every one of us at the unpredictable other end of our lives. Are we simply snuffed out, and that's the end of the world, history, and everything? Because if I don't know anything, then as far as I'm concerned, the world is at an end, even though I know it goes on regardless of me and everyone else. To think that I will one day be lost in that great ocean of time without any points of reference is unbearable. And I don't like the idea of being laid in the cold ground. My body may not notice the cold, but it would if I were alive, and the thought bothers me.

I'm no great reader, but I'm no fool and I take things in. Do you know what they mean by 'to sleep – perchance to dream'? I expect you do. To be reborn into a new world and learn from scratch, in what may or may not be a nice place – that is not a prospect I find easy to contemplate. But at least then I'd know I'd died. It worries me that if death is just the end of existence after all, then I'll never actually know it. I'll never even know I'm dead.

It makes my head whirl just thinking about it. Mostly I just get on with my life and don't spend a lot of time dwelling on these matters. But the presence of death, in particular the death of those I have known, brings it all swirling back to the surface. I realise that's not a pleasant experience for anyone, but for me it creates a very special kind of unease that worms its way into my soul and awakens me with nightmares for weeks at a time. I'm pretty sure that some of this, at least, is bound up with my own experiences of death and the dead, and so if you can bear with me, before we come to the story of Bethlehem Hall, I'll tell you about the ones that affected me most. There were three of them.

I was ten when I saw my first body. We were still living in our cottage in County Wicklow, and Grandpa had died and was laid out in the front room. I didn't want to go in and see him, but our friends, neighbours and relatives had all been in to pay their respects. They were hushed and being unnaturally kind to me. All, male or female, would lean over the coffin and kiss Grandpa on the forehead, as I observed through the open door of the room that I would not enter. I didn't want to look at Grandpa, and I certainly didn't want to kiss him. Some of the friends and relatives had to travel a considerable distance, and they couldn't all just drop whatever they were doing and come straightaway, so we had to leave the coffin open for several days.

Each night four candles, at the points of the compass, would be lit so that Grandpa did not have to spend the night by himself in darkness – it's one of our things. It was summer, and it had been quite warm for the past few days. That evening, as it began to grow dark, it was time to light the candles. It was my mother's job, but tonight she wouldn't do it. A thunderstorm had been building for some time, and in the late afternoon it had finally broken.

Mother and I were alone in the sitting room. The last visitors had been to the house today, and now dusk had turned into darkness. The rain had eased off a bit, but was still falling steadily, pattering through the warm air. Up to now my mother had been lighting the candles, but tonight she said, 'I can't go in there tonight and light the candles. I can't face it!'

'But Mum, you must! You can't leave him in the dark!'.

She looked at me with something in her eyes I hadn't seen before. 'I can't do it. You'll have to. You don't have to look at him, Eileen, just go in, light the candles and come out again'.

I could see it was no use arguing. Someone had to do it, and there was only me. It never occurred to me to refuse. So, I took the matches, went out of the living room and closed the hall door behind me. Then, with a peculiar sensation that was not quite fear but certainly included unease, I opened the heavy wooden door to the front room.

People who've lived in the country, or indeed anywhere before the days of refrigerators, will know that a thunderstorm can turn milk. It can also turn a body. A horrible gagging stench came out of the door in a great waft and straight into my nostrils. I retched, heaved the door shut again, and flattened my back against the cool white wall of the hallway, taking several breaths as I recovered. But I knew I had to go in. I turned my face away from the door and took a big deep breath, opened the door again and plunged into the room.

The dim moonlight at the end window made little impression on the darkness, and I was only aware of the coffin on its table as something semi-visible in the deep shadows. I looked away from it, struck a match, and saw the first candle on my right. I lit it, hurried down the room to the next one behind the head of the coffin, lit that too, and dropped the match onto the bare floorboards. With averted eyes and clenched teeth, I passed behind the coffin and on to the third candle, struck another match and lit it, and then onto the fourth, lit that, shook the match out and hurried to the door, still holding my breath. All that took only a few seconds, but as I reached the door something made me turn and look at Grandpa. In the uneven light from the four candles I could see his face, all blotched and discoloured. I didn't want to look, but I just couldn't help it. It was like when you go past a car crash and you know you shouldn't look, because you might see something you don't want to, but you have to look anyway and then you wish you hadn't. I rushed out and slammed the door behind me.

That night my mother put a bucket of scented disinfectant in the room with the coffin before they came to nail it down the next day. The sweetish smell of the disinfectant, and the decaying-meat smell of Grandpa, was a much worse combination than either alone. It never got entirely out of my system, and to this day I can picture it, if that is the right word, and the remembering, if I dwell on it too long, brings back the picture of what my dear, loving Grandpa had turned into in such a short space of time. Perhaps I told myself he'd gone to heaven, because whilst he wasn't a saint, he was still a kind person, well, he was to me anyway. I don't remember exactly what I thought, but I do believe that somehow this lit the fuse to a fear, a dread that's never really left me even now.

To move on to the next time. I was eighteen and working as a hairdresser in Liverpool. I'd finished for the day and had to go and collect something, I forget what, from Aunty Barbara, who had a fish-and-chip shop nearby. It was early evening in November and already dark. A modern glass front, surmounted by *Stone's Fish and Chips* in red-on-white early '60s italic, contrasted with the rundown brown-grey upper storeys. Some youths were lounging about on the pavement with their bags of chips. I ignored their stares and hurried in. Inside the brightly-lit shop the windows were already steamed up. Everything was yellow and silver, and oil hissed and spat as Barbara's assistant poured in a load of chips. Battered fish, fishcakes and sausages of various sorts lay behind the glass, staying more or less hot on the metal grilles.

'How are you then Eileen?' Aunty Barbara was cheerful.

'I'm fine, thank you Aunty. We had quite an easy day today.'

'That's nice Eileen. Well, you know, Minnie's upstairs. Would you like to go and see her?'

Minnie was – had been – the owner of the building. She must have been well into her eighties and had died in her sleep two nights previously. I didn't specially want to go, but the open, smiling way Barbara looked at me as she asked seemed to indicate that it was expected. I didn't quite know why I was supposed to want to take a look, but her tone was totally natural, just as though she'd asked me to pass the gravy boat at dinner, and you wouldn't refuse to do that, would you? I suppose that's why I immediately, instinctively agreed, not taking time to think about it. 'Yes, all right. Which room is it?'

'She's in her bedroom, dear. It's right at the top of the house, first door on the left.'

Before I knew it, I was climbing the stairs in a sort of daze. Leaving behind the glare and heat of the shop, I closed the hall door and was immediately in another, much older world. I had not been in this part of the house before. The bare, creaky wooden stairs were lit by a dim bulb from the landing above, and the walls, anciently painted dark brown I think, bulged in places and were uneven to the touch. On the first landing a worn strip of old carpet was the only furnishing.

I wanted to turn around here and go straight back down, but I was ashamed to seem so weak. So, it was on, up another flight decorated in much the same style, and I was at the first door on the left, cream coloured and showing signs of multiple coats of paint over the years. It was ajar, and a faint light glimmered through the crack. Cautiously, I pushed it open.

The light was from the candles. The room was sparsely

furnished, with only a dark wooden dressing table against one wall and a trestle table in the middle of the room. The walls were papered with a faded old green-and-cream lattice pattern. Rust-brown curtains adorned the window, and there was a snip-rug on the floorboards. The whole room spoke of shabbiness, of worn-out furnishings that had served their time and should have been replaced long ago. But the central feature was Minnie in her coffin, on the trestle table, tilted slightly so that as soon as you came in the door, she was looking straight at you.

Except that she seemed to be looking from the dark shadows of empty sockets, before I realised that two pennies had been placed over her eyes. I stepped forward reluctantly. She was dressed in a sort of cream-coloured, frilled and panelled nightdress that reached from her neck to her feet, and a similar frilled bonnet, done up under her chin, covered everything but her face. Her hands rested on her hips. Minnie seemed shrunken, smaller even than in real life, and quite unnaturally still. Her mouth was open, her lips fallen in without her false teeth. She looked like a gruesome wax doll from a nightmare.

I can still see it all now. The sight struck me to the heart, and I turned around and hurried back down to Barbara in the shop.

'Oh my God, what's happened to her?'

Barbara looked puzzled. 'What d'you mean?'

'What did you put pennies on her eyes for?'

'They wouldn't close.'

'But her mouth's open, you can see inside it!' I couldn't seem to stop.

She gave me a patient, slightly weary look, and smiled tolerantly at me. 'Eileen love, that's what they look like when they're dead'.

I railed at her. 'What did you make me go up there for? I didn't want to see her!'

I was quite angry at Aunty Barbara, because I felt she had pressured me into something I really didn't want. Minnie wasn't even a relative, and there'd been absolutely no reason for me to see her. I could have hit my aunt for being so stupid. Except I'd been just as stupid in not saying no, and that made me angry at myself too. And I couldn't shake off that image for days. Whenever I shut my eyes, there would be Minnie, tilted up on her table and looking just like she was about to get up and the pennies would drop off her eyes. That placid, comforting old Edwardian lady who wouldn't hurt a fly had turned into something hideous, like a doll one of your relations gives you, and you hate it, but you can't get rid of it because it's a present and you have to keep it put away, so it doesn't keep on giving you the creeps. Maybe that's why I can't bear dolls, clowns, or other grotesques, as I call them.

There is just one more time to tell you about, and then we're done with the background. It must have been nearly twenty years later, and in those years, I'd been married, divorced, remarried and separated. I seem to have attracted violent and abusive men. I don't know why that is. Anyway, at this stage in my life I'd left Liverpool and was living in Southport. I had returned by train for the funeral of Aunt May - we Irish seem to have lots of aunts - and was going to the Chapel of Rest, where she was laid out for burial. Penny, my fourteen-year old daughter, was with me. We held hands for support as we entered the room.

It was the afternoon before the funeral, and we were the only ones here. The Chapel of Rest was white and hushed, except for the sombre classical music that played softly in the background. Lilies and other strong-smelling flowers were on a table in the corner, and there were blue drapes at the window. There was also a scent dispenser, which wafted continuously. For weeks after I could smell that odour of perfume covering the stink of the cancerous tumour that had finally killed Aunt May and had left a great seeping hole in her side.

In the middle of the room was Aunt May in her coffin on a trestle table, clad in a powder-blue lying-out gown. Her hands were folded over her hips, and her fingers were black from the second knuckle down. Her long fingernails, which she had painted in life, were just plain black now and gave her hands a pointed appearance. Her eyes were not quite closed, and in that narrow space under the lids I saw that they were black all over, just like pools of black ink. It looked as if you just needed to prod her around the eye and all this liquid would come flowing out down her cheeks and onto the satin padding of the coffin.

It was the first time Penny had seen a dead person. She clung tightly to my hand and moaned 'Oh Mum, she looks awful! I don't like this! I wish we hadn't come. I don't want to stay here, can we go please? Please Mum!'. Well, I didn't want to stay either. So out we went, me and Penny, into the fresh air, both of us thoroughly shaken. We had to find a cafe and sit down over a cup of coffee to recover, before we went back to Irene's, where we were staying. And I swore to myself then that I would never, ever look at another body again. I didn't give a damn whose it was. I told Penny to make sure they screwed the lid down on me and don't let them come and see me all false and distorted. I don't want that, and I don't believe they really do either. And if that bothers anyone, it's just too bad.

After many difficult years, in which there'd seemed no prospect of anything approaching a normal life, I finally found fulfilment and happiness with a good man. Penny and her brother Michael had grown up and left home, and Paul and I lived in a nice part of Southport, where we ran a small shop. We made a profit, not much but enough for us to live on, and we were quite comfortable with that and Paul's Army pension. Paul's life, too, had been a troubled one, and this newfound stability was the foundation of a happy time for us both.

One day my friend Viv came into the shop. Viv is younger than me, pretty in a dark sort of way, clever, and always smartly dressed. She's a bit cheeky and great fun, and we share a sense of humour that can be quite down-to-earth at times. 'Hey Eileen, guess what! How do you fancy a girls' weekend in a country house for nothing? Well look no further, 'cos I can fix it for the both of us'. She laughed, shook her body and jangled an imaginary set of keys in the air. 'So, go on then, ask me all about it, I know you're dying to!'

Viv made me smile. 'What's this devilment of yours, are you planning a weekend away, so we can swap secrets and consume loads of drink?'

She pulled a face. 'Oh no, you know me so well! But really, I have got this house for a weekend next month, and won't you come along? It would be great. Poor old Paul, you'll have to leave him alone, but he won't mind, he can get on with the accounts. Come on, I'm between men now and you may not get another chance!'

I wanted to laugh but didn't, and said, 'Now then Miss Vivian, just because you're free and single there's no call to be rude about my man, who I might add is very good to me.' She gave a look of exaggerated alarm and I cracked up.

Hopefully I've given you an idea of what Viv's like. She's quite dark, and someone had told me she has Arabic blood. Not that she'd said so to me, and I'd never asked. I do remember thinking, before I got to know her properly, well, we're both from ancient peoples and I know your little secret, but you don't know mine. But that's by the by.

To get back to the story. Some friends of Viv's had a big old place in the country that they were renovating. They were going away for a couple of weeks and had offered her the run of it if she would go down for a couple of days, to keep it looking occupied. Viv works in the week, and she planned to go down for the middle weekend. Did I want to come? Yes, I did. Much as I love Paul, a girl needs a bit of space now and then. Besides, a girly weekend away sounded like fun and was something I hadn't done for a very long time, in fact I couldn't remember when – perhaps never! Yes, I would arrange it with Paul. No, he wouldn't mind.

'What is this place anyway?' I asked. 'Is a butler provided?'

'Mmm, possibly not,' Viv said. 'It's called Bethlehem Hall, but I don't think it's a mansion, more a big house in a village. We may have to scrape along without a ballroom.'

So, there we were on a Friday evening in summer, driving down in Viv's car to this place, which turned out to be in the depths of rural Cheshire. I won't say any more than that, just in case someone recognises it. Viv had the keys, and in our cases were wine and a nice bottle of brandy, just on the off chance we might need them. It was a beautiful evening as we sped down to our destination with carefree talk, laughter, and relaxing music on the car stereo. I felt like a kid going on holiday. It was a nice feeling.

We left the motorway and joined the country roads, winding through flat open farmlands. This area was strangely attractive in a backward kind of way. Big old farmhouses among trees, all red brick and pantiles, sheet-metal barns and occasionally the wooden skeleton of an ancient tumbledown brick one, all amid fields of wheat, greens and maize which filled the landscape under a big empty sky. Here and there was a village, here and there a tractor would slow up the traffic before eventually pulling over to let the queue pass. There weren't many hedges, but there were trees, and on the skyline rows of poplars and little copses added to the charm of the landscape. It reminded me of Ireland.

At the village we wanted, I scanned the road and the fields for our turning and then, across a field, I saw what must have been the Hall. It was not what you'd call country mansion size, but it was big, big enough to be called a Hall. I caught a glimpse of a great square structure with white windows, before the trees hid it again. A short distance further on was our turning. A little way down a narrow lane, fields on one side and bungalows on the other, the top of the Hall rose into sight and then there we were. A high hedge with a small iron gate fronted the house, and to the side was the drive, gravelled and blocked in by a much larger pair of iron gates. I opened them, and Viv drove in and round to the side of the house. As she got out and opened the boot, I took a good look at Bethlehem Hall.

It was dark red brick, with an imposing three-storey presence and a parapet round a pitched roof. It looked like a big cube, as if someone had wanted a country house without paying an architect. Its age was hard to tell, but I wouldn't have known that anyway. I could only see that it was old. The front and side had rows of windows, some bricked up. It was surrounded by privets, and I glimpsed a long lawn at the back. The garden at the front looked small, but only compared with the size of the house; anywhere else it would be considered generous enough.

My first impression was a bit of a shock at such an old house, obviously meant to be grand, built with all corners and no curves or arches. You don't tend to see houses like that in the country. Perhaps it would be okay in a town, alongside others like it, but here it stuck out. It was grim and austere, but at least the bricks were mellowed by time. Bethlehem Hall must have been ugly when new, but it had aged along with the landscape and now I suppose you could say it belonged here. No, I couldn't see any beauty about it, but it was grand in a harsh sort of way.

There was something else. I had an uncertain feeling about this house, as if something were radiating off it. It was not necessarily a bad feeling, but not a good one either. What was it? And then I knew. It was 'the gift', and it wanted to tell me something. I tried to listen but couldn't, and after a few seconds I gave up trying. And the moment I gave up was the moment I heard it, the little voice in my head that I'd heard before but not for some years. It wasn't male or female. It was a voiceless voice, as if I were hearing the impression it made in my mind rather than the voice itself. But it spoke to me clearly enough. It said simply: 'There's something here.'

Viv lugged the bags out and banged the hatch shut. 'Well, this is different!' she said, in the cheerful tone you use to describe something you're supposed to be pleased about, but don't actually like very much.

'Come on, let's see inside,' I said, as we carried our bags across the front garden to the little front door. There was a big old lever lock key and a Yale key. I opened the door and we stepped in.

We both gasped in surprise. Suddenly we were in a quite different, and beautiful house. A long hall led through elegant archways to a fine old wooden staircase with balustrades. Old panelled doors with decorated brass handles led off the hall to the rooms at the side. The contrast with the outside was startling. We put down our bags and Viv opened one of the side doors. Here there was another surprise, as we looked into a grand front room with an ornate plaster ceiling and a big marble fireplace. There were oriental rugs on the parquet floor, white wooden shutters, candy stripe wallpaper and worn, comfortable furniture that looked to have started life expensively. It was the kind of house I'd always have loved but could never have afforded.

'Wow!' said Viv. 'When they said they were doing up an old place I didn't know it was like this'.

I couldn't think of anything to say but 'It's fantastic!' And it was. The room opposite was done out as a library. There were green leather chairs, antique glass-fronted bookcases and deep red walls. The country house effect was complete.

We explored with the excitement of two children. The kitchen was vast, with hooks for game still hanging from the roofbeams. The wonderful staircase was all barley-twist and huge round finials. I now know that it was late sixteenth century, but at the time I would never have guessed that a brick house would be that old. Halfway up, a great window looked out onto a long lawn enclosed by poplars and rhododendron bushes. Viv went straight past it without stopping to admire the view. A central corridor ran down the first floor, with bedrooms leading off it. Our bedrooms, on different sides and at opposite ends of the corridor, were helpfully marked with notes. Mine was a good size and looked comfortable, if not as richly furnished as the rooms downstairs. We went on and had a look at the third storey, which presumably was once the servants' quarters, but these were very obviously still unfinished, big empty rooms with bare dusty boards and patched walls.

Once we'd got unpacked and settled, and I'd rung Paul to say we were safely there, Viv and I took a bottle of wine out onto the terrace that overlooked the lawn. It was 8.30 on a fine evening, and we sat and rested for a while, unwinding from the trip down and not saying much at first.

'We'll have to eat something, you know', I said at last.

'I know', Viv said. 'It's so beautiful here, not what I expected when I saw the house. I just feel like sitting and taking it all in for a bit longer'. And so we did. We sat and watched the sky turn red and deepen behind the poplars, which gradually turned into silhouettes. It was very pretty.

In the end, about nine it must have been, we went in to the kitchen. After a late meal, when it was completely dark, we sat in the front room. Not much was left of the first bottle of wine, and when Viv offered to open another I didn't even pretend to object. The washing up could wait. We were too comfortable to move now. We just talked, starting off with trivial stuff before getting onto more serious matters.

The wine made us open up, and I found out quite a bit about Viv, as I'm sure she did about me. Viv is a hard drinker, and despite putting away over a bottle of wine she was in control of herself and didn't reveal any big secrets. Just the same, you get quite a good look at someone's character when you spend an evening drinking seriously with them, especially if you go in till two in the morning. I saw in Viv a tough character who'd been through a lot, but was holding on tightly – too tightly, perhaps – to stability, and wasn't entirely happy with herself. I already knew she could never hold down a relationship for long, and now I wondered if this was because she was too needy for constant reassurance, perhaps even desperate, once she got beyond the initial stages. Behind the brave, strong front, she reminded me of a lost child.

I don't want you to think I was sitting there coolly assessing my friend. I'm not that callous and calculating! It's just that over the years I've learned to size people up pretty quickly. I've had to, sometimes for my own safety, and now I find it's become automatic. Even when I'm having a good time, as we were that evening, part of me seems to detach and note things down as they happen and present me with answers about people as it works them out, and that's what it said about Viv. I sensed unresolved anger, which with her insecurity would make her a tempestuous person to be with. Men would put up with it for a while, and maybe enjoy it, because Viv is clever, funny, and sexy, but after a while I imagine they found it all too demanding, got fed up and moved on. Poor Viv. She is a person of real integrity and deserves better than this, but that's how her life's gone up to now.

I also learned that her father was Egyptian, but her parents had divorced when she was young and she seldom saw him. She told me had an exaggerated fear of stairs or steep slopes - bathmophobia, it's called, so she said matter-of-factly. 'I'd never make a mountaineer, I get giddy just looking at them!' She'd been married once, and still was. He had left her years ago, she had no idea where he was and had never bothered to get a divorce. She had no children and had never wanted any. She had a first-class degree in mathematics from Cambridge University. This came as a shock to me. She'd never mentioned it before, and I'd always thought of her as being on my own level. I tend to feel a bit inferior to educated, clever people. My education ended at sixteen, and I don't think I'd have done a lot more even if I'd stayed on. I'm not an academic sort, and my parents and I had, for once, been united in the wish that I should leave school and start earning as soon as possible. But don't go thinking I'm stupid, just because I don't have the education you do.

Towards the end of the evening I recollected what my voice had said to me outside the house. And then I thought how strange it was that I'd heard and sensed nothing, nothing at all, since I'd been inside. Maybe there wasn't anything to worry about and the voice was just alerting me to its presence, so I wouldn't be startled if I came across it. I was quite drunk by then and shrugged it all off.

In my bedroom, the little bedside lamp was warm and reassuring. I climbed into a very comfortable bed, switched the light off and almost instantly fell asleep, peaceful and undisturbed for the entire night.

Next morning, we got up late. I felt pretty muzzy - we both did. We had breakfast at a truckers' cafe a couple of miles up the road, and back at the house I suddenly felt fit for nothing and so did Viv. We retired for a nap, she to her bedroom and me to one of the big chairs in the library. I've always found it easier to nap in a chair during the day. If I go and lie down on a bed, it seems deliberate and calculating and the odds are I won't go off. But just let me sit and watch TV or read something, and I'll doze off for sure. Viv seems to have no such problems.

I started to read a book, and sure enough I soon started to feel heavy and sleepy, so down went the book and I rested my chin in my hand and began nodding off. Just as I was at the point of falling asleep, I felt something. Like my voice – but it wasn't that, it wasn't something from me – it was soundless. It was as if someone nearby had taken a deep breath and let it go again. Like you might do in bed at night – you're breathing slowly and easily and then, unexpectedly, your body grabs just the one deep breath without asking you and goes back to slow and easy again. Well, it was like that. It was weird, but I was tired, and I let it pass.

The next thing I knew it was a lot later and I woke up in the chair feeling groggy. Some coffee got me feeling better, and in the afternoon, we didn't do much, just lazed around, watched TV and mooched about the house and garden. We went out later on, managed to find somewhere passably decent to eat, and came back to Bethlehem Hall. We had a glass of wine each, but I didn't finish mine. We were still pretty hungover.

We sat and talked again, more quietly and thoughtfully, perhaps, than the previous night. I won't bore you with the detail, other than one thing. Viv was up before me after we got back from breakfast, and she mentioned that she'd woken up in tears, feeling very emotional and shaky for no reason. I thought it was probably because she was tired and didn't think anything more of it at the time. It was only later that it seemed to fit into what happened.

So, there we were, determined to wring maximum pleasure out of the rest of our girly weekend, especially me. It was the longest Paul and I had been apart since moving in together, and whilst it wasn't exactly freedom, it was a change and I wanted to savour it. I'd had a nap and I should have been full of energy. But we'd overdone it the night before, and it wasn't long before I gave up, and at an embarrassingly early time – not that long after ten – I told Viv I'd have to go to bed. She didn't seem to mind, and I think she was still feeling the effects herself, though she's pretty good at hiding that sort of thing. Off I went and got into bed. I switched off the light and lay there, wondering what Paul was doing just now. I knew he was fine because we'd texted earlier on. But this was the second night away, and I missed him.

I woke up in the early hours. One moment I was asleep, and then I was awake and fully alert. I hadn't heard my inner voice, but I had this bristling feeling that something wasn't right. I lay without moving and listened as hard as I could for a minute or two. I could hear nothing, but the sense of danger did not go away. Then there it was. There was that same intake of breath I had been aware of in the library, but longer, and deeper. I hadn't sensed any mood about it before, but this time there was no doubt. It was threatening, and it chilled me with a deep, primal fear.

Something started happening. I wasn't sure what it was at first, and then I realised the air was getting colder, and I didn't feel comfortable in my bed any more. I wanted to get out of it, but I found that I didn't dare. It wasn't the fear of whatever was in the room with me, because I knew I was no safer in my bed than outside it. But I was afraid that if I got out, the floor might not be there, and I might step into a void. At the same time, the bed seemed to be getting narrower. I knew this couldn't really be happening, but it was, or at least I thought it was. Looking back, I doubt I was properly awake, and maybe I was in that state where you believe you're awake and you're thinking straight, but actually you can't tell dream from reality. I was convinced though, and I still am, that there was something in that house beside me and Viv, and that it was drawing on me, weakening me. What it intended to do next, I could not imagine.

There was a strange darkness in the room. I don't know if my eyes were open or closed, but I was certain now that beyond the sides of my bed there was no floor, no bedroom, only an awful abyss, the black pit of terror I knew of old made real and sitting there with a gaping grin, waiting for me to fall in and be devoured. I mustn't let that happen! But the bed was shrinking even more. Desperately I pulled the bedclothes into the centre, to give myself something to hold on to. But it was no good. With what felt like a soundless laugh, the bed seemed to give one last contraction and reared itself up in the middle, with me hanging onto it. I was on a high ridge, balanced on the knife edge of an infinite sloping height, petrified with terror and unable to move or get down.

I heard a scream from the corridor, following by a slamming door. Viv was in trouble and I forgot everything else and leapt out of bed, landing on a firm and solid floor. I ran out shouting 'Viv, it's me', to find the corridor light on and her door shut. In her room, Viv was face down on the bed, arms up level with her head, and shaking. She didn't acknowledge me, not even when I lifted her half up, talking and reassuring her all the time. She was beyond hysterical; she was unreachable, and I could have slapped her hard and still got no response. I didn't do that. I kept telling her it was all right, there was nothing there, and I'd stay with her, and eventually she stopped shaking. When she looked at me and said 'Eileen', I knew she was back.

I stayed in Viv's bedroom for the rest of the night. After a couple of hours, she fell asleep, and I went back out to check on the corridor and my room. All was empty and silent. The corridor light was still on, and whatever it was had departed, for the time being at least. I went back into Viv's room and I don't think I slept till shortly before dawn.

We were due to leave Bethlehem Hall the following day anyway, but even if I'd invested my life's savings in it I wouldn't have spent another night there. Everything was hurriedly packed the following morning with a minimum of talk, and by ten we were on our way back. We'd had nothing to eat, but luckily, considering it was a Sunday, the trucker's cafe was open.

Sitting there in a quiet corner amid the mundane normality, Viv told me some of what had happened to her. She too had woken up suddenly in the night. She'd heard a sound in the hall, like scratching. She told me she'd wondered if I was alright and had gone into the corridor and switched on the light. Someone was hunched in the shadow at the other end of the corridor, but it didn't look like me. She took a step forward and peered at it. It must have realised she was there, because it turned around and came towards her.

Viv found it difficult to describe exactly what she saw that night. I got some of the story then, and the rest of it later. She said something about a shuffling female figure in an old granny nightdress, clawlike hands outstretched before it. There was wispy grey hair, yellowish skin, and a rattling noise from its throat. The face was blotched, but the worst thing was the eyes. They were just dark spaces, like pools of ink. Viv said it seemed eager for something. And it stank appallingly, which she said was almost worst of all, as she could not seem to get it out of her nose afterwards. (There was nothing when I ran out into the corridor, only a faint odour of floor polish, or something like it.)

I hardly dared ask about the nightdress, but I did, and I think I managed to make my question sound casual. What was it like? Viv thought for a moment. Well, it was a sort of creamy colour, she said. It went all the way up to the neck, and it had frills on it, and a panel down the front.

We never told the owners of Bethlehem Hall about their sitting tenant. Perhaps they still don't know about it. How and why it all happened is beyond me. It could be that Viv is mediumistic, and maybe it was that, alone or in combination with my gift, which enabled those things to happen. I think I found it easier to deal with than she did, because I'd already accepted the idea of an existence beyond the physical world. People have no idea how hard that is to come to terms with the first time you encounter it.

I am also sure that something was protecting me and wouldn't have let me come to any harm, like the lantern that bobbed along behind me all those years ago. In a strange, twisted way, it all feels a bit like a practical joke that was played on us. Do discarnate entities possess a sense of humour? That's another question I don't have the answer to. But I'm glad to say that Viv's still my friend, even if the friendship's a bit different somehow. We know each other better, and we're quite open with each other. Some things don't need to be discussed, though. We don't talk about that weekend, and we don't mention Bethlehem Hall.

LORD COMBERMERE'S GHOST

Snapshots of ghosts are big business these days, thanks to the existence of high-performance computers and advanced onscreen applications, which enable even talentless amateurs to create realistic hoax images. Perhaps this is one reason why those ghost photographs still taken most seriously by paranormal investigators date back to earlier eras, when fakery – though it did happen then – was a more complex process and much easier to detect.

One of the most famous of these was the image apparently captured at Combermere Abbey, Cheshire, in the December of 1891.

Given the seriousness with which it has been treated over the years, the photograph of Lord Combermere's ghost is at first glance a startlingly unspectacular thing. It depicts a typical late-Victorian era library complete with lush furnishings and hanging plants. There is nothing overtly unusual about it, except that, if one looks closely at the foreground, the faintly distinguishable outline of a well-dressed gentleman is seated in an antique armchair.

On first seeing this photograph, friends and family immediately declared that the half-discernible form was Lord Combermere, which was rather odd as the picture was taken in the Abbey library by keen photographer Sybell Corbet at a time when Lord Combermere was four miles away – being laid to rest, having died a couple of days previously. But the mere fact that there is nothing outlandish about this image is maybe its hidden strength. No bizarre incidents accompanied its capture, and unlike Raynham Hall in Norfolk, where the so-called 'Brown Lady' was photographed in 1936, and the Queen's House in Greenwich, where the 'Tulip Staircase Ghost' was shot in 1966 – probably the two other most famous 'authentic' ghost photographs – Combermere Hall, located between the market towns of Nantwich and Whitchurch on the Cheshire/Shropshire border, was not, and still isn't, regarded as a haunted house. Moreover, the lack of sensation accompanying the tale lends it an air of genuineness. The household would have had nothing to gain from creating a hoax of this kind, and in fact, in terms of bad taste alone, quite a bit to lose.

The whole occasion was a sombre one. Lord Combermere, aka Colonel Wellington Henry Stapleton-Cotton, 2nd Viscount Combermere, was 73 when he died, having enjoyed a distinguished military and political career at the heart of Queen Victoria's Empire. A popular figure locally, and by this time in retirement, his death was the result of a tragic accident when he was run over by a coach and four. As it happened, Sybell Corbett, his sister, was staying at the Abbey at the time, hoping to make a photographic record of the house, which, having once been a Benedictine monastery, was of some historic value. Despite her brother's death, Corbett continued the project and on the day of his funeral had set up her camera to photograph the library. While it's possible the long exposure this would have required could have meant that someone, maybe a servant, had entered the room unaware and sat in the chair in question, and that this would have explained the spectral image, the entire household were adamant that the house was empty at the time because everyone was attending the funeral. There is also the significant fact that numerous witnesses described the spectral figure as strongly resembling the late Lord Combermere.

As a footnote, the Combermere family were no strangers to the supernatural. In 1819, Lord Combermere's father, another Lord Combermere, who happened to be Governor of Barbados, personally investigated the mysterious case of the 'Moving Coffins', wherein a number of heavy burial caskets apparently moved around of their own accord despite being kept in a sealed vault.

WRITER'S CRAMP
David A Riley

The Literary Editor of the *Digest of Horror* swung round lazily on his well-worn swivel chair as the morning's mail was brought in. Cartwright-Hughes looked askance down his long, thin, fastidious nose at the heap of battered manila envelopes that were unceremoniously dumped in front of him by the office boy. Another batch of horrors, he thought languidly, and in more ways than one, no doubt! With a quiet sigh of resignation he picked out one of the slimmer envelopes, sliced it open down one edge with a blunt, bone-handled knife and extracted the enclosed batch of densely-typed sheets of paper. His teeth should twinge every time he received one of these, he thought as he surveyed the closely packed lines of typescript. The half dozen foolscap sheets were almost black with thick, smudgily typed letters. Lesson one for all would-be writers, he sermonised acidly, should be: always, but always type with two spaces at least between each line and just now and then, perhaps once every forty years or so, clean the keys of whatever decrepit, pre-Adamite typewriter was being used. Really he shouldn't have to read something like this. It was appalling. Even the edges of the paper were furred from wear. But, unfortunately - the Literary Editor's eternal bane! - the *Digest of Horror* was short, as usual, of publishable material and something would have to be found soon to fill the remaining eight pages in the March issue, which was due at the printers this week.

Cartwright-Hughes settled back as comfortably as his long spine would allow, propped his feet precariously on the edge of his desk and looked at the title heading of the story: *Paper Doom*. At least the title was reasonably original, he thought, pressing gamefully on. But his expectations quickly began to sink into a welter of unreadable Lovecraftian clichés - bad Lovecraftian clichés of the worst type. This was impossible! Yet, as his eyes scanned further lines, he had to concede that there was, even so, the germ, the merest germ of an idea in it. In some peculiar way the author's grasp of what he was writing about, clumsy though it may have been, did contain a dim air of authenticity. It was difficult for Cartwright-Hughes, who preferred his stories slick, to see just how this was being put over, yet it was there nevertheless.

Finally, he flung the manuscript down onto the desk, surprised at himself for having stolidly ploughed all the way through it. Normally he would not have bothered to read more than a couple of pages of any story which was obviously unusable after the first two paragraphs. Reluctantly, he had to admit that the basic plot was good, but the writing, in almost inverse proportion, was horrifically bad. He pulled out a standard rejection slip from a drawer in his desk, clipped it to the manuscript and slid it into the stamped addressed envelope which the author had wisely supplied.

There the tale would have ended had it not been for the equally disappointing input of submissions to the *Digest of Horror* in the rest of the morning's mail. By noon, Cartwright-Hughes was exasperated and tired. His eyes ached from deciphering the badly typed piles of manuscripts, some of which were blurred with coffee rings and other, less easily identifiable stains, which made him wonder whether some of the putative authors had had sudden, short-lived fits of good taste before sending their manuscripts to him and temporarily made more appropriate use of them for mopping up the floor.

At 12.30 Sykes, the office manager, strolled in with a list of schedules. '*Digest of Horror* is getting awfully close to its deadline, old man,' he intoned portentously. He was a bald-headed Yorkshireman whose round spectacles seemed to reflect the light like spherical mirrors in a way which Cartwright-Hughes found mildly disconcerting.

Cartwright-Hughes tapped the pile of rejected manuscripts with his foot. 'Literary merit seems to have escaped our hopefuls for the moment,' he said, 'though I suppose something might turn up in the second post.'

'The Last Post will be more appropriate if it's not ready on time. This isn't the only magazine we've got to get ready for the newsstands, you know, old man, nor is it our biggest money-maker these days from all accounts, eh?' This was a rather crude reference, delivered with typical Yorkshire bluntness by Sykes, to a sharp but, in Cartwright-Hughes' opinion, temporary slump in the sales of the *Digest*. 'Market fluctuations,' he had said breezily when tackled about it earlier, though he had felt an undeniable twinge of concern. Cartwright-Hughes yawned. 'If the worst comes to the worst I could always write something myself to fill it out.'

'Just so long as it's ready for Thursday,' Sykes said. 'That's the deadline, the *absolute* deadline. We can't wait any later than that.'

By the end of the next day Cartwright-Hughes had taken to gnawing his thumbnails. Tuesday now, there was only one more day to go in which to get the *Digest* finished. To judge from the dismal calibre of amateurish contributions he had been inundated with for the past few months he had no illusions as to what to expect in tomorrow's post. It was like that poem by Yeats, he thought:

> *The best lack all conviction, while the worst*
> *Are full of passionate intensity.*

There was only one thing for it, he thought reluctantly as he gazed gloomily at the secretarial staff in the general office through the dusty windows of his own Sanctum Sanctorum, and that was to dash something off himself. It would mean having to burn some of the proverbial midnight oil unfortunately, but there did not seem to be any realistic alternative. He could, he supposed, have used an old, out-of-copyright reprint, perhaps something from Poe or Bierce, but the *Digest of Horror* was basically a magazine of contemporary fiction. The larger than normal number of old reprints over the past few months had almost certainly been the main reason for the magazine's drop in sales. The task now was to win back its readership. More reprints wouldn't do that. Far from it!

No, there was no other feasible choice. He would have to write something himself.

But what?

Cartwright-Hughes let his fertile imagination amble back over plots he had come across amongst the dirge of unprintable material submitted to the *Digest* recently. Perhaps there was something amongst these which could be quickly chiselled into some kind of presentable shape, but it was usually the hackneyed plots of the contributions that had them skittering back through the post to their authors with rejection slips tagged to their tails rather than just poor or inferior writing. Imagination and, in particular, originality were the things they mainly lacked. Yet there was one recently which he seemed to remember having been impressed with at the time, though its lamentably bad writing had earned it a well-deserved rejection slip.

Abruptly he reached across his desk for the typewriter, tugged it towards him with a triumphant grunt. *Paper Doom* had had a plot he could use, updated with a few amendments and additions. The bare bones of its plot would do nicely for the kind of filler he wanted, though he would have to change its title.

With practised ease Cartwright-Hughes' fingers tapped out the title at the head of a clean sheet of A4 paper; *Hand-Pressed,* he'd call it, in reference to the affliction the main protagonist in the story would literally have cursed upon him.

The story, which was reasonably straight forward, concerned a man's revenge against his wife's lover. Here Cartwright-Hughes diverged radically from the original story, but *Digest of Horror*'s most popular items often figured tales of gruesome, matrimonial revenge, sometimes, though not always by any means, involving the supernatural. The emphasis was strictly on horror and plenty of blood, digestible or otherwise.

The method of revenge was the only real act of plagiarism involved, although Cartwright-Hughes did not feel guilty of even this. After all, he thought defensively, the original story was unpublishable anywhere.

Sticking to the original theme of *Paper Doom,* the vengeful husband, who is depicted as having an academic knowledge of certain forbidden 'Black Arts', sends an old book on demonology to the unsuspecting seducer. On opening the book, the man's attention is drawn to a short phrase on the first page which has been written in what looks like brown ink. The ink, of course, is blood. This is the key which immediately unleashes the terrible nemesis that has been sent to him.

The page is not paper at all but some kind of thin, leathery substance disturbingly akin to tanned human skin. No sooner has the man read the inscription to himself than the page suddenly starts coming to 'life', wrenching itself free from the binding of the book and hurling itself at the man's right hand, which it completely envelopes. So tight does it cling to him that it seems more like an undersized leather glove - or as if his own hand had suddenly aged into the claw of an ancient corpse.

The repulsive skin cannot, he discovers to his horror, be removed, nor can it be seen by anyone else, as if it was only there in his own imagination. But the real horror comes when he finds, not only has his hand, in his own eyes at least, been hideously disfigured by the raddled, corpselike skin, but that whenever he is not in complete control of it his hand can unexpectedly act with an apparent will of its own - a will which it soon becomes clear is determined upon his destruction.

The culmination of the story, aimed unerringly at as gruesome a climax as possible, comes when the unfortunate seducer discovers that the only way in which he can rid himself of the curse is to turn it back on its creator. This, sticking again to the plot of *Paper Doom,* is achieved by the victim reciting backwards the original phrase which brought the page to 'life' and severing his hand from his wrist with one chop of a machete. This drives the demonic skin back onto its creator, whose throat is ripped out in a ghastly welter of blood.

With the final gory paragraphs completed Cartwright-Hughes heaved the typewriter back across the desk with a sigh of contentment - a tired sigh of contentment. It was now 12.15

a.m., but at least the *Digest of Horror* could go to press complete. And Sykes would have nothing to grumble about for another month.

To Cartwright-Hughes' satisfaction there were no more hitches in the March issue of the *Digest*. Eventually, as sales figures started to come in, they even showed a slight but significant upwards climb, confirming for him his diagnosis for its recent slump. From now on, God willing, there would be no more reprints from the 'mouldy oldies', as one irate reader had referred to them, but brand new, garish, matrimonial bloodbaths, of the type the *Digest*'s readership apparently lapped up with enthusiasm - but then Cartwright-Hughes had never had any great respect for the readership of the *Digest of Horror*. As he had once expressed it to a colleague: 'Always presume that your average reader is about twelve years old, spotty, sadistic and partially illiterate, and you can't go far wrong.'

Less than a week later he received a small, buff envelope in the post addressed to him by name. To his surprise he found that it was from the author of Paper Doom. Cartwright-Hughes read it silently to himself, his face growing pale. Finally, he jerked back in his chair and swore. 'Cheeky bastard!' he exploded.

'Anything the matter, old man?' Sykes, who had been strolling past the office when Cartwright-Hughes gave vent to his outburst, poked his head through the doorway. Cartwright-Hughes waved the hand-written letter towards him angrily. 'This cheeky son of a bitch is accusing me of stealing his story!'

'And did you?'

Cartwright-Hughes snorted. 'The damn thing was that badly written he couldn't have given it away, never mind have it stolen. The worst I did was to use a couple of his ideas in the last issue of the *Digest*. And ideas aren't copyright, whatever this nut might think to the contrary. He should have felt flattered that I'd used them. At least when I'd finished they were readable, which is more than could be said about the gibberish he wrote.' Cartwright-Hughes reached into his breast pocket for a handkerchief to wipe away the spittle from his lips.

'Write back to him then and put him in his place,' Sykes said.

'If you're right in what you say, he hasn't a leg to stand on.'

Cartwright-Hughes grunted. He had already decided to do this anyway. As Sykes ambled down the general office, shaking his head, Cartwright-Hughes lunged for his typewriter, angry phrases smouldering through his mind. The man had almost threatened him, he thought indignantly. Threatened! He'd see who threatened who. When it came to cutting phrases, there was one thing being an amateur and quite another thing being a professional, and Cartwright-Hughes hadn't got where he was without learning a trick or two.

Cartwright-Hughes glanced at the address on the letter:

A.J. Dymchurch, Esq.,
The Laurels,
Watery Lane,
Oswaldtwistle,
Lancashire.

Well, Mr Dymchurch, Cartwright-Hughes thought harshly, we'll now see what you're made of. His fingers dived aggressively at the keys on his typewriter, venting his feelings in a machine-gun-like clatter of invective. The cheek of the man had been unbelievable. To demand - to actually demand - that he publish an apology in the next issue of the *Digest of Horror* for stealing his story! Cartwright-Hughes growled between clenched teeth. And then, adding insult to injury, to warn him of the consequences if he didn't in vague and bewildering terms like he did! Any psychiatrist, given that letter, would have had the poor fool locked up. Cartwright-Hughes' fingers quickly typed out this point, ending with an explosive exclamation mark which almost broke the key from the typewriter.

'Put this in the first post,' he called out to the office boy as he meandered aimlessly past, throwing the letter, now signed, sealed and addressed, across to him. 'First class post.' That would show that he meant business!

To Cartwright-Hughes' satisfaction the next couple of weeks were spent peacefully on holiday. When he eventually returned to the office, happy, relaxed and sun-tanned after a much-needed break in the Austrian Alps, he found a pile of mail on his desk. 'Good grief,' he muttered as he disdainfully looked over the parcels of manuscripts. He pulled one out. This must contain a novel at the very least, he thought as he weighed its heavy bulk in his hands. It was hardly worth the effort of opening it since the *Digest of Horror*, as everyone should know by now, he thought, never used anything longer than a ten thousand-word novelette. Shaking his head Cartwright-Hughes cut the parcel open to see if return postage had been enclosed. To his surprise he found that the parcel didn't contain a typescript at all but a hardbound book. 'What on earth is all this about?' he wondered as he pulled it out.

Clearing the rest of the mail to one side he rested the volume on his desk. It was very old and rather ugly; its wrinkled binding looked as if damp had at one time or another take a firm grip of it and ravaged it with decay. A thick, noxious odour rose mustily from it. After touching it he carefully and fussily wiped his fingers clean on a handkerchief of the clammy feeling the book's cover had coated them with. Something about this disturbed him, but he could not figure out what ... or why. Perhaps it was the smell, which was as if some small animal had crawled into the book and died.

Cartwright-Hughes flipped the book open to see if there was anything tucked away inside to indicate who had sent it. It was then, quite suddenly, that warning bells - or their mental equivalent - went off inside his head. He knew instinctively, without any shadow of a doubt, that he must not look at the page facing him, but it was already too late. His eyes were almost compulsively drawn to the dark red letters scrawled across it:

Mutato nomine de te fabula narratur.

Change the name and the tale is about you? Cartwright-Hughes' fingers briefly touched the jagged writing to smooth the paper, which had begun to wrinkle oddly. As he did so there was a sudden ripple of motion across it and the start of a tear appeared at one end. Cartwright-Hughes jerked his hand from the book in revulsion, but the page came with it. Like a tattered, wind-blown moth the parchment flapped about his hand. It was stuck, as if glued to his fingers. Vainly he shook his hand to throw the thing from him, but the wrinkled parchment clung tenaciously to him, enfolding itself about his hand. Cartwright-Hughes knew that this was ridiculous. It was as if he had blundered into that trite story he had had so much trouble about. But stories like that never happened, not in real life! He clutched, frantically, at the page to tear it from him, but as he pulled it was like trying to rip his own skin from his hand. He cried out in pain and fell back, bewildered, against his desk, slipping to the floor where he wrestled with the thing, but it seemed to have him trapped in an iron vice moulded to the exact shape of his hand. And the vice was tightening. Crushed, his fingers were already starting to go numb. No! Noooo! He grunted with exertion, but his fingers could do nothing against the hideous, fleshy parchment that had trapped them.

For a moment Cartwright-Hughes, who was not a strong man, felt dizzy and he knew that he was falling into a faint. When he recovered moments later he saw a circle of faces staring down at him.

'Are you all right, old man?' Sykes asked as he pushed a folded jacket beneath his head. 'Take it easy. Don't rush to get up.'

Cartwright-Hughes breathed deeply. He had passed out, that was all, he thought. Overwork probably. A feeling of relief passed over him. It had, after all, been nothing worse than a nightmare as he lay sprawled out on the floor.

Slowly, Sykes helped him to his feet while someone fetched a chair. As he sat down, Cartwright-Hughes glanced at his hands.

'Is anything wrong?' Sykes asked; he gripped Cartwright-Hughes' shoulder to steady him, certain that he was about ready to collapse again. But Cartwright-Hughes rallied himself, though he remained silent for the moment as the full horror of it all started to sink in. He knew that there was no point in saying anything now, not now, because no one, no one but himself, would ever be able to see it. He stared in horrified silence at the wrinkled 'glove' that covered his hand like a membrane of ancient skin.

When he finally felt strong enough to stand up he asked Sykes if he would drive him home. 'Anything to oblige, old man,' Sykes responded with the kind of over-enthusiasm people often adopt towards those they consider invalids. Subduing the irritation he would have normally reacted to this with, Cartwright-Hughes walked with him to the car park. Sykes' amiable if aimless chatter passed him unheard as he pondered on the situation he now found himself in. Every moment or so he glanced at his hand as if hoping that eventually he would find that there was nothing there and that it had all been a hallucination after all, but the wrinkled skin was there every time, and he knew, deep down, that this was no hallucination. It was real. Horribly, horribly real!

He thought back over the plot of *Paper Doom*. He had no doubts as to the source of the thing that had afflicted him. A.J. Dymchurch, Esq., he was the man. He was the man all right, the dirty, vindictive ...! Cartwright-Hughes drew his lips back taut across his teeth in a fit of fury. Yet at the same time a grim chill of foreboding crept through him as he looked back over the story he had partially purloined. As Sykes turned the ignition in the heavy Wolseley saloon and drove them out onto the busy main road, heading towards St Johns Wood, Cartwright-Hughes wondered whether the rest of the 'curse' as depicted in Dymchurch's story would follow, in particular the determination of his disfigured hand to kill him. He stared distrustfully at it. While he was in conscious control of it he knew he was safe, but how could he possibly keep this up all the time? It was impossible, and he knew it. Yet, would he have to go to the violent extreme depicted in the story to free himself of it? He shuddered nauseously at the thought. A squeamish man at the best of times when faced with reality, he found the whole idea inconceivable.

Sykes left him outside the entrance to the select block of flats in which he lived. As he hurried in, the doorman called out: 'Just one letter today, sir.' Thanking him, Cartwright-Hughes accepted it from him and hastened to the lift. He clutched the small, buff envelope in his left hand, having developed a sudden aversion to using the other 'contaminated' hand for anything, especially this: one glance at the crabbed handwriting on the front of the envelope was enough to inform him of the identity of the sender.

Safely back in his flat, with its broad view of St Johns Wood, Cartwright-Hughes poured himself a strong gin and tonic and put a record on the music centre, choosing a favourite Mozart concerto to help ease the tension that had gripped him and to restore at least the semblance of some kind of normality. Gripping the gin gratefully he settled back in an armchair by the window and carefully unsealed the letter.

'Dear Mr Cartwright-Hughes,' it read, 'You will have by now received the book I sent to you and taken possession of the page enclosed in it. After the way in which you criminally stole the story I sent to you I doubt whether you are uncertain about what will happen next. You have been warned once already. That should have been enough. Yet I am not a heartless man. There is still time. If you carry out what I set out in my previous letter to you I can reverse what has happened. But time is short. And getting shorter. I must have your reply, in writing, soon or it will be too late. Yours, etc., A.J.D.'

Cartwright-Hughes sank back despairingly in the armchair. He knew that he was faced with an insoluble problem. How could he possibly confess publicly to having stolen another writer's story? Not only would that mean his professional ruin but, even more importantly perhaps, it would make him a laughing stock from now on with everyone he knew. It was downright impossible for him to do anything like this. Impossible! He might just as well cut his own throat. There was no way in which he could expose himself like that, whatever the cost.

Abruptly, he jumped to his feet, put away the gin and strode into the study in the next room where he unlocked the writing bureau in which he kept his personal mail and laid out a clean sheet of paper. Drawing up a chair, he started to write out a reply to Dymchurch, a reply that was radically different to the one he had sent to him before. As he wrote he avoided as much as possible looking at the wrinkles and creases of dried skin that covered his hand. Instead he concentrated on trying to write something conciliatory to Dymchurch, something which would enable him to avoid the personal and professional suicide of confessing to plagiarism. Ideas floated through his mind as he wrote. An offer of money - a substantial offer of money - was one. Another was the offer of a series of stories in future issues of the *Digest,* although that was certain to send sales plummeting to an all-time record low. Play on his vanity, he thought cynically. That was the thing. If Dymchurch could go to the extremes he had in revenge for taking a couple of ideas from his story the man must have an obsessive ego. He must have!

Cartwright-Hughes paused to trace back over what he had written. As he glanced at the letter his face became deathly pale, and a tremor started to pulse in his lower lip.

'Don't waste your time pathetically pleading. The terms have been stated. Either accept them or face the consequences. There is no other choice.'

Cartwright-Hughes stared at the crabbed handwriting bewilderedly. His right hand felt even more alien to him now than before. It wasn't his at all any more. It was possessed, stolen!

He picked up a paper knife and gently tried to prise the 'skin' away, but it was no use. The thing wouldn't budge except if he cut his own skin away at the same time. Was that the solution then? Get some back-street surgeon to cut the skin, both skins, from his hand? If he did that, though, he might just as well have his hand cut off, since he doubted if so much skin could be replaced through skin grafts. He might be better off, then, having his hand amputated, properly carried out under anaesthetic by a surgeon. At least that way it would be relatively painless. Though he couldn't just go to any ordinary surgeon for a job like that. He'd more likely end up being certified by any reputable doctor. The only kind he could approach. he knew, would be someone who had been struck off, someone crooked.

Fortunately, Cartwright-Hughes had his contacts, built up over the years from his habit at one time of sniffing cocaine. Erosion of the nasal passages due to 'snorting' the stuff resulted in the not unusual necessity of having to have plastic surgery performed on his nose. Since cocaine was illegal, he had had to take the prudent step of arranging through a 'friend of a friend' to have the operation performed in a discrete clinic somewhere in Brixton. He remembered the anonymous-looking redbrick tenement where the squall of some God-awful rock music all but drowned the screams of untended babies in the surrounding slums.

Although he didn't know the 'surgeon's name, he was told at the time by his contact that the man had once been highly placed in his field until struck off for unethical and somewhat immoral practices.

Cartwright-Hughes thumbed through his personal phone book, then dialled. Half an hour later, an appointment had been made for that evening for a large sum of money. He felt sick in the pit of his stomach at what he would have to undergo, but there was no choice. He flexed his fingers. It was almost inconceivable that anything had really changed. It still felt like his own hand. It still felt under his control. But the wrinkled skin sheathing it and the alien writing on the note paper were clear enough proof that his hand had been possessed. He dared not wait for it to act unexpectedly against him, as he knew it eventually would, to bring about his death. It was like walking about with an assassin attached to the end of his arm.

When, later that day, he ordered a taxi to take him to Brixton for his appointment, Cartwright-Hughes vowed to himself that somehow, in some way he would get his revenge. However clever he might think he was, Dymchurch would not get away with this.

The diesel train drew up at the station, where it was instantly battered by blasts of rain. Cartwright-Hughes glimpsed a dispiritingly small, untended platform through the dirt-smeared window of the carriage door as he tugged it open. A plain sign read: *Church and Oswaldtwistle.* He shivered as he stepped down onto the platform at the cold, penetrating winds, and clutched his briefcase to him like a shield in his left hand as he hurried to the steps which brought him down to the road. He hurried along till he saw a sign for Union Road. An old man, the flat cap on his head bowed against the rain like a battering ram, was shuffling past. Cartwright-Hughes called out, asking the way to Watery Lane. The old man looked at him with glassy, red-rimmed eyes.

'That'll be up the'er,' he pointed waveringly. 'Tha goes past yon shops o'er there – D'yer see them? You go on past the Co-op, then a sandwich bar, *Scoffs,* then a pub, right on till tha gets to th'end – then tha turns reet. Keep on goin' after that till tha comes t'th'end. Then keep on goin' to tha left.' He rambled on a few more directions which Cartwright-Hughes carefully noted.

'Thank you. Thank you very much,' he said.

'Think nowt on it.'

Cartwright-Hughes thought for a moment, then said: 'I don't suppose you know someone up that way called Dymchurch, do you?'

The old man cocked his head to one side and looked at him shrewdly. 'Albert Dymchurch?'

'It could be. I only know his initials: A.J.'

'Aye, that'll be 'im. Albert Joseph Dymchurch.' He spat eloquently into the gutter. 'If'n I were you I'd steer clear o' that on'. Should 'a' bin locked up years ago.'

'Why?'

'Why? 'Cause 'iz brains are addled, that's why. Always 'ave bin.' He grinned confidentially. 'If you're 'ere to certify 'im you'll no' go short o' volunteers to back up what I say. Iz that what you're 'ere for?'

Cartwright-Hughes hesitated, uncertain now whether under the circumstances he had been wise to let anyone know that he was here to see Dymchurch, especially a garrulous old man like this. There were certain to be plenty of questions asked later, and the less anyone knew about him the better.

Noticing his hesitation, the old man chuckled good-naturedly. 'Don't worry yoursen, lad. I'll not press you if'n you don't want to say nothin'. I respects a man 'as'll keep a secret. Too much loose talk these days az it iz. But if'n you are 'ere to lock th'owd blighter up then you've got my blessin's lad. Aye, that you 'ave, all reet.'

Following the old man's directions as the wind and rain gradually died down from being vilely unpleasant to a kind of persistent dreariness, Cartwright-Hughes came some fifteen minutes later to a narrow lane leading between a line of trees. A small terraced cottage faced him there, its neighbours blatantly derelict. Dead ivy covered its stone walls like dried varicose veins. A musty smell of unwashed linen, cats and other domestic animals hung round the door, indication enough of how it would smell inside. There were no curtains at the windows, only discoloured newspapers held in place by crinkled strips of equally discoloured tape.

On the unpainted, splintered and damp-swollen door was a small plaque, *The Laurels* pretentiously painted across it in crumbling 'Olde English' letters.

Cartwright-Hughes rapped officiously on the door and tried to adopt the stance appropriate to a local council official. This, he thought, would give him the best means of gaining entry into the house without rousing any undue suspicions. Browbeat the bastard first, he thought, with a load of domineering bullshit – sanitation and hygiene, appropriately enough, were obvious targets he could use. Then ...!

There was a muffled creak at the door, quickly followed by another, though neither had any noticeable effect. A further creak followed, impatiently this time, and the door was suddenly tugged open. It jammed just as suddenly on the uneven flagstones inside, leaving a gap barely wide enough to squeeze through.

The odour of unwashed linen and animals became appreciably stronger and was joined by a further smell of cooking – this appeared to consist mainly of some kind of boiled vegetable, probably cabbage, though Cartwright-Hughes was by no means certain.

'Yes?'

An elderly, narrow-shouldered man in a threadbare cardigan peered round the doorway. His thin, angular, unshaven jaws were clamped tight, tensely, while his pale grey, rather watery eyes scrutinised Cartwright-Hughes through slightly misshapen horn-rimmed spectacles perched at an odd angle on the bridge of his nose. Tiny tufts of greyish hairs sprouted like a kind of sparse, miniaturised sedge from the tip of his nose and the lobes of his reddish ears, accentuating his definitely unkempt appearance.

'Mr Dymchurch?' Cartwright-Hughes enquired, briefcase held tight against his abdomen in bureaucratic fashion. 'Mr Albert Dymchurch?' he added pedantically.

'Ye-es.' Apprehensively Dymchurch glanced at the briefcase much as a downtrodden Roman citizen might have once looked upon the fasces of a Senatorial magistrate.

Despite the hatred and anger which had driven him here all the way from London, Cartwright-Hughes realised that he was now beginning to enjoy himself, yes, despite everything.

'I've been asked to see you,' he said, 'to check your sanitation. There have been complaints ...'

Dymchurch stepped back into the house. 'Please come in, please come in,' he said, ineffectively tugging at the door to widen the gap. 'I shall 'ave to get this fixed someday,' he muttered apologetically as Cartwright-Hughes squeezed through the doorway and followed him into the dim room beyond.

Confusion and dust lay about him in the living room - or whatever Dymchurch chose to term it. An old fashioned sideboard cluttered with books that looked equally old; an open coal fire from which a few sickly looking flames periodically spluttered; several armchairs, of which all but one were covered with piles of still more books; and a 1950s style bicycle propped against one wall, while above the fireplace there hung a framed portrait in oils of a thin-faced man with a yellowish complexion and slightly protuberant eyes. The whole room filled Cartwright-

Hughes' fastidious soul with revulsion - a revulsion born from the dreary, defeated squalor of it all. Dymchurch stood watching him, his baggy trousers and patched cardigan so in place amongst the upheaval that it almost acted as a kind of camouflage, blending him into the background. Cartwright-Hughes studied this man who had hated him so much as to do what he had done to him. He looked too ineffectual, too old, too decrepit, like a worn-out and senile schoolteacher, to have done all of that.

Dymchurch waited patiently for him to speak.

There was no point now in any further prevarication. Cartwright-Hughes, looking down on Dymchurch from an advantage of an additional six inches, said: 'We've never met before, but you know me. At least, you know me enough to have tried to have me killed.'

Dymchurch's eyes opened wide, apprehensive again and perhaps just a little afraid. His hands fluttered uncertainly to his lips as he spoke, carefully choosing his words. 'You are, I take it, from London - not the Council?'

Cartwright-Hughes admitted the obvious. 'Cartwright-Hughes is the name,' he said, unclipping his briefcase. He thumped the heavy book he had been sent onto the floor. Spurts of dust erupted from beneath it, fogging the light from the windows. He reached into his briefcase again and brought out a small package wrapped in oilskins. In carrying out all of these actions he used only his left hand. His right arm was used solely to hold the briefcase pressed to his stomach. Suddenly he let the briefcase drop to the floor and held his arm towards Dymchurch, revealing the stump that terminated at his wrist. The flesh was still covered with gauze from the operation. A dark stain tinged it.

Dymchurch clucked. His eyes peered speculatively at Cartwright-Hughes. He was plainly surprised.

Cartwright-Hughes held the oilskin package to his chest and picked it open. Inside lay a wrinkled hand, his hand, his stolen hand. He threw it down at Dymchurch's feet.

'You know what will happen next,' he said.

Dymchurch shrugged. 'Whatever will be ...' he murmured. 'I can do nothing to stop you, not now.' He shrugged carelessly. Cartwright-Hughes noticed for the first time a steely glint in the man's otherwise watery eyes. Was that indicative of the harder, tougher part of the man, the part that had given him the will to delve as deeply as he had into whatever realms of forbidden knowledge he had chosen to master?

Cartwright-Hughes straightened his back. 'The tables are turned now, and you can learn what it is like to be cursed. And learn how careless you were to use the same curse against me as you used in your story.' Cartwright-Hughes opened a slip of paper, from which he read: '*Narratur fabula te de nomine mutato!*

Dymchurch stepped back as the wrinkled skin covering the severed hand started to move. It seemed to heave itself up from the hand, and Cartwright-Hughes could see the red perforations beneath where it had clung, leech-like, to his flesh. Like a deformed moth, the 'skin' flapped itself and rose unsteadily into the air. It was then that Cartwright-Hughes began to suspect that something was wrong. For a start off Dymchurch had developed a tight, little, satisfied smile which threatened momentarily to grow. Why? But worse, he saw that the 'skin' was starting to move, not towards Dymchurch, but towards himself!

Cartwright-Hughes stumbled back, falling over the arm of the chair behind him. The 'skin' suddenly flapped forward. Instinctively he brought the stump of his right hand up to shield his face, but the thing wrapped itself about his wrist for the merest moment, biting into the unhealed wound, before slithering past and flapping towards his face.

'Why?' Cartwright-Hughes cried out in bewilderment. 'Why?'

The 'skin' slapped hard into his face. Where its abrasive underside touched his flesh it left bright red weals that trickled blood. He clutched at it with his left hand, but the perforations beneath it seemed to burn his fingers as if it was covered with thousands upon thousands of tiny, venomous, razor-sharp mouths that sucked at him. He rolled over as it tightened itself about his throat, as the room began to spin before his eyes and the air seemed to boom inside his ears. 'Why? Why?' he choked out, his words all but meaningless as the 'skin' tightened its grip, and blood spurted in hundreds of tiny jets out from beneath it.

Dymchurch strolled curiously over as Cartwright-Hughes collapsed, convulsively choking on the floor. His face was now purple above the livid 'skin' wrapped round his throat, and small, bubbling, mewling sounds were all that escaped from his lips, drawn back agonisingly from his teeth. Dymchurch smiled as the Literary Editor's feet kicked out ineffectually, weakening quickly.

It was fortunate, Dymchurch thought, that he had not stuck to fact all the way through the story he'd submitted to the *Digest of Horror,* otherwise Cartwright-Hughes would never have tried, without the protection of a pentacle about him, to order a gaunt back to its inhospitable world between the planes. They became terribly, even nastily aggressive about things like that.

'But you should have known,' Dymchurch chided reprovingly to the shuddering remains of Cartwright-Hughes, whose swollen eyes had already started to cloud over, 'that there is a world of difference between fact and fiction, and the two should never be confused. You, of all people, should have known better than that.'

SCREAMING SKULLS

Allegedly, there are a number of screaming skulls in England. According to popular folklore, these grisly relics of humanity - in each case a dried-out, desiccated skull, normally kept behind a curtain or panel in some venerable old country house - are testimonies to grave injustices done in the past, usually of a religious or sectarian nature, and they'll indicate their extreme displeasure if any attempt is made to remove them.

The Northwest of England, with its grim history of Reformation era violence and the brutal massacres it witnessed during the Civil War, boasts two such artefacts. The screaming skull of Wardley Hall, a listed medieval manor house in Worsley, on the northwest outskirts of Manchester, is one of them. The other is the skull of Skull House in Appley Bridge, a Lancashire village located close to the Leeds/Liverpool Canal just north of Wigan.

In the former case, the skull of Wardley Hall has various colourful legends attached to it. One holds that it belonged to 17th century royalist adventurer and drunkard, Roger Downs, who supposedly lost his head in a fight he pointlessly picked with an armed guard on Tower Bridge in London. In fact, the truth is sadder. The skull has actually been traced back to Father Ambrose Barlow, a Catholic priest who in 1641 was arrested while saying a secret Mass in Astley, Manchester. King Charles I had recently passed new legislation reinforcing the rules against Roman Catholicism, and even though Barlow had been crippled by a stroke, a decision was taken to make an example of him. He was hanged, drawn and quartered at Lancaster Castle.

Afterwards, Barlow's head was boiled in pitch and displayed on a pike over the castle gate. It finally found its way to concealment and veneration at Wardley Hall, when smuggled away from Lancaster by Catholic sympathisers. Ever since then, legends have insisted that the skull must remain in this its final resting place. For a time, its whereabouts were forgotten, but then, in the mid-18th century, a servant discovered it whilst engaged in refurbishment. He was so revolted by the grinning object that he tossed it into the manor moat – and that night the most terrible shrieks were heard around the house, the ground shook, and fearsome poltergeist activity was experienced. When the servant confessed what he'd done, the moat was dragged and drained until the skull was rediscovered and returned to its cobweb-filled cubby hole. Repeated attempts to remove the skull and even to destroy it were made in later years, all resulting in the same paranormal chaos. On one occasion it was supposedly smashed to fragments with a hammer, but the following morning was found on the Hall's front doorstep, completely intact, still grinning.

Since the 1930s, the curse or blessing, or whatever one feels inclined to call it, appears to have lifted. The Wardley skull has been removed from the building on several occasions, usually for religious purposes, once by the Bishop of Salford, who was temporarily a resident there, and there were no reported disturbances, though folklorists have suggested that this may be because on these occasions the reasons for the removal were benign and it was always the intention to have it replaced afterwards.

The second of the two skulls, the one resident in Skull House, Appley Bridge, is a less visible and in some ways more mysterious artefact.

Skull House is not some ornate country manor, but a privately-owned farm cottage in what was once a remote district, though this too played its role in the tragic, tumultuous affairs of 17th century England. In 1651, Oliver Cromwell's Roundhead forces scoured the area between Preston and Manchester, hunting down and routing those contingents of Royalists still scattered across the county in support of Charles II. One additional purpose of theirs, at least according to some of the histories, was to root out what remained of Lancashire's monk and priest population and finish them off once and for all.

According to the folklore, one such attack was launched on a priory quite close to Appley Bridge. A sole surviving monk is said to have fled to a nearby cottage, where he hid by climbing the interior of its chimney and lodging himself in an aperture half way up. The Roundheads finally smoked him out, literally, by lighting a fire in the hearth, and once they had him in their grip, they beheaded him.

As with the legend at Wardley Hall, the skull was only kept on the property over the following ages through sufferance - because whenever an effort was made to dispose of it, dire consequences would follow. One owner of the house allegedly threw the skull into the River Douglas, which runs close by, but though the skull supposedly returned of its own volition, he later fell into the river himself and drowned. Another simply abandoned the object in local fields, but later found that it had returned - he duly fell down the staircase and suffered life-changing injuries. Other disasters have included sickness and bereavement.

These days, perhaps inevitably, the skull remains in the house, though not on public view. It has been investigated, however, and evidence suggests that the tale of the unfortunate monk is fabricated. To begin with, the story about Cromwell's troops razing what remained of Lancashire's Catholic churches and monasteries is nonsense - there were none remaining by the 1650s, and in fact there hadn't been any such institutions in that district for over a century. It is entirely possible that the early storytellers had got their Cromwells confused. Possibly, the wrath of Thomas Cromwell, Henry VIII's infamous church-breaker of the 16th century, had been the cause of the frightened monk's flight, though a recent scientific enquiry has revealed the skull to be female.

This does not of course mean that the tales of hauntings are lies, but whoever the unfortunate woman was, whatever tragedy reduced her to little more than a wizened, featureless skull, it will likely remain a secret now for evermore.

WET JENNY
Christopher Harman

The dank chill could have seeped up from the canal, four floors below. Three months since Anita Shaw had sold the apartment and her successful accessories business, abandoned Lancashire and returned to Lincoln. Reeds Properties hadn't shifted no. 47 off their books and were unlikely to this bitter January. Other apartments were empty too, three at bargain basement prices and one offered at a greatly reduced rent.

The Waterside had been a derelict flax mill before its conversion. Its vivid red brick, wrought iron balconies and big picture windows rose above warehouses and sheds, depots and bleak empty yards, defunct factories and decayed terrace housing. Development of the immediate locale had been in Urblough Council's Local Plan for three years but hadn't advanced much further than that.

The estate agent's patter had died off in the face of Gurdow's token questions as he cast his gaze over the decor, the fixtures and fittings. In the plush office off Urblough's main shopping street she'd told him they didn't conduct viewings on a Saturday afternoon. Fixing his gaze on her and mentally crossing his fingers, Gurdow had said he was viewing on behalf of an elderly relative thinking of moving back up north. Adding another untruth, that he had a train ticket back to Lincoln first thing Monday morning, he'd stood with arms folded, resolute as the bobby he'd been three decades before at Lincoln City football ground. After a phone call to her boss she'd arranged to meet Gurdow at the Waterside an hour later.

Miss Shaw had left the place fully furnished but it was hardly a selling point. The blocky sofa looked sculpted from hard cheese. The coal-effect gas fire was an intimidating chrome citadel. With coarse textured carpet tiles, mustard-yellow walls and beige Venetian blinds the living room was as homely as an office. She'd given the wall-mounted plasma television to the neighbour who'd helped her that terrible day in October; the rectangular pallor left behind would be an apt representation of her vanished son until the wall was repainted or another TV or a painting was hung up.

Gurdow caught the estate agent sneaking a glance at her watch. 'Chilly,' she said, unapologetically stuffing her hands into the pockets of her plaid woollen coat.

'Can you let me out please?' Gurdow said.

A flicker of disappointment as she realised he meant out onto the balcony. Her hand flurried in her shoulder bag for the key which she jabbed and turned in the lock. Gurdow slid the door and stepped out. She joined him, both hands back in her pockets.

Nobody on the tow-paths. Leftwards the canal fed eventually into the docks a mile away where cranes formed slender upturned L's and a solitary funnel smoked before the nothing of estuary, sea and winter horizon.

Movement below, a fragmentation of yellow froth on the canal's surface. A low breeze must have disturbed it, or missiles flung by the children whose laughter rang off the dank drear verticals and corroded fire-escapes, fading as they found other mischief to get up to.

A monotone remained – traffic in the city centre. It rose a tone, dropped, rose again. Gurdow gripped the balcony rail. The sky slid on the roof-scape. Gurdow pressed his fingertips to his ears, turned his back on the threatening blight of Urblough, the hum of traffic trying to become a tune. The estate agent frowned.

'Something wrong?'

He dropped his hands. A single note of distant vehicles. Restless sleep last night, dreams of suffocation and biting teeth, then four hours on the earliest train that morning and he'd never been a good traveller. 'No,' he said with pretend puzzlement.

She went back inside, Gurdow following. He slid the door and in the second before it sealed away the outside with a sharp bang there was a splash, lingering in his inner ears as he said, 'Bathroom?'

It was spacious and in pale green porcelain tiles but for a wall of mirrors and a shower unit of frosted glass. Gleaming brass taps at one end of the deep, claw-foot bath. A snapshot in Gurdow's head of Miss Shaw under a layer of soap-bubbles.

In his Lincoln office she'd been immaculately turned out; trouser suit, silk scarf, tear-drop earrings. Her shiny blonde bob left a shape like the glass in a diver's helmet for cheek bones, lip-glossed lips and large icy-blue eyes.

A friend with a wayward husband had recommended Derek Gurdow, private investigator. She agreed with a touch of impatience to the travel and hotel costs he stipulated on top of his fee. She said she almost regretted leaving Lancashire. Out of sight, out of mind as far as the police and *Urblough Messenger* were concerned. The liaison officer had stopped ringing. Platitudes from the lead officer on the investigating team.

Gurdow had tape-recorded her account of the October evening.

Alex had been in the living room watching *Finding Nemo* on the Disney Channel, while his mother dozed in her own watery world. She'd had a hard day attending to teething troubles at her new shop in Lancaster before rushing down the M6 to collect Alex from Infants. She'd become aware of a primitive, folk-like tune, slow as a dirge, the voice female but low and harsh. From the living room, she realised, the words muffled by the intervening door. *Finding Nemo* didn't have any songs as far as she could recall - and if it did there surely weren't any like this one.

She was thinking there was something vividly present about the woman's voice when it stopped. She'd never known Alex to switch off the TV himself - or to be so silent. With a terrible sense of things not being right she'd got out of the bath and put on her bath robe. Gurdow had steepled his fingers and pictured that all too well. She went dripping into the living room.

No sign of Alex. The TV was on, no sound coming from it, the screen frozen on a green underwater twilight vertically striped with kinked narrow reeds. She'd called out, frantically searched behind furniture, inside cupboards, under the beds. The child-proof window locks were all secured, as was the door to the balcony. Dismay then, at the sight of the front door, open a few inches. Alex was tall enough to have reached the door handle and let himself out - but why? He'd no friends in the Waterside, nor anywhere in the vicinity. Frantically she'd called out his name in the corridor. At this point in Gurdow's office one of her ice-blue eyes had welled with a tear.

Her immediate neighbour had emerged and accompanied her down in the lift. There had been a deluge of rain outside the building. Soon as wet as she had been getting out of the bath, she'd cursed Alex and pleaded with him to show himself. She hurried to the rear of the building, cast her gaze on the drab black band of the canal. Nobody on the tow-paths; a few atoms of relief at there being no indication of a floating shape in the water.

She rang the police, insisting the singing woman had taken her son. They searched that night and volunteers assisted the next day. No sign of Alex alive or dead, no clues to his possible fate. No evidence of an intruder; no fingerprints other than Alex's and his mother's. If anyone had witnessed the boy, alone or accompanied, they hadn't come forward.

He was the lead story in the *Urblough Messenger*; in the online version, trolls opined on neglectful mothers, hinted at ones who were even worse.

Mid-morning three days later came the phone call.

'Hello?' she said and thereafter didn't repeat. Children playing, laughing, calling to each other. Not close - maybe out on a street. A series of rapid clicks puzzled her until the realisation they were chattering teeth. Some wretch in a cold dismal bedsit, with nothing better to do than hound a name in the news? The phone went dead before she had a chance to say what she thought of them. A crank with the wherewithal to withhold their number. She phoned the police, but they could do nothing on the basis of one untraceable call. Neither to them nor Gurdow could she offer a clue as to the sex of the caller.

A day later a letter in the *Urblough Messenger* referred to a spate of disappearances in the 1890s, children labeled the Water Babes, and a fabled bogey-woman known as Wet Jenny. The next day an old article was reprinted on the subject by a local historian called Len Luft.

Miss Shaw learned the police had spoken to him but any theory that some deranged woman had taken on the mantle of Jenny, even to the point of abducting a child, hadn't been at the forefront of their investigation. She'd gone to speak to Luft herself, more than once until advised not to. 'He was polite but shifty,' she'd told Gurdow. 'Kept rubbing his eyes and blinking. He knows everyone by the canal. I still think he knows more than he lets on. I mean – what if he's protecting someone?' It was more an order than a suggestion that Gurdow should speak to him.

Gurdow left the Waterside and returned to his room at the Premier Hotel. Sipping complementary tea he re-read Luft's account of Wet Jenny in *Bricks and Water: Urblough's Canal-side Past.* It was a stapled booklet with tiny print that made Gurdow's eyes prickle and water. He packed his knapsack with his tablet, camera and phone and walked through the late Saturday afternoon shoppers to Apprentice Square.

The Farmers' Market was packing up. Teenagers sitting on the steps of the Cenotaph tipped back bottles in preparation for the evening ahead. On the steps of the City Library were half a dozen people, all middle-aged to elderly and wrapped up for a winter hike. At the mid-point in the age-range, Gurdow was welcomed with nods and half-smiles, his dyed hair and successful resistance to middle-aged spread fooling nobody. One man had a belly that pushed out his unbuttoned mackintosh. His eyes gleamed under the brim of his pork-pie hat. He had a staff with a tiny hurricane lantern on the top, unlit for now. He nodded a welcome and brushed a finger against a welling eye, taking Gurdow in. This must be Luft.

Gurdow guessed his trench coat marked him out from the others as the private investigator who'd rang that morning from the train to confirm the time of their meeting. Luft had again expressed his sympathy for Miss Shaw and would be 'only too glad' to discuss the case later that evening. Gurdow doubted that. He said he intended to join the History Tour that afternoon. With suspect pleasure in his voice, Luft said he was welcome, 'But I can't promise my old canal tales will be any more helpful to you than they have been to the regular police.'

Luft was doing a quick count when another couple arrived, a stout woman ostentatiously puffing and a lanky bespectacled girl. An hour, he said, ending at the Tow Rope pub. He didn't go on to say he part-owned the place on the proceeds of a hefty redundancy payment from his college teaching post. If running the pub accounted for half his time, then the other half mixed working for the council's Tourism and Leisure directorate and continuing to unearth Urblough's smoky past. He'd been researching a former chapel on a bank of the canal on the evening of Alex's disappearance.

Luft moved off at the head of a line of ones and twos. Past the granite law courts, they entered a street lined by imposing properties housing law firms and accountants. After a quarter of a mile it ended at bollards like peg teeth. The group passed under a curved sign - Ripley Pier.

An antiques shop, wine bar and hair boutique were amongst the up-market establishments on both sides of the canal. Brickwork had been pointed and cleaned, paving stones were in pastel colours. People strolled over an aluminium modular bridge, some window-shopped and others leaned against the black-painted railings and stared into the water. A family posed for a photograph under a fake Victorian street lamp.

'Oh can't we stop,' said a woman, lagged head to foot in wool, jocular in her pleading as she eyed the shops.

'No we can't.' Luft was humorously prim. 'We're here for history not rampant commercialism.' He set forth.

Drabness past the lamplight. The sky was a fine grey sand over the black drooping geometry of the roofs. 'Keep together and tread carefully,' Luft said breezily over his shoulder. 'I don't want to be fishing you out of the drink.'

A row of cottages had a homely charm; chintz curtains, a

decorative wagon wheel, a beer barrel water butt. Withered contents of a window box were excusable at this time of the year, but not splitting black plastic bags piled under a window, the bottles and cans littering the patio next door. Further on an edifice of brick had soaked up too many nights. Luft said it had been the lair of a forger and counterfeiter in the 1920s.

A scrabbling in the dark interior sounded like quill pens and was probably rats. A woman in a cape and gloves made a 'Eugh' sound and a lone, bony man in a balaclava rolled his eyes and half-smiled at Gurdow.

Pockets of activity alongside the tow-paths but commerce had largely fled. A poster for a rock gig in a window; glass and water shivered to a deep bass beat. Further on, a hammering of nails but there were more piles of planking than craft behind a huge rusting iron gate with a 'Boat Yard' sign. Luft said barges were manufactured for pleasure these days, and it was decades since they'd transported coal to the factories. Ho hum, Gurdow thought to himself, as others nodded soberly and balaclava man stroked his chin.

The party crossed a footbridge and entered a path between warehouses. Windows were teethed in broken glass coated in a plaque of green lichen. Weeds flourished in piles of perished tyres. The path brought them to a run-down terrace with a wavering roof ridge. Formerly dockers' cottages, Luft said.

They seemed no longer homes until the party was passing the one at the end. In an open window a tap gushed. Splashing and giggles from a whole shoal of little ones elicited 'ahs' and sad-happy faces from a couple of the women. A telephone wire hummed.

A hundred yards on a great dilapidated pile was stained black, maybe by the abandoned coal depot next door. It had been a workhouse, then a children's home, Luft said. An empty shell now, holes without glass or window frames, a dark gash in the roof. The place had drawn a new generation of children, bubbling with laughter as they stamped through puddles inside. 'Dangerous,' a woman said, her brow wrinkled with concern. Others muttered agreement and looked to Luft. Coal

Row, he informed the woman when she asked. She held back as he moved on, his itinerary more important than the welfare of wayward kids. Gurdow heard the woman asking for the police on her mobile phone, explaining and giving out the address.

Single file between high walls, then a turn took them into a channel which Luft said was an interesting offshoot from the main stretch. Opposite, a bakery was like seed cake in its coat of pebble dashing. In a gloomy entry were towers of crates. Children giggled and Gurdow thought they'd squeezed into them to spy on passers-by. But no - polythene lined the crates and droplets shone, not eyes. He'd nearly commented and was glad he hadn't.

Luft spoke of a bankrupt baker in 1920s who'd weighed himself down with bags of flour and stepped into the canal. He was describing the circumstances of other drowning tragedies when a woman in furs and heavy make-up interrupted.

'Come on, Len,' she said, over-familiar after only twenty minutes. 'When are you going to talk about the Water Babes?'

Luft didn't reply for the space of a breath. 'I'm never sure where to,' he said. 'But here's as good a place as any.' His face blushed in the red light of his lamp but Gurdow noticed no untoward emotion or tension in his expression or voice.

'Over a five-year period in the 1880s, a number of children disappeared. Searches by police in the district revealed nothing. And the canal never gave up any bodies. Rumours began to circulate of a woman seen lurking by the canal, a lank and dank creature with a wild shock of hair as colourless as water. 'Wet Jenny' they called her. A poster was circulated with an artists' impression. The police followed this line of enquiry for a time but with no results.'

Gurdow recalled the poster reproduced in Luft's book. A scribble of hair widening downwards to bony shoulders. Hunger in round, otherwise empty eyes. A big swollen jaw.

Luft was walking on when the lanky girl piped up. 'Wet Jenny's surely a variant of Jenny Greenteeth?' Behind her thick lenses her eyes darted timidly from her mother to Luft's rounded shoulders which heaved as he turned back to face the party. He wiped a watery eye with a handkerchief. A preparatory sigh as if for a wearisome subject hardly worth discussing.

'Jenny Greenteeth is a north country demon - in case any of you haven't heard. A haunter of rivers and ponds. A stealer-away of the offspring of agricultural labourers. And with the influx of impoverished country dwellers into the grimy machine shop cities of the burgeoning industrial north there was a quaint theory that the twilight folk of the northern moors and meadows had followed after, some of the less savoury ones intent on the rich pickings in the dark seams of the streets and alleyways.'

Rebounding off the decrepit walls, the group's wry chuckles were high and bodiless, like the ghosts of their younger selves.

'Didn't Wet Jenny sing?' the lanky girl asked, disingenuously. Clearly she knew the story.

'Singing,' Luft said. He surveyed the canal path ahead. 'Is reported to have been heard at each of the times of the disappearances - make of that what you will.'

'A kind of inner city siren,' the man in the balaclava said.

'Those poor children,' a woman said with a sympathetic tilt of her head.

'Nobody here has anything to worry about then,' a man murmured for everyone to hear, bulky in his car coat, prompting mock scoldings from the women around him.

'Speak for yourself,' the lanky girl said, with an eager smile, looking at home in the group now.

'She's long dead. Nobody has cause to worry,' Len said, with a stiff smile. 'The spate of vanishings ended and so too did reports of Wet Jenny.' He glanced at his watch, the topic for him at an end.

'Didn't a group of clergy of various denominations get together and enact some ritual they thought would get rid of her?' This, from balaclava man, startled Gurdow.

'Never been any proof of that,' Luft said, shortly. 'Shall we move on?'

Gurdow noted something self-conscious in the deliberation of his pace.

'I read about it in a contemporary article in the *Messenger*, peripheral to some family history research I was doing.' Balaclava man muttered to Gurdow, 'Our Mr Luft doesn't know everything.'

Or he does, and he's holding back, Gurdow thought. Real or apocryphal, the 'ritual' was the most intriguing piece of information he'd heard since arriving in Urblough. He doubted it could have any bearing on his investigation but resolved to check out microfilm of the *Messenger* in the central library tomorrow.

'Wet Jenny' bonded the group in light-hearted chatter until they came to slimy green stained steps leading down to what Luft claimed to be a former gin den. Not much farther on a lorry groaning in low gear pushed a funnel of light up the curve of a bridge. Windows in a tenement opposite gaped until the lorry had gone.

It had loosened stones. Splashing impacts in the darkness under the bridge, then ripples appeared. A snow-haired man asked if there were fish and Luft confirmed there were, adding 'careful' as the man leaned out over the stone bank. After a moment he was pointing like an excited child. They all looked into the water.

In a forest of weed two dim gleams were as close together as eyes. More gleams –appearing to blink as the ripples arrived. There were exclamations. Fingers were pointing at bulky shadows that must have been fish, standing on their tails, reaching for the surface.

'Aren't they big?!' a woman said, delightedly. Gurdow wasn't so sure. The water magnified, the weed obscured. Luft said the weed 'grew like wild-fire' in places.

'Gone now,' the snow-haired man said. Nimble fish, the gleams of their eyes darting away as quick a fireflies.

The canal widened to a dock the size of tennis court. On the far side, windows filled with broken panes had ledges bearded with green silken slime.

'That was a smelting works,' Luft said. 'Iron ore was lugged here on barges.' He added with little enthusiasm, 'The council wants to clean up here too. They want to build a water park and swimming baths. I think you can have too much water.'

Wet Jenny hung motionless from her heels in the water, hair curtaining her inverted face. Gurdow's gasp attracted some attention.

'Cold air - gets me here.' He patted his chest, smiled the shock out of his face. Attention away from him, he gave an accusing look at the iron mooring post on the opposite edge of the dock which had cast the reflection; olive green, its upper reach wrapped in a head-dress of no-colour plastic sheeting from some craft no longer present.

History in obscure objects in the dark aspic of the canal where it continued, but nothing from Luft. He seemed more intent on the water than the buildings alongside.

A junction had brought them back to the main canal. Off to the right the Waterside was suspended on a busy floor of roofs and chimneys.

A train clattered over a series of brick arches. Past the bridge people remarked on an imposing stone building. Inside, voices declaimed and a tambourine was bashed. Somebody said it was a chapel.

'Wesleyan until the '50s,' Luft said, not stopping. 'Urblough College owns it now. Used for drama club rehearsals. It'll be part of the regeneration if it happens - an actual theatre venue. Beautiful octagonal design.'

'You did some work here, didn't you, Len?' balaclava man said.

Old news, Gurdow thought, looking at his watch.

'I did, yes,' Luft said, his voice sounding squeezed.

'Find anything interesting?' balaclava man asked.

'Interesting to family history researchers maybe - registers, Sunday school rolls. They're at the Record Office now.'

Balaclava had another question. 'Didn't those religious men meet in the chapel? Ostensibly to discuss the matter of Wet Jenny but weren't there rumours they enacted some hocus-pocus and from about that time there were no more reports of Jenny?'

'What rumours were these?' Gurdow asked as casually as he could manage.

'Oh, just reported in the *Messenger* at the time and vigorously denied by the individuals named,' balaclava said.

Luft's head was bowed: he looked harried. 'Tittle tattle, conjecture ... All nonsense, even if they did resort to - as you say 'hocus pocus'.' He fluttered a hand distractedly.

A phone call to Urbough Record Office had given Gurdow the background to Luft's work in the chapel. A student had accidentally put his arm through a wooden panel in the cellar and discovered a narrow space serving as some kind of document store. It had been damp and smelled of mildew. Luft had been contacted on the same afternoon by a teacher at the college. He'd gone to have a look, stayed for hours and his efforts had been rewarded with a mass of documentation, gratefully received by the Record Office, and a chill that in the days after turned into pneumonia. Nobody could say why the space containing shelves of mundane documents should have been hidden by the panelling.

Could Alex Shaw's disappearance on the same day as Luft's investigation at the chapel be anything other than a coincidence? Whatever the case, Luft was plainly unsettled and couldn't be viewing with ease the prospect of more questions later.

Past a bend was the Waterside on the far side of the canal; flashing TVs and mood lighting in the few apartments that weren't in darkness. After crossing a bridge, they walked in gloom interspersed with sporadic street-lamps until the Tow Rope came into view, its lights a shuddering cluster of squared-off moons in the water.

After thanks and farewells only Gurdow followed Luft inside. Luft spoke to the barman, then went into the back.

Beams and a staircase might have been ship's oak. There was a wood burner by the far wall. In black and white frameless photographs, dockers sat on casks and toasted each other with upraised tankards. Resembling descendants, a few men on bar stools eyed fresher faces eating, chatting and laughing at round tables.

Gurdow bought a beer and took it to a corner table. An hour to fill before he was due to meet Luft at his house. He got his tablet from his knapsack and downloaded Google Maps. Luft's street wasn't far off, a matter of five minutes or so.

In the extreme corner of his eye an emphatic gesticulation drew Gurdow's attention.

The woman had her back to him and faced Luft at a round table. She wore a shiny green housecoat. Her mop of frizzy hair looked hastily cut short at the shoulder and wasn't exactly grey, nor any other colour. Straight, bending well back from the knuckles and widening at the tips, her long fingers made rapid gestures. It could have been a sign language, not least because Gurdow was certain that in the general rumble of voices she wasn't making a sound. She had Luft's complete attention until he noticed Gurdow looking across. Showing no surprise or indignation, he stared back steadily. Shocked, Gurdow looked down to the menu. Luft's eyes, thickly filmed with moisture, had looked not just vacant, as at some terrible shock, but bleak, trapped in some awful situation he was unable to resolve.

Who was she? Luft was unattached as far as Gurdow knew. The housecoat suggested she was an employee. Silent, but in her heated gestures demanding something of Luft.

Gurdow concentrated on the menu. When he'd decided he looked up and saw Luft and the woman had gone. He went to the bar and placed his order. Conversationally, he mentioned to the barman he'd been on Luft's history tour.

'Oh aye?' the barman replied guardedly, passing the order slip through a hatchway.

'The lady he was with just now. I don't recall her in the group today.' Disingenuous – Gurdow knew she hadn't been.

'No, she's staff. She cleans. She's … new.' The barman gladly turned to another customer.

Gurdow had finished eating forty minutes later. He paid a visit to the basement level WC then took his leave of the Tow

Rope. A lifting sensation inside him, a mixture of elation and apprehension.

He'd turned left on the tow-path, gone fifty yards and could see the opening into the street off which Luft lived when he heard the wordless tune. A dash of cold, like droplets on his spine as the voice intertwined with his recollection of the wavering pitch of the traffic he'd heard from the Waterside apartment earlier that day.

She was close, the singer, but there was no way he could get to her easily. The tow-path ended where the façade of a massive brick edifice jutted out a good couple of feet and dropped sheer into the water. 'United Cottons' in huge flaking white letters on the side of the building. Beyond was the concrete slab of a bridge. On the bridge or was she nearer, on the tow-path? By the time he'd found his way around the building, she might have gone, but there was a possible solution.

A skiff was tied at the prow to a wooden post embedded in the stone bank. It could have been intended as a makeshift means to get by the interruption to the tow-path. No oars or paddle, but if he let the back end drift out some way he'd be able to see to where he presumed the tow-path continued.

He gingerly lowered one foot down into the shallow well. Water seeping through the cracks gave him pause for a moment, but the boards held. His other foot joined the first. Crouching, he pushed gently from the bank and the skiff's back end swung out.

He gasped, his mouth more a gape than a smile. It was Luft's employee, and in the same green housecoat. She was sitting on the stones lining the bank, her white feet kicking the water with a sullen force while yet in time with the dirge-like tread of the hummed tune. She was looking towards a pillar of the bridge around which dirt and detritus had gathered. Her hair hung forward, covering her cheeks.

What possessed her to be here? He could have called out but startling her with his presence now might be counter-productive. He'd talk to her tomorrow. For now, her behaviour was worth a photograph.

He swung the knapsack off his shoulder and took out his camera, his fingers clumsy in the cold. He aimed, steadied the image in the display, was puzzled. He looked up at the gathering of rubbish around the pillar.

Cardboard, newspaper, rotten fruit, cans and bottles had washed up along with blackened objects not immediately identifiable but resembling burst footballs. One or two twitched as if at a stray surface breeze not felt where Gurdow was hunkered down in the skiff. He looked down at the display again and was on the point of pressing the switch when the humming opened out into sung words:

Where shall we wander
In the water and the weeds
Where the black eels and white fishes are –

A high voice, its timbre hard; an old woman's voice, strong, weathered, elemental.

A soft click when he pressed the shutter button. No flash, he'd turned that function off. She continued to sing. Maybe he should have brought a tape-recorder. He stuffed the camera back into the knapsack.

Job done – for now, he thought. He'd be compromised if she saw him, but something in her whole aspect and demeanor made him pull hard on the rope, keen to be out of her line of sight should she turn.

He'd partly stood preparing to reach for the bank when his right foot suddenly went through the boards with a vicious splitting. A shock of cold up to his thigh. With no alternative but to push up with his other foot, that one too punched through the remaining boards. His feet were precarious on slippery submerged stone. His shocked heart filled his chest. He thought things could have been worse – and immediately were. His feet skidded under him and he was sitting up to his midriff in liquid ice, gasping for breath. He felt around him for his knapsack, found it, lifted it dripping out of the water.

Light laughter like skimmed stones stopped his groan. With

a start he remembered he hadn't been alone. He was now. She'd gone. Whatever the discoloured objects by the bridge pillar had been, they'd gone too.

He stepped over the side of the skiff and moved carefully on the slimy stone floor. Clambering onto the bank he felt cold, wet, wretched and a fool. She can't have failed to hear the disturbance and seen the comical shambles - probably recognised him from the Tow Rope. But she would have the greater part of the explaining to do when he interviewed her tomorrow.

A shiver rattled him. Cotton liked the damp, he'd read in Luft's *Bricks and Water*, but his aching hip bones didn't. He was due to meet Luft about now but there was no way he could present himself in this state. He'd ring him from the Tow Rope then call a taxi to take him back to his hotel. When he was dry and warm again he could enjoy the progress he'd made tonight.

He shivered back to the lights of the Tow Rope.

It was three-quarters empty with most closeted in the side booths. The barman rubbed a tea towel into the mouth of a tankard and it squeaked laughter.

'Crikey - what happened?'

Gurdow's response was to regard him darkly. A giggle from someone unseen and surely too young to be in the pub. He extracted his mobile phone from his water-darkened knapsack. It was no surprise to see nothing in the display when he switched on.

'Got a payphone? I want to ring for a taxi.' Definitely kids he could hear in a corner booth, parents not shushing their unpleasant chuckles, not hissing at them to mind their own business.

'Ten years back we did. Use ours.' He indicated a wall-mounted phone to one side, under the optics behind the bar.

'Phone book?' He'd have to think of an excuse for asking for Luft's number if he was ex-directory.

'Got a list here.'

It was on a laminated piece of card. Taxi firms, hospital, brewery, names - probably staff. Good, Luft's too. Gurdow keyed in the number and Luft answered almost immediately.

'Can we meet tomorrow morning?' Gurdow asked. 'Something's come up –'

'What has?' Luft sounded tense, guarded, when he might have been expected to sound relieved at the ordeal being put off if only for a few hours.

'Had a mishap. Took a wrong turning, slipped and ... got wet. Redevelopment can't come too soon – better lighting for a start.'

'What kind of mishap?' Luft's voice was up a pitch or the phone was making it so.

'Just what I said,' Gurdow replied, his calm reasonable voice undermined by a sudden chattering of his teeth.

'You should get back to your hotel. Damp and cold isn't good at your age.'

Your age? 'Yes, well you'd know about that,' Gurdow blurted before he could stop himself.

'What?' Luft said almost inaudibly.

Gurdow felt compelled to make his point. 'The cold damp basement in the chapel, that evening. Made you ill, didn't it. Though things were worse for Anita Shaw, it has to be said.'

'Of course. A bad day. The chapel is the part of the History Tour I like to gloss over – if I mention it at all.'

'I might go back there – just to look around –'

'You mustn't –' Luft broke in urgently before correcting his tone. 'I mean ... not tonight.'

With no intention of going tonight, Gurdow said, 'I'm sure the young thespians wouldn't object.'

'No. No, don't. Stay where you are. I'll come down. We'll talk in the office.' After a heavy pause he said. 'I'll tell you what else I found at the chapel.'

Gurdow was startled from speaking for a second. Luft went on as if Gurdow needed to be persuaded.

'There was an iron chest in the cellar, crosses scored onto it. Inside it was full of stinking water.' A few panting breaths down the line. 'There's more –'

Whatever it was, white noise covered it, rushing into Gurdow's ear more like a fury of white water. A strumming in his chest; excitement and incredulity that he was on the cusp of some revelation, yet the discovery of 'stinking water' was hardly going to shed light on Alex Shaw's disappearance. He was convinced Luft's employee was going to prove a hugely more fruitful line of enquiry. He replaced the receiver.

A violent shiver went through him. The barman looked sympathetic.

'I'll sort some dry clobber for you if you like. Cabbies can be a bit fussy about their upholstery.'

'Could you? Thanks.' Luft had got the staff well trained. Gurdow would call for a taxi after he'd finished with Luft.

'Drink? A whisky might warm you up.'

Gurdow gave a palsied nod. These shivers attacked from nowhere. 'I'll be by the wood burner.'

The barman brought the drink over. Gurdow paid, said 'keep the change' and stopped him as he was turning to go. 'Saw your cleaning lady, out by the canal.'

The barman frowned, scratched his wrist.

'Can you tell me anything about her?'

Rubbing the back of his head and staring past Gurdow, the barman was a picture of awkwardness. 'I *could* do,' he said uncertainly.

'I'd appreciate it if you did,' Gurdow said with an unyielding edge to his voice. 'I'm investigating the disappearance of Alex Shaw. You'll have heard about that?'

The barman nodded. 'Gina, she's called. She's local. Lives out by the docks, Len says. She's only been working two or three weeks. He took her under his wing.'

Gurdow made a puzzled frown. 'Did she need to be?'

'Maybe. Has some kind of … problem.' An uneasy little burst of laughter. 'Doesn't talk - well, I've never heard her.'

'Have you heard her sing?'

'Sing? No way!' He looked mystified, then smoothed that out of his face. 'Len deals with her.' Plainly, he didn't like to. 'Some kind of sign language between them when I've seen them together - which isn't often.' He added with an effort to be positive. 'Does a good job though. Comes in, works, goes home.'

While Gurdow took a sip of his whisky, the barman took the

opportunity to head away. 'I'll get your stuff.'

He came back with a full plastic bag. Gurdow peered inside, stood. 'Tell your boss I'm here. He's coming down. We're going to have a talk.'

'I'll do that.' The barman looked towards the door to the lavatories. 'Take yourself downstairs.'

'Wasn't going to change right here,' Gurdow said, tipping back the rest of the whisky.

He went to the door on which a stick man and woman held hands. His second trip inside an hour. Behind the door he descended the stairs and it struck him, as it hadn't the first time, that they must drop deeper than the canal. At the bottom there was a narrow vestibule veined with pipes and with doors to 'Ladies' and 'Gents' on each side.

Inside the latter, three stalls faced bone-white urinals. Three washbasins and a band of mirrors over them at the far end opposite the door.

Gurdow went into the nearest stall. Scuffed shoe prints on the damp floor, indicative of a day's worth of drinkers. He sat on the seat cover and prised off his shoes. He stood to peel down his trousers and held them before him, a drowned man's, heavy, as if his flesh and bones were still inside them. He drew on the overalls pants and pulled the straps over his shoulders. He was feeding an arm into the sleeve of a chunky Fair Isle sweater when the main door opened, then knocked back into the frame as someone entered.

A metal bucket clanged onto the floor. A wet mop slapped abruptly. Shivers nearly unbalanced him until with an effort of will, he suppressed them. He put his shoes back on. His coat over one forearm, with his other hand Gurdow touched the door catch.

Saturday night seemed like a peculiar time to be cleaning, but he'd seen that the cleaner was anything but conventional. He let go of the catch when rat tails of the mop slavered in the gap under the door. After a long moment they headed away in the direction of the wash basins. Gurdow noticed he was breathing again.

A tap was turned on, then another, then the third. Water

pounded loudly into the three basins.

He'd slip out, now. Likely she wouldn't hear him leave in the din. And what if she did? Whether or not she recognised him from upstairs or in the skiff, he doubted she'd want to converse with him, or any man come to that, here. And from what the barman said, she was as good as mute. Some way would have to be found to communicate - but that was for another time. He didn't care for a sudden aural imagining of her singing in her defence. She was unsettling him badly right now - that was for sure.

He took a breath as if he were about to dive into a pool. A slight tremor of his fingers as he slid the catch. It made no sound against the noise from the taps. He stepped out carefully onto the glistening floor. A glance and his foot skidded a heart-stopping shoe-length.

Yes, it was her. Tall, thin in her pea-green work coat. Her hair looked like long hair hacked short. And it was wet, the colour of water under a grey sky. As she worked her hand energetically into the central wash basin, steam wreathed her, misted the band of mirrors.

Three paces to the door. Gurdow pulled and his fingertips slid off the slick handle. He tried again and the door was rock solid in the frame. It was locked, presumably to prevent entry while she completed her work. Something frantic in the way she scrubbed at the middle basin that even an ingrained ring of grime wouldn't warrant.

He must have been watching for half a minute. *Speak. Now.*

''scuse me.'

No let up in her scrubbing. Was she deaf? Cold water in his veins, beads of it on his brow, when she started to hum. The melody was hard in the throat, it prowled behind tight closed lips.

He shook his already shuddering shoulders like an athlete warming up. From the mentally unstable to the plain mad, they were the ones who'd always tested his professionalism. This was such a test.

Again, louder, ''scuse me. Can you let me out please?' A

shake in his gruff request, but it had got through.

Ceasing to scrub, ceasing to hum, and with her hands grasping the sides of the basin, she stared into the mirror. Just a pair of dark patches in the condensation.

'Yes.' Getting somewhere at last. 'Can you let me out, please.'

Long reedy fingers whisked rapidly, clearing a small patch in the mirror. Eyes as round and unblinking as a fish's, and gradually dissolving as the mirror misted over again.

Fingers rapid again, almost an otter-like motion. More of her face now, confirming that she was very like the picture of Wet Jenny. A face raw and pale as a nun's. The circles of her eyes fierce in their vacancy. In her square pugilist's jaw her lips were clamped shut on the teeth pressing out.

The water was steaming the mirror again as her lips parted and she sang. Her voice cut through the hissing of the taps, rubbed over his skin like pumice stone. The tune was ancient; stones and trickling water might have composed it. Her mouth in the mirror was making bigger shapes than the words needed:

Play below
My bonny bairns
Your bones, yours smiles way under –

Like excited children, the rasping whispers of the taps. Splashes as water overflowed the rims of the basins. Gurdow yanked frantically at the door handle.

We are forever
My little fishes
Let none put us asunder

Nothing more - an end - and Gurdow feared what might ensue. He looked back. In the mirror, her vague cloudy mouth remained wide and in motion as if the tune continued solely in her head.

Off her head. The barman knew that. Was his spying on her from the skiff enough of an outrage to her craziness for her to respond with violence? Whatever the case, those spindly arms couldn't do much damage, with or without the mop. Such thoughts going through his head resulted in a smile that felt like a gash, a fish's mouth.

'Door ...' he said falteringly, as she faced him in clouds of steam. Glittering curtains over the edges of the basins; an inch-deep pool on the floor tiles.

'At last,' he said, but 'last' was more a gasp that drained him of breath as she approached, her bone-white ankles swishing through the pool, eyes streaming, fingertips dripping.

Old as water, he thought, but her teeth put her beyond any question of age. Plentiful, sharply pointed - and in a rapid biting motion. And so *green*. Green as the earliest days.

A wet cold stone in his chest pressed on his heart. Tears sprang from his eyes.

To the waters lapping over his shoes, he added a warm gush all his own.

LAND OF MONSTERS

Located in the heart of the Irish Sea, almost equidistant between Northern Ireland and mainland Britain, the hilly and richly wooded Isle of Man, or Mann to use its local name, is an official part of the United Kingdom, but at the same time a self-governing British Crown dependency. It possesses its own unique language and culture, and a complex polyglot mythology derived from the beliefs of the Stone Age settlers who arrived there in 6,500 BC, the Gaels who followed in the 5th Century, the pagan Saxons who invaded in the 7th, and perhaps most influentially of all, the Norse Vikings, who finally incorporated Mann into their powerful Kingdom of the Isles in the 9th.

Little wonder its ancient lore comprises so wide a range of supernatural beings, though it is still something of a mystery that so many of them are evil.

The faeries of Mann were said to be among the most vicious in the whole of the British Isles, damaging farm-stock with their faerie hounds, stealing horses and replacing human babies with their own deranged, deformed changelings. But even these malign entities pale to insignificance when compared to the island's monsters.

The Manx 'bogey beasts' as they were known, were in some ways indistinguishable from the faeries as they too were gifted with magical abilities, but they varied considerably in appearance and manner. In addition, and almost without exception, they were held by nervous islanders of former centuries to be very real and very dangerous.

The 'buggane' is the best example, a creature of near-demonic disposition. Adopting the form of a monstrous, misshapen ram, it would linger in the precincts of abandoned churches and chapels, intent on preventing any repair work, thus holding back the forces of light. St Trinian's, near the foot of Snaefell Mountain, is one derelict structure long said to be haunted by a buggane. In fact, the buggane allegedly drove the small rural congregation away in the first place, smashing in the chapel roof and vowing that forever after it would prevent a restoration of Christian worship on that blighted spot. Long into the 19th Century, the ruin of St Trinian's was shunned. When a local tailor claimed that he would stay there overnight, he was apparently chased away by the creature, which pursued him on two legs and flung a rock after him that was so large it almost killed him. The heavy rock can still be viewed today, as can St Trinian's chapel, which remains roofless and desolate.

Equally sinister was the 'glashtan', a kind of twisted, malformed brute whom medieval Manx farmers were rumoured to once have recruited to perform heavy work on their land, though most often it was notorious for kidnapping and ravishing women. Scholars consider that this primitive being represents folk-memories of an ancient race, possibly the original prehistoric islanders driven into second class citizenship by the arrival of the Celts.

Less sympathetic maybe is the 'cabbyl-ushtey', a ferocious water horse that would tempt riders to mount it and then dash into the nearest body of water, to drown them. The cabbyl-ushtey was allegedly even fiercer than its Scottish cousin, the kelpie, and could be identified by its backwards-facing hooves. One such horror supposedly lurked by the secluded Nikkesen's Pool in Glen Roy, where it claimed many lives. An even more terrible presence was said to be the 'tarroo-ushtey', a water bull that roamed the shallow waters off the island's shore. Bathers, beach-combers and fishermen were this beast's prime targets; the first (and probably last) they ever knew of the impending attack was the glow of its burning red eyes as it approached under the waves. Folk tales tell how the tarroo-ushtey once came ashore on the Calf of Man, in the island's southwest corner, and, rather than fleeing, a posse of farmhands attempted to kill it, only to be led a merry dance all along the coastline, before the thing leapt nimbly into a river and swam swiftly down to the sea.

Even more bizarre are the 'phynnodderee', the 'gruagach'

and the more prosaically named 'Jimmy Squarefoot', all of which were used by Christian preachers on the island as object lessons regarding the fate of the extremely sinful. The former is actually referenced in the Manx Bible, described as a satyr – half man and half shaggy goat – and was believed to be the horned and hideous offspring of men and faeries, but neither one nor the other and thus doomed to spend a solitary life in the deep, gloomy woods. Anyone who came upon it, either by accident or design, could expect to be rent limb from limb. The gruagach meanwhile was supposedly a druid or sorcerer cursed by God for his dabbling in the forbidden arts, and transformed into another mindless half-animal also condemned to forage in the woods, living solely on roots and insects. Jimmy Squarefoot, on the other hand, is the hexed remnant of a boorish husband who stoned his own wife to death, and now is doomed for eternity to wander the back-country around Ballagilbert Glen as a pig-headed man whose natural instinct is to stone anyone else he encounters (and there are reports of this very thing happening).

In addition to all this, Manx myth is riddled with tales of goblins, devil dogs, trolls and giants. All aspects of the traditional pantheon of British and Irish legendary creatures are represented.

Today of course, Mann is a holiday haven, famous for its quaint coastal towns, its cottages and hotels, and of course for the annual pilgrimage made to the island each June by the world's motorcycle enthusiasts. In that respect, these horrible denizens of a fearsome past seem far, far away. But there are still lonely paths on the island, empty moors, dreary woodland abodes and isolated ruins where, when evening looms and the mist comes down, it is much too easy to believe that ancient, malevolent presences are skulking close to hand.

THE DRAIN
Stephen Gallagher

Sometimes I still think about it.

I know it was a long time ago, but you don't forget a night like that; not when it shaped you a little and changed you a lot and then took someone away. It was also the scariest thing that ever happened to me, and that's how I'd like it to stay.

I'm damned sure I wouldn't want to go through anything worse.

It began, I suppose, when I met up with Spike outside the gates of the city park just after dusk. There were supposed to be three of us, me, Spike, and Michael, but Michael was late as always and so we moved down to the corner away from the road to wait for him. We felt that somebody might get suspicious if they saw us hanging around. Two dirt poor kids with no elbows in their sweaters and the backsides worn out of their trousers; latchkey children out after dark, what could they be wanting but trouble?

Spike showed me his hammer.

'I got it out of the shed,' he explained. 'I'll put it back later, and no one'll know. What about a torch?'

I showed him my father's cycle lamp. 'It's nearly new,' I warned him. 'If I lose this, I'm dead.'

That wasn't all of it. Spike had scrounged up a bottle of cream soda and I'd made some paste sandwiches. They were a little grey from handling and I'd skipped on refinements like butter on the bread but please, you've got to make allowances, I was eleven years old at the time. As far as anybody at home knew I'd gone to the fair, which was midway through its once yearly stopover on some rough ground at the far end of town.

Later on I was going to be wishing that we'd all done exactly that.

Michael arrived after about another ten minutes. We could see him standing by the gates, bewildered and looking around like some abandoned thing, but then Spike gave him a whistle and he came down out of the streetlighted area to join us. He'd brought a carrier bag that hung like a bowling ball in a sling and banged against his legs as he moved.

'I had to walk it,' he said morosely. 'Bastard conductor wouldn't let me on the bus.'

Of any of us, Michael lived the furthest out. His house was in a cramped terrace and beyond it was marshland with distant power lines and, arched like a silver bow in the far, far distance, the motorway bridge that ran on over into the next county. On foot, it would have taken him nearly an hour to get in from there. A while ago he'd hit upon the trick of boarding the bus with no money and sitting as far away from the conductor as he could get, so that by the time he was thrown off he'd already have covered a good part of the journey. Tonight he'd obviously been remembered, but he seemed to feel that he'd somehow been cheated of a right. That was Michael all over - just enough imagination to think up the scheme, but not enough to realise that it wasn't going to work every time or forever.

We both ribbed him a little and he got hot and angry, and then we got down to business.

'First we check all the torches,' Spike said and he tested his own, which was an old rubber coated thing that looked as if it had been around since wartime, and then I did the same with the cycle lamp, and then Michael reached down into his carrier bag and brought out the biggest, ugliest looking flashlight that I'd ever seen. It was made out of tin that had been plated to look like silver and it had three sliding buttons on the handle. These operated filters that would change the colour of the beam. Everything about it screamed *piece of junk*, but Michael showed it like it was his grandfather's watch or something.

Then he switched it on. The bulb gave off a weak, urine coloured glow which faded to nothing in less than five seconds.

'Oh, great,' Spike said sarcastically and Michael, immediately on the defensive, said 'It's not my fault.'

'Of course it isn't,' Spike said reasonably, and then he took the flashlight from Michael's hands and lobbed it as high and as hard as he could over the park wall and into the darkness. It flew like one of those German grenades, tumbling end over end, and I heard it come down in bushes quite some way inside. Michael gawped at Spike in disbelief, and even I felt that he'd overstepped some invisible mark.

'You rotten sod!' Michael said.

And Spike said, 'Shut up.'

'You can come back and find that, tomorrow!'

'You'll be able to buy a hundred like it by then,' Spike told him. 'And with decent batteries, as well.'

Everything went quiet.

Michael wasn't exactly mollified, but stopped his protesting. I expect that the prospect of such riches was enough to distract and entrance him for a while. I have to admit, I found it pretty overwhelming myself. Spike looked at Michael, and then from Michael to me. In that moment we were as aligned in our thinking as compass needles. We were a team, we had a purpose.

In stealth, we scrambled over the low wall and entered the park.

I went back and took a look at the park again a couple of years ago. The gateway's still there, a big triple archway of sandstone in the Victorian style, but these days it doesn't seem quite so monumental as it did then. There's a carved plaque above the middle entrance to commemorate the fact that the ornamental fountains were presented by the mayor of the borough in 1857. The gates lead through onto a broad central walkway of dull red tarmac, powdered along its edges by fallen debris from the overhanging tree branches. The walkway climbs gently into the heart of the parkland.

I should imagine there's something like it in nearly every Northern industrial town; some long ago civic gift from a factory owner or a mine boss, tamed and decorous and mostly deserted. I'd guess that this one had perhaps once been a streambed and valley that had been tidied up and transformed, the stream culverted and the contours of the land flattened out to accommodate a bowling green, a big old conservatory, an ugly playground, some red shale tennis courts, and enough rolling landscape to lose them all in. You could stand in the middle and believe you were in another country, anchored only by the sounds of traffic coming from the road as if from some near distant amphitheatre.

Back when the park had first been laid out, it had been surrounded by a low wall topped by some elaborate cast-iron railings. But the railings had gone for the war effort leaving only faint, well-worn stumps in the stonework, and making a boundary that didn't even slow us that night. I expect Michael snagged his pants on the way in. I don't remember for sure, but it was the kind of thing that he was always doing.

And I think there was probably a moon. I remember that we were following the main walkway and that there was stuff in the asphalt that glittered like pantomime dust. Nobody was saying much at that stage. Spike was carrying his hammer and I had the cycle lamp at the ready, but I wasn't using it. We didn't need it yet, and we didn't want to risk being seen so early in the expedition. Michael was grousing a little at the rear, but mostly under his breath.

A couple of hundred yards up the walkway, we came to the first of the ponds.

At a guess, these had been created as a system to deal with the original drainage from when the land had been open fields, or woodland, or whatever. The lower pond was the smaller of two, and it was a mess; stagnant greenish brown water with a few branches sticking up out of it like the ribs of drowned ships. Low railings enclosed it, although there was nothing inside them to defend. Until a short time before it had been fed by a steady trickle from a brick lined shaft that ran under the path. Now nothing came through, and the level of the pond was dropping.

We went on by. We were heading for something bigger.

The upper pond was almost a lake, and had been the centre of some intense activity over the past few weeks. Now, as we approached it, I risked the light.

A new fence, probably the first new feature in the park for years, stood before us. It was six feet high, made of chainlink on white concrete posts, and it was topped with three parallel rolls of barbed wire. It looked like something you'd find outside a prison, or surrounding some really grim holiday camp. But what made it unusual was the line that it followed; it seemed to cut across the layout of the park with no logic or reason. It ran through flowerbeds, it took a chunk out of the walkway, it sealed off a complete side path and then crashed onward through the woodland taking account of nothing. It was like a hasty barrier thrown up around some nuclear accident. Something drawn on a map without too much consideration, and then made real.

We followed it for a while, until a gap in the bushes on the other side gave us a view down onto the lake itself. Here Spike raised his own flashlight, and shone it all the way across to the fountain.

'It's still there,' he said, his voice barely louder than a whisper.

The beam faded almost to nothing over the distance. But not quite. The fountain was big and ornate, stained green and streaked with rust from the iron fittings that held the stonework together. The bowl was silted up with dead and rotting leaves and above this, two intertwined serpents raised a cherub on their tails. The cherub held a burning torch; atop the torch, a golden flame.

It *was* gold. Even with the light from so far away, you could see.

Michael said, 'How do you know for sure that it's real?'

'It's real,' Spike said.

Of course it was real. It was a part of our backstreet mythology, one of those certainties that was handed down and which you never even thought to question. Like, there were king sized rats in the cellars of the school that had once killed and eaten a caretaker. No one had ever seen them, but everyone knew of someone who had. Or that a raid on one of the restaurants in town had once turned up the half butchered carcass of a German Shepherd dog, and then the whole thing had been hushed up. Or that the man who fixed old refrigerators in a wooden shack down by the railway sidings was a convicted child molester with a special taste for smooth skinned little boys, and under his coat he carried a fisherman's gaff to hook them and drag them home. Or - well, I could go on, right down to the one about how rubbing the sleep grains out of the corners of your eyes could make them fall out, but you get the idea. The flame on top of the big fountain in the park was made of solid gold.

And last week, for reasons that I'll tell you about in a minute, they'd drained the lake.

Spike led us on around the perimeter fence, shining his own light along where the wire and the ground met, and as I followed I could feel my heart hammering so hard that I could almost imagine it throwing a piston and blowing out a chunk of my ribs. Getting into the park after hours was no big deal, but entering this inner enclosure would be different. The park was big, it was familiar, there were at least a hundred ways out if you were chased. But on the other side of the wire you could be cornered and, try as I might, I couldn't think of any excuse or explanation that would sound convincing.

Michael, with no light of his own, had to stumble along behind us. I wasn't paying him much attention. Only a few months before, any of us could have crossed the line now marked out by the wire and walked down to the edge of the lake with no problem; but its presence now seemed to have changed the nature of the territory beyond, making it into alien country. I wasn't the only one who felt this way. There were scorched patches of ground on the far side of the wire, small blackened arcs of a couple of feet or less where kids had reached through and set fire to the grass. Why, I don't know. The blazes must have been small, and had hardly spread. There were other things too, including a traffic cone that had been tossed over to land just inside. All that stuff, it was like, I don't know ... tributes. As if you couldn't look upon the barrier without feeling something primitive move within you, and you were driven to respond accordingly.

'Here it is,' Spike said. 'The point of no return.'

He'd stopped and was shining his flashlight at the section of fencing that he'd noted the day before. Where the wire met the post, it had been unhooked and peeled back to make a triangular gap of about eighteen inches. Someone of our size or smaller would just about be able to wriggle through. We didn't know who'd done it or why, but we *did* know that they hadn't made it to the fountain and so it didn't really matter.

We gathered around the gap.

The point of no return.

I heard myself saying, 'We could still call it off and go to the fair.'

I was half expecting Spike to jump in and say something scornful. He didn't speak; but Michael did.

He said, 'Then we'd never be happy again.'

We both looked at him, or what we could see of him in the darkness. He was like a point of stillness, surrounded by night sky and clouds. He went on, 'We'd always wonder. There'll be lots of fairs. But there won't be many chances like this.'

I didn't know what to say. He was right, of course. Nobody moved for a moment, and then Spike's response was to dive to the ground and squirm his way under the wire. He moved like a weasel, sleek and skinny and infinitely flexible, and he came up on the other side as if on springs. I crawled after, dragging the sandwich bag and my cycle lamp, and as I got to my feet I could see that he was already on his way down the banking.

The grass in here had been neglected, and had grown knee deep in places. Michael was grunting and squeaking his way through after me as I followed Spike. I saw him stop, his flashlight beam picking up something on the way, and then he went on.

This was a mess. Beyond the grass was a stretch of broken rubble pierced by coarse, springy rushes, and it wasn't easy to keep a footing. As I approached the place where I'd seen Spike hesitate, my beam picked up the sight that must have stopped him. It was a simple wooden sign, a board on a stake that had been driven into the ground, and it read

DANGER
Explosives

and I felt the same little kick of fear that Spike must have experienced. But it was nothing unexpected and so I pressed on, and a minute later caught up with him at the edge of the pond.

Michael took a minute longer to reach us, floundering a little without the help of a light. We could track him in the darkness almost every step of the way.

He said, 'You might have waited.'

'And your mother might have fucked a chimpanzee,' Spike replied, and he turned his flashlight out across the bed of the pond. 'Feast your eyes, boys. We're gonna be rich.'

Rich.

It's hard to say from here what the word must have meant to me then. Big cars, big houses, servants? Plane rides and casinos? Or simply a weekly comic that no one else had read before me, and maybe that tin moonwalker toy in the newsagent's window that I'd been aching over for almost a month? Something somewhere in between, I expect. Or maybe nothing more than an indefinable hunger; we were provincial inner city kids set to go nowhere and we didn't even know it, but something in us was responding to the call of treasure and it drew us along. The spotlight picked out the golden flame and I swear, dulled and dirty as it was, it seemed to shine back at us with a light of its own.

Moonlight showed up what was left of the pond. It had never seemed like much of a size but now, as a drained basin, it appeared huge. Some water was still pooled at the lowest point. The rest of it was mud and black shale, and showing in just a few places was the exposed masonry of its man-made lining. The water had always been so murky that it had seemed bottomless, but I could now see that in some parts it could never have been more than about three feet deep.

'Look at that,' Spike said, indicating the shallows. 'We could have walked over any time.'

'Yeah,' Michael said. 'And got blown to pieces.'

From here I could see a ring of the danger signs. They were all around the edge of the emptied lake. Most looked as if they'd been knocked and tilted, as if they'd been used by knights on horseback for jousting practice.

About six months before, some boy whose name I forget had cleared a place on his bedroom mantelpiece for his newest find. He'd told his mother that he'd found a 'space wocket' in the park and she, in the way of parents everywhere, had said something vaguely encouraging while making no real effort to remember. Two days later, while straightening his room, she'd found herself face to face with the wocket and the strange, green-grey corrosive puddle (*like melted brains*, I heard somebody describe it) that had leaked out of its casing. It was a mortar shell, and not exactly a healthy example of its type; it was, in fact, decayed and unstable, and that same afternoon it had exploded scattering thirty pounds of sand, the galvanised metal of the fire bucket that it was standing in, and much of the planking of the stray dog pen in the police station yard where the bucket had been placed to await the arrival of a bomb disposal team.

Patient questioning revealed that the wocket had surfaced in the mud on the edge of the pond, where the banking was at its lowest and a kind of marshy area had formed. They checked it out, they found about a dozen brass cartridge cases of a similar age. They closed the pond, and the army moved in.

The lake, it seemed, had been used as a postwar dumping ground for the unused munitions of the LDV (the wartime Local Defence Volunteers, civilian part time soldiers whose initials to just about everybody of my parents' generation meant Look, Duck, and Vanish). Nobody knew for sure exactly what was involved, or what might still be simmering in the depths; but the safety wire had been hastily erected by council workmen and the bomb disposal men began a thorough sweep of the exposed mudflats.

They'd found some stuff but it wasn't much; certainly nothing as spectacular as that first discovery, and now they'd declared the pond to be probably clear but with no guarantees. The plan now was that it should be filled in, and the surface grassed over.

Just to be certain.

Which meant that anyone hoping for a grab at the golden prize was going to have to do it now, or else find himself staring at the new ground and thinking of all the might-have-beens.

Spike was taking off his shoes.

'Do we all have to go?' Michael said, eyeing the foul looking mud in the bottom of a basin that resembled a Sargasso without wrecks.

Spike said, 'You stay here and hold the lights. Otherwise you might get mistaken for a hippo, and shot.'

That was fine by me because I didn't much like the look of the mud either. Even though we were a team, I think that any of us would probably have agreed, if pressed, that this was Spike's show. He was the driven one among us, he was the visionary. Michael and I would always be in there with him, but he was the one whose impulses gave us somewhere to go.

Spike was a strange one, in many ways. His father had been in prison, once; nothing glamorous or anything, just a small-time handling offence, but the old man had come home looking as shrunken and as sad as an old shoe. We never talked about it; Spike, I knew, had set up a vision of the world in his own mind where the entire thing had never even happened. But that was Spike all over; sometimes he could see a thing and believe in it so hard that, after a while, you didn't have any choice - you had to believe in it, too. He was tall for his age, skinny and fair, and his hair was like a brush. These days it's fashionable to spend money to look that way, but on Spike it just grew. He had a younger brother called Snotbags. I don't know what his real name was. I think even his parents called him Snotbags, at least some of the time.

After he'd taken off his pants and laid them on his shoes Spike took a first, careful step off the bank, and sank right in to above his knees. We shone the lights on him, almost as if he was in some kind of a circus act. I could see him tense up and stiffen with a sharp indrawing of air, and I knew that the mud had to be even colder than it looked. Then he started to wade out toward the middle, the hammer in his hand, picking his way with care. He was wearing hand me down Y-fronts that hung on him like Ghandi's loincloth.

Progress was slow. I don't know how much help the lights were because he was walking straight out into his own, long shadow. When he was about halfway, Michael called out in a raised whisper, 'Watch out for mines, Spike.'

Spike glanced back, his face pale in our lights. 'What?'

'They found all sorts in there. Bombs, hand grenades, all kinds of things. There could be other stuff they didn't find.'

'Bollocks,' Spike said, but he said it without any terrific sense of certainty.

He picked his way onward, more nervously now.

When he reached the podium at the centre, it took him a moment before he was able to get a good grip and hoist himself up; but once clear of the mud, he was in his element. He swarmed up the fountain like a monkey. The overhang of that six-foot bowl was no challenge to him at all; he simply grabbed its edge and swung himself out to dangle in space and then he pulled himself up and over, swinging and kicking all the way. He got to his feet and stood in the bowl, grinned and waved to us with the hammer, and turned his attention to the flame that was now almost within his reach.

'The Golden Fleece,' I heard Michael breathe beside me.

And I said, 'Yeah.'

We were all agreed that *Jason and the Argonauts* was the best film ever made, better even than *Hercules Unchained*. Michael didn't have to explain the sense of the moment, because I felt it too.

By now Spike had hooked one leg around the serpents and wrapped his free arm around the lower part of the cherub, so that he could lean out without falling and get a clear swing at the target. It was a stretch, but not impossible. From where we stood it seemed that he merged with the sculpture, flesh and stone intertwined; the question flashed across my mind, what if it couldn't take his weight, what if the whole thing were to come crashing down and bringing Spike with it, and then the thought was forgotten as I saw the hammer flash and make a clean swipe through the air.

He missed. I could hear him cursing, although it was mostly to himself. Spike knew words that I couldn't even imagine meanings for. He repositioned slightly, and tried again.

Sparks flew. The ring of metal on stone was shockingly loud, and the hammer bounced off leaving no apparent damage. But Spike had the range now and he started whacking at it, hard and regular.

Michael said, 'Someone's going to hear him.'

'No one's around,' I said, but without much certainty; Spike was kicking up a racket like a blacksmith at his forge.

'You could hear that from the road,' Michael said.

And then suddenly it stopped, with a crack that was unlike anything that had gone before, and I saw Spike grabbing to keep his balance as he threatened to topple; both lights wavered as Michael and I reacted and when they'd steadied again, I could see that the cherub's entire hand - including the torch and you know what - had sheared away completely. The arm was now just a broken stump thrust up into the air, and Spike was cursing again as he scrambled down.

'Anyone see where it went?' he called across to us.

I hadn't, but Michael reckoned that he'd glimpsed it as it flew. He pointed Spike's flashlight toward a particularly unwelcoming area of mud about twenty feet out from the fountain's base. It looked as if it had been heavily trodden and churned over, probably by army men with metal detectors.

'Oh, great,' Spike said wearily, and he dropped from the bowl and started to wade out.

I prised off my shoes and took off my pants. I was thinking that in a way the mess had to be reassuring, because it meant that the area had been thoroughly swept and was unlikely to be dangerous. Trouserless, I felt terribly vulnerable. I stepped out from the bank, slid right in, and felt as if I'd been part swallowed by some seabed creature of cold and slime. Leaving Michael still struggling with his shoelaces, I slowly headed out for where Spike had already started to search. With no light of his own he had little hope of finding anything, but he was looking all the same.

'Got it,' I said.

I'd picked it up in the beam even before I'd gone halfway. It was nowhere near where Michael had indicated, but it had landed and stuck and fortunately hadn't sunk more than halfway in. I reached it first, and dug it out. It was heavier than I'd imagined. As soon as Spike reached me I held it out to him; didn't even think of doing it any other way.

Spike said, 'Where's mucous brain?'

'Still folding his trousers,' I said, and I shone the torch toward the bank. There was Michael, doing exactly as I'd guessed, and blinking uncertainly in the beam as it fell upon him.

Spike said, 'Look at those drawers. They're holier than the Pope.'

'With more skidmarks than Brands Hatch,' I added.

And Michael scowled and called out, 'Spunkface,' and then he was about to say something else when the three of us froze.

Car headlights, up on the highest point of the banking.

I killed the cycle lamp and Michael, over on the shore, switched off Spike's flashlight. The car was climbing the access track to the mesh gates that were the only official entrance to the enclosure; we could hear its engine labouring as it bounced up the rough ground, and a few seconds later its headlamps came fully into view. They were like the eyes of a beast, coming up to press its face against the wire.

At the wire, they stopped.

I heard Michael hiss, 'It's the police,'

'It isn't the police,' Spike said quietly.

The lights raked along the fencing, grew to a peak of intensity, and then faded away. We could still hear the engine, still hear the crunch of tyres upon stones, but now it had the sound of something that was prowling around rather than making a head on approach. Some security man, at a guess. We knew all about security men. Some of them were fat and few of them were fit, and most of them despised what they'd been hired to protect. Spike had already checked out the site over a couple of nights and had reported that there was no permanent watchman, so this was probably a patrolman from some cheap and corner-cutting firm who'd drop by a couple of times a night to see that the padlock was still on the gate, and otherwise would tend to leave the place alone.

We'd have nothing to fear. Spike touched my elbow, and we started to wade for shore.

The three of us gathered on the banking. Spike wiped the object clean and I wondered with what until I heard Michael muttering *Hey, where's my trousers?* and then we took our first real look at our prize.

The cherub's hand had come away in a neat break across the forearm just below the wrist, and the surface of the cut stone was as clean as new concrete. The hand and the base of the torch were weathered and green, pitted by almost a century of soot and air pollution, but the flame ... the flame, under a surface coat of grime, was of the purest gold.

'It is real,' Michael said, as if until this moment he'd been unable quite to believe it.

'Told you it was,' Spike said. 'Touch it, and see.'

'No,' Michael said.

I glanced at him then; he was round eyed and scared looking, and I remember thinking that he was a peculiar kid in lots of ways, but I didn't think about it any more deeply than that ... at least, not right away. Spike was about to say something, but it never came out.

Because what we heard instead was a stranger's voice, and it came from somewhere frighteningly close.

It said, *'Come on out, boys. I know you're in there.'*

We each looked around sharply, each of us in a different direction. I felt as if I'd swallowed a weight of guilt whole and it had suddenly jammed in my chest. The man, wherever he was, couldn't be much more than forty or fifty yards away. Michael was the worst. I'd never heard anyone fart in terror before. If the man needed a fix on our position, the sound alone was probably enough to give it to him.

But we didn't move, and none of us responded. Except for Spike, who whispered so that only we should hear.

'Don't get rattled,' he said. 'It's a put on.'

Michael was shaking. 'What if it isn't?'

'I know what I'm talking about. Stay calm, and he'll give up and go away. We're winning. We already got what we came for.'

And then we heard him again: *Come on, lads, let's have you*, only now he was further away. It seemed that Spike was right. The man, security man or whatever he was, appeared to be walking the outside of the perimeter fence and calling at random. Throwing bait, waiting to see if any fish might rise, moving on, and trying again.

'He knows,' Michael insisted.

The man tried again, now even further away.

Spike said, 'Even if he does, there's only one of him. He can't be everywhere.'

Silently, we dressed. The filth I'd been wading in wasn't going to do the inside of my trousers any good, but at least it wouldn't show when I got home. We dressed by moonlight alone, saving our lights so that the watchman wouldn't see; every now and again we glimpsed his beam, about ten times more powerful than either of ours, probing the undergrowth in some distant part of the enclosure.

When he'd reached a point that was as far from us as it was possible to be, we started out for the fence.

We moved in single file, Spike leading the way. There was no sense of adventure any more although later, I knew, this would be the high spot of the story that we'd tell. But that's how it is, with stories. Hearing about it and doing it just aren't the same thing. Right then I wanted to be out of it, I wanted to be safe, I didn't even want to *think* of some of the consequences that could lie ahead of us if anything went wrong. We scrambled over the rubbly patch, pushed our way through the waist-high grass, and reached the fence somewhere within a few yards of our point of entry.

Spike shaded his flashlight with his hand, and checked for the position of the gap.

The gap was no longer there.

For the first time that night, I saw that Spike was thrown. He'd come prepared for anything other than this; this was something that defied sense and logic.

'It's here,' he said. 'It's got to be.'

I said, 'He came and closed it up.'

'How?'

'Wire, something, I don't know.'

It would have been straightforward enough, the work of only a few seconds; just roll the wire back down to the ground, hook a couple of loose ends through the adjacent links, and then twist them tight. See the gap one night, bring along the tools the next. It was probably just routine business to the watchman but it meant that we were caught, as surely as if we'd triggered some spring loaded trap.

'We'll have to climb,' Spike said, looking upward and with an edge of desperation in his voice that I wasn't used to hearing.

'I can't,' Michael said.

And I was pretty sure that I couldn't either. The fence itself could be managed, but not the wire along the top. Even Spike would have trouble there, and I'd have been prepared to believe that Spike was capable of anything.

I didn't for one moment think that he was afraid. No, his desperation didn't come from fear. I think his apprehension was that the biggest enterprise of his life - a venture into forbidden territory with a fabulous prize at its end - was suddenly going to end in the cold plunge of mundane reality. We'd grabbed the Golden Fleece, and in doing it we walked the ground of heroes. The prospect of having that taken from us was far worse than that of any material loss. I mean, what you'd never had, you couldn't miss. But this was more like a kind of self-esteem. Lose that, and you'd have a loss that you'd remember forever.

He said, 'Wait a minute. I have to think.'

So we waited, and after a few moments we again heard the

call of the watchman.

He said, *There's no other way out, now, boys. I'm not going to wait all night. Come over to the gate, or I'll have to send in the animal.*

His voice drifted down to us, like something on a night breeze. Then we heard the distinct rattle of a heavy chain, and a shrill, *whup-whup-whup* whistle.

Pretty much the kind of whistle you'd use to call in a dog.

Maybe even a big one.

Michael said, barely audibly, 'Throw it back in the lake, Spike.'

Spike shot him a look. 'It's too late for that,' he said.

I didn't have to ask what he meant. It was like the needle in the base of Talos, or the eye of the giant Buddha – you steal one of those suckers and you *know* you're not just facing a slap on the wrist ... you're drawing the attention of something great and terrible, pulling the plug on hell to let demons come streaming out, and there's no way that you can get away with dropping what you've grabbed and so dodge the consequences.

Michael said, '*Spike* ...' and Spike said, 'Fuck him and his dog, we'll get out through the drain.'

'What drain?' I said.

So Spike showed us.

'I won't go down there,' Michael said.

The entrance to the drain stood at what had been the water's edge. Its function, as far as I could see, had been to keep the pond level more or less constant by drawing off any overspill. It was flush-fitted into the masonry of the banking, and it was barred by an iron gate. The gate had been thrown open, but I wouldn't exactly have called it inviting; it looked like the way into the world's smallest, darkest prison.

Spike said, 'What's the choice?'

'I won't,' Michael said shakily, and I was surprisingly glad that we had him along. Perhaps it occurred to me then that a lot of the time, Michael's fears were pretty much the same as my own; the difference between us was that he frequently saved me from having to express mine, so that I could be scornful along with Spike and seem just as tough.

But this time Spike said, 'It's nothing like it looks. It just goes through the bank and under the road and then comes out into the lower pond. It's nothing.'

Michael was unconvinced. 'What if we get stuck?'

'Look, we'll try it. If it's no go we'll come back out.' He lifted the golden flame, which we'd wrapped in Michael's empty carrier bag. I still had the sandwiches, Michael was now carrying the soda. 'I'll throw this back into the lake, and we can all go up to the gate and get a leathering.'

I couldn't see much of Michael's expression because we weren't using the lights, but I could sense the strange tension between the fears that held him back and the fears that drove him on.

And then somehow, his terror seemed to make a deal with itself.

'I can't go first,' he said.

'I'll go first,' Spike said, and slapped him on the shoulder as he started to move. If the guard was letting a dog loose into the grounds, there was no time to be debating about it. As Spike went by me, he added in a low voice, 'Make sure he follows me.'

Spike bent almost double, and went in first. The tunnel fitted him like a sleeve. Michael hesitated at the entrance, and as he stood there looking into darkness I heard the far-off sound of a gate hinge squealing and then a reverberating crash as the gate presumably fell shut again. I gave Michael a hard shove on the rear, and he yelped and pitched forward.

I waited about one second, but there was no way of telling whether or not he'd been heard. So then I put my head down, and followed.

It was a tight fit, all right. I couldn't raise my head even though I was almost squatting, and the walls brushed my shoulders on either side. Spike had switched on his flashlight so there was a kind of rim of illumination getting back along the tunnel sides ahead of me, but I couldn't see much past Michael.

The stonework was dank and slimy, the floor angled downward. We couldn't walk, we couldn't run, all we could manage was a kind of restricted shuffle. I didn't even want to think about how far we had to go. I pretended that the end was in sight, only a few yards ahead.

But I knew that it wasn't so. Try as I might, I couldn't help thinking about the width of the banking and then the rough ground and the grass and only *then* the broad main walkway of the park; and I tried to remember how far down on the opposite side it was to the lower pond, and it seemed like forever. Long enough so that, for a distance somewhere in the middle, we'd have lost sight of the way in and yet still be a long way short of seeing the exit.

I could feel my chest tightening in panic. I felt as if I was in a deep, dark fist somewhere miles under the earth, and the fist was closing. I used to have this nightmare. I was in a big block of concrete and there was just my nose and mouth showing. I couldn't move, I couldn't see, I couldn't hear, but I could breathe and I could scream. In a number of ways this was almost as bad and in one it was worse, because it was real.

Ahead of me, the light opened up. Michael had dropped to a crawl, following Spike who had done the same. What the hell, I thought, and did likewise.

This was better. Now there was space around my head and the feeling of oppression wasn't quite so fierce. The light swung and bobbed as Spike led the way, shadows cast by the uneven stonework zooming back and forth along the walls as the light moved.

'All okay?' I heard Spike gasp, and the two of us grunted in response.

Now that I could I glanced backward, for some reassurance. The entranceway was a small rectangle of moonlight, already impossibly far off. It was almost as if I was lying in the bottom of a well and looking up at the night sky; it was just faint square of a different kind of darkness, and no reassurance at all.

And then, as I was about to turn away, I saw something move across the rectangle and block out the night sky completely.

'Oh, shit,' I said.

'It's all right,' Spike whispered, the tunnel echo making the sound almost loud. 'There's nothing to worry about.'

'Like hell,' I said. 'There's something in here with us.'

We all stopped - yes, I know, but the other two had stopped and I didn't have any choice - and listened, but the three of us were breathing so hard that it was impossible to make out any alien component. So then I switched on the cycle lamp and aimed it back down the length of the tunnel, and that wasn't much use either; I might as well have been aiming it at the stars, for the distance that its now weakening battery was able to cover.

'Everybody hold their breath,' I said, and we listened again.

Now we could hear it.

Panting hard. Gasping. Grunting.

'It's in,' I said. 'But it's stuck.'

And Michael said, with awe, 'How big does that make it?'

Spike said nothing, but turned to go on.

Easy for you, Spike, I thought ... you ain't the last one in line, here.

I aimed the cycle lamp all the way back again. Did I see eyes there, two dull points of reflection at the furthest extent of the beam, or did I only imagine them?

If it was stuck and it stayed that way, then there was nothing to worry about. But say it wasn't; say it was just a really tight fit, and it was inching forward, and that it would pick up speed as it advanced with the mossy sides of the tunnel greasing it like a piston, accelerating and accelerating to come thundering down on us like an Underground train, jaws opening and spit flying and nowhere for us to dodge or hide; say that happened, then who was going to be first course on the menu?

I scrambled on as fast as I could. And if Michael was going to be too slow then tough shit, I was just going to scramble right on over him.

Everyone ahead of me stopped, and Michael squawked as my head rammed into his behind.

'What's the matter?' I said. 'Keep moving!'

'We can't,' he said, breathlessly.

I looked around him.

We had a problem.

Just ahead of Spike, the tunnel appeared to divide. A narrow branch - even narrower than the one that we were in - went off to the left, while the main descending shaft went on ahead. Or rather it didn't, because the roof had fallen.

'We're trapped,' Michael said.

The blockage was like a jumble of stone that had been tipped from a wheelbarrow. Not a wall but a sloping pile, and a gap at the top that went on into darkness. I could maybe have slid my arm into the gap, but nothing more of me could have followed.

Spike picked off one of the surface chunks and tossed it aside, saying, 'Nah, it's just loose stuff. And it can't be solid or we'd be up to our necks in water.'

I glanced back. 'We can't piss around, Spike,' I said. 'It's getting closer.'

'Wait a minute.' He pulled his way up the pile, making a small avalanche of masonry debris, and peered through the space at the top. He pointed his flashlight in and then, with a flick of his wrist, tossed it through. Then he squinted through the gap again.

'It's clear further in,' he said. 'But there's a lot of stuff to shift.'

Michael gave me some support. 'He said there isn't time.'

Spike looked at us both. Crowded together in a space too small to turn around, I could almost sense what he was thinking; were the loyalties shifting here, was his grip on the troops beginning to slip? We'd always been a balanced threesome but, given sufficient pressure, perhaps that could change.

Nothing happened for a moment.

Then he said, 'This way, then. Pass me the lamp.'

And he started off down the leftward branch.

I felt my heart sink when I saw how he had to turn his shoulders sideways, simply to be able to get in at all. From here on it wasn't a tunnel, it was hardly more than a slit. Michael followed him almost with eagerness. For a moment my imagination ran a little more freely than I would have wanted it to – I saw this branch leading to a smaller shaft, and on to a smaller, until we were flat on our bellies with the earth pressing down on our backs and we'd come to a dead halt against solid rock and then we'd try to inch back, and there'd be *nowhere to go* ... no light, no air, no space, just a fit as snug and as close as the grave ...

'It gets wider,' Spike called back.

Just before I entered the branchline, I took a quick look through the gap at the top of the rockfall. It was like looking into a long, deep letterbox. But there was some sense of air and space at the far end, because Spike's flashlight had rolled on through and dropped on the other side to illuminate the open area where the unblocked shaft continued.

Well, it *did* get wider along the branchline. But not by much.

I was consoled by the thought that if the beast behind us was having trouble squeezing itself down the main shaft, then it was going to have no luck at all down here. All we had to do was keep our heads, keep on going, and we'd be all right. I squirmed along, and endured the odd kick from Michael's flailing shoes for the sake of being not one inch further back than I needed to be. Every time he kicked me he said *Sorry,* and every time he said sorry I told him to keep going.

We were ascending again, and quite steeply. That was fine by me, because it meant that we were heading back for the surface. At a guess this channel served some other part of the park, I don't know where, and emptied into the main drain. I tried to visualise where it might lead and I thought, Oh God, I hope it's not the toilets. Anywhere but the toilets. It was bad enough to be crawling in slime, without having to entertain the thought that it might be something worse. And how would we get out? I'd always thought of it strictly as a one-way system. Once the crap was around that U bend, I didn't want to know.

But I was quickly saved from any further speculation, because we'd gone no more than twenty yards when Spike said, 'Dead end.'

'What?' I said. 'Let me see.' And Michael pressed himself against the side so that I could get a look through.

Spike was telling the exact truth. An end could get no deader. I was looking at a wall of bricks, not exactly new but nowhere near as old as the tunnel itself. They'd been sloppily laid, probably from the other side, and the mortar had squeezed out and set around the joints. Nothing short of a pickaxe could have got us through, and there was no room to swing a pickaxe anyway.

Michael said, 'Now what?'

And I said, 'Well, I don't know about anyone else, but I'm sick of dragging these sandwiches around.'

The fact of it was that we were close to exhaustion. We must have travelled something approaching a quarter of a mile underground by now, although it felt like a lot more. We were three blind mice and we'd run about up to our limits, and this brief enforced halt made us realise it.

So we lay there in the darkness, and broke out the picnic.

I was ravenous. I'd guess that the others were the same. Nothing was wasted, anyway. Afterwards I felt faintly sick, as the white bread sat in my stomach like a party guest who won't get the hint and go home. We lay in silence, passed the warm soda back and forth, and listened for the beast.

Being the last in line, I was the one best able to tell how it was going. I didn't much like what I could hear. I couldn't see back to where the tunnel divided, which was fine because it meant that anything standing there wouldn't be able to see me; and that was a distinct possibility, because by the sound of it the beast had worked its way right in and was dangerously close.

Heavy breathing. Panting. A few grunts.

And a persistent, slithering, *sliding* sound.

I tried to tell myself that it couldn't be as near as it seemed, that the echo of the tunnel itself was having a distorting effect both on distance and direction. But then my efforts at self-delusion came to nothing, because the beast started to dig.

Big stones rolled, gravel moved, and I knew that this could only mean one thing; that it had reached the rockfall, and believed that we were on the other side. Big and fierce it might be, but it couldn't be too bright. It was pawing and scratching in high speed bursts, snuffling, pawing again.

Still, nobody moved. The sound - bounced, amplified, and made hollow - was all around us. Every now and again bricks and stones would fall, filling the tunnel's end with a noise like that of a bowling alley. Michael flinched when it happened, and I suppose I did too. And just a few yards away, our pursuer worked on with a patience and persistence that were almost demonic.

Sometime, we were going to have to emerge from this dead end. Suppose the beast dug onwards, suppose it even broke through. Assuming that its master was waiting back there at the lakeside, we'd have no way out at all; not forward, not back, not anywhere. The beast would hold one end of the drain, its master would hold the other, and we'd be helpless in the middle.

Face it, we were pretty helpless now.

There was a glimmer of light from down the tunnel. The beast had managed to open up the gap a little, and a faint wash from Spike's abandoned flashlight was leaking through. A long shadow moved on the wall. I heard its breath, rank and heavy and filled with a growing sense of elation.

Behind me, Michael moved. I glanced back, trying to shoot him a look of warning in case he should make any sound, but it was far too dark; I could only sense him rather than see him as he turned his face to the back of our branch tunnel, and what he did then was probably the last thing that I ever would have expected because he stuck his two fingers into the corners of his mouth and emitted the loudest and probably the last *whup-whup-whup* whistle that I ever expected to hear.

He was *calling* the bastard thing to us!

I remember wondering if there would be enough time left for me to get hold of him and strangle him before the beast was upon me, and I expect that Spike was thinking the same; suddenly I had no confidence at all about the narrowness of the drain keeping it out and, anyway, even if it did, now that the beast knew where we were it needed do nothing more than sit tight and starve us out. I could hear it responding, trying to turn in the restricted space, yelping as it stuck; it sounded as if someone had run a charge through it and sent it into overdrive. Stones were kicked, claws scraped ...

And the beast frantically started to back off down the tunnel, returning tail-first the way it had come.

I couldn't believe it. And I couldn't understand it, not straight away, and when I did it brought a respect for Michael's nerve that I'd never thought I'd have any reason to feel. He'd given the same call that the beast's master had given, back there at the lakeside; and because of the tunnel's acoustics, the beast had failed to realise where it was coming from.

And so, thinking that it was being recalled, back it had gone.

I gave it a while, listening hard. And then, as quietly as I could, I started to shuffle my way back to the main drain.

It was strange, but after the extra confinement of the branchline I came out into the main tunnel with a sense almost of relief. I fought off the fear that it was all a trick, that the beast was playing a sucker game like my father pretending to go downstairs when all he was doing was marking time on the top step, with me holding my breath in anticipation until he flung open my bedroom door and shouted *Boo!* – how long ago was *that*, I wonder – and I eased myself around to look back along the drain.

It was gone. I could see clear all the way to the end, the entranceway no bigger than the size of a penny.

With my voice as low as I could keep it, barely more than words and breath, I told the others.

Michael stuck his head out to look for himself. Spike wanted to do the same, but Michael was in the way and I wasn't going to move to let him out, not yet. No way was I going to back off down the tunnel to be last in line again. If we were going to dig through the blockage and go onward, then I'd do the shifting and I'd be the first one through, and let Spike come out last and be the tailgunner for a change. He was the one who'd wanted the flame in the first place, the whole thing had been his idea.

Looking down the tunnel, Michael said, 'Remember what he said? He didn't call it a dog. He called it *The Animal*. It's something worse than a dog. We called it up when we took the golden flame.'

'I'm not giving it back,' I heard Spike say from the other side of him.

'We could vote,' I suggested.

'No! We're not voting for anything. I didn't come this far for that. You sound like a couple of girls.'

Well, it may not sound like much, but there was no better way to close an argument amongst eleven-year-old boys. Tentatively, I switched on my cycle lamp and turned it onto the rockfall to see how we stood. The beam came on with about half of its original power, now, and we only got that much because the battery had been resting for a while. When I looked at the bulb, I could see the glowing shape of the filament wire inside instead of just a brilliant source.

The 'animal', as its unseen master had called it, had barely scratched at the surface of the fall. It had pawed and clawed and opened the gap out a little, but only by taking out the earth and gravel; the big masonry blocks that had once formed part of the tunnel roof still lay untouched. Pawing wouldn't do it; they'd have to be lifted. I set down the lamp somewhere flat, and began to work by its light.

Imagine four bricks together, with slightly more weight; then dusty them up and break off the corners, and you'll have some idea of what I was working with. I couldn't lift the blocks easily, I could only bunny-hop them along in six-inch steps and then, when I had one clear enough, roll it end-over-end to Michael. Michael dragged it through to Spike, and Spike did his best to stack it together with the others in a makeshift wall behind us. There was no way of avoiding noise, but we kept it down as much as we could. I wasn't trying to clear the tunnel completely; I was simply trying to make us a way through, and probably at an inevitable cost of torn clothing and scraped hands and knees. But they were the least of our worries; real ones, to a child, but deferred in the face of other dangers.

It wasn't too bad. The worst that I'd feared – that of hitting a whole chunk of maybe half a dozen blocks still held together with the original mortar, and impossible to shift without a chain and a bulldozer – didn't arise. The stone lining of the drain had collapsed in on itself but the earth above had kept the tunnel shape, like a mould; all I'd have to do was clean out the gap just a little more, and we'd have a wriggling space.

It wasn't just stones and dirt and gravel that I had to clear. There were weeds and old rubbish as well, washed down from the lake whenever and trapped here as if in a filter. It hardly mattered, I was probably already as filthy as I could get. Just as long as I didn't stick my hand in a dead duck, or anything.

I dug out what had once been an old tin can, and passed it back to Michael. Michael nearly fumbled and dropped it and I felt my heart leap, but he caught it again. We couldn't fool ourselves that we were safe. Whatever patrolled the lake shore, looking for some other trace of our passage, need only hear one brief call to return to the burrow.

I turned back to what I was doing. Something was sticking up out of the debris, and I pulled it clear. When it came out, it was bigger and heavier than I'd expected.

It resembled a toy rocket, a fat little body with tail fins. It was badly corroded, with a surface that looked more like pitted old stone than metal.

I'd found one of the old mortar bombs.

'Look at this!' I whispered, holding it up.

'Put it down,' Michael said hoarsely, and I looked at him. 'One of them went off already.'

I looked at my prize with some curiosity. I'd no sense of danger. It just looked like a really, really neat thing to take home. But I wouldn't, of course, because I knew that Michael was right; so I just held it out to him to pass along with the other debris, and Michael shrank back as if it carried the plague or something.

'Not me,' he said, and so Spike reached past him and took it.

Michael hunched further back against the tunnel wall. I heard the crack as his head met the low stone.

'OWWWWWW!' he yelled.

'You fucking idiot,' I said, and I gave him a shove on the shoulder, and he cracked his head for a second time and yelled again.

We all froze. Except for Michael, who sat rubbing at his lumps with a scrubbing sound like sandpaper until Spike hissed at him to stop.

We heard it enter the tunnel.

We could hear that it was heading our way.

And it was moving at three times the speed that it had been before.

Spike said, 'Is it wide enough yet?' And I said, 'It'll have to be.'

I hauled myself up into the gap and started to force my way through. My chest stuck and I breathed right out and then Michael was behind me pushing, and I started to slide. I got a hold on something, and dragged myself a little further; and then suddenly I was tumbling forward in a shower of debris and I was out into the chamber that had been formed on the other side. I got up to my knees and turned around to face the gap; Michael's hands were already waving around and searching for something to grab, and I caught hold of his wrists and pulled. It wasn't easy, he was heavier than I was. Ever pulled a tightly packed duvet out of its box? He came, but it took everything I had.

He came out suddenly and all in a pile, like a foal at its birth, and as he scrambled aside I looked for Spike.

The gap looked impossibly narrow from this side. And Spike wasn't in it.

I called to him. His face appeared at the other end.

'Take this first,' he said, and he pushed through the bag containing the golden flame.

He looked like a monk who'd been walled into his cell, passing out some valued relic. I took it and slung it to Michael, and then reached to help Spike through.

He didn't come.

'Spike ... !' I called, only too aware of what was bearing down on him. Silence wouldn't help us now.

His face reappeared. 'Carry on,' he said. 'I'll catch up with you.'

'There isn't time!'

'I've got a plan.'

A plan? What was this, *Mission Impossible*? The only worthwhile plan was to move as if our tails were on fire. What did he mean, he had a plan?

'What's he doing?' Michael said from behind me.

'God knows,' I said, and I hoisted myself into the gap to take a look.

Even as I was doing this, a sound began to ring out. For a moment I was confused because it was almost exactly the sound that I'd heard when Spike had been up at the top of the fountain, taking shots at the flame with the hammer; a blacksmith at the anvil, beating out a white-hot shoe. Then I got to see.

The cycle lamp was still where I'd set it. By its light, Spike was working. He'd set the mortar bomb between two of the fallen roof stones so that it was held pointing out towards the entrance of the tunnel. With the hammer in his hand, he was pounding away on the rusted nub of the detonator cap.

I got one other brief impression, of the beast that was bearing down on him from the deeper shadows and it was everything we'd feared it might be; the Hydra, the Gorgon, the Big Bad Wolf, a tunnelful of viciousness thundering toward Spike with the momentum of a train, eyes like baleful headlamps and teeth like knives; and then there was a flash like a photograph that sent me back dazzled, and then a half second later a bigger, more powerful shockwave that bucked the ground and brought all kinds of shit cascading down from the ceiling while beyond the wall the entire tunnel seemed to be falling in on itself.

And then, after a while, everything settled into silence.

I know what he'd intended. An improvised bazooka, a one-shot launch that would arrow straight into the face of its target and wipe it away. It might have worked for Sean Connery, but it didn't work for Spike; all that he got was a big bang with no particular direction to it and a one-way ticket to wherever. After the dirt had stopped raining down and while my ears were still ringing I tried to scramble back through the gap to see what I could do, but it was useless. I dug with my hands until my fingers bled and then I dug a while longer, and then finally Michael had to pull me away.

'The batteries are going,' he said, wiping the dust from the flashlight's lens. 'We have to get out.'

At first, I wouldn't leave.

'There's no point,' Michael insisted gently. 'He's dead.'

We crawled out of that brick sleeved culvert above the lower pond no more than five minutes later, but I felt as if I'd spent a lifetime underground. No bars awaited us, just a flimsy wire grille that was no challenge at all after everything that we'd been through. There was a lot of activity at the upper pond by then, but none as yet down here; we melted off into the night and left the park via the garden of one of the big houses that looked over it.

They say that the explosion sent a column of mud and stones about thirty feet into the air, like a geyser. They sifted through it in daylight and for a while it actually seemed that they were reassembling evidence of some strange mythical beast, until the pieces resolved themselves into the mingled remains of an eleven year old boy and the watchman's Doberman.

That's what they called it, anyway. Personally, I've got my doubts. It may have been a Doberman when it went in, but I know what I saw down there and it was something more.

I arrived home to an empty house. There was no hot water but I sat in the bath and scrubbed myself clean anyway. I hid my ruined clothes, intending to burn them when I could. I lay in bed and heard the rest of them arriving home; in fact, I think I heard every sound in the house that night. I don't think I slept at all.

I don't know the details of how Michael covered himself, but he seemed to get by. They swallowed our story about Spike not having shown up to meet us at the fair, mainly because a few of the stallholders looked at our photographs and said Yeah, they'd seen us hanging around that night. To them, we were probably just two unremarkable faces amongst thousands. Maybe they'd seen us, maybe they hadn't; what did it matter, as long as the police heard what they wanted and left them alone?

We met up again a few days later, down by the canal. Michael had brought the golden flame, wrapped in a piece of crumpled brown paper. Close up and in daylight, it didn't look like much. Michael scraped at it with his penknife.

Some of the gold paint came off to expose the stone underneath.

We were on a quiet stretch of the canal, where two old barges lay half sunken in a backwater with rushes growing up through them. It had been one of Spike's favourite places.

So that was where we dropped it in.

CHINGLE HELL

Chingle Hall, in Goosnargh, a rural village just north of Preston, does not claim to be the most haunted house in England, or even the most haunted house in Lancashire, but it certainly has a reputation that has travelled far and wide. So much so, in fact, and not a little bit because its spectres are of the distinctly spooky variety, that certain ghost-hunting societies have re-christened it 'Chingle Hell'.

Though 13th century in origin, it isn't much to a look at. None-too-large as medieval manor houses go, it admittedly retains several of its original interesting features - an encircling moat (though the original timber drawbridge has now been replaced by a permanent bridge), an interior chapel and several priests' holes - but there is something rather drab, even dreary about its plain whitewashed exterior.

Despite this, the ghosts of Chingle Hall are among some of the best documented on the modern paranormal trail, with mysterious but extensive evidence collected on tape, video and still photograph. There are said to be 21 ghosts here in total. One of these, the spirit of someone allegedly bricked up deep inside the house can still be heard attempting to scrape its way out, and if you bang three times on the inner wall, it will bang back. Another, a young woman who apparently wanders the upper floor, weeping, has the power to infect those who encounter her with overwhelming sadness - one visitor had to be restrained from throwing herself out of a high bathroom window after such a meeting.

Other entities inside the hall are of a more violent persuasion. The kitchen area is the haunt of a poltergeist that has reputedly hurled pans and dishes, sometimes for hours on end. On one occasion it stacked crockery until it reached the ceiling. Investigators claim to have photographed inanimate objects floating in this part of the house. But far more worrying is a presence that seems to revel in starting fires. Researchers claim to have recorded piles of logs exploding into flame in the hearth, apparently of their own volition. Subsequent examinations found no trickery; no accelerant of any sort was discovered, and no means identified by which a hidden flame could have been applied. Likewise, when a support beam in the house suddenly commenced burning when there was nobody even close to it, the Fire Brigade were called. They doused the fire but were unable to explain how it had started.

Perhaps more unnerving still are the weird monastic apparitions for which Chingle Hall is nationally famous. Curious hooded apparitions are regularly spotted in the building or around its grounds, and if these are the shades of long-departed monks they are not always of a benign disposition. While some are simply glimpsed praying or walking down passageways and vanishing through doorways that no longer exist, others are said to be more threatening. One in particular has been seen glaring in through various downstairs windows with strange dark features that are more beastlike than human.

It may be, if one is keen to find explanations, that this monastic aspect is a big clue. The house is strongly associated with Saint John Wall, yet another Lancashire man who was executed for the 'crime' of practising his Catholic faith. Wall, who was born in Chingle Hall, grew up to be a learned and likeable Franciscan friar – many who met him were charmed by his good humour and educated manner – but in 1678 he was falsely named as a conspirator in Titus Oates' imaginary Popish Plot, and sentenced to death unless he would repudiate his faith. Refusing, he was hanged, drawn and quartered the following year – a scene of such horror that even the largely Protestant crowd rioted afterwards.

Though eerie noises have been heard in the building's John Wall Room, there is no guarantee that these have anything to do with the saint himself (beatified in 1970, one might have expected Wall to find peace in the afterlife). But his terrible fate deeply angered the Catholics of the county, especially the Catholic clergy, and as Chingle Hall had previously been a secret meeting place of Catholics, with clandestine Masses said there and precious relics stored in its hidden chambers, it became a focal point for Catholic belief and practice, and maybe others who'd died in sectarian violence were less circumspect about returning after death and making their feelings felt.

But there is another possible explanation behind the spirits of Chingle Hall.

Sometime in the 20th century, when the Hall was undergoing minor restoration, it was noticed that a number of its beams and joists were engraved with very old, indecipherable symbols. Examined by experts, these were later identified as Viking runes. A further investigation revealed that much of the timber used in the initial construction of the house had been pillaged from the hull of a Viking longship. The house was first constructed by Adam de Singleton in the 1260s, but the land had been captured from its original Saxon owners by Uthred de Singleton in 1066, which also, coincidentally, was the year of the last great Viking invasion of England – and that one came through the north. So, it's not really implausible, if a genuine Viking artefact was incorporated into the structure, that the spirits haunting Chingle Hall date back to a much earlier, even more violent age than the Reformation.

It could also be that they are nothing to do with Christianity whatsoever.

ONLY SLEEPING
Peter Bell

It was the long dark corridor in the boarding house, amongst other things, that made Robert not look forward to going on holiday with his parents to the Isle of Man again.

For two weeks in August every year, as far back as he could remember, Robert and his parents visited the seaside. They had visited various resorts, all so similar he could not recall the names of the dreary places. That, at least, had been the case until this year, when they would be revisiting the scene of last year's holiday.

It had been the first time they had visited an island. The sea journey, gulls circling the ship with plaintive calls, the mysterious approach from over the horizon of the emerald cliffs and hills had caught his imagination. The beaches were good and there was plenty to do. At first the holiday had been genuinely enjoyable.

That, however, had been before the footsteps on the landing, the landing by the long dark corridor ...

Lying awake the night before the return to the scene of his unease, he couldn't stop thinking of the awful guest-house ... He went over the events in cold, precise detail ...

The taxi from the pier drove the two-mile arc of Douglas Bay before climbing up Summer Hill to their bed-and-breakfast in Onchan. The sweeping terraces of tall hotels that curved around the promenade spoke of better times. Though many still wore a superficial air of affluence, here and there a crumbling discoloured facade and the occasional unsightly gap made Robert think of a once fine set of teeth beginning to decay. The Isle of Man, however, in contrast to the drab resorts they had visited in recent years still seemed to be making an effort to look festive and respectable.

That at least was how he felt until, alighting from the taxi, he saw looming before him *Sunny Bank*.

The name *Sunny Bank* had conjured an image of a pleasant homely cottage, roses rambling over a rustic porch, but the dwelling before him stood tall and grey upon a corner, long terraces extending on either side in infinite tedium. *Sunny Bank*, in insolent defiance of its name, moreover, was heavily shrouded behind a screen of unkempt sycamores and a riotous uncut privet hedge. Dismay besieged him as he beheld this gloomy abode.

His apprehensions were mitigated somewhat by their jolly hosts. Mr Moore, a rotund, sun-tanned figure, made Robert think of a small and friendly bear; Mrs Moore was grey haired and thin with ruddy cheeks, an absent-minded air and an appealing laugh. Their congenial hostess, talking unceasingly, showed them round. The hallway, lit by a stained glass window on the stairs ahead, managed to avoid being too sombre, despite the guest-house *bric-à-brac*. The wholesome dining room opened to the left. The lounge, opening to the right, was bright and airy, with two bay windows.

There was a youngish couple there. They had their backs to them, briefly turning in acknowledgement. The man looked pale and tense; his manner was perfunctory. She, raven-haired and beautiful in profile, was more effusive, smiling as she slowly turned her head and held Robert in a long and curious regard. Full-faced, however, her beauty was flawed by an odd asymmetry of features. And there was misery in her hollow eyes. Her steady penetrating gaze made Robert feel naked and uncomfortable, and he was mightily relieved to depart.

'Mr and Mrs Dennison,' Mrs Moore was whispering to his mother. 'She was born in Russia. She has a lovely accent! Like Marlene Dietrich! Her baby died earlier in the year and they've come away to help get over things. Very sad! We sometimes hear her crying in the night. They sleep just down the corridor.'

The corridor that Mrs Moore was referring to was reached up five steps left from a small landing on the staircase ahead. The main flight also turned up from here, reversing direction, leading to a broader landing above the hall, and this is where she led them first. A window overlooked the front garden. Two bedrooms opened off. In the bright front room his parents were to sleep. With its pink and white-patterned paper, and its two windows it looked instantly agreeable.

This was not the case with Robert's room. Mrs Moore's repeated reference to it as 'the master bedroom' could not mitigate its uninviting aspect. Maybe it was the faded green wallpaper that made it so dismal; or the fluttering density of the trees outside the narrow window. The room felt very overcrowded. The bed made up for him was flush against the window. Another, of immense proportions was close by the door, and there was not much space to get around its foot past a huge oak wardrobe. And he didn't like the way the loose brass doorknob went through several turns before it would engage the catch.

He was relieved, though, that his bedroom was not off the long dark corridor. The first was occupied by their hosts; the next by the young couple. The passage seemed extraordinarily long, and he could not quite equate the geometry of the upper floor with the size and layout of the space below. It felt horribly cut off and it crossed his mind it would be very awful to be trapped there. Any relief, though, was quickly dashed as Mrs Moore explained the position of the bathroom – at the far end of the long, dark corridor.

'You've got a long, long walk,' she laughed, 'if you drink too much before you go to bed. So! Tread carefully in the dark! The light's not working.'

In the dark! He didn't fancy going down there in the middle of the night. He had no wish to hear the sound of mournful tears reverberating in the darkness.

Doubtless due to the soporific maritime air, Robert slept right through till morning. His slumber, though, was by no means dreamless; and in one of those dreams he thought he had wakened, suffused with unease. The detail, when he tried to recall it, remained obstinately vague, yet connected in some sinister way with footsteps on the landing outside his door. The next few nights brought undisturbed rest. Midway through their stay, though, anxious dreams returned, all connected in some eerie way with the long dark corridor and Mrs Dennison.

Mrs Dennison, in truth, was starting to bother Robert. Every morning over breakfast she gazed at him with an avidity that was not quite wholesome. She tried to catch him, every time he caught her eye, with her dismaying smile, part tragic, part exultant. Such a smile in a normal face might have been engaging, but that ghastly asymmetric facial twist lent her an expression not far short of appalling. Worse still, these past few days she had taken to waylaying him, touching him, once even cuddling him - as if he was a baby. Just because she'd lost her own!

'She's unhappy,' his mother chided when he raised his fears, 'you must be nice to her. It's a terrible thing to lose a child ... And don't be so silly! She's harmless.'

Yet, for Robert, the knowledge of the tragic woman's plight did not ease the horror of her importunity.

The real trouble began at the weekend.

It was the end of a mellow day; the family was ambling along Douglas Promenade. The sun had dropped behind the hills; the sea-front illuminations were coming on, rendering the bay a luminescent golden crescent. Across the shimmering waters the lighthouse on the headland was sending out insistent beams of light. It was quieter here away from the town, the silence broken only by distant sounds from over the sands and the rasping passage of a tramcar on the Manx Electric Railway. They were looking down on a rocky cove strewn with pebbles and seaweed, separate from the main sweep of the shore. A faded wooden sign guarded a concrete stairway that crumbled down the cliff to the strand:

PORT JACK. BEWARE!

The steps were not so bad as they looked, but there could be no doubt they needed care. Care was required on the beach as well, where one false move on slimy rocks could mean a broken ankle, and there were dire warnings about high tides. The cove was attractive in its own way but, isolated as it was from the distant swirl of coloured lights and the carnival sounds of the promenade, it felt too lonely to be comfortable, and in the evening shadows rather dismal.

There was one other person, over near the water's edge, a woman by the look of it. Her face was partly hidden by a mass of unkempt hair, and there was something about the angle of her neck that didn't look quite right. It was difficult to be sure in the twilight, but the features glimpsed appeared ravaged, as of someone maimed or prematurely wasted. The woman looked distressed. An innocent wanderer along the shore, no doubt, but she conveyed an air of weirdness that coldly touched Robert. His mother and father appeared not to have noticed the eerie figure.

The light was fading fast as they left, the illuminations along the curving promenade now dominant, the hills silhouetted against a pink-streaked dusk. Over the bay hung a single flickering star. The tide was on the turn, the waves surging and falling boisterously against the pebbled shore. The ill-clad family, dressed to suit the vanished summer heat, shivered in the rising breeze, hastening precariously across the seaweed-strewn cobbles. Robert took a last look behind. As he scaled the unstable steps, gripping on the rusting handrail, he tried to tell himself it was just the dying light that made it seem as if the figure's devastated face was staring up at him.

That night in bed Robert's mind was restless. Every time he was on the point of dropping off, the figure on the beach flashed before his eyes, blending into that of Mrs Dennison. It had been a mistake to bring on holiday that book of ghost stories; his father had been right, all nonsense! There was a frightful one set in a boarding-house, to do with a whistle on a beach and a sheeted figure rising up from a bed. He wished there was only one bed in his room. And he wished he hadn't seen the woman on the shore …

Suddenly, he awoke. It was still pitch dark. So far, he had managed to avoid going to the bathroom in the night, but there was no alternative: he would have to brave the perils of the long dark corridor. It was not a pleasant prospect. As he struggled with the door-knob he heard, indistinct at first, a sound, coming as far as he could tell from the stairs; the sound of stealthy footsteps, as if the plodder strove for secrecy. The ominous tread halted. As he listened, heart in mouth, he tried to tell himself it was only the noises one heard in a large old house at night as its beams and rafters settled in the falling temperature before the dawn. He was about to proceed when, horror of horrors, the steps resumed again, moving, now it seemed, along the corridor – the way he needed to go! An interminable time passed, until a brooding silence prevailed.

Robert waited in the dark. Eventually, he could hold on no more; the imperative of nature triumphed over terror.

The corridor appeared even darker and longer than he remembered. The sobbing from the room beside the bathroom was no less harrowing for being muffled. Mrs Dennison had not diminished her advances, reaching out every day to clutch him. She was looking more and more haggard as each day passed. He'd heard his mother discussing her plight in whispered tones to Mrs Moore. As he hurried back down the long dark corridor the sobbing turned to wailing. His foot creaking on a loose floorboard as he reached his door startled him, and for a dreadful moment he thought the handle had jammed completely, exiling him on the tenebrous landing. Behind him yawned the black vacancy of the stairwell. A wild and terrible thought gripped him: was there something out there, lurking in the shadows? The house, cluttered and confined as it appeared during the day, now felt infinitely vast, a labyrinth where who knew what might hide.

In the purity of the summer morn, the gulls' insistent calls shrilling outside, Robert tried to put his night-time fears in perspective. Fancy getting scared of that woman on the shore! Reading those ghost stories! The beach story was bad enough, but what was that other tale, something about children with no hearts and long fingernails? That involved a boy visiting a grim bathroom in the middle of the night … The story had terrified him so much he hadn't finished it.

It was, therefore, somewhat disconcerting when Mrs Moore lent over him at breakfast and whispered, 'I hope you weren't disturbed last night by the ghost?'

Mrs Moore glanced behind her surreptitiously; her voice fell lower, she was almost miming. 'Bill often stays up late and has a little tipple – I hope he didn't waken you?'

Only Mr Moore! Going to bed, drunk, at some unholy hour of the morning.

Mrs Moore's explanation might be reassuring; but the same could not be said of Mrs Dennison, whose pestering remained voracious. Next morning Robert came down to breakfast late, hoping to avoid the couple. To his consternation his sinister admirer remained at the table after her husband had left. She said little, and when she did speak he couldn't understand a word she said: that funny foreign accent Mrs Moore found 'lovely'. Most terrifying was her eager, complicit smile, as if she shared a secret with him. She was looking visibly more wasted. Her greying raven hair, no longer tied back, hung loose in disarray; and he didn't like the incongruity between the smiling lips and the haggard lines about her eyes, or the ghastly asymmetry of her features. Day by day, the pallor of her face was becoming more pronounced, the dark hollows round her eyes ever deeper chasms. He had no wish to be embraced by this crier in the night.

And it was that night he jumped awake in an extremity of terror …

He sat bolt upright, listening in the darkness; he could hear what he hoped was an inebriated Mr Moore on his way to bed. But the footsteps, he was sure, weren't ascending from downstairs, but from the direction of the dreadful corridor; plodding softly, slowly and purposefully, stair by stair, with intervals of silence as their unseen owner paused. The pauses were even more frightening than the steps, conjuring an impression of deliberate purpose and furtive malice. A terrible conviction assailed him: *they were coming up the steps to his room …*

At last, there came a long respite; he began to hope the steps had ceased, or he had imagined them … But they resumed. The banister creaked and there was the unmistakable crack of the loose board outside his door ... He awaited with beating heart, the awkward revolutions of the broken doorknob. But there was nothing but the ominous silence of the night ...

It was their last evening on the island. For the past few nights, the footsteps had stopped, or else Robert had slept too deeply to notice them; and though Mrs Dennison's importunity persisted, the imminent prospect of his departure would soon bring to an end this nuisance. But in the night Robert woke, drenched with horror ... There were the footsteps again ... creeping up the stairs, firm and sly ... *Only Mr Moore* ...

But something was wrong ...

A shocking thought besieged him ... something Mrs Moore had said at supper-time ...

Mr Moore was not at home that night. He remembered Mrs Moore complaining: he was off to Liverpool for a football match, and staying over ... Whoever it might be out there on the landing, it could not be Mr Moore ...

Then who on earth could it be? A ghost? Nonsense! No such thing! They were only stories in a book. Dad was right, a load of old rubbish. He'd throw it in the bin first thing tomorrow!

Was it one of his parents? ... Mrs Moore?

No, not them. His shivered as he grasped the awful logic of the explanation ...

Mrs Dennison did not sleep well. He'd heard her himself, weeping in the dark hours. An insomniac, perhaps she prowled the house at night after everyone had gone to bed. But was it just insomnia? What was that story in his horrid book about a boy staying with a friend with a terrifying aunt? Hadn't that grim woman walked the house at night, spreading terror? Maybe the fearsome lodger was loitering outside his door, ready to come in and smile her tortured smile at him, to reach out and cuddle him ... or worse ...

Was she out there, lurking on the landing, biding her time, relishing her wicked moment, ready to steal into the room and pounce upon him ...

And, my God, there she was ...

The door-knob. The door-knob that was faulty. The door-knob that went through several revolutions before it would engage the catch ... was revolving and engaging ...

The next thing he knew was the light on in the room; his father asking what on earth all the shouting about. Robert's halting efforts to describe events did not elicit sympathy. And he realised that, even had he been sufficiently composed to give a clearer explanation, an account of plodding footsteps and a predatory lodger hardly carried conviction, except as the fantasia of nightmare.

Their return to the island did not begin auspiciously. It was clear, as *The Lady of Man* left the storm-wracked River Mersey, that it was going to be a rough crossing. The contrast with his maiden voyage, the magic summoning of sun-lit hills from over the horizon, could hardly have been more severe. The island was invisible behind sea-level cloud until they buffeted into Douglas Bay. The booming of the foghorn, dour and muffled, fell like a leaden weight upon his soul, presaging menace indefinable. A cold dank blanket hung everywhere as the exhausted family, pale-faced and irritable, queued outside the terminal for a cab. Robert didn't like it when he heard a local sailor call the mist, in almost reverential tones, 'Mona's Shroud'.

Robert felt confused when they arrived: for *Sunny Bank* looked different. Then he noticed: the sycamores had been felled. It made the house look more wholesome; there were bright flowers in the garden. In striking contrast to this welcome rebirth, however, the door was opened by a Mrs Moore looking ten years older. Her greeting sounded forced, all her gaiety had gone. Deep lines furrowed her rosy cheeks. She had noticeably lost weight. He could tell from his mother's expression that she too was shocked.

An explanation was soon forthcoming.

'Bill passed away last month,' she gasped through her sobs. 'Suddenly! A heart attack! I didn't like to mention it when you rang in case it put you off. The doctor had been saying for years he should drink less!'

His mother's commiseration was swept aside by a cataract of tears. There was more to come.

'It's been a bad year. Well … I suppose I ought to tell you,' she stammered, 'You remember that young couple—you know, the Russian girl? … The Dennisons? … '

She was pausing, as if unsure whether to proceed, eyeing Robert. Her voice dropped to a whisper. A shiver passed over him even before the words came tumbling out.

'One night, a few weeks ago – they'd come again for a holiday – she got up in the middle of the night while her husband was asleep. You know she suffered from insomnia? She used to have these fits, poor soul, when she'd cry and cry about the baby … the one she lost … Well, they found her in the morning … At the bottom of those old steps at Port Jack; broke her neck! Everyone thought she'd fallen, those steps being so dangerous, but they found a note …'

Mrs Moore sat down upon the hall chair, bereft of speech for some moments …

'She's buried in the graveyard over the road. The vicar wasn't keen. With it being a case of, well … you know … And not being a member of the parish. But her husband wanted her to stay on the island – the funeral and everything. It was where they'd had their honeymoon, see? Very sad.'

There was another tearful pause.

'But they had to lay her in unconsecrated ground,' she whispered.

'With it being … you know … The vicar was very firm – they stick to the old customs here … At the back of the church, near the shed where they keep the spades and things. Just a mound with a little stump of a cross, poor soul!'

Robert went cold all over. He recalled the graveyard: with its snub-nosed, mildewed angels peering through the brambles, its deadly-nightshade thickets, the briars and the nettles, the looming crosses … They had used it as a short cut to the shore, it cut off a big detour along the road.

Mrs Moore had shifted to more material concerns.

'It's been terrible for business,' she moaned, 'Word gets around. Rumour has it that it was here in this house she'd done it! Things had been getting bad enough anyway, what with people going to Majorca nowadays. We'd just begun a facelift on the house when Bill died. The place is still in a state.'

One welcome consequence of the disorder at *Sunny Bank* was that Robert would not have to sleep again in the dreaded 'master bedroom'. It was still only half-finished - Mr Moore had been doing the decorating himself. His parents were in their old room next door. Where then was Robert to sleep?

Already their hostess was leading him along the long dark corridor. Despite the freshly painted walls, it was as dark as ever, and the facelift had evidently not included repair of the electric light. Robert's heart sank. They had reached the end, next to the bathroom. Mrs Moore was ushering him into the bedroom - the bedroom where he had heard the night-time strains of bitter tears.

That night, as he climbed the stairs to bed, the horrors of last year returned with vivid clarity: the padding footsteps, the creaking board, the wailing, the brooding peril of long dark corridor - which had certainly lost nothing of its power to terrify.

His new bedroom had been the first to be re-done, said Mrs Moore. It sported gaily coloured floral wallpaper; though it was evident that Mr Moore had been no craftsman. There was one disturbingly huge double bed - the very one, probably, from which the crier in the night had arisen for her final journey to oblivion! ... Uneasily, he huddled beneath the covers, trying to muffle sounds.

Sleep did not come easily. He heard his parents shout 'goodnight' to Mrs Moore; and she retiring to the bedroom next to his. Faraway a dog barked, a car went past, and then there was a yowling - a cat no doubt on the prowl, yet dreadful to hear. Then, silence - the silence of the midnight hour, broken only by the muffled boom of the foghorn on the misty headland. Each time when he was on the brink of sleep, the dread visage of Mrs Dennison kept appearing in his mind ...

Then, horror of horrors, came the sound he didn't want to hear: footsteps, sidling down the long dark corridor – just like last year! *Only Mr Moore* ... Yet Mr Moore was dead! One more tread, terrifying in its finality! Whoever or whatever was responsible was now lurking on the threshold. Crouched, stooped or strutting on hind-legs, it was all the same – abomination was awaiting. But would it merely wait? Pray God, it wouldn't touch the door-handle ...

Breakfast was nearly over by the time he joined his mother at the table next morning. They were the only guests. It was a fine day, ideal for the beach. His father had already gone ahead. Robert's suggestion they take the longer route along the road got short shrift.

'What's wrong with the short cut?' his mother laughed, 'You're not afraid of a few old graves, are you? There's worse things to worry about than ghosts – you'll learn!'

Rooks were wheeling round the misty spire as they trod the narrow mossy alley to the church. An incessant croaking and a wild fluttering cut the morning air. The sun was shining through the lofty trees. Remnants of a heavy dew dripped from unkempt bushes, catching jewels of light. A metal gate led them first past recent graves, densely packed, glistening in the sunshine like a too-white set of new false teeth. Black and gold-lettered epitaphs leapt out, incongruously optimistic. They had reached the rotting wooden gate leading into the old part of the burial ground when his mother stopped.

'Damn!' she declared, 'I've forgotten my sunglasses, I'll have to go back ... You go on!'

Robert hesitated. 'No, go on, don't be silly!' she insisted, 'You know where we're meeting.'

Robert hurried ahead amidst the grim monuments and the mossy slabs swathed in briar. Some of the tombs were massive, too massive for the human scale, enclosed by iron railings; he wondered with a shudder what on earth they were hemming in. The canopy over one grave had cracked six inches wide: *Only Sleeping* read the lettering on the head-stone. Robert felt relieved, once past the yawning gap, that no unearthly claw had seized his ankle.

It must have been because he was in a hurry that he mistook the way. Momentarily, he could not recognise where he was. Black cypress sentinels and blood-red yews crowded round. Weird statues, winged or hooded, faces ravaged by weather, age or worse, loomed horribly. Instead of arriving at the main gate on the far side near the road, he found himself before the church, towering above the gaunt cypresses in ponderous gloom. He could see the wooden shed beyond the tower – the frontier of unconsecrated ground … Some yards away loomed the high crosses by the exit – but to get there meant passing near the awful woman's resting place – if resting was what happened in unconsecrated ground. Yet going back would involve wandering again amongst the gloating statues and the caged-in tombs, not to speak of braving the passage of the ankle-snatcher's crumbling abode.

Summoning his courage, he hurried on, to the sanctuary of the road. The scratching on his shoulder was only holly, but it distracted his attention. For a fraction of a second his eyes betrayed him: he scanned with fearful curiosity the rough wasteland at the back of the church, tearing his glance away with sufficient speed to make uncertain just what it was he thought he saw …

As he made his precipitate exodus, slipping on the green-slimed flagstones, he tried to tell himself that all he'd glimpsed – he could hear the echo of Mrs Moore's hushed tones – was 'just a mound with a little stump of a cross'.

All that evening Robert dreaded going to bed. When at last he did, he seemed to lie awake for hours, as the silence of the night settled like a shroud. He tried to think of pleasant things but couldn't rid his mind of the graveyard. *Only sleeping!* He tried counting sheep, dozing, jumping alert as he saw them leaping over a stumpy cross into a shallow grave … *Unconsecrated ground!* He tried not to recall what it was he thought he might have seen beyond the church.

Mrs Dennison's wasted features floated before him with a dreadful crystal clarity … the haggard eyes … the ghastly smile … the misshapen face … the tangled hair … the babbling English … the clutching and the cuddling …

At last he drifted off into a troubled sleep, awaking with a start, in the uneasy hinterland between sleep and consciousness. An evil dream lingered …

The sequence of the nightmare, if nightmare it was, unravelled before him: a crooked figure moving with a see-saw motion over the road from the church; twisting with repulsive gait up the garden steps; a wan grinning face tilting up towards the window; an awkward yet deliberate plodding down the long dark corridor, its abominable approach slow but inexorable …

Robert turned his eyes to the door …

He noticed with a surge of terror that the door into the room was open …

Approaching the bed was a hunched shape …

But it was not approaching … it was upon it …

As the pale fingers of the dawn caressed the room, the figure arose, ragged-haired, tall and menacing, eager arms reaching over, stretching out to grasp him …

OF GODS AND GHOSTS

Chester isn't just one of the oldest cities in Britain. In pure historical terms it is also one of the most dramatic. First built as a fortress by the Romans around 70 AD, a heritage that would be vividly remembered a thousand years later when in medieval times it was still referred to as the 'City of the Legions', it continues to flourish in the 21st century, its current population standing at 350,000. In the meantime, it has experienced almost everything the tumultuous last two millennia of British history could throw at it, and yet its ancient walls, as constructed by Emperor Vespasian, stand as dominant now as they ever did.

It is surely no surprise that Chester folk can tell hundreds of stories about their town in which the souls of the dead play prominent roles.

To start with, there has been much bloodshed here. The city's amphitheatre, which, with seating for 10,000, is the largest ever excavated in Britain, staged mass executions and brutal gladiatorial games for the best part of a century. In 616, at the height of the Dark Ages, King Aethelfrith of Northumbria slaughtered a massive Welsh army at Chester, and then massacred an entire monastery of local monks in retaliation for their offering prayers against him. Later on, invading Vikings captured the city and held it against numerous Saxon counterattacks, until Alfred himself drove them out by scorching all the city's farmland. Even more violent events occurred during the English Civil War, when Chester was subjected to an apocalyptic siege, which saw the population all but starved, and thousands upon thousands of troops killed trying to storm the walls or at the nearby battle of Rowton Heath (1645).

In simple architectural terms, Chester – so many times damaged in battle and rebuilt again, often in quick, arbitrary fashion – is now a curious hotchpotch of the old, the new and the ancient. The city centre, particularly the area around Watergates, comprises buildings representative of all ages and styles, many of them mixed together. It is said that numerous rooms and floors here are separated only by inches of wood and stone but also by centuries.

And ghosts and spirits walk through all of them.

The esoteric history of Chester dates back to its origins. The fortress from which it sprang, Deva Victrix, was named after the goddess of the nearby River Dee, who was believed to wield great power in the district, which Roman worshippers tapped into, while one of the best-preserved monuments from that era, the Shrine to Minerva in Handbridge, has been the centre of mystic beliefs and arcane practices since the second century. There are other traces of the Roman supernatural: sightings of a cloaked, spear-carrying legionary pacing between Vicars Lane, where the amphitheatre stood, to the old watchtower at Newgate, were reported as long ago as Tudor times, and are still reported today. Legend tells that this was Decurion, a junior officer whose desire for a local lass led him to break the fort's security and accidentally enable a raiding party of Britons to sneak inside and cause chaos, killing Decurion in the process. The tramping of booted feet, possibly the sound of other Roman soldiers on the march, has been heard in the cellars of several Chester pubs now known to have been built on the site of an ancient military cemetery.

The medieval period also provided Chester with notable ghosts.

Shadowy monastic figures have been seen and heard praying and chanting in various of the antique religious buildings in the city, but also in modern structures, such as garages and workshops, which were erected on the site of earlier churches and shrines. Chester Cathedral boasts what is possibly the eeriest tale of this sort, when in the 12th century, a demonic presence was invoked in the city, causing hideous hauntings, but also poisoning crops and bringing illness to the animal population. Eventually, the bishop managed to exorcise the entity, and had the image of a chained imp carved high in the clerestory window of the cathedral's nave as a memento of the city's successful struggle against evil, and as a warning to any further demons planning similar forays.

Despite this, infernal horror was never far from Chester.

Three women – the so-called Boughton Witches – were hanged on Gallows Hill in Chester in 1656, having been convicted of causing death through sorcery. The grim tale had an unexpected sequel in 1898, when a certain Michael Globe, who was researching the case, claimed that he'd been visited by the trio's malignant spirits, which ordered him to desist. Globe allegedly refused and died later while visiting their execution site.

But despite these lurid and rather sensational events, most of Chester's paranormal past comprises tales of the miserable and mundane, from the Elizabethan maid who still gazes in through the windows of the property where the family lived who had made her homeless and caused her death by exposure, to a young man whose spectre lingers in the public toilets where he slit his wrists back in the 1960s, from jilted lovers to drunks, drug addicts, destitute sailors and shell-shocked soldiers, all of whom failed to find happiness in the afterlife; an indication maybe that, despite its history of arcane mystery and epic event, Chester's biggest problem, like all modern cities, is, and always has been, a surfeit of social issues and the subsequent fallout of human misery.

PEELING THE LAYERS
Sam Stone

'We saw her this morning,' Meeks said.

'Where?' Edwin asked.

'In the lake, Sir. Floating.'

Edwin stared out of the window down across the vast gardens. He didn't own Heaton Hall or the estate beyond but was responsible for another inherited legacy nonetheless.

The house was opened up occasionally by the 'Friends of Heaton Hall'. This was one such day, and Edwin always made sure he was there on open days. 'You know what to do,' he said to Meeks.

Meeks nodded and went away to take care of the task.

'There hasn't been a body for a while,' a voice said behind him.

Edwin turned to see Elise standing in the doorway. She was wearing a long flowing dress in the Empire Line style. 'Not getting into the part today then?' he said.

'Not unless you think it will help.'

Edwin turned back to the window. The sun was rising, dawn was almost upon them, soon the staff would arrive to unshutter the house in preparation for open day.

Elise came to his side and looked out at the flowing landscape.

'Almost show time.' She was amused. She always enjoyed the drama.

Edwin saw no humour in what would happen in the next few hours.

'I've always loved this place,' said Alex as they walked up the huge staircase. 'I really wanted to show you it. It's part of my childhood. Part of my life here in Manchester. Long before we met.'

'I know,' said Victor. 'And I want to know everything about you.'

'It's odd though. They stopped opening the place regularly to visitors. And I haven't been since … I was about thirteen, I guess.'

'Why does the place mean so much to you?' Victor asked.

'Perhaps I had a romantic view of it. As a child … Linked to puberty probably. Why else?'

'That's the shrink part of you talking,' Victor said as he smiled at her. Something he rarely did.

Alex didn't respond. She too was given to being serious. Instead she considered why Heaton Hall still intrigued her.

'I like old houses,' she said as though speaking her thoughts aloud.

'This is more a folly though … Like Penrhyn Castle. Which you also loved as I recall.'

'Not as much as this place.'

They passed through a roped-off bedroom that appeared ready to sleep in. Alex studied all of the old furniture but made no comment. It amused Victor, because no one embraced the modern world more than her. She never liked anything in their house that wasn't in vogue and the style of these old castles and houses she wanted to visit was so far removed from her own personal taste that it was impossible to reconcile her fascination with the old against her obsession with the new. She loved to see these places. Even now her eyes glowed with interest as she paused at the rope and stared into the gloomy room.

Victor found himself wondering what it was she sought in the darkened corners of the space. Did she imagine the original owner's wife lounging on the chaise? Did she romanticise the apparent simplicity of their opulent wealth? He tried not to analyse her but it was difficult not to. Alex was, on the surface, just as calm and collected and professional as Victor, but often he felt that she had layers that one day he may peel away. What was underneath intrigued him the most. There was something about her past, something from her childhood that led her into the psychiatry profession and it wasn't the same thing that motivated his career choice. Victor wanted to learn what that was.

'Do you like history?' he asked her.

'I'm interested in it of course. It's part of what makes us who we are … the baggage our parents brought from the past.'

Alex turned away from the bedroom and moved on deeper into the house. Victor followed. She ensnared him.

'Tell me about the last time you came here,' he said.

'I don't remember the last time exactly. More a culmination of times. There was a summer spent paddling in the children's pool in the kids' play area. I haven't shown you that yet. But there's swings, slide, seesaw … the usual. But also this shallow paddling pool. It was a very hot summer that year. I recall going on the boats on the lake … a few times over the years too. Not many. Lots of walking around the grounds. I always loved looking in the house. I probably did that most. Yet … I didn't remember the rooms. This feels like I'm seeing it all for the first time.'

'What else did you do here?'

'Horse riding. I wasn't very good, but I came here on the occasional Saturday. I was at high school by then. Maybe eleven or twelve. I had a friend who had a horse and once or twice I'd spent a weekend helping her muck out the stable. But as girls are, she and another friend were cruel. They laughed because I had to wash my hands before we ate our lunch. I don't recall if that was why I didn't help again. But I liked the horses. Wanted to ride. So I came here instead.'

'Who brought you to the park on Saturdays?'

'No one.'

'Did you come with friends?'

'No.'

'Totally unsupervised?'

'I was never afraid to be alone.'

Victor knew that this was true. Alex was comfortable in her own company. Perhaps more so than in his.

He took her hand but her fingers slipped from his grasp as she hurried on into another room.

Why was it she was still so elusive? Even after all this time. He followed her. She was a shadow, a ghost, a flame that would never burn out.

'Can I help you?' said a voice beside him.

'I'm here with ...' he pointed in the direction Alex had flown. Then he turned to find a beautiful woman watching him. She wasn't the usual type to work in a heritage site - usually retired volunteers were on hand to give historical context.

'This part of the house is off limits,' the woman said. 'I'll show you back to the Friends' tour guide.'

'But my fiancée ...' he said.

'Don't worry. Someone will guide her back.'

Victor followed the woman down a staircase he hadn't previously noticed. It was a back entrance - a servants' staircase perhaps.

'Through that door,' she said, pointing to a large framed, oversized door ahead.

Victor went towards it. As he opened the door he turned to thank the woman, but she had already moved on. Probably through some secret passage-way. He would enjoy telling Alex when she finally found her way back to the group.

'This way,' said the guide.

Victor tagged on at the back. He searched the faces of the others on the tour. Then followed a half an hour of history, and explanations, none of which he could take in. The truth was he was growing more and more concerned that Alex hadn't found her way back.

The tour came to an end and the group was escorted outside of the house. Victor looked around with dismay. 'Where is she?' he muttered to himself.

'You okay there?' said a teenage girl who was walking a small dog.

'My fiancée ... I think she's still inside.'

The doors of the house were now firmly closed. Victor tried them. They appeared to be locked. He knocked. But no one came.

'She can't be,' said the girl. 'That place has been shut for ages. They don't let anyone look inside anymore.'

'But I just went on the tour.'

'What tour?'

Victor looked back at the door from which he had just left the house. There was a sign now pasted on it.

HEATON HOUSE. CLOSED FOR RENOVATION.

Victor was confused. He walked towards the car park and searched for his car. There were cars of all kinds there. But not his sparkling new Jaguar. The area looked different too. Unkempt. Dated.

He became aware of the clothing that the people around him wore also. It was wrong somehow. Though not being much for fashion he couldn't be sure why.

He returned to the house. Walking the perimeter, he searched for Alex. Where was she? How had she simply disappeared? He was frantic and then he recalled his mobile phone. He went into his pocket. He'd call her. This had to be some kind of prank.

The phone was warm in his cold hands. The weather had gone from very warm summer to a cold early autumn. He dialled Alex's number, but the phone rejected it.

There was no signal.

He went back to the house. Banged now on the door. No one came to open it. Victor's nerve cracked when he looked around and found the grounds now totally deserted. Unlike Alex he did not like to be alone. Especially in open places.

Victor experienced a feeling of vulnerability. His head hurt. His eyes stung and panic tightened his throat.

Where was the teenager with the dog at least?

Not knowing what to do, Victor reasoned he must find a park employee to help him find Alex. He walked down the long driveway from the house toward the boating lake. But this place was deserted too. The payment booth was closed. No boats were on the lake. Instead they were all stored and tied up on the island in the centre. Victor climbed over the fence and walked toward the edge of the lake. Then he saw her. *Floating*. Like an angel in a calm sea. Beautiful and … dead. Very dead …

'*Sir?*'

Victor snapped out of his reverie.

'Did you want to hire a boat?'

The area was buzzing with life once more. Victor blinked. He saw the row boats and pedalos working their way around the lake. He found he was squinting into now glaring sunlight. Gone was the autumnal air that had stung him.

'Body …' he said.

'Oh, that old tale …'

'Tale?' said Victor.

'About the woman who was found in the lake. About twenty years ago now. She was thirty-two. With her fiancé. They went into the house but she vanished. Then, later, she was found drowned in the lake.'

'A story …?'

'Well. No one ever really found a body here. But the fiancé insisted he saw her. They dredged the lake but they never found her.'

Victor looked down at his hands. He saw now the markings of liver spots. Markings that hadn't been there before. Confused he headed back up to the house. There he saw a sign saying 'Open Day'.

'Hello,' said a woman standing by the door. 'We have one space left on the final tour if you're alone.'

Victor looked up and recognised her from somewhere. She wasn't the sort he'd expect to find working a heritage site. They were usually retired folks who had lots of historical information to impart.

Victor had a feeling of *déjà vu* as he followed her inside.

They went up a staircase. He didn't speak as he followed. But the more they walked, the more familiar the woman became to him …

'Victor?' she said.

She gave him one of her rare smiles.

'*Alex* …'

She took his hand. 'What did you want to know?'

'Know?'

'There's a reason you wanted to visit something from my

childhood. Are you having second thoughts?'

Victor shook his head. 'Never.'

'Not even ...'

He pulled her to him. 'Never Alex. I love you.'

She slipped from his grasp. And though she was a grown woman of thirty-two, she ran on through the house like a schoolgirl being chased by a horny, unwelcome suitor.

Victor rose to the bait and gave chase. He forgot who he was sometimes. That serious side faded. Listening to the crazed minds of those he treated could alter a man. It could taint your soul. But Alex ... she *freed* him.

She ran downstairs. One of the old volunteers came out of a room in the house to frown at them. But Alex didn't notice. She was clear of some burden that her childhood had given her. Now she let that inner, frightened creature loose.

He followed. He felt like a dog in heat. He had to possess her. Always. But she was light on her feet, and Victor, not being the sporty type, struggled to keep up.

He caught her - because she wanted to be caught - by the boating lake.

By then the mid-afternoon sun was fading, the park rapidly emptying. Victor kissed Alex in an uncharacteristic display of public affection.

'What's got into you?' she asked.

'You have. The layer we just peeled.'

'What layer?'

'I know Alex. I know what happened to you.'

Alex frowned.

'I know now why you became a shrink. You genuinely feel you can help.'

'Of course. That's why any of us went into the profession isn't it? That and interest in the human psyche.'

'Murderers fascinate me. So do victims ...'

'You work with the darkest ... I know,' she said.

Victor noted that Alex's frown remained. He could see that vulnerable child now. The one who couldn't remember what the rooms in the house looked like. But so wanted to return to look into the dark shadows for that deep horror she had faced.

The layer he had been hoping to peel fell away as he saw the fear and doubt appear on her face.

'What happened in the house?'

'What do you mean?'

'You ran away … got lost.'

'I could never get lost in there,' she said. 'It's outside that …'

She fell silent.

Victor picked the scab. 'The horse riding …'

'What about it?'

'It's a metaphor for another memory.'

'Don't be ridiculous.'

'What was the name of the horse you rode?'

'I don't recall …'

'You don't recall because it never happened. How many times did you go riding?'

Alex's frown deepened. 'What is this?'

They were by the boat house now. Alex looked away from him, over at the lake. 'Should we hire a boat? I like to row,' she said.

She took his hand, but Victor could still see the frown. His fascination with her grew. Maybe he hadn't peeled the right layer yet. But there was abuse there. He knew it.

Her bravado had gone. For the first time he saw her uncertain and the normal confidence she exuded appeared to be a distant memory. She examined his face with an expression akin to *fear*…

'The lake …' he murmured.

'What?'

'*Floating*. In the lake.'

'Stop it Victor!'

Victor stared out over the water. There was no body in the lake. But he knew she had been there twenty years ago.

'Sir?' said the boat attendant. 'Did you want to hire a boat?'

Victor turned away and walked back up the hill towards the house. The door was open and the beautiful girl who had guided him down the back stairs earlier was waiting.

'Is this hell?' he asked her.

'Come inside Victor,' she said. 'I'm Elise.'

He followed her in. They passed the tour unseen as they walked back upstairs.

'I saw her in the lake. I peeled and prodded the wound of her childhood. *I caused it.*'

He noticed that Elise was wearing an Empire Line gown. She took his hand.

'You come back here every year, trying to make sense of Alex's disappearance,' she said, 'but still you don't remember what happened.'

Victor shook his head.

'It's time we peeled *your* layers ...' said Edwin behind them.

Victor turned and looked at the man. He was familiar, but Victor did not know why.

'*Remember* ...' said Elise.

Edwin took Victor's other hand ...

'Stop it Victor!' said Alex.

'Come on Alex, we're getting married next week ...'

'Not here. What's the matter with you?'

The boathouse was deserted and the park was just a short time from closing. Across the lake the boats were already moored, and the attendants had left, locking the barrier to prevent anyone coming into this area unsupervised. Victor and Alex had hidden for devilment – Alex's idea.

'There's no one around. We could go for a swim at least. Maybe cross to the island and borrow a boat for a little while.'

'Okay,' Victor said.

Alex stripped down to her bra and pants and Victor stripped to his underpants. They left their clothing by the boathouse and then, sitting on the edge of the concrete mooring, they dangled their feet into the water.

Alex braved it first. Victor wondered if it was because she felt vulnerable in her underwear. Once submerged, she pushed away from the side and began to swim.

Victor slid into the water. It was cold and his breath caught as it engulfed him. Then, following Alex's lead he swam out into the lake. It was bracing and fun. Moving made him less aware of the cold and his limbs naturally warmed up as he followed her. Alex was a good swimmer, better than Victor, but he was secure enough that he knew he could make it all the way across to the island.

'We're professionals,' he thought as guilt for any misdemeanour often reared its head in the middle of the fun. 'We shouldn't be here.'

One of the things that Victor loved about Alex was her spontaneity. But it also worried him. She seemed so serious and controlled and then, there were these moments, flashes really, of … he couldn't even think of the correct word but the closest was rebellion.

Alex reached the island and was carefully selecting a boat. She pushed one into the water and then she watched Victor as he swam towards her.

Before untying it, Alex placed the two oars in the boat.

'Come on Victor you slow poke!' she called.

That layer again flashed across her face. Bravery, strength. She wasn't afraid of anything.

Victor reached the boat.

'Get in,' Alex said. She untied the mooring rope as soon as he was in place. Then she climbed in beside him.

Victor was tired from the cold water and the lack of practice in swimming such a distance. He rowed the boat into the centre of the lake though, and there they sat, floating on the water.

Then Alex took over the rowing for a while. Victor watched as her arms moved with ease. His future wife was strong mentally and physically.

'Tell me more about your childhood …' he asked again.

'Oh, that old chestnut!' she laughed. 'As much as you'd love to be rescuing me from a horrific past, I will have to disappoint you, darling. I didn't have a terrible childhood. In fact, my parents were pretty boring. Dad, as you know, was a paramedic. Mum, a nurse. They both wanted me to become a doctor. But I don't think they expected me to be a psychiatrist.'

Victor knew this. She'd told him several times. But what she didn't like to talk about was the day they both died. It was a layer he really wanted to peel ...

'Darling,' he said. 'How did they—?'

'You're tired,' she said. 'I'll drop you back near the boathouse.'

Victor didn't argue because he really believed he couldn't make the swim back.

After he climbed out of the boat, he pulled on his clothes as Alex rowed back to the island. She dragged the boat back into place and firmly tied the mooring rope. Then she waved to him and waded back into the water. He watched her silent grimace as the cold touched her skin. She mimed a shudder for him and then laughed, plunging confidently back into the water.

She took up a strong crawl but as she reached the halfway point she paused. Treading water, she began to look around her. Then Victor became aware of a vibration that flowed through the water. The land beneath his feet shook. Surely it couldn't be an earthquake? Not here, in England!

He cupped his hands around his mouth and called to her. 'Keep swimming!'

Alex began again and then the cold of the water found the tiredness in her limbs. She wasn't as strong as she thought she was.

Cramp! Victor thought.

'Lie back!' he yelled. 'Float, Alex!'

She tried to.

Victor was rooted to the spot with fear. He'd never faced any real adversity and now, not being the best swimmer, he was torn between self-preservation and the fear that she would drown.

'I'll get help!' he cried.

Alex turned, she fought against the cramp and struggled closer to the boat house. But the pain swallowed her, as did the water.

'Alex!' he yelled. 'Oh God! Alex!'

'What are you doing here?' said a voice behind him.

Victor turned to see the boat attendant.

'There's a woman. Drowning in the lake!'

The attendant looked out. 'I don't see anyone.'

'She went under! Please you have to help her!'

The attendant went and unlocked the boathouse. Inside, a petrol-powered boat was moored in a shallow gulley of water. He climbed in and drove the boat out.

'Over there!' shouted Victor. 'She was over there!'

The man steered the boat to the spot. He even jumped into the water and swam under.

But there was no sign of Alex ...

'It was my fault,' said Victor to Elise.

Edwin and Elise released his hands.

'No,' said Edwin. 'It was unfortunate. She was in the wrong place at the wrong time.'

'If I hadn't pushed her to talk. If I had been brave enough to go back in the water for her ...'

Edwin and Elise exchanged a look. *Tell him,* Elise thought. Edwin nodded. It was time.

'Alex is caught in a rift,' Edwin said. 'A time-shift. And you are linked to her. It's why you come back every year and relive this same moment over and over. It's also why you'll leave here today and not remember coming back.'

'I don't understand,' said Victor. 'I lost the love of my life. She drowned.'

'She's not dead,' said Elise. 'Take comfort, Victor. She'll never be dead.'

'This is old land,' said Edwin. 'It belongs to creatures who choose never to be seen. But sometimes their world leaks out into ours. Alex is caught there. Eventually they will pull her across into their world permanently. Time moves differently in the underworld.'

'Who are you people?' asked Victor.

'Guardians,' said Edwin. 'We're here to make sure this never happens again.'

Elise escorted Victor out of the house, and back to his own time. Then she returned to the upstairs room that overlooked the gardens.

'He'll be all right,' Edwin said.

'I know. But how many more years must he suffer?'

'You know what they are like. They'll take her in eventually. It just takes time. For *empathy* to set in.'

'Do they even understand emotions as we do?' Elise asked. 'After all the fae aren't human and never will be.'

'Unlike us, who once were ...' Edwin said.

Elise stood beside him and gazed out over the gardens as though she were remembering a time when she too was caught between worlds.

'It's time,' said Elise.

A light brighter than human eyes could tolerate burned in the corner of the room. Elise and Edwin turned and walked towards it. Elise suspected they'd be back. Not too soon, but certainly in a year's time when the *flow* happened and the other dimension leaked into the world of humans. Then, Edwin and Elise would have to return. So may Alex and Victor, to live their day over again.

'I hope they free her soon,' Elise said.

'So do I. The pain of being caught ... like that ...'

'Don't think of it,' Elise said. 'We've done the best we can.'

They melded with the light and then Meeks, following behind, watched as the two unnatural beings became part of an old and faded painting. As the couple turned to face outward, he threw a white cloth over the frame plunging the picture into darkness.

The portal had closed.

Meeks looked around the room confused. He couldn't recall what he had done all day. He picked up his broom and began to sweep away the dusty footprints left by the visitors.

THE BORGIAS OF THE SLUMS

Though they may lack the bloodlust of other serial killers, though they don't go for rape or torture or dismemberment, though they don't offer their victims to the Devil, or send cryptic letters to the police, perhaps the most reviled mass murderers in the modern world are the so-called 'black widows'. Invariably female, these scheming, cold-blooded individuals tend towards a much subtler modus operandi, befriending, caring for and sometimes even marrying lonely, isolated men, and then disposing of them at the first opportunity, usually by poison, to take possession of their wealth and property, or to benefit from any insurance policy that might be in force – and in many cases, to make a good living from this heinous activity.

Maybe the most shocking aspect of this type of crime is the perceived unnaturalness of it. With females normally held to be the nurturers in society, the mere thought that they might use this reputation to inveigle their way into the trust of innocent persons with the sole intent of killing them and acquiring everything they own is quite shudder-inducing. Thankfully, they are a rare breed of criminal, and yet every one of them scores highly on the scale of evil, none more so than two of the original role models for this kind of thing, two Liverpool women of the late-19th century.

Margaret and Catherine Flannagan were a pair of Irish sisters, who, in 1880, managed a run-down boarding house on Skirving Street in the north of the city. Various other characters lived on the premises at the same time, but few of them were destined to live for long. The first to die in mysterious circumstances was Catherine's 22-year-old son, John. Previously a specimen of good health, he declined overnight and expired without explanation. At this early stage no alarm was raised, even though Catherine was awarded a handsome insurance pay-out from the Burial Society. Margaret, meanwhile, had entered a romantic relationship with another lodger, Tom Higginson, whose eight-year-old daughter unexpectedly died in 1882, shortly after the two of them were married, for which the Burial Society again made a generous payment.

More deaths occurred the following year. Margaret Jennings, a young woman who lived at the same address, was the next to expire, compensation again provided by the Burial Society. By this time, neighbours were becoming suspicious even if the authorities weren't. In fact, so pressurised by gossip did the two sisters feel that they moved house - not once but twice, though they remained in Liverpool and otherwise appeared to make no change to their lifestyle.

It was later that same year, 1883, when Tom Higginson collapsed and died. A doctor diagnosed alcohol poisoning, but Higginson's brother did not believe this and held a private investigation, discovering that his deceased sibling had been insured with five separate Burial Societies, the net result of which was that his widow, Margaret, became a wealthy woman.

When this evidence was brought to the attention of the police, an investigation was launched. In fact, the Liverpool Coroner interrupted the actual wake to take charge of the body. Very suspiciously, Catherine Flannagan immediately fled the premises. Margaret remained, but when arsenic derived from fly paper was found in the corpse, as well as on both her and her sister's clothing (in addition to being all over their house), she was arrested. It took another few days to track Catherine down - she was hiding in a rooming house in Wavertree at the time.

Not long after this, the other corpses were exhumed, and they too contained traces of the lethal substance. In an apparent effort to muddy the waters, Margaret confessed that she and her sister were guilty as suspected, but also claimed responsibility for seven other deaths not immediately connected to their family from which they had also obtained financial benefits. She added that she and her sister had not acted alone, implying that a circle of five or six 'black widow' murderesses and corrupt insurers was operating in the city, offering support and assistance to each other as they profited from killing. Several names were named, more arrests were made, and fearsome police interrogations held, but it was clear from the outset that evidence would be thin against all but the two sisters.

In due course, it was Catherine Flannagan and Margaret Higginson who were charged, convicted and who mounted the gallows side by side at Kirkdale Prison, Liverpool, on March 3, 1884.

An air of horror had surrounded the trial, not least because suspicion was strong that other felons had escaped justice and maybe that other victims were still unaccounted for. Only 1,000 subdued spectators attended the execution, which was a small crowd by the standards of the time, the population of the city appalled that two women could have performed such ghastly deeds. So intense was the revulsion that the sisters were later referred to by former friends and neighbours as the 'Borgias of the Slums', while their death masks were among the first wave of exhibits added to the new expanded Chamber of Horrors at Madame Tussauds Wax Museum in the late 1880s.

ROOT CAUSE
Ramsey Campbell

I sat behind my second pint of beer and pretended to be unaware. Over by the billiard table a man in motorcycle leathers was selling a Japanese television: next to the fruit machine three sharp-faced youths in impeccable pastel suits seemed to be muttering about the supermarket across the road. Whenever I glanced at my book in case they thought I was watching, Vladimir said 'We're waiting for Godot.' They must have suspected I could hear them, for suddenly all three were staring at me across the archipelago of tables, the frayed beermats and greying ashtrays. I headed for the door while gulping the last of the beer. In the doorway a girl of about sixteen was loitering. I hurried, anxious not to be late for work, and had reached the wasteland of the intersection when I saw the children beneath the overpass.

They were clambering up the concrete pillars as though the tangled graffiti were vines, towards the roadway overhead. Precisely because I was nervous, I had to intervene. I mustn't flinch away because their lives weren't like mine.

As I reached the concrete island in the middle of the crossroads, the children came scrambling down. They had almost dodged into the traffic before they saw I wasn't following. 'He isn't anyone,' said a ten-year-old, the daytime mother of the group. 'He's only the library man.'

'You mustn't play under there. You might hurt yourselves.' I felt absurdly pompous, but I could only be true to myself. 'If you come to the library, I'll find you some books to read.'

'Come here till I tell you something,' the ten-year-old hissed to the others. When she had finished whispering, one boy peered beadily at me. 'Are you a queer, mister?' he said.

'Certainly not.' But I knew how my middle-class accent,

stiffened by years of elocution classes, must sound. The concrete gloom pressed down, the muffled hissing of the cars overhead made the pillars sound like trees, and I was afraid that if I went towards the children they would run into the traffic without looking. 'Don't come to the library if you don't want to,' I said, turning away.

Of course I hoped that would lure them in. Certainly the library needed enlivening. Presumably the plate-glass walls had been intended to attract readers to the tens of thousands of new books, but when I arrived the place was almost deserted. The librarian gave me and the clock a sharp glance, and I hurried to deposit my coat in the staffroom, burping loudly enough to wake an old man who was dozing over the racing pages.

When I emerged, the children were swaggering toward the junior section. The uniformed attendant went after them at once, eager as a policeman on his first beat. Within a minute they were eluding him in four directions, punching the books as they ran, until the shelves looked gap-toothed. The librarian helped chase them while I served a pregnant woman who was returning an armful of overdue books. I didn't charge her a fine, for she already had three children, and I'd seen her husband a few minutes ago, drinking away his unemployment benefit in the Viscount of Knowsley. All at once my neck felt exposed and red-hot, for the librarian was frowning at me, but she hadn't seen me waive the rules. 'Brian, did you tell those children to come in here?'

'Yes I did, Mrs Smullen. They didn't seem to have anywhere else to go.'

'They most certainly have. They ought to be at school. If they choose to play truant, they mustn't think they have a refuge here. And apart from that, you saw how they behaved.'

If the attendant had left them alone they might have found themselves books to read, but I refrained from saying so: I was on probation at the library for the first six months. As the afternoon wore on I stuck labels in books, dealt with a few readers, woke up a snoring drunk, read a landlord's letter to an old lady. The girl who had been loitering in the doorway of the

Viscount sat waiting for her mother, a plump pink woman with the fixed thoughtless smile of an inflatable doll. At last the mother appeared in the lobby, beside a man who was averting his face, and beckoned her daughter out. I tried to watch where they went, but Mrs Smullen was saying 'You weren't to know about those children, I suppose. You'll learn when you've been here a few weeks. I know it comes as a shock that anyone can live the way these people do.'

But they had no choice, I thought as I waited for the bus that night outside the library. They were trapped here in the new town, miles out of the city from which they'd been rehoused. Half the firms which had promised jobs had set up factories elsewhere instead. That was why the overpass was empty now, robbed of the heavy traffic which had been supposed to feed the town.

The April twilight settled on the tower blocks - you couldn't tell it was spring out here, except by the green tips of the saplings beside the intersection - and I grew nervous about whether the bus had broken down, leaving me to wait another hour. Nothing moved on the narrow fenced-in pavements, the pale roads. Few people went out at night here, for there was nowhere to go. The overpass stood like a huge grey humped insect, a dozen legs supporting its midriff, and I found its utter stillness oppressive. It was enough to make me nervous all by itself.

Ten minutes later it was smudged by darkness. Now it looked like a petrified clump of trees. If I stared at it long enough I thought that the children were back again, clambering. Once I was sure that they were, and made a fool of myself by hurrying to look. For a moment I thought they had dodged across to the trees and were peering out at me, as if anyone could hide there: the saplings were no thicker than the poles which were teaching them posture.

I didn't give them a second glance, for I had almost missed the bus. The driver grudgingly opened the doors, and sped up the overpass ramp. I could never understand why buses used the overpass, especially now when the roads were deserted. As the bus reached the top, he grimaced - perhaps at the sight of the miles of tower blocks with their racks of windows, or the way the bus juddered in a stray wind, or the only other passenger, who was complaining to nobody in particular that his nose was bleeding again. Neither of them worried me. Now that I was on the bus, I felt safe.

I felt safe until the next morning, when I saw the police cars outside the supermarket. The shattered hole beside the main lock made it clear what had happened, but I already knew. A policeman was talking to the manager, who wore a dark suit and five o'clock shadow. 'Nine televisions, eight music centres,' the manager was saying, like a belated carol of Christmas spending. I hurried into the library as if I were the culprit, averting my face.

I felt as if I were, but what could I have done? I had only suspicions to offer, and yesterday I would have had even less. Certainly I had no proof. Still, I felt on edge to speak to the police as I unlocked the front door to let in the old men. In they trooped, to squabble over the first read of the newspapers.

I was stamping books at the counter when the police found the guard dog on the island beneath the overpass. As they carried it back to the supermarket I saw how its glassy-eyed head lolled, how the fur of its throat was darkly matted. I was angry, but I was more afraid, and very glad to be helping someone search for books when the police came to ask the librarian if she'd noticed anything suspicious yesterday. Until they left, I was afraid they would ask me.

And as soon as they left I was furious with myself, of course. The three youths would never have known that I was the one who had told the police. But then, I realised as lunchtime approached, they weren't the type that would need to be sure, and that made me nervous enough to stay away from the Viscount of Owsley in case they had seen the police in the library.

I was too tense to stay with Mrs Smullen when we closed for lunch. Instead I went walking among the tower blocks. Draughty doorless entrances gaped everywhere, broken glass glittered on stairs, graffiti dwarfed the walls. Here and there I passed terraces with ragged lawns and crippled fences; most of the houses were boarded up. On one of the few larger areas of green I saw children dragging a large plastic letter K and an N through the mud, which explained what had happened to the Viscount. Around the green, injured saplings tried to lean on splintered poles. It occurred to me that the only untouched saplings I'd seen were by the overpass.

I was on edge all day, and glad to leave. A teacher reserved all our junior books on ancient Britain for a school project, the teenage girl and her doll-faced mother strolled along opposite sides of the main road, slowing whenever they heard a car. That night as I waited for the bus I saw how the road stood over the place where the dog had been found, like a spider photographed in the act of seizing its prey. Had the thieves hidden the dog over there, or had it dragged itself? I found that until the bus was beyond the overpass, everything made me nervous – the way the driver grinned to himself, the smell of the raw meat which the woman at the far end of the bus must be carrying, even the distant chanting that drifted up from below, no doubt football songs in the Viscount. Once they'd begun singing football songs when I was in the pub, and I'd felt more out of place than ever.

At least next day was Thursday, my day off in the week. That afternoon I sat for a while on the pavilion and watched the bowlers, old soldiers and retired businessmen whose moustaches were neat as the green. I could almost believe there was nothing more important than the unhurried click of bowls. Later I strolled through the house of the family which owned the estate: elegant roped-off rooms, portraits safe in the past. Usually while I was there I could pretend I had stepped back in time, but now the house reminded me how I was trying to forget about tomorrow.

When I arrived at the library, it was worse. Overnight half the windows had been smashed. Mrs Smullen watched the workmen, her lips pursed, as they nailed boards over the gaps. She looked furious with everyone – no doubt the police had wakened her during the night – and I hardly dared say good morning. Besides, I was trying to ignore a secret fear that the windows had been smashed as a warning to me.

Now there was no daylight in the library. I was boxed in with relentless fluorescent light, like a laboratory animal. At lunchtime I sat on the far side of the staffroom from Mrs Smullen and tried to hush the pages of the Vonnegut novel I was reading. I was afraid to show my face in the Viscount of Owly.

All at once, halfway through the afternoon, I was enough on edge to say 'Shouldn't we do something about that girl?'

She was sitting at a bare table, waiting for her doll-faced mother and whoever she might bring. 'What do you suggest we do?' Mrs Smullen said.

I ignored her sarcastic emphasis. 'Well, I don't know, but surely there must be something,' I pleaded, fighting to keep my voice low. 'She can't be more than sixteen years old, and her mother seems to sell her to anyone who comes along.'

'As a matter of fact I happen to know she's thirteen.' Before I could react to that, she turned on me. 'But what exactly are you implying? Are you alleging that I would allow my library to be used in that way?'

I might have been too shocked to pretend that I wasn't. In particular her words dismayed me: suggest, imply, allege – the language of a cautious newspaper. I hadn't replied when a woman came in with an armful of books. 'See to the counter, please,' Mrs Smullen said.

The books were overdue, and I felt frustrated enough to take a sadistic delight in counting up the fines. When I announced the total, the woman stared unblinking at me. 'My friend owed more than that the other day and you didn't charge her,' she said.

Mrs Smullen intervened at once. 'We aren't authorised to waive fines. If your friend wasn't charged it must have been an oversight, and she should count herself lucky.'

When the woman had gone, leaving her ticket with the unpaid fine and muttering that she'd rather watch television anyway, Mrs Smullen demanded 'Is that true? Have you been waiving fines?'

'Well, there was one lady, that woman's friend.' In fact there had been several. 'She was pregnant for the umpteenth time, and her husband's unemployed.'

'I pay quite enough tax to keep people like her without

encouraging them. Because you're new I'll overlook this, but if it happens again I shall have to mention it in your probationary report,' she said, turning away.

I might have retorted that it was also public money that paid her wages, but of course I didn't dare. Instead I tried to lose myself in work, though I was neurotically aware of every one of her movements, wherever she was in the library. The sky darkened, the fluorescent light seemed to intensify, the glossy spines of books glared discordantly. By the time Mrs Smullen went for her afternoon break, it was pouring with rain.

As soon as the staffroom door closed behind her, I glanced about. Apart from the old men snoozing and mumbling at the tables, the library was deserted, and I didn't think that anyone else would come in until the rain eased off. I hurried to the phone at once, and called the police.

Immediately I heard a voice, I told it about the young girl and her mother. I'd hoped that would make me feel I had achieved something at last, but I only felt uncomfortably furtive, as guilty as if I were making a hoax call. Of course I didn't give my name, and wouldn't let the owner of the voice put me through to someone else. I replaced the receiver hastily, and spent five minutes worrying that Mrs Smullen had heard the ring.

The girl at the table had found a picture book of Spain and was leafing through it rather wistfully, but I couldn't spare much time to watch her, for I was too busy watching for the police. Whenever the library doors opened, my stomach felt wrenched. I might have been the person they were looking for, not her at all.

I was glad when Mrs Smullen reappeared. At least I could take refuge in the staffroom. But I couldn't read; I could only gaze out at the dark afternoon, the streaming road, a few cars ascending the overpass, their headlights swollen with rain. I was so nervous that I saw a figure being slashed with knives beneath the overpass. It must have been the shadow of a sapling, knives of rain and headlights. The rain made the graffiti on the pillars resemble huge blotchy faces.

When I emerged from the staffroom, the girl had gone. For a moment I felt guiltily relieved, then I realised that it didn't mean the police would stay away. Suppose they assumed the call had been a hoax? Suppose they recognised my voice? I was afraid to look up when the doors opened, and by the time the library closed I was near to panic. It was almost a relief to stand outside in the last of the rain and wait for the bus, even though I couldn't help peering across at the overpass. I saw nothing unusual, even when I hurried to the window of the bus and stared down from the overpass. There were only the saplings, glistening darkly.

I didn't sleep well that night. I dreamed I was in the staffroom, unable to look away from the overpass outside the window, while someone came into the room behind me. I jerked awake when I felt an icy touch on my throat. After that I couldn't sleep at all, and perhaps that was why, next morning on the bus, the noise of the engine seemed to turn into chanting as the bus reached the overpass.

At least there was no sign of the young girl. Perhaps Saturday was her day off. I managed to behave as if everything was normal: I asked people to keep their voices down, told readers I would put out the returned books in a few minutes, said 'Staff only behind the counter' when they tried to grab returned books from the trolley. Mrs Smullen could have had no reason to suspect that anything was wrong, until I came out of the staffroom at the end of my morning break and saw her talking to the police.

My reaction gave me away. I hesitated long enough in the doorway for her to see that I wanted to hide. I snatched a handful of reservation cards and tried to look as if I were searching for the books on the shelves, but as soon as the police left she hunted me down. 'Was it you who called the police?'

'Well, somebody had to do something ...' I kept my voice low, and wished that she would do the same; readers were glancing at her. 'You said she was only thirteen ...'

'Let me make one thing perfectly clear to you.' Her face was growing red, her voice was rising. 'I am in charge of this library. From now on you will do exactly as I say, no more and no less. If that girl comes in here again you will tell her to leave at once.'

'But that won't achieve anything,' I hissed. 'She'll only go elsewhere. What are the police going to do about her?'

'Will you go back to the counter and get on with your work.' She turned her back on me at once and strode to her desk.

When I had to give a reader his tickets, I almost dropped them. My fingers felt swollen, my face was burning. Not only had all the readers heard Mrs Smullen, some of them had given her approving smiles. When she went into the staffroom for her break I mouthed obscenities at her, but that didn't make me feel any less enraged. I was still standing at the counter, digging my fingers viciously among the book cards and readers' tickets, when the three sharp-faced youths came in.

They hardly glanced at me, but one of them murmured something. All of them sniggered as they sat down at the table furthest from the counter. They began to mutter, heads close together, a low blurred sound like the noise of a fly trapped in a room. Even if they had been three other people I would have found it nerve-wracking. As soon as an old man turned to glare at them I strode over. 'Will you keep your voices down, please,' I said, my lips trembling.

They took their time before they looked up at me, smirking. 'All right, squire,' one said. 'You won't even know we're here.'

As soon as I turned away they burst out laughing and resumed talking. All at once I felt safe; they were on my territory here. I was in charge of the library while Mrs Smullen was away, whatever she might think. 'That's enough,' I said with all the violence I felt. 'I told you to keep quiet. Get out and make your plans somewhere else.'

'And what'll you do? Hit us with a book?' one said. As they rose to their feet, the chair legs screeched over the linoleum. They were no longer smirking, because I'd revealed what I knew about them. One of them reached in his inside breast pocket, and my felt and throat already felt raw.

Before he could withdraw his hand, the library attendant returned from a surreptitious visit to the Viscount of Owl. He saw what was happening, and intervened at once. 'Go on, the lot of you,' he snarled, exhaling beer over me and the youths alike. 'Don't try it. I'll have the law on you.' For a moment the youth stood there like Napoleon, then the three of them marched out, kicking all the chairs within reach.

I was relieved that the attendant had intervened - not only because he'd prevented whatever they might have done to me, but also because he had decoyed their hostility away from me. At least, I hoped he had. Certainly Mrs Smullen assumed that I had been helping him throw out some troublemakers. It wasn't until the library closed for the night, and I was waiting for the bus, that I realised fully how blind my hope was. The youths had every reason to cut me up like the dog, and now was their chance.

I hid beneath the overpass and watched for the bus, but I felt by no means safe. Clouds were blackening the twilight; it was very dark among the pillars. I was surrounded by graffiti, incomprehensible as runes. They were confusing the edge of my vision, for there seemed to be far too many pillars, disfigured by huge looming faces. I wouldn't look up, even though I kept thinking that children were clambering overhead; I knew it must be an illusion of the graffiti - no children had ever had such bright red mouths. I had enough trouble convincing myself that the spidery saplings weren't fat and darkly glistening.

When the bus came in sight I felt safe at last, but not for long. As soon as I sat down I caught sight of the driver's face in his mirror. The bus was racing up the overpass, and he was grinning mirthlessly, grinning like a wooden mask. He looked insane.

As the bus reached the top, it swerved. For a moment I was sure he was going to drive straight through the concrete railing. When I opened my eyes, we were a hundred yards beyond the overpass, and he looked perfectly normal, almost expressionless. Perhaps it was only my lingering nervousness that made him look anything else.

My nervousness wouldn't go away. It loomed over me all Sunday while I tried to enjoy the spring among the large scrubbed houses near my home. I thought of calling Mrs Smullen in the morning to say I was ill, but I knew she wouldn't believe me. My probationary report would no doubt be bad enough as it was.

I didn't get much sleep. On Monday I was tense long before I arrived at the library. Everything made me anxious, even a child who had fallen near the overpass and was crying about his bloody knees. But there was a surprise waiting for me. Someone had been sent on relief from another library, to make the staff up to three.

Mrs Smullen must have known in advance, but it didn't matter that she hadn't mentioned it to me; I was too relieved not to be on my own with her. Jack, the new man, was an expansive sort who asked the readers what they thought of the books they were returning, something Mrs Smullen never did. He joked with everyone, even with Mrs Smullen, until her face made it clear that joking was against the rules. I felt at ease for the first time in days.

Perhaps Mrs Smullen resented our rapport. Halfway through the morning she showed me an item in the local newspaper. The woman I hadn't charged fines had been arrested for shoplifting; her flat had proved to be full of stolen goods. 'I hope that will make you think a little,' Mrs Smullen said, but I was less depressed by the report than by how triumphant she seemed. When Jack saw I was depressed he winked at me, and I felt better.

'Coming for a drink, old son?' he said at lunchtime. I didn't mind us going to the Cunt of Owl now that there were two of us. Jack challenged me to a game of billiards, which I lost hilariously. He insisted on a third round of beer, and we were gulping it down with barely a minute to go before the library opened when the three youths appeared at the far end of the bar.

I choked on my beer, and stood coughing and spluttering while Jack thumped me between the shoulders. One youth was dawdling ominously towards me along the bar, but it didn't feel at all like a scene in a Western to me. Then one of his companions caught his elbow and muttered something that turned him back, and at once I felt impressive as John Wayne. I wasn't scared of them or of Mrs Smullen. I took my time finishing my drink; I wasn't about to start coughing again.

When we returned to the library it was already open, and the doll-faced woman was flouncing out with her daughter. 'You pack while I tell Reg we have to stay with him,' the mother was saying. So the police and Mrs Smullen had made the move elsewhere, but what had that achieved? Still, I felt resigned to its inevitability, thanks to the beer.

The beer helped me amble through the next hour or so, chatting with readers and fumbling for their tickets in the narrow metal trays, but by the time I went for my afternoon break I felt sleepy. I sat and blinked at the rain that was striping the staffroom window. Before long I was nodding. I thought there were too many pillars in the gloom beneath the overpass, but then I saw that what I'd taken for a mass of pillars was something else: a glistening tangle of roots or branches or entrails, that were reaching for me. They might have caught me if I hadn't been woken by a crash of glass.

I sat and stared, and couldn't move. Just a couple of feet in front of me, the staffroom window had been smashed. I heard footsteps running away, and the clang of a metal bar thrown on the pavement, but I could only stare at my reflection in the fragment that remained of the window. I could feel glass in my throat, which was wet and growing wetter. Reflected against the streaming overpass, my chest was darkening with a stain.

Mrs Smullen strode in almost at once. I managed to stand up, my feet crunching broken glass, so that she could see what had happened to me, but she hardly spared me a glance. She seemed almost to blame me for the damage. Perhaps she was right – no doubt the broken window was the revenge of the sharp-faced youths – but couldn't she see that my throat had been cut? At last I ventured to the mirror above the sink, and made myself look. There was a tiny splinter of glass under my chin, but no blood. My chest was soaked with rain.

Perhaps I should have been able to laugh at my panic, but the anticlimax only worried me: it seemed the worst was yet to happen. After all, I would have to wait by myself for the bus. The hammering of workmen at the staffroom window resounded through the library. Before long it felt as though they were hammering my ears.

But I didn't have to wait for the bus. Though he didn't live near me, Jack offered me a lift home. I felt limp with relief, even when he headed unnecessarily for the overpass. 'Here goes the roller coaster,' he cried.

As the car reached the top, it veered alarmingly. I thought there must be a crosswind, though I couldn't feel one. I glanced at Jack to make some such remark, and at once I was afraid to speak. He was grinning stiffly, showing his teeth. His eyes were fixed as glass.

I watched him because I couldn't look away, until we were off the overpass. At once his expression began to fade, and a hundred yards further on he looked at me. 'What's up?' he said.

He seemed back to normal. 'What were you thinking about when you made that face?' I said, trying to relax.

'What face?'

'You made a face just now on the overpass.'

'Did I? I'll take your word for it, old son. I can't recall thinking of anything. This bloody place, I expect.'

He obviously thought he hadn't told me anything, but I felt he had: it was just that I couldn't define it, especially while his hand kept touching my leg whenever he changed gear. Soon he let his hand rest on the gear lever and my thigh, until I drew away. Once I was alone I tried to pinpoint what I should have noticed, but my mind felt like a lump in my head. That night I kept waking, convinced that the prickling of my throat meant it had been slashed.

Next morning I almost fell asleep on the bus, but I alighted before it reached the overpass. Though I couldn't see the driver's face, I was almost sure that he lost control for a moment at the top. I didn't feel any more confident for having escaped the bus. As I hurried past the intersection the buds of the saplings looked too green, violent as neon.

Jack clapped me on the shoulder when he arrived. 'How are you today, old son?' I tried to stay away from him and Mrs Smullen; I didn't feel at ease with either of them. Old ladies jostled in front of the shelves of romances, the attendant threw out several children for giggling at picture books. I searched for adult books on ancient Britain for the class that was coming in later. Through one of the remaining windows I could see the overpass, rearing up as if to pounce.

When I went for my morning break, I wasn't conscious of taking a handful of history books with me. I sat in the boarded-up staffroom and tried to relax. Flats in the tower blocks must feel like this, like cells. More than the glaring light, it bothered me that I couldn't watch the overpass. I closed my eyes and tried to find a reason for all the tension and frustration I was suffering. If I could understand them, perhaps they would go away. If the lingered they would grow worse, and I couldn't imagine what I would do then.

My hands were clenching. They clenched on the books, which I realised at last I was holding – and suddenly I realised what I'd overlooked.

For a while I stared at the unopened books. I had to know, and yet I was afraid to find out. Eventually I turned to the index of the first book. There wasn't much to find: most of England had been Celtic in the fourth century, the Druids had performed human sacrifices in sacred groves. Perhaps I was wrong, perhaps my impressions had no historical basis after all. In any case, how long could an area of land retain its character? Could any influence survive so long?

I opened the second book, and there it was: a Roman description of a sacred grove. Barbaric rites – 'Barbara ritu sacra deorum' – every tree sprinkled with human gore, altars heaped with entrails. Trees were carved to represent gods – 'simulacra maesta deorum' – and I knew how the Romans must have felt to be hemmed in by the huge looming faces, for I had felt it myself. I was sure of myself now. Jack had said more than he knew when he'd called it a bloody place.

I was sure of myself, but not what to do. Who would I tell? What could I say? I hurried out of the staffroom, trying to think whether there was anything at the intersection that might convince people, and saw the school bus full of children in the distance. It was heading for the library – for the overpass.

At once my sense of danger was so intense that I began to shake. There wasn't time to explain to anyone. I had to act, I mustn't fail again. My whole body was tingling with apprehension, and yet deep down I felt relieved, capable of dealing with the miles of concrete and everything within them at last. All at once everything seemed clear and simple. The bus came speeding down the long straight road as I ran panting towards the intersection. Before I reached it, my lungs felt raw.

By the time I stumbled to the far side of the intersection, the bus was only yards away. I stood in front of the overpass and gestured wildly for the driver to go round. When the grin formed slowly on his face I knew what I'd failed to anticipate, but it was too late. As he drove straight at me my vision blurred, and the saplings seemed to bend towards me like the tendrils of a carnivorous plant. As the bus knocked me down into darkness, I thought I heard the children chanting.

But perhaps I was wrong. Perhaps I was wrong about everything. When he came to visit me in hospital, the driver said that the steering had locked. He'd managed to brake, though not in time to prevent the impact from fracturing three of my ribs. Perhaps he had been grimacing as he fought the wheel, not grinning at all.

Yes, I think I was wrong. Now that I read over what I've written, I think that the unfamiliarity of everything distorted my view of it – of the intersection most of all. I can hear the birds in the trees outside the window, singing with their bright red beaks, and it seems to me that the saplings by the intersection may be the most important factor in the lives of all those people. When they grow into trees, surely their green must brighten those lives. Once I leave the hospital, I must do what I can to help the saplings grow as they should.

THE HORROR AT THE GATEHOUSE

One of the most frightening ghost stories in the whole of the British Isles comes to us from south Lancashire and is dated to the mid-1970s. It is not a widely told tale as the land-owners have long been reluctant to publicise it, firstly because they fear they would lose staff – they certainly lost staff back at the time – and secondly because parts of the estate are now up for sale and there is concern that if this story became well known, there would be a dearth of customers looking to buy.

For all these reasons, no names of specific persons or places shall be mentioned here, but the privately-owned estate, which still covers some 20,000 acres in the lush countryside between Wigan and Preston, was partly a shooting estate and partly farmland, its centrepiece a magnificent 18th century hall, now fully restored and modernised. One might have expected that there'd be some scope for spooky phenomena here, but apparently there was no history of disturbance until the date in question. As well as the hall, the estate encompassed numerous cottages and outbuildings, and employed hundreds of local people, and at no stage had there been any reports of supernatural or paranormal occurrences.

Until 1976.

That summer, a decision was made to clear one particularly overgrown corner of the estate, for which purpose various students were temporarily employed. By all accounts, the project started well. The weather was hot and dry, so the youthful workforce would labour all day, spend the evenings drinking in the village pubs, and sleep free of charge in various of the lodgings dotted across the enormous property. One such lodging was a 17th century residence known simply as the Gatehouse. It wasn't really a house, more a tower with a single door downstairs, a single spiral stair, and a single bedroom at the top with one window. Despite its name, it was no longer attached to a gate. It had been once, but the estate had grown since then, the gate finding itself 'inland' and thus becoming redundant. Eventually the gate and the other gatepost were demolished, leaving only the solitary tower where the gatekeeper had once lived. The entrance road also fell into disuse and soon was nothing more than a secluded, grassy lane.

By all accounts, it was an idyllic location for a billet, especially during that infamously hot summer, though because there was only one room and one bed, only one person could stay there at a time. The first person lucky enough to draw this straw was an exchange student from Hong Kong. For several days he worked the land and slept in the Gatehouse tower. By all accounts, he wasn't much of a socialiser, but he was friendly enough and the other students came to like him.

Could what happened to him next have been a student prank?

For various reasons, it seems unlikely.

About a week in, at around three o'clock in the morning, the estate manager was woken in bed by a hysterically screaming man banging on the door of his cottage. When the manager opened up, he found the Asian student outside in a wretched state: white-faced, sweating and wearing pyjamas, the bottom half of which he wasn't even aware that he had soiled. The manager and his wife gave the student brandy, cleaned him up and finally managed to calm him down sufficiently to get a story out of him.

The student said that he had been in bed in the tower when he'd suddenly heard hoof-beats approaching along the lane. There were horses on the estate, so this didn't bother him. But then the animal halted directly outside. A second later, he heard the most ferocious equine shrieks below his window, accompanied by a terrible pounding on the downstairs door. He knew instinctively that these blows weren't struck by human fists, but by an animal's hooves. A moment later, he said, the door crashed inwards, literally splintered from its hinges. Incredible though it seemed, he then heard those same hooves ascending the spiral stairway, enormous blows following on his bedroom door. This also was broken down in the darkness and an immense grunting something forced its way into the room. The terrified student climbed from the window and attempted to scale down the ivy, falling at least half the distance - about eight feet - before running across the estate barefoot.

When the estate manager and his wife examined the student, his pyjamas were full of thorns, his hands and legs covered in scrapes, and his feet badly cut.

The manager gathered some farm-hands, and they went down to the Gatehouse together, where they found the front door not only intact but still closed and locked. The same applied to the bedroom door. Aside from a very faint musty smell, there was nothing out of the ordinary - except of course, for the bedroom window, which was wide open.

It was a total mystery.

The young man was adamant that he'd been telling the truth. If someone had been playing a prank, where was the evidence of it? If he'd been perpetrating a hoax of his own, he'd imperilled himself climbing from the window - he could easily have fallen the whole distance and broken his neck. And would he really have soiled himself just for effect?

Whatever the case, he left the following day.

The estate owner closed the Gatehouse, but now more and more students were being brought in to work and it became obvious that bed-space was needed. Shortly before the end of the summer break, having finally decided that the Hong Kong student had either had a nightmare or maybe even had been taking drugs, estate staff reopened the building.

The new occupant, a Londoner this time, was not told what had happened previously, and initially everything was fine. However, about one week before the end of the summer holidays, with many of the students returning to university, exactly the same scenario played itself out again. The estate manager and his wife were in bed when they were disturbed in the middle of the night by a wild shouting outside. The latest student was in a similar state of terror to the first. Without any apparent knowledge of the previous incident, he described the same hooves galloping up to the

Gatehouse, breaking the outer door, clopping up the spiral stair and smashing into the bedroom. As before, he too had climbed from the window and run barefoot to safety.

The manager and his men returned to the property, but again it was closed and silent. The only sign of disturbance was the open upper window.

When the summer was over, attempts were made to investigate the building properly. Members of staff held vigils in the upper room all night to see if anything would happen – but nothing ever did. Even so, the building was closed again on the owner's instructions, and it would not be put to any other use for the next three decades.

Perhaps the eeriest aspect of this tale is that it has no beginning, no middle and no real end. Nothing like this had ever happened before, nothing like it has happened since, and no explanation has been found.

In the 1990s, an enterprising journalist attempted to link the case to atrocities committed in the area during 1648. That year, Oliver Cromwell fought the battle of Preston, a bloody struggle indeed, which extended for miles along the main highway, and left 12,000 casualties. Cromwell was successful, and as so often happened on both sides, the victors showed little magnanimity to the defeated. Many Royalist prisoners were executed on the field, in the actual vicinity of what would later become the country estate in question. The journalist surmised that a series of odd pock-marks on the base of the Gatehouse tower were evidence of firing squad activity. But no definitive proof of this was found. In any case, much Lancashire ghost-lore centres around the depredations of Cromwell and his Roundheads, who in a heavily Catholic county always seemed worthy of blame, so any such explanation must be taken with a pinch of salt.

The tale remains a fascinating but frustrating one. We are no closer to an explanation now than we were in 1976.

FORMBY POINT

Anna Taborska

'The Northwest is like the body of a beautiful woman. North of Liverpool lie her breasts. And Formby … Formby is her nipple.'

'Which nipple?'

'What do you mean, which nipple?'

'Well, is it the right nipple or the left nipple?'

Irritated, Pete switched off the radio. He was born in Formby but hadn't been back since he'd left for London University (and stayed) and his parents had moved to Manchester. Twenty-five years ago now. He'd just been visiting them for the long bank holiday, but some twang of nostalgia for his modest, but occasionally magical childhood spurred him to say his goodbyes early on the Monday morning and head off west down the M602.

He'd told his parents that he had to get back to London early to prepare for a presentation the next day. This tiny lie seemed easier than explaining that he wanted to get to the beach quickly and walk at his own pace, not constrained by anyone's arthritis or rheumatism or dodgy knee, and without the constant worry that one of them might tumble and do themselves an injury. A nagging feeling of guilt accompanied his deception - after all, they'd taken him to the beach on many an occasion when he was little, and now perhaps they'd be grateful for being given the opportunity to revisit the seaside themselves. But as he turned off the M62 onto the M57, the guilty feeling dissipated and he started to look forward to the trek across the sand dunes, rewarded by the stunning view of the sea off Formby Point and the sea breeze as he approached the water. He wondered whether the tide would be in or out.

Serendipitously, there appeared to be a programme on the radio about Formby; or, more accurately, two sports commentators seemed to be engaging in some increasingly annoying banter, but Pete felt like he needed something to occupy his thoughts, so he turned the radio back on.

'Of course, Formby is now best known as the residence of the late Phil Rafferty, the footballer who had his foot cut off by his lover's jealous boyfriend.'

'Ex-boyfriend.'

'For those of you who haven't been following the story, the ex-boyfriend of Rafferty's girlfriend Linda Frome broke into the footballer's £2.5 million Formby home, overpowered him while he slept and cut off his famous left foot.'

Pete wasn't much of a football fan, but he'd heard all about Rafferty of course. The mutilation and subsequent suicide of the footballer had caused a media feeding frenzy the world over. The promising young Irishman had been signed by Liverpool only six months earlier.

'The foot was never found.'

Pete switched the radio off again.

Eventually the motorway came to an end and Pete continued up Broom's Cross Road, the flat green fields on either side a familiar, welcome, yet disconcertingly desolate sight. Once Broom's Cross Road gave onto the Southport Road, Pete was on the home stretch, yet the feeling of unease persisted. By the time Southport Road became Ince Lane, then Moore Lane, it took all of Pete's willpower not to put his foot down. No matter how many times he drove down this stretch of road, childhood fears surfaced to spook him. The Round House - an eighteenth century brick building with a conical stone slate roof - to his left marked the approach to the stretch of Ince Woods allegedly haunted by the so-called Grey Lady. To Pete's mother's despair, a helpful aunt had told little Petey about how a mysterious female figure would wander out onto Moore Lane from Cross Barn Lane just beyond and across the road from The Round House, causing vehicles to swerve off the road. Petey had taken the story to heart, and the subsequent designation of the stretch of road running through Ince Woods as an accident black spot, and the discovery one winter of the frozen body of a school friend's grandmother in a ditch at the side of the road where the Grey Lady was said to walk, just served to strengthen little Petey's terror. Fits of hysterical tears from age six to age eight had forced Pete's father to take an inconvenient detour every time the family left Formby for a day out, and even now Pete chastised himself for not having taken an alternative route. But, as usual, there was no Grey Lady (not that he expected one), he managed to avoid any hint of a possible accident, and he was soon quickly and efficiently heading for the Formby Bypass and Liverpool Road beyond, then turning left onto Raven Meols Lane.

Pete drove all the way to the end of Raven Meols Lane, which turned into Queen's Road and then into Bushby Lane, stopping just before Bushby Lane turned into Lifeboat Road, and parking up in a side street. He set off up Lifeboat Road on foot. To his left was a fair-sized fenced-off area of woodland, which housed Shorrocks Hill nightclub and what was once a members' only day spa with indoor and outdoor pools - now turned paintballing headquarters. To his right were a couple of millionaires' houses, one of which had previously belonged to the unfortunate Phil Rafferty. Pete frowned at the FOR SALE sign nailed onto the gate post, and found himself wondering about the last resting place of Rafferty's left foot. He shook off the morbid reflection, annoyed at himself for allowing the imbecilic radio presenters to get under his skin.

Soon the dead footballer's estate gave way to woodland, and Pete wandered off the road into the pine trees that constituted Formby's famous red squirrel reserve. Pete had loved playing in the woods as a kid, and the Scout troop in which he'd been a Cub often went hiking in the picturesque landscape, collecting pine cones to sketch and learning about the glorious variety of fauna and flora. But as Pete now walked deeper into the woodland, orienting himself to stay parallel to Lifeboat Road, there seemed to be something different about the woods. Something Pete couldn't put his finger on it. Something not quite right.

Pete slowed his pace, peering into the trees, listening intently for any sound out of the ordinary. He couldn't shake the feeling that he was not alone. Each time he took a few steps, he thought he heard something moving in the undergrowth nearby, but, when he stopped, there was only the sound of distant birdsong and the breeze sighing in the pine tops. Pete listened for a while, distinctly ill at ease in the place that had formerly brought him solace and joy. Then he hatched a plan: he'd walk quickly for a bit, then stop abruptly enough for whoever might be following him to be caught off-guard and take at least one more step so that Pete could ascertain where the footfalls were coming from. But the plan backfired when Pete stopped suddenly and nearly jumped out of his skin as a startled woodpecker which had been keeping pace with him burst from the bushes to his right and flew off into the trees.

Relieved, but irritated with himself for being frightened by something as innocuous as a ten-inch bird, Pete continued through the pinewoods in the general direction of the beach. And yet he still couldn't recapture the carefree, light-hearted feeling he'd always experienced here as a child. He'd only walked a dozen or so metres when he noticed a red squirrel - dead, lying on the ground, its eyes decomposed, flies and bugs swarming all over it. Great. He'd never so much as caught a fleeting glimpse of a red squirrel before, and now here was one oozing putrescence before his very eyes. Disgusted, Pete headed left - back onto Lifeboat Road. Perhaps it would be simpler to stick to the path. But he hadn't got far when he passed a dead baby rabbit on the side of the road. Then another and another. Christ. Where were all these dead rabbits coming from? Perhaps they'd wandered out onto the road and been hit by cars, but the road leading up to the beach was narrow and cars here drove too slowly to hit so many rabbits ... surely?

To say that Pete wasn't enjoying the walk to the beach as much as he'd anticipated would be something of an understatement. Eventually the pine trees gave way to grassland and the odd low, squat tree, weirdly misshapen and growing crazily in the direction dictated by the constant battering of the wind. Soon the road became a dirt track, and Pete was walking through another area of special interest: an area fenced off to protect northern dune tiger beetles and Formby's famous natterjack toads. Pete had never seen a natterjack toad. But wait: what was the putrid thing lying at the side of the track, front legs curled over its chest, two disproportionately large hind legs pointing lifelessly at the sky? No ... really? Pete wasn't even going to contemplate the bizarre possibility of another dead animal. It was a children's toy - he told himself: a toy dropped, forgotten and trodden into the dirt. He looked pointedly ahead and strode as quickly as the increasingly sandy constituency of the path would allow.

Soon the whole path was covered in sand, and on either side of it rose the famous Formby sand dunes, dotted here and there with spiky marram grass. The path - what there was of it - now wove up and down amongst the dunes. Traipsing through the sand was increasingly heavy-going and Pete had to stop a couple of times to tip thousands of tiny grains out of his shoes. After a while he started to doubt himself: had the path to the beach really been this long? It seemed like he was lumbering through the sand forever, although in actual fact it couldn't have been more than ten minutes or so. He stopped and tried to catch his breath. This next dune was surely the last one, and of course it had to be the biggest. He was glad he'd given up smoking for New Year. If he hadn't, he'd be filling his lungs with tar round about now, and the trudge uphill would probably be even harder. Pete braced himself and climbed the last few epic metres up the final sand dune.

Finally, at the very top, Pete was rewarded by a view that took his breath away no matter how many times he saw it: laid out before him, the golden-white sand of Formby Beach and beyond it, in the distance, the steel blue-grey of the Irish Sea. A relatively recent addition to the scene was the Burbo Bank Offshore Wind Farm - a constellation of twenty-five wind turbines on a vast sandbank - straight ahead and to Pete's left, towards Wales and the Mersey estuary. At 300 feet high, each turbine was nearly as tall as the Blackpool Tower, but their distance, at four miles off Formby Point, belied their imposing stature. Pete looked south down the coast, towards Crosby. He knew there was an extraordinary art installation there: one hundred cast-iron,

650kg, life-size figures spread out along three kilometres of the foreshore and stretching almost one kilometre out to sea, made from casts of artist Antony Gormley's own body, embedded in the sand and staring forever seaward. Perhaps another time he'd visit the Gormley statues, but that would have to wait - there were other wonders for Pete to explore today. His unease about the dead animals lifted slightly and he gazed out to sea.

The tide was out - as far out as Pete had ever seen it - and to his delight the receding sea had uncovered the eerie black skeleton of the *Ionic Star*. Pete knew there'd been a solar eclipse on Friday, and he'd read in the *Liverpool Echo* about how the subsequent gravitational pull of the sun, moon and planets had caused a supertide, the extreme low tide that followed exposing some of the dozens of shipwrecks off the Mersey coast. But the article hadn't prepared Pete for the breath-taking spectacle of actually seeing the desolate remains of the *Ionic Star* embedded in the mudflats off Formby Point. Pete could clearly see the tiny silhouettes of people exploring the unfortunate cargo ship's giant ribs. Enthralled and unnerved in equal measure, he made his way down onto the beach, determined to investigate the vessel from close-up.

The Blue Star Line Company had been building ships since 1891. Throughout the many years of the company's illustrious existence, numerous of its ships met a sticky end - sunk by enemy torpedoes or wrecked on foreign shores. The fate of two of these sister ships spring to mind if only for the reason that they perished within two months of each other. These steamships were the *Ionic Star* and her younger sister the *Doric Star*, but lucky Stars they certainly weren't. The *Doric Star* was sunk by the German Battleship *Admiral Graf Spee* off the West coast of Africa on December 2nd 1939. Less than two months earlier, on October 16th, the *Ionic Star* had almost made it home and to her Liverpool destination with her cargo of fruit, cotton and meat before running aground on the treacherous sands of Mad Wharf, a mile west of Formby Point. The position of the ship made salvage nigh-on impossible and so, to add insult to injury, she was used for target practice during the Second World War.

As he walked out onto the pale golden expanse of Formby Beach, Pete paused for a moment at the ruins of the old lifeboat station. Built in 1809, the lifeboat station - now reduced to melancholy grey and terracotta brick foundations - had itself been built on the site of Britain's first lifeboat station dating back to 1776. Depressing and strange, the fractured remains jutted red and orange from the golden-white sand. But Pete had inspected them a hundred times as a boy, and now his heart was set on the vast black ruin that he'd only seen a couple of times before, and never this exposed. The *Ionic Star's* dark carcass was usually completely covered by the sea, and, although Pete had seen parts of the wreck a couple of times before, it still unsettled him.

He started walking out towards the sea and that's when he noticed the dead jellyfish. One, then another, and another - until it seemed that the whole seaward side of the beach was littered with slimy tentacled corpses. Dead jellyfish on the beach were nothing new, of course, but Pete had never seen so many at once. Then something caught his eye. A gelatinous pink-beige blob some half a metre in diameter. Flaccid arms spread out from its centre like a grotesque knobbly star. As Pete stared at the hideous spectacle in fascination, a couple who'd been strolling on the beach behind him noticed the transfixed man and followed his gaze.

'Oh my goodness!' exclaimed the woman. 'It's huge.'

Pete couldn't help but smile at the woman's words, but quickly composed himself and gave the couple an acknowledging nod.

'Hi there.' The couple smiled back at Pete, then proceeded to take photos of the decomposing barrel jellyfish and of each other with it. Pete left them to it and continued towards the *Ionic Star*, careful not to tread on any of the decaying monstrosities. Soon he was out of the 'dead zone' and heading across the wet sand to his goal. For a moment there was total silence - not even seagulls calling overhead. And then the wind blew from the sea - cold, loud, humming and whistling around Pete, until it felt like its persistent eldritch wail was right inside his head. And then a voice rang in Pete's ears - distant and shrill, the desperate cry of someone in mortal peril.

'Help!' the voice came from up ahead and a little to Pete's right. Pete looked back to see if the couple he'd met had heard it too, but they were nowhere to be seen. 'Over here!'

He looked around in alarm and eventually spotted what looked like a barnacle-covered rock protruding from a pool of water in the sands ahead of him. Pete had never noticed the rock before; then again, he'd never seen so much of the beach exposed before. Alongside the rock curved a row of what looked like rotting grey-black wooden stumps, and Pete realised that he was looking at another wreck – one that he'd never previously seen. The rocklike structure was the sunken vessel's two-cylinder vertical engine, completely covered in mussels.

The *Bradda* had come to rest – if that's how the ill-fated steamer's desperate, violent end could be described – about 300 yards north of the *Ionic Star* and three years earlier than the larger vessel. On January 9th 1936, the Dutch-built, Isle of Man based steamer set off from Birkenhead with her cargo of coal, bound for Rogerstown in the Irish Free State. It was already dark and the weather was poor when the small coaster headed off down the River Mersey. Within minutes, a terrible gale ensued and hurricane winds of a hundred miles an hour lashed the *Bradda* mercilessly.

Arthur Cregeen had experienced many a storm in his years as master mariner at the Ramsey Steamship Company, but never anything as swift and violent as this. He knew better than anyone how to handle himself and any vessel in his charge, and he recognised that this was a battle they weren't going to win. To make matters even worse, he hadn't been able to keep course along the deep centre of the Crosby channel – two boats had passed the *Bradda,* and the smaller vessel had been forced to keep to the Formby shore side, too close for comfort to the limestone training wall designed to stop shipping from becoming grounded in the shallows. They'd just passed the Great Burbo Bank; the guiding light of the Crosby Lightship, moored off the northeast elbow of the vast sandbank, glowed faintly to their port side. Any further and they'd be blown out into the open sea. It was now or never.

'We're turning back!' the captain shouted to his crew of five. But the storm had the vessel in its deadly grip, and when Cregeen tried to swing her round, the *Bradda* did not respond. 'She's refusing to answer the helm! Brace yourselves!'

At sixty-two years of age, Robert Harrison had been an able seaman for more years than he cared to remember. It had been exciting at first, but lately all he could think about was making retirement age so that he could spend more time with his wife and fifteen-year-old daughter. He'd served as helmsman under Cregeen before, but this was the first time he thought he could detect a note of concern underpinning the customary calm of the forty-five-year-old captain's commands. The other sea veterans – sixty-year-old chief engineer Thomas Tasker and fifty-four-year-old second engineer William Clewis – were also too well aware of how quickly their current predicament could turn lethal. Able seamen Samuel Ball and Isaac Skillen were much younger than the others. Isaac still lived with his parents in Douglas. He'd been looking forward to his twenty-first birthday next month and to spending time with his fiancé.

The wind whistled and screeched, driving waves of stinging rain and icy spray into the light-built vessel. The gale raged all around, whipping the dark waters into a frenzy. Then an enormous wave struck. There was a back-wrenching jolt and a shudder as the *Bradda* was blown stern-first into the Mersey training wall designed to keep shipping in the Crosby channel. Now quite out of control, she breached the wall into the shallower Formby channel and ground to a halt on the sandbank beyond.

From his post at the wheel, Cregeen fought valiantly to free the *Bradda* from the sandbank, but the violent, churning sea and the cloying, hard-packed sand pinned her in.

'Get the flares!'

Wrestling not to lose their footing on the slippery deck in the face of the tempest's onslaught, the *Bradda's* crew sent up flare after flare and rocket after rocket, in a desperate attempt to summon help. The Crosby Lightship wasn't far; surely someone would spot them? They must have sent about fifty distress signals, but help did not come. Cregeen was starting to despair for his crew.

'Put on your lifejackets!' he shouted over the maelstrom.

Soaked through and despairing, they continued to send up flares and rockets in the hope of attracting the attention of the lightship, a lifeboat, or any passing vessel. Their signals tore through the miasma of the storm-black sky, scant competition for the thunder and lightning that crashed and streaked overhead. Boats passed no more than half a mile away, and each time a glimmer of hope flickered for Cregeen and his crew.

'Help! Over here!'

But the passing boats took no notice. Perhaps they failed to spot the *Bradda*. Perhaps they knew that following her into the shallow Formby channel would entail meeting the same fate as the doomed vessel.

When the boat's supply of flares and rockets ran out, the men soaked towels and rags in paraffin and fired those instead. After two hours of continuous assault from the elements, the boat began to list very badly and the men used the last of their strength to climb onto the port side of the bridge. Then a great wave struck the *Bradda,* and she went right over. Physically strong and athletic, Samuel Ball managed to climb further up. The next wave washed Harrison, Tasker and Clewis away. Harrison hit his head hard as he went over; for him the fear and pain was over before the swell took him. Another wave struck the vessel, then another, and Ball was ripped right off the bridge to which he was clinging. Out of the corner of his eye he saw Skillen washed overboard as well.

'Isaac!' the Captain cried out after the last of his men, and then he too was gone, into the black and angry sea.

But the waves parted long enough for Ball and Skillen to swim clear of the stricken vessel and the danger of being battered and crushed against her bulky, wave-swept corpse. Ball, the strongest swimmer of the crew, spotted the younger man.

'Skillen! Over here! Isaac!'

Ball noticed a piece of timber that had broken off the *Bradda* and was being thrown about by the waves nearby. He grabbed it and swam towards Isaac, pushing it out in the young man's direction.

'Grab a hold!' he shouted, planning to pull Isaac to shore.

Isaac reached out - as far as he could. For a moment his fingers almost touched the sodden timber, but then a huge wave parted the two men and Isaac disappeared from view.

'Isaac! Where are you?!' Ball called out over the hurricane. Was that a human voice in the darkness? Isaac's faint cry for help? Or just the wind shrieking? 'Isaac!'

Battling the swirling, heaving waves, Ball swam towards what he thought was the spot where he'd last seen the other youth, but there was nothing but wild, inky water all around. Unable to swim any further, he drifted for a while, calling out, listening, trying to keep his head above water. The sea was pitch black. The best thing he could do was bring back help. He scoured the horizon, and oriented himself towards the Formby Lighthouse, and then a smaller, closer light that glowed in a window of the tide gauge attendant's cottage on Lifeboat Road. In the dark sea behind him, unheard by Ball, Isaac surfaced one last time.

'Help! Over here!' Then he was gone for good.

The *Bradda* lay considerably closer to shore than the *Ionic Star*, yet while Pete could distinctly see people walking right up to the *Ionic Star*, much of the closer wreck was submerged in water. Pete figured that the smaller vessel must be in a trough or lake of sorts. The sands off Formby point were anything but flat - their shifting, treacherous surface concealed all manner of gullies and channels. In some places you could walk right out to sea, at others rivulets connected deeper pockets of water, and an unwary rambler, unaware of the tides, could easily become cut off from the shore.

The sound of the wind increased, though not its strength. Pete was perplexed when he realised that the wail of the wind was out of all proportion to the feel of it against his skin. He strained to hear the voice again through the whistling and howling. And it came.

'Help! Over here!' Definitely from the direction of the mysterious wreck.

Pete walked as fast as he could over the wet sand, trying to see who it was that was calling out.

'Hang on!' he shouted, 'I'm coming to get you.'

But as he neared the wreck, Pete couldn't see anyone in the water.

'Help!' The voice grew weaker as the sound of lashing rain merged with the ululating of the wind, but no raindrops fell on Pete and, as he looked up, he saw that the sky was still clear. Pete cast a glance towards the *Ionic Star* and saw to his dismay that the people who'd been taking photos of it were no longer there. He looked around and saw the last of them disappearing up the beach, way out of earshot.

'Where are you?' Pete called out as he ran towards the fading voice.

'Over here!'

A thunder clap echoed overhead, but no lightning, as the phantom storm seethed around Pete. And suddenly the wet sand beneath Pete's feet gave way to a sharp drop, and Pete plunged down into icy water. His startled cry was cut short as his head submerged for a moment, then he was partially out of the water again, struggling to stand. He could no longer hear the pleading voice; only the lashing rain and howling wind of the ghostly storm that raged somewhere on another plane of time. And then Pete was screaming, begging for help, as the viscous mud of the gully into which he'd fallen closed around his feet, clutching, pulling, sucking him down into the seabed. And the crabs were scuttling towards him along the hard, wet sand above him and the soft silty quicksand beneath him.

'Help!' It was Pete who was crying out now, arms flailing, voice carried away on a non-existent storm. 'Over here!' But there was nobody to hear or to help, and Pete sank slowly, helplessly, his terror prolonged and elongated, as if he were trapped in an eternity of fear and despair. As the tide came rolling in and the dark water closed over his head for the second and final time, Pete's mind mercifully took him out and up. In a split second, he was gazing down at the spot where his own body had disappeared from sight beside the dark wreck of the *Bradda,* then standing on the sand dune, looking at his favourite view, then passing the house in which Phil Rafferty's foot had once landed with a thump on the bedroom carpet, in his car listening to the radio, standing with Bridget at the altar, graduating from university, sharing his first kiss, gazing up at the kind, smiling faces of his parents towering above him. Then one final moment of terror, and it was all over.

Pete drowned before the crabs surrounded him and started to feed.

HILL OF MYSTERIES

Bidston Hill, on the Wirral peninsular in Merseyside, may not be the highest hill in the Northwest of England, but it is certainly one of the most mysterious. At 234 feet, it is a mere pimple compared to the likes of Pendle Hill, 1,827 feet, and Winter Hill, 1,496 feet, but its reputation for eeriness stems from the plethora of strange events and spooky rumours concerning it, and from its association with a notorious Satanist.

Purely in appearance terms, Bidston Hill comprises several curious features.

A flat boulder on the hill's northwest face bears a 1,000-year-old engraving of an ancient goddess and is believed to have been carved by a Norse-Irish raiding party in the early 11th century. Directly to the north meanwhile, a similarly engraved rock depicts an immense snouted animal, which has been identified as either a horse or wolf. Buildings on the hill include a derelict windmill, the evocative Bidston Observatory, and even though the summit is over two miles from the sea, a 19th century lighthouse originally erected to guide ships up the channel to Liverpool.

On moonless nights it is rumoured to be the meeting place of cults and covens, while the windmill is allegedly haunted by the ghost of a man who was either murdered or sacrificed in the vicinity. In the 16th century, a kind of werewolf supposedly dwelled here, a child born out of wedlock and abandoned in the hilltop woods, where he gradually grew up but at the same time deteriorated into an animalistic creature that fed on the local wildlife. According to the myths, after terrorising the surrounding villages for quite some time, he was subdued by a band of huntsmen, who spared his life at the request of a local priest on the condition he would be forcibly removed from the district. As with all good horror stories, though these events are said to have occurred in distant antiquity, echoes appear to remain. As recently as 2014, local people have reported chilling howls from the hilltop late at night.

But while carved stones and gambolling wildmen are redolent of an older world of scary apocrypha, Bidston Hill also sits at the centre of some distinctly modern legends. It is an apparent hotspot for UFO phenomena, weird objects – including a pitch-black something reputedly the size of a battleship – sighted hovering above the summit in 2012.

But it is the story of Richard Tilly that most interests paranormal researchers.

One of a wild breed in the 18th century, Tilly was an adherent to the code of the Hellfire Clubs, where wild disregard for the rules and conventions of society were the order of play, and prosecution by the authorities rarely resulted. Of course, he perfectly suited this tradition, being a country squire who was also a rake, gambler, drinker, womaniser and devil-worshipper. Despite this reputation, little actual detail is known about his activities during life, but there was plenty written about him after his death, which occurred around 1730.

For decades after Tilly had left this mortal coil, there were reported incidents of young women crossing Bidston Hill alone after dark, and, often close to the old windmill, being approached by an unsavoury character, a ragged, foul-smelling man in a long wig and the rotted, dingy garb of the early 18th century. Invariably, he was described as having a leering, cadaverous face, and being full of filthy suggestions. Physical attacks were even launched upon some unsuspecting victims, several of them later able to display livid red claw-marks. It could be assumed that some lustful vagrant was responsible for these crimes – and indeed several investigations followed along those lines – if it hadn't been for the fact that reports of this nature continued to be made until the early 1960s.

It may be relevant that Richard Tilly lies buried somewhere in the vicinity of the windmill.

BELOW

Simon Bestwick

Manchester's a city of layers; over the years it's been knocked down and built over, again and again. Now and then, something comes to light. They dig a new building's foundations, find an old one's. Coins, earthenware and glass, mixed in sand and clay.

If you're lucky, that's all you find.

Of course, you can find other ways in, too. And sometimes - sometimes it's what's down there that finds a way out.

I was walking to school along Dunham Road in Altrincham, one cold misty morning in November 1986, when Martyn called out to me. We walked in together sometimes, depending on whether or not he was late, getting a lift, or just not bothering to turn up.

'You all right, Stumpy?'

From someone else, that might have been an insult, but I knew Martyn didn't mean it that way; by then I had a pretty good radar for insults, subtle or otherwise.

'Yeah,' I said. 'You?'

'All right.' He leant against a lamppost. 'You going in?'

'Yeah,' I said. 'Course.'

I didn't *want* to, but playing truant was as unthinkable as murder to a good little boy from a middle-class South Manchester suburb. Martyn didn't care. He was always in and out of trouble - bunking off, fighting, keeping girlie mags in his desk. He'd even told Mr Briggs the Games master to fuck off. We'd thought Briggs' head was going to explode.

Martyn had caught hell for it – as always – but didn't give a shit. I dunno how he escaped expulsion, but he did. He was a big lad, athletic, successful – for a thirteen-year-old – with girls, and nothing scared him. He was everything I wasn't.

'What for? Just gonna get the shit kicked out of you.'

Not if you stop them, I wanted to say, but didn't. When Martyn helped me out it was because he felt like it; other times he couldn't be arsed, or he was busy making one of his famous non-appearances. He was something I was grateful for when it happened, not something I expected, much less took for granted. Besides, he'd have had to be nearby every minute.

I didn't want to go in that morning, or any other; it's a shit feeling, to hate and dread going somewhere but having to. Every morning I dragged myself in, wanting to stay in bed, or take a bus into the countryside, wander through a field. But I couldn't.

Martyn looked at me and shrugged. 'I'm not.'

My stomach clutched; the worst days were the ones Martyn wasn't in school.

He saw my face. 'Don't go in then,' he said.

'I can't.'

'Why not?'

Because, I wanted to say, but didn't.

'Come with us,' he said. 'I'm going town.' *Town,* if you live near Manchester, means the city.

'Can't,' I said.

He scowled. 'Don't be a poofter.'

I just looked back at him miserably. He snorted. 'Fuck off, then.'

When you don't have any power, those who do are scary. Like gods: you live or perish by their whim. I could say that's why I called after him – I was scared of losing whatever favour he held me in, and with it the little protection it gave me. But that wasn't it. Just for a second, I'd visualised the possibility of a day away from school. Another path. One where I wasn't picked on. Being a goody-two-shoes hadn't got me anywhere; maybe I'd be luckier as one of the bad boys.

'Hang on!' I said, and ran after him. Martyn looked back at me and grinned.

About three months before, Barry Rigby had been duffing me up while one of his mates emptied my schoolbag out all over the yard. Martyn had dropped Rigby with two quick punches; when he did that, his mate ran away.

Afterward, he'd helped me pick my stuff up. I had a Douglas Reeman book - one of my Grandpa's, who'd been in the Navy in the War - and it turned out Martyn liked Reeman too. Maybe that'd been why he waded in. Or maybe it was just because he could.

I dunno why he liked me - if that's what it was. It wasn't a friendship as such, but now and then he told people to fuck off when they bothered me. I was grateful but scared too. Martyn Barrett was the kind of lad they meant when they said *loose cannon*; you never knew which way he'd go.

We caught a double-decker into town, bagsying the front seats on the top deck.

I spent most of the journey staring out of the window. Back then, I went to Manchester maybe once or twice a year with Mum and Dad, so it was like a voyage to an unknown land. The 108 bus route from Altrincham led up through Fallowfield and Moss Side into the city centre, but they might as well have been Outer Mongolia or the surface of Mars for all I recognised them. It was another world.

It was the first time I'd ever done anything like this. I was the one whose Mum and Dad would be shocked when it came out. Mum would shake her head and be disappointed; Dad would bark and glower. Never mind the teachers. But I didn't let myself think about that. Instead, I thought about the view from the bus's top-deck window, about where the streets that bled off from the main road went, who might live in the tall Victorian town houses along Princess Road as we went into Moss Side – anything but what would be waiting for me later.

'What we gonna do?' I asked Martyn. He slouched in the corner of the other seat; he was looking out of the window too, but I don't know if he saw anything much. He glanced at me and shrugged.

'Dunno,' he said. 'We'll see.'

Every morning I was given bus fare and dinner money; I'd a little of that left, while Martyn had a fiver – a small fortune by our standards. I didn't ask where he'd got it. We'd find some use to put it to.

We got off at Piccadilly. I'd stuffed my blazer and tie into my backpack; Martyn had pulled his tie off and zipped up his parka against the cold.

We bought some chips and ate them in Piccadilly Gardens. Nearby were a bunch of scruffy-looking homeless types, and a few punks in studded jackets. When one of them looked at me I looked away: I was afraid of both groups, but at the same time I was excited. This was living; this was adventure.

We finished eating. Martyn crumpled up his chip wrappers and tossed them away. 'Let's go to Shudehill,' he said. 'They've got nuddy mags in the shops there.'

I followed him, stopping only to chuck my chip wrappers in a nearby bin. I had a good-boy instinct to pick up his and dispose of them too, but resisted it.

Shudehill's different now. There's a shiny new bus station and Metrolink stop there these days, but back then it was just a grubby stretch of dirty-fronted shops laid beside the Arndale Centre. And the Arndale then was a dull squat box of grimy-looking beige tile that looked more like the world's biggest public toilet than anything else. Stayed that way till 1996, when an IRA bomb wrecked the place; after that they rebuilt it as the shiny steel-and-glass thing it is today.

I followed Martyn into one of the second-hand bookshops

and a smell of old paper folded round me. A couple of books caught my attention: science fiction, horror. But I was trying not to look at the stuff on the other side of the shop. There were cardboard boxes of glossy magazines; the tops of girls' faces peered over the rims of the boxes, eyes warm and inviting. Dyed-blonde hair, black eyebrows. Above them were shelves, some of them with magazines facing out.

Then as now, Shudehill was full of second-hand bookshops, half of each one given over to girlie mags. Some dealt in harder stuff, and if you knew who to ask you could buy actual videos – usually grainy, third or fourth (at least) generation copies. Today, of course, there's no act you can't view at the click of a mouse on the internet, but back then sex still had something of the air of a sacred mystery. Was that better or not? I couldn't tell you, but back then getting hold of a picture of a girl with nothing on was like finding the Holy Grail, never mind anything else.

I'd seen a couple of dog-eared second-hand magazines at a friend's house one afternoon the previous year; it'd left me with an ache in the groin I still hadn't yet found the means to get rid of. But here it was all on display. I went over to the shelves; couldn't help myself.

'Would you come away from there, please?' said the man behind the counter. He probably wasn't much more than twenty-five, but to me he was a giant with all the authority of adulthood. 'That's for over-eighteens only.'

I mumbled an apology and drifted back to the bookshelves. I saw a Douglas Reeman book and smiled. Maybe I could buy it for Grandpa. But that just made me think of what would happen when I went back home and I stopped smiling, feeling my stomach clutch again.

'Oi!'

The man behind the counter bellowed it – a full-throated blast of adult rage – and I knew Martyn had done something stupid, something really bad.

I probably knew what it was even before I saw, of course – what else could it be? He ran past me towards the door, shouting 'Come on!'

I saw the magazine clutched in his hand, and I ran after him. Behind me I heard the counter flap flung back as the man came after us. I hadn't taken anything, but that didn't matter; I was playing truant, after all, so I was already Martyn's partner in crime.

We burst onto Shudehill and Martyn tore across the street. Normally I looked both ways before I did that – I'd been raised on the Green Cross Code adverts – but I was bloody terrified at that point. The counter-man yelled behind us.

A horn blared – a big orange and white GM bus, coming straight at me. I ran away from it, heard tyres screech as an Austin Montego coming the other way braked. Somehow, I didn't freeze up but ran on to the far pavement, trying to keep up with Martyn.

It wasn't easy. Martyn ran with the school cross-country team, while I was about as far from being 'sporty' as you could get; PE and Games held a special kind of terror for me, above and beyond even what school normally had to offer. Still, I was scared shitless, which helped.

Even so, as he cut down one of the narrow side-streets that squirmed off from Shudehill, my lungs were burning and I was starting to flag. I couldn't even tell if the counter-man was still behind us – we might have lost him when the bus roared past, darting down the side-street before he had a clear view of the street again – but I didn't dare look around.

The back streets off Shudehill – well, most of them are called the Northern Quarter now, and a few years later they'd be full of quirky little shops and bars, but back then they were a hive of grim pubs, run-down shops and derelict buildings. Narrow, cobbled streets, filthy with dogshit and puddles of stagnant water. I saw a rat scuttle out of my way as I ran, following Martyn around a corner.

Around the corner – and the side-street was empty. I looked around, still running, close to tears now: if the counter-man was gaining, I'd be left alone to face the music.

Bastard, I thought.

'Stumpy! In here!'

I swung round; the board covering what had been the doorway in a derelict shopfront had been prised back, and Martyn's face showed in the darkness inside. I wondered if the counter-man had heard the nickname. It was the kind of thing, I suddenly thought, that criminals called each other. We *were* criminals now, both of us.

'Quick!' Martyn hissed.

I stumbled over the threshold; he grabbed my arm and let the board flap back into place. 'Shhh,' he whispered.

The inside of the shop was black and the air so damp I felt it settle on my skin. It reeked of piss and decay, stale smoke and other things I couldn't name, but which made me want to tear back the boarding and run out into the street, gulping air.

Martyn gripped my arm tighter, as if he knew what I was thinking.

From outside came the slap of running feet, a gasping for breath. 'Little shits!' roared a wheezy voice. 'I'll fucking have you!'

The counter-man. I heard him huffing and puffing - right outside the shop, by the sound of it. 'Fuck!' he yelled, and there was a thud as he kicked a wall. There was a soft rattle and hiss from above us, as if the blow had dislodged something. I shrank back; there was no knowing how stable or solid the building's structure was. It might fall on our heads any second.

Outside, the counter-man wheezed. 'Bollocks,' he muttered again. He spat. Then, after the longest time, we heard his footsteps recede.

'Let's get out of here,' I whispered.

'Shhh,' Martyn whispered back. 'Not yet. Give it another minute. Make sure he's gone.'

He was right; I knew that, even though all I wanted was to get out of the place. So I waited, breathing that poisonous-smelling air. I could hear my wristwatch ticking in the dark. It seemed ridiculously loud, all of a sudden; I couldn't believe that counter-man hadn't been able to hear it.

'Can we go now?' I whispered.

'Yeah, okay,' said Martyn, but even as he said it there was

another noise. A creaking, cracking noise, then a splintering: wood giving way.

I realised where it was coming from at the same moment that the floor buckled and sagged under us.

'Fuck!' said Martyn.

I tried to jump for it, but it was already too late. The rotten floorboards collapsed, and we fell.

I know I screamed. I know, too, that I had time for a moment's surprise at how long the fall was: even a basement wouldn't be this far down. Then there was just the scream, the fear sweeping everything else away.

I knew I was going to die, and that I didn't want to. A silly, childish thought, as if not wanting to would change a thing. I would hit ground and then –

Except that I didn't hit ground, not exactly. What I landed in was thick, wet and deep, and I plunged through it, but it cushioned me. I *did* sort of hit ground in the end – my hip cracked hard against something solid, and I screamed in pain – and the thick cold wetness covered me, but I coughed and flailed and broke free of it and there was air. It was colder and damper and smelt worse than the air in the shop had, but it was air.

'Fucking hell. Fuck. You okay, Stumpy?'

In the dim grey light, I made out Martyn; he was slathered with filth. We were in some sort of round chamber with earth walls. The floor of it was awash with mud; sitting down in it, it came up almost to my neck.

I realised I was crying. 'My hip ...'

'Bad?'

I struggled about in the mud and managed to stand, groaning in pain. 'Fuck, that hurts. Think it's broken.'

'You couldn't fucking walk if it was.' Martyn floundered upright too. We peered up; the shaft we'd fallen down vanished into the dark above.

'Help!' I shouted.

'Shut up for Christ's sake! You want that fucker coming

back?'

'Do you wanna stay here?'

Martyn scowled. 'Don't want either,' he said. He chewed his lip, then spat mud. 'Well, he'll have fucked off, anyway.'

'Maybe someone else'll come past, then.'

Martyn squinted around, dug an old lighter out of his pocket and flicked it into life. The flame's glow crept up the walls. 'The fuck are we?' he said.

'Maybe a well?' I said.

'Nah.' He pointed at the walls. They were mostly earth; bits of brick and wood poked out of them. 'There'd be bricks or tiles or something. Wouldn't there?'

'Dunno.' I didn't much care either, not right then. I was cold, wet, scared and my hip was throbbing where I'd banged it. Even school seemed preferable right then.

Martyn started shouting for help. I joined in too. But none came. There was only the rustle in the dark above us; bats and rats and creeping things.

Martyn flicked the lighter on again and inspected the walls. He dug his fingers in experimentally, and loose wet earth crumbled and fell to the floor. More slid down from above and spattered us. 'Bollocks,' he said. 'Not getting out that way.'

'*Where*, then?' I could hear the whine in my voice and despised it, but I couldn't seem to make it go away.

'The fuck should I know?' he shouted. I cringed from it, and hated myself for cringing. But I couldn't help it; for the second time that day, I was thinking that I was going to die – this time slowly, starving down here.

I turned away, looking at the greyish mud we stood in. Puddles of water had formed on its surface; they gleamed in the light.

What light?

'Hang on,' I said.

'What?' Martyn snapped.

'Put the lighter out,' I said.

'What you on about?'

'Please,' I said.

He did – and there was still light there. Of course there had been; we'd been able to see each other even before he put the lighter on. We could see each other down here, but I hadn't been able to see a thing up above.

'See it?' I said. 'Where's it coming from?'

'Fucking hell.' Martyn crouched down; so did I. When I did, I saw there were holes in the walls – big round ones, just above the surface of the mud. They were deep, stretching away from us, and the pale silverish light gleamed on their damp earth walls.

'They're *tunnels*,' I said.

We stared down them. The question of who'd built them never really occurred, not then. Of course there were tunnels. You got tunnels underground, didn't you?

There was a shallow slope from the bottom of the nearest tunnel mouth to the mud-pool. I got on my hands and knees and tried to climb up it but slid back. Martyn grabbed me so I didn't fall. 'The fuck are you doing?'

I pointed down the tunnel. 'There's light down there, right?'

'Yeah, so?'

'Where's it coming from?'

'Well how I should I fucking – oh. Right.'

This time, Martyn helped push me up, then clambered up after me with a grunt. The tunnel was pretty low, but I could stand almost straight; he had to stoop down. The floor was sludgy, but not as bad as what we'd just left.

The light, wherever it was coming from, still glistened on the damp of walls and floor. We started down the tunnel towards it.

There was no sign of any supports, nothing to shore the tunnel walls up; they were just round passages of hard-packed soil that snaked through the earth. The air was stale at first, but soon I could feel a very faint breeze, cold but comparatively fresh.

We kept trudging towards the light. I'm not sure how long for, as my watch had broken in the fall. I began to wonder if we shouldn't have stayed back at the bottom of the shaft and called for help. Sooner or later, someone would have heard us. Wouldn't they?

We were both bitterly cold and shivering, teeth chattering: shock, coupled with the dip in the cold mud bath, followed by the traipse through the damp, draughty earth tunnels.

Something changed. It took me a few moments to realise what it was, because it wasn't one thing. The ground underfoot was becoming harder, more solid, and the air's cold dampness less. Something about the light up ahead had changed too.

A few more steps and I saw why; the walls of packed earth were giving way to reddish-coloured stone. I reached out and touched it; it had a gritty, sandpapery feel, and was dry. Sandstone.

'We're getting somewhere,' I said.

Martyn grunted. He didn't sound convinced, and that made me wonder if I was wrong. But we went on.

'Listen,' he said suddenly.

'What?'

'*Listen.*'

I did, and then I heard it too; a distant thumping and clatter of machinery. I twisted round to look at Martyn and he grinned. I found myself grinning back. He clapped me round the shoulders awkwardly. 'You're a genius, Stumpy. A fucking genius!'

I didn't feel cold any more as we pushed on; a warm glow lit me up. A *genius,* he'd called me. Till now, I'd always been a follower, a hanger-on, like one of those pilot fish that hovered around the sharks as they swam, picking food from their teeth. But now *he* was following *me.*

The noise got louder and the light brightened with each bend of the tunnel; soon the racket was deafening. Martyn looked back.

'What's up?' I shouted – I had to, over the noise.

He shrugged. 'Thought I heard something.'

I shrugged too. An echo, running water, rats; could've been anything. Didn't matter, anyway; we were nearly out of here.

One more bend, and now the light was sharp and bright, the noise thunderous. Even shouting at the top of my lungs, I'd have struggled to be heard. God knew what we were coming out into – a factory of some kind? – but there'd be people surely, somewhere near.

Only as we rounded the bend did I stop to worry – what if the tunnel ended in a grille, something we couldn't get through? Even if there were people on the other side, how would we make ourselves heard?

But the tunnel opened straight out into a huge, wide room. I saw a white-tiled floor and ranks of tall machines. Long strands of some material stretched up over frames, and shuttles whizzed back and forth across them.

Weaving machines; warp and weft. We'd had a school trip to Quarry Bank Mill in Styal the year before, and they'd had a machine a bit like these running.

Martyn prodded me in the back, and I went forward. There was a two-foot gap between the tunnel mouth and the floor, and I was already feeling stiff from the cold and the walking, so I climbed slowly down. Martyn jumped down and landed flat on his arse.

I laughed weakly – I don't think he heard it over the racket – and looked around for a person. I saw several; small figures in white smocks and black trousers, tending the machines. I started towards the nearest one, but even as I did, I realised something was wrong.

Partly it was the light. At first, I'd thought there were fluorescents, but the ceiling was bare sandstone, and the light seemed to come from everywhere and nowhere. And there were huge skeins of cobwebs stretched out between the tops of the machines – years' worth, it looked like.

I told myself it was just a scruffy basement, somewhere where they weren't fussy about appearances. The important thing was that there were people here, and we'd be able to get help. I was so sure the worst of our problems were over that I found myself worrying about what would happen when we got back to the surface, over the stolen magazine and our bunking off school.

But as I came near the figure in the smock, I realised that it wasn't just the surroundings; there was something wrong with it, too. It was no taller than I was. And its hair was pale – not white, like Grandpa's was, but *faded* – and dry, like straw. Its feet were bare and looked like splayed white claws.

And then it turned towards us.

Its head was a papery bulb. That's what it looked like; damp paper that had dried, brushed with a thin layer of muck like that which coated Martyn and me, only dried and cracked and flaking. It didn't have a face, that was the horrible bit – no nose or mouth, just taut empty skin. It had no eyes either – just black empty sockets, but the worst thing of all was that they seemed to see us, and they seemed to beg us for help.

I took a step back, bumping into Martyn. I heard him say something – I don't know what it was but felt him move backwards. The child – I suppose that's what it was, or had been – moved towards us, but was pulled up short. I saw that it couldn't move away from the machine, because its hands were being pulled into it. I don't mean that they were crushed – the substance of them seemed to be pulled and stretched, like chewing gum, dragged into the machinery's churning guts. I looked up at the threads being woven.

'The tunnel,' I heard Martyn shout, and I nodded. We backed away. All along the line of machines, other children like the first turned to stare at us: empty faces, holes for eyes.

We reached the entrance we'd come through, and Martyn started climbing in – but then I grabbed his arm. A moment later, he saw what I'd seen; shadows moving at the bend in the tunnel. Something was coming down it.

I turned back to the machines. The children were staring at us. Shadows disrupted the pale light, moving across the ceiling and spilling across the floor; something was moving between the ranks of machines, coming our way.

'Oh *fuck*.' I heard Martyn shout that even over the machines. 'Come on.'

We ran away from the tunnel, past the row of machinery and staring eye-sockets. Martyn yelled and pointed – I saw another tunnel entrance, up ahead.

He jumped straight inside and ran in – it was lit by a pale glow, the same as the other had been – but I hesitated. What was going to be down *this* one? What if something was coming the other way, the same as there'd been in the one we'd come in through? But when I looked back, I was just in time to see something else emerge from between two weaving machines and turn to look my way. I don't know what the hell it was, but it wore long dark robes with a hooded cowl, and it was very thin and very, *very* tall; its head almost brushed the ceiling twenty or thirty feet above. Inside the cowl there was only darkness, except for two eyes – I assume they were eyes – glowing palely.

'Stumpy, come *on!* yelled Martyn, and I did as he said, scrambling down the tunnel. I didn't dare look back again. I didn't want to know how fast that thing could run.

The thunder of the factory – or whatever that place had been – died away as we ran. As it did, there was a humming in my ears that slowly faded.

We ran until we collapsed; for the first time ever, I kept up with Martyn. Then again, I was well-motivated. Tall as it was, the thing in the robes had been thin enough to fit inside the tunnel if it crawled on hands and knees. Assuming it had either.

'Jesus. Jesus.' Martyn was shaking. 'Jesus.'

He didn't ask what it was. Neither did I. An adult might have, but we were still young enough for much of the world to be an unknown place. A monster, a bad thing; that was explanation enough.

'We should have stayed in that fucking well,' he said, glaring at me. But his lips twitched, and his eyes were wet: to see Martyn Barrett nearly crying was almost more frightening than what we'd seen in the factory. Almost.

'Well we didn't,' I snapped back. He glared, and I thought he was going to swing for me, but then there was a noise from back down the tunnel and we both shut up. We froze there, waiting, but nothing came.

Martyn tugged my arm, and we moved on.

The light grew brighter, but we didn't hurry towards it this time.

It was the same silvery glow we'd seen before, and we'd seen what had been at the end of *that*. Unfortunately, what we'd seen was right behind us and possibly gaining, so we hadn't much choice but to move.

The air became colder again; I could see my breath in front of my face and began to shiver once more. The walls glistened with moisture, and soon the sandstone was giving way to packed soil. Water trickled along the tunnel floor and seeped, icy-cold, into our shoes.

There was a smell too; stagnant water, sewage, rotten things. The light brightened, and the tunnel opened out.

What we could see beyond wasn't pretty. A flagged stone floor, brick walls blackened with soot and slimy with moss, and water trickling down them. There was an archway almost directly opposite us. I could see a table laden with filthy, mould-covered pots and pans and wooden chairs green and spongy with rot.

I glanced at Martyn; he didn't look any happier about the place than I did, but then he looked back down the tunnel, and so did I. We hadn't heard any more noises from behind, but that didn't change the fact that our only way now was forward.

Martyn took a deep breath and jumped out, landing with a pained grunt on the flags. He turned back to help me down, and we looked around us.

The brick walls curled up overhead, but not that far – the ceiling was seven or eight feet high, at most, and the cellar or undercroft or whatever it was we'd found couldn't have been more than twelve feet wide. I breathed in and gagged on the stink, despite the cold.

'Breathe through your mouth,' said Martyn. 'Come on.'

As in the 'factory', the pale silvery light seemed to come from everywhere and nowhere at once. It didn't light the whole chamber, though; thick shadows filled its corners and could have hidden anything.

The chamber through the archway was the same size as the first, but the floor was unflagged, just raw earth, wet and soft and oozing. The worst thing was that there were blankets spread out on straw on the ground, each with a bundle of rags at one end. Beds and pillows for whoever or whatever slept down here. Across the chamber was another archway still. If we were lucky, I thought, the undercroft might lead out to a way back. Assuming we could keep going; my teeth were chattering, and my toes and fingers were numb with cold.

Martyn stopped. 'What is it?' I said.

'Listen.'

I did. 'I can't hear –'

'*Listen*, Stumpy.'

I did, and this time I heard it: a very soft, wet sound that came from behind.

We turned as it moved to fill the archway we'd come through. My first thought was that it was a maggot, a huge maggot; it was pallid and pulpy with a body of soft, mealy-looking segments, and its face was a white, featureless blob, except for two round black eyes. But the shape of it was manlike – or perhaps apelike would have been more like it. It had a hunched back, huge shoulders, long arms with massive hands that almost dragged along the ground.

We backed away as it slouched through into the second chamber. There was something boneless about it; I thought that if punctured with something sharp it might deflate in a gush of warm fluid, but didn't feel confident enough to test it. Its long, flabby fingers flexed and clasped, clenching tightly; I didn't want to test the strength of their grip either.

'Come on!' Martyn bolted through the archway at the end of the chamber, but braked to a halt on the other side and I nearly cannoned into his back.

The third chamber was flagged like the first, and also featured a table and chairs. But these chairs were occupied; three creatures like the one we'd just fled from turned slowly to face us and rose to their feet, shambling forwards.

'Fucking hell!' I ran back through the archway, but stopped again; the first creature was halfway across the chamber and closing in.

Martyn jostled into me, also retreating from the family of

flabby creatures. We stumbled back into the unflagged chamber; closing in on us, the first creature lifted its head and a wet, gaping hole slowly tore in the featureless pulp of its face. A slow hollow moan rang out; it was echoed behind us and I looked back to see the other three squeezing through the archway, similar maws yawning open in their faces.

'Shit,' said Martyn. 'Oh shit shit shit.'

I looked around for an exit, but there wasn't one.

Except that there was.

In one of the brick walls was a large round hole. Beyond it, the same silver light gleamed down another sandstone tunnel.

'Martyn!' I shouted and ran for it. He overtook me on the way, jumped as he reached it and landed on the hard stone with a yelp of pain. I jumped too and landed inside the tunnel in a crouch. I had to laugh; Briggs wouldn't have believed his eyes if he'd seen some of the feats I'd managed today, bruised hip or no – the pain of that had faded almost to nothing.

The four pallid ape-maggot things lumbered towards us, moaning, arms outstretched – and then stopped. They lowered their arms and stood there, staring at us. But their mouths stayed open, and the moaning didn't stop.

I looked back at Martyn; he'd already backed several yards down the tunnel. I looked back at the moaning creatures and backed away too. We kept backing away till they were lost to sight.

The tunnel became earth and then sandstone once again, drier and even a little warmer. My teeth stopped chattering, and feeling seeped back into my fingers, although my toes stayed numb.

It didn't do much to lift our spirits, though. Neither of us had spoken since getting out of the undercroft, but I didn't doubt Martyn was thinking much the same as me: wherever this tunnel led, there'd be something else waiting for us. We'd been lucky the last couple of times, might even be again next time or the one after that, but sooner or later we'd be too tired or slow to outrun whatever we encountered.

The tunnel shivered; at first there was a gentle vibration, then thin dust fell from the ceiling and it shook. I steadied myself against the wall.

'What's going on?' I turned and stared at Martyn; there was a quaver in his voice and he looked as if he'd start crying any second. 'What's *happening?*

The tunnel shook harder, and Martyn opened his mouth to cry out. I don't know whether he did or not, because there was a cracking, splintering sound. It wasn't like the noise the floorboards in the old shop had made - this was harder and *louder*. The tunnel jerked and shifted - and then, as in the shop, the ground under us gave way and we were falling.

I was screaming, and heard Martyn doing the same. But this time it was different. We hit solid earth almost at once but continued falling: we'd dropped through the sandstone tunnel into an earth one below it. This was steeper than any of the others, though, angling sharply downwards. Wetter, too - the floor was a river of slippery mud so that we shot down it as if was a log-flume.

The same silvery light bathed everything as we went down. Even if there'd been anything to grab hold of - and there wasn't - we'd gathered so much momentum there was no arresting the descent. At this rate, we'd be killed whenever we reached whatever was at the end of the tunnel - we'd be fired out of it like bullets.

But the tunnel was levelling slowly out. By the time the small disc of light that marked the tunnel's end showed, we were slowing down, finally coming to a halt about a dozen yards from the entrance ahead.

Martyn gripped my shoulder to push himself to his feet. I could feel him shaking. 'Bloody hell,' he said, and gave a weak laugh. I stood up; my legs felt wobbly. We couldn't see what was beyond the tunnel yet.

'What do you think?' he said.

'How do you mean?'

'I mean, what do you think we should do?'

I didn't say anything. I mean, what was there *to* do? Climb back up the way we'd gone? We'd have only come slithering back down. And even if we *had* been able to reach the sandstone tunnel, that would have led us to some other buried pocket of old lost things.

Martyn sighed. 'Yeah,' he said. The quaver was back in his voice, but then he pulled himself up, stuck his chest out and said: 'Right then.' His voice was as hard and steady as he could make it. He strode past me towards the entrance.

The cold here was worse than it had been anywhere else; my teeth started chattering again within seconds. The tunnel entrance was set into a damp stone wall, and that wall looked... *old*.

Overhead – fifty or sixty feet above us – the light gleamed on stone buttresses and slabs. Thin white stalactites hung down from them. At ground level was a narrow, cobbled street. I don't think it could have been more than five feet wide. On either side were buildings with mullioned windows – houses, or maybe shops. There was faded black and white paint on them; I thought they might be Tudor. Rats scuttled along the street, but they were different from the ones I'd seen up above: they'd been sleek brown-furred things, while these were hump-backed and jet-black. Black rats, I realised; I'd seen pictures of them in a book. The kind that used to be everywhere in Britain but had been displaced by the brown rat hundreds of years ago.

The buildings had iron-bound wooden doors that looked ready to fall apart from rot, the stonework was cracked and the windows filthy – but lights gleamed inside them nonetheless, yellow and greasy-looking.

Shadows moved on the cobbles too, from inside the houses. Dark things moved close to the windows and peered through at us. The windows were dirty and foxed; the faces behind them were just blurs.

And then, with a creak, the door of one house swung open. The light spilled out across the damp cobbles; rats scattered from it, squeaking. A shadow stretched out, and inside the house something began to move.

It was silhouetted against the glow from inside, so I couldn't make out its features, but its clothing resembled that of a seventeenth-century Cavalier. A wide-brimmed hat with a bedraggled feather in it; a heavy rapier hanging at its waist. Leather boots that clacked loudly on the cobbles; breeches, a faded sash. Long, dead-looking hair fell around its shoulders. It wasn't completely made of bones, but the light shone through its dry, papery skin as it turned to face us. It didn't move after that or make a sound; it just stood there, watching.

Another door swung open; another followed, then one by one the rest, till washes of yellow light illuminated the entire street. More men dressed like the first, women in bonnets and dresses. There were at least a dozen of them, and still the yellow lights flickered as shapes moved in the windows. They didn't move or make a sound, but I felt a greater sense of threat from them than I had from anything else we'd seen down here.

Even the rats now made no sound. The only thing I could hear was water dripping somewhere. And a very muffled, distant sound that might have been machinery. Perhaps we'd gone full circle and ended up near the factory. But then the Cavaliers stepped forward; they moved as one, in a mass, and in complete silence.

'Shit,' said Martyn, his voice going high. We both backed away but were up against the wall in two or three steps. I peered up the tunnel – if the mealy things in the undercroft hadn't been able to follow us, maybe the Cavaliers couldn't either. But the tunnel was gone – all but the first few feet, anyway. Beyond that was only a mass of wet earth.

I turned as there was another sound from the street – it was a sort of dry rustling, like the wind blowing through leaves, but with a kind of *rhythm*. I'm not sure, even today, but I thought then – and now – that it might have been laughter. I don't know which of them made that sound. All of them, maybe. Then it died away, and the Cavaliers, still in silence, took another step down the street towards us, all together.

Martyn grabbed my shoulder. He was pale. 'Gotta go through them,' he said.

'What?'

'If we can get past 'em, there might be a way out.'

A way out to what? Surely the best we could hope for was another tunnel, which would lead us to somewhere else like this. But I decided I'd rather take my chances with the factory or the undercroft than these. 'How?' I said, as the Cavaliers took another step.

'Rush them,' he said. 'Knock 'em down or dodge 'em.'

It sounded ridiculous, but what else could we have done? 'Okay,' I said.

'On three,' said Martyn. 'One, two ...'

The Cavaliers took another step. Martyn didn't speak, his grip on my arm tightening. They took another, and then he found his voice again. 'Three!' he shouted, and ran at them, head down.

I ran too, not at them but at one of the gaps between them. One moved sideways to close the gap, but in doing so opened another gap between himself and his neighbour, and I veered left and plunged through that. Then I was in amongst them; they stank of dust and age. A bony hand clawed my shoulder; I screamed, tore free and ran on.

Martyn screamed too, but he didn't stop.

I wasn't the fastest runner in school, far less the strongest boy, but I was good at dodging things; it was a skill I'd evolved out of sheer necessity. I dived and rolled to the cobbles to avoid another clutching hand, then scrambled to my feet as bony fingers snagged my hair. I screamed again as I pulled one way and they the other, till the hair came out and I went charging up the street.

'Stumpy!'

Almost at the far end, I looked back. Martyn hadn't stopped screaming, and now I saw why. Most of the Cavaliers formed a line across the street, now turned towards me, but behind them was a knot of a half-dozen, male and female, who had hold of Martyn and were shepherding him into one of the houses. I couldn't see all of their hands – I'm not sure, and I keep trying to tell myself I *couldn't* have seen it, but it looked as though some of their hands were *in* him, rather than *on* him.

He had an arm free, and was reaching for me with it, and he

kept screaming my name until they bundled him through one of the doors, which swung shut behind them with a dull, final *thud.* Even then, I could still hear him.

The other Cavaliers stood in silence for a moment, then took a step towards me.

I turned and ran – but all I found in front of me was a blank wall. I clawed and pounded on it, but of course nothing happened. I looked for something, anything, even another tunnel entrance, but there was nothing. And when I turned around, they were only a few feet from me. I could see their decayed, half-mummified faces. Their hands reached out.

And the wall beside my head exploded.

I screamed. I don't know if anyone else did. But light burst through the hole, and it wasn't the same light as before. I registered that but didn't understand what it meant as I fell to the floor, curled up and screaming. I'd reached my limit. I just wanted to be somewhere else. Away from here. Even if it was only in my head.

I vaguely registered the light getting brighter, heard voices shouting. But I was still past understanding what they meant, and when hands touched me, I screamed and fought them, till finally someone stuck a needle in my arm. And no matter what happened, no matter what anyone said, I wouldn't open my eyes.

I never went back to that school. I enrolled at a new one in the summer of '87, after some home tuition to help me catch up on what I'd missed. I was a quieter kid than I had been, and no-one picked on me; when I hid inside myself from the Cavaliers, not all of me came out again. At least not then. There'd been a lot of therapy, of course. To help me get over Martyn.

I don't know if they found a body. If there was a funeral or memorial service for Martyn, it happened while I was still hidden away inside myself. Martyn and I, I was told, had fallen down a disused drainage shaft under the derelict shop, got lost in some maintenance tunnels before emerging partway across the city near Cateaton Street, where as luck would have it some workmen had been digging a new gas main.

Years later, someone told me that there are stories of an old cobbled street, buildings and all, under Cateaton Street.

Part of the tunnel had collapsed, burying Martyn, but the workmen had broken through into the area where they found me.

No-one believed me about the factory, the undercroft, or the Cavaliers. A hallucination, they told me, caused by a terrible trauma.

I almost came to believe that. In fact, I *did*, for years; I suppose it was the only way I could get through the rest of my school years and all that followed. By the time I'd left University, you couldn't see the join any more between who I was and who I'd been. It was later that it came back.

I keep trying to push it away, with work or drink or drugs. I've have had all the associated ups and downs along the way, and I've come out in reasonably good shape, all things considered - but it's never stayed gone for good. And the last year or two's been particularly bad. That's why I've written this down; hoping it gets it out of my system. Gets the factory and the undercroft, the cobbled street and the Cavaliers, out of my dreams. And Martyn, too; Martyn most of all.

I keep seeing stories on the news, you see, about sinkholes opening in Manchester. It could be anything, of course, but I keep thinking about how that sandstone tunnel gave way under us. How the floor of the old shop did, come to that.

Like I said: sometimes it's what's down there that finds a way out.

THE VENGEANCE OF BANNISTER DOLL

The strangely named 'Bannister Doll' is not, as some may assume, a possessed toy or mannequin, but the name given to the spirit of a murdered flesh and blood girl; a run-of-the-mill ghost, one may think. And yet it has such evil connotations in the town where it allegedly resides – Preston, in Lancashire – that the mere mention of the name is believed dangerous, tantamount almost to an invocation.

The tale dates back to the early 19th century, when Preston was an industrial blot on the landscape and its overworked population forced to live in cramped, dirty hovels. It even begins in mystery, because the crime that started it all – a heinous one even by Dickensian era standards – was horrific in the extreme and yet, apparently, it went unpunished.

A man who we know only as Mayor Bannister had a daughter called Dorothy. It seems highly unlikely that Mayor Bannister was actually mayor of anything, let alone Mayor of Preston, as he and his family were said to be very impoverished. However, Dorothy Bannister was a famous beauty – her nickname 'Doll' derived from this, and her hand was sought by young men from all over the town. Mayor, who was ill-tempered and possessive, was determined to keep her in his own family, and on the day she confessed to him that she had taken a lover and had fallen pregnant, he flew into a homicidal rage. Dragging her onto open ground at the rear of their property, he tied his daughter to a post and literally whipped her to death, leaving her corpse there as a warning to all.

Given his low status, it is particularly startling that no apparent retribution followed, at least no retribution from a human agency. Dorothy was laid to rest in the graveyard at Holy Trinity Church, and that seems to have been the end of the matter. Except that shortly afterwards, Bannister and his wife are said to have fled their home, which was in the Snow Hill district of the town, though what caused this was not specified.

A short while later, the murders began.

The first was a young man found in a gutter in the town centre, so brutally beaten that his ribs and skull were crushed and many of his other bones broken. The authorities investigated, but no solution was provided. A second such killing followed in the next few weeks, another young man battered to death and to the point where his corpse was almost unrecognisable. A third killing occurred a short while later, very similar to the first two.

In retrospect, it looks as if the police in Preston – assuming there was a police force there at this date (Preston Borough Police were only inaugurated in 1815) – were inexperienced at investigating murder, given that, as in the case of Doll Bannister, these other three slayings also went unsolved. How the various tragedies became conflated is another puzzle, but not long after the last of the three young men died, rumours were running wild that Doll Bannister, or 'the Bannister Doll' as her vengeful spirit was now referred to, was responsible. Of course, it could just be that the rumourists were having a field-day, attempting to connect the victims by hinting that these young men were the three who had dishonoured the unfortunate girl, or maybe had known her merely as friends and yet had failed to save her from her fiendish father. But reports were soon coming in that the angry spirit – a tattered, bloody wreck, grinning dementedly – was actually seen prowling the backstreets of Preston in the early hours, looking for drunken toughs tumbling out of the town centre pubs. Amazingly, these reports continued until the 1960s, when a milkman doing his rounds one misty dawn sighted her mutilated form lumbering up Snow Hill.

Without written documentation, much of this tale must be classified as folklore rather than history, though the death of Doll Bannister certainly occurred. All through the 19th century, the whip-marked post upon which she was killed remained on the rough wasteland to the rear of her family's old home, even long after the house itself was demolished, and other matrons of the town would bring their daughters there to lecture them about the perils of wanton behaviour.

The evil memory of the murder has only contributed to the notion that simply mentioning the unfortunate victim's name is enough to summon her ghost.

OLD HUEY
Solomon Strange

Lancashire, 1965

Old Huey worked in the Chingleton town dump. It was little more than a large expanse of wasteland at the end of Dark Lane four miles from St Paul's Church, near the outskirts of Preston. He'd been custodian for fifteen years and lived near the tip in a stone cottage badly in need of renovation.

Huey was born malformed, a physical condition due to a traumatic birth. As he grew older the deformities became much more distorted. His forehead hung over deep-set eyes, a Neanderthal protuberance that scared most people. His jaw jutted out, a cruel defect which caused his lower set of crooked teeth to be on permanent display. But the deformity didn't end there. Huey's hunchback gave his hairless head a curious cocked look and while one of his arms was slightly withered, the other dangled apelike to his knees. Although he walked with a hobbling lurch, he was incredibly strong. God's only attribute to someone many considered a monster. Perhaps that was what drove him to do what he did.

Huey liked the dump and made a good living from it. The mountains of rubbish could on some days be a veritable gold mine. Dump picking was his privilege and he excelled at it. In his brown hip waders, leather gloves and with a sack over his back, he would scavenge like a man possessed. There were busted sofas, chairs, bureaus, things that could be restored with time and effort and sold to antique shops in Manchester. Huey used his disabilities to his advantage; there was nothing wrong with his brain, he conned the dealers and they in turn ripped off the punters. Then there were the junked cars at the west side of the tip; various makes and models, it was incredible the parts people left on their vehicles when they'd dumped them. Carbs and radiators were a good earner, not forgetting windscreens, spare tyres, distributor caps, head and tail lights. Local garages couldn't get enough of spare parts.

The dump was good, a place he could hide and feel comfortable in, but all that had changed. Not even the stash of money hidden away beneath the creaky floorboards of his crumbling home could prevent the growing resentment he felt. After all this time, people in Chingleton still sneered at him whenever he went shopping. It was a journey he hated, the looks, the remarks. He knew what they said about him behind his back, and it was true, he was a bastard. Many townsfolk had known his mother, the local whore who had died during childbirth and they wondered if that had been a form of punishment for spewing out such hideous spawn. But it was the group of teenagers who'd appeared at the dump in recent times that got to him. Every night they threw bottles at his home and he'd pleaded with their parents to make them stop but had just received verbal abuse in return. Unhindered, they continued with their taunts, snarling their hatred, followed by howls of laughter. He was the town freak, there for the amusement of boozed-up fools.

Huey hoped that sooner or later they would get bored, but the ritual dragged on for weeks and then months. Eventually unhappiness festered into bitterness and twisted his thoughts.

One unfortunate Friday night they returned.

The huge fire, the roseate glow which bloomed earlier had now diminished, and the dump was smouldering, black greasy smoke rising up and merging with the darkness above.

He heard them coming, the sound of bottles crunching beneath their feet. He stopped prodding the remnants of the fire with the poker in his hand and closed his eyes for a moment before turning to face them. The light on the wooden shack behind illuminated them. They swaggered, drinking cans of beer.

'Hey humpback,' the one nearest him shouted, amid howls of laughter.

There were seven maybe eight youths, although he couldn't be sure because the light was insubstantial. But he took in their shapes, could make out their leather jackets, jeans and unruly hair.

'Mind you don't fall over, Quozzie. You'll rock yourself asleep trying to get up again.'

Laughter was followed by more remarks. 'When did the freak show arrive?'

More insults were spat out. 'What do you do in the tool shed, spazzie, make friends?'

Each youth seemed to inspire the next with a barrage of humiliation.

A globule of spittle hit him in the eye. Huey wiped it away quickly with his withered arm, smearing it across his cheek.

'Hey, we're talking to you Quozzi!'

Flickering anger began to rise.

'Look at the gormless git.'

His eyes narrowed.

'Cat got your tongue Quozzi?'

Someone struck Huey on the side of the head and he fell to his knees. He rummaged around in the dirt and gripped hold of a familiar tool.

'Games over, where's the money?'

Huey got to his feet, his shirt sleeves rolled up past his elbows, glaring at one of the thugs. When he lunged forward, the teenager's mouth dropped open, but it was too late to cry out. Huey had already raised the machete into the air. It came down with a bone crunching *crack*.

As another of the leather-clad gang tried to rush him, Huey withdrew the bloodied machete from the thug's head, the twitching body dropping to the ground. He swung the weapon again, catching another teenager in the neck. The young man stood impossibly still, his body now ending in the bloody stump of a neck. Blood squirted from between his shoulders, drenching Huey.

The others watched, limbs rigid with fear.

Huey laughed, holding the blood-speckled head by the hair, thrusting it towards the gang. As they goggled, the headless body slumped into the glowing ashes of the fire.

Huey moved amongst them, slaughtering everyone.

Ten years later

Mary Webb checked the battered signpost through the window of her Rover.

'Bloody Hell,' she muttered, 'it's almost as if this place doesn't want to be found.'

She consulted the map balanced precariously on her lap. Chingleton had to be in this general direction. She looked right, paused for a moment and then decided to go left. Ahead lay woodland. Mary engaged first gear and set off slowly along the country lane.

The drive from Gloucester had not been pleasant at all; an accident on the M6 had caused a huge tailback and had wasted most of the day. If there was one thing she hated it was being stuck in a shitty traffic jam. She'd driven through the whole day and now at night her thoughts started to drift. During the journey she'd found herself fighting the tears that welled up, blurring her vision, threatening to send her car crashing into the lorry that had been in front for most of the way. What a stupid death that would have been, especially now. It was true James had almost destroyed her; he'd made her fall in love and then had shattered her emotionally. On more than one occasion she'd had to pull off the motorway to regain composure.

Why?

The thought exploded in her head. They'd been together for three years, living together, sharing each other's lives with a joyous intimacy but things had suddenly changed. He'd became distant and cold. The first signs came when he began to reject her caresses, blaming his mood on stress from overworking. Then came the arguments, fuelled by growing suspicion. Questions were met at first with a stonewall denial and lies. Only when she'd begun pleading with him, had she learned the awful truth.

He'd fallen in love with another woman.

The words had struck like a slap in the face.

As the lonely months dragged on, the numbness subsided, replaced by hurt, rejection, self-pity, and this in turn gave way to anger and frustration. Then, finally, it was over.

Ironically this whole mess had resulted in a holiday in Torremolinos with three co-workers from the bank where she worked. During this vacation Mary had met someone else and was introduced to a kind of love she had never known: a kind of love, unacceptable to some, which could only be shared between two women.

They met at *Jenga's* disco, a stomping ground for straight and gay alike. Feeling a little low that night, she'd decided that a long walk along the beach and some fresh air would do her good. The night was warm and the sea breeze gentle, she recalled. She'd listened to the voices of people rising from the large open areas outside, café-bars and restaurants along the main strip. It was lively, bristling with gift shops, bars and clubs. Life here was incessant, vibrant and all encompassing, and that in itself had raised her mood.

She'd made her way across the road, dodging a few Spanish youths on scooters, to *Jenga's,* an ultra-modern building with red neon lights blazing fiercely against the blackness of the night. The music, laughter and the babble of life coming from that place was almost ear busting, but fun, especially for an attractive young woman of twenty-four. She entered hesitantly at first, feeling intimidated and overwhelmed by the size of the place, joining the throng of people heading down a flight of stairs into the heart of the club. She sat, sipping a vodka whilst listening to *Jive Talkin'.* The dance floor was bustling; wall to wall people; lights spun; flashing and kaleidoscopic beams of laser light flew from one end of the room to the other. Mary caught sight of her own reflection in the oblong mirror beside her and swept a hand through her bobbed hair, and just at that moment she met Sam, a tall, incredibly beautiful woman. They'd laughed, danced and made love several times during what little time was left of the holiday and although she'd found someone else, her so-called friends already began to distance themselves.

Sam dismissed them as a bunch of ignorant cretins. And she was right but as the final days approached, they started discussing living together. Mary had known things would be hard, although nothing had prepared her for how tough it would really be. Her family and friends rejected her as Sam had warned. So, not long after returning home, she made the decision to move in with her partner.

Mary had thought she'd driven all the memories of her previous relationship from her mind but the journey here to the north of England had proved otherwise. The fact that she'd had to pull over a couple of times and cry hadn't in anyway undermined her feelings toward Sam, but this old wound still ran deep.

She uttered a soft groan as she shifted position. The loose joints of the car seat creaked, her back ached and she was uncomfortable. Her mind was drawn to the road again and her eyes flicked towards an approaching signpost:

Chingleton Secure Hospital

A slender arrow indicated the way down a winding lane, which was made to appear incredibly narrow by the tall hedgerows at either side of it.

Mary shuddered, although it wasn't from the cold. Perhaps it was because of the signpost to the institution. It reminded her of Sam's story about the gruesome legend connected to the old asylum's most infamous inmate.

Mary's thoughts returned to the road and she shook her head, trying to wake herself up. The atmosphere was humid with the threat of thunder, but it was the mist that now concerned her. Thickening veils of it lay across the road in front. But Chingleton had to be close now.

The road tilted downwards and narrowed, and as she rounded a tight bend near the bottom of the hill, she saw another misted signpost:

Dark Lane.

'Thank God,' she muttered. Sam was standing a few hundred yards farther along, wearing a green fleece and walking boots. She gave a little wave as the Rover pulled up alongside her.

'I thought you'd never get here,' Sam said with a smile.

'Sorry,' Mary replied wearily. 'I got stuck in some really bad traffic.'

'Well, tomorrow I'm going to take you to Blackpool. The Tower is great fun and the Pleasure Beach is a real buzz. On Sunday we can go for a walk around the Trough of Bowland. It's a beautiful area with fells, hills and deep valleys. Or we could visit Pendle Hill. Presumably you know the witchcraft stories.'

'That sounds great.'

'I've got another surprise,' Sam announced. 'I've got two tickets for *My Fair Lady* at Chorley Little Theatre.'

'A theatre?'

'It's only small and run by volunteers but it's such an intimate venue I couldn't resist.'

For the next twenty minutes they chatted, catching up on things. Mary was about to share some really exciting news about a job offer in Preston when the car juddered and spluttered to a halt.

'Oh crap,' she said, eyes drawn to the fuel gauge. 'I've run out of petrol.'

Sam forced a smile. 'It's okay. There's a garage a couple of miles away. If you've got a fuel container, I can take a short cut through the woods and be there in no time.'

'No! I can't let you do that.'

'Yes, you can.'

'Are you sure?'

'Absolutely, I know this area like the back of my hand. I'll get the fuel and you can have a rest and before you know it, we'll be at my house enjoying a stiff drink and warm bath.'

'Sounds good to me,' Mary said.

'So, where's the container?'

'In the boot.'

Within moments Sam had grabbed the petrol canister, slammed the boot shut, waved and was off walking quickly through the misty woodland.

Mary looked at her wristwatch, an hour had passed with no sign of Sam.

She gazed into the inky woodland. Nothing there moved. There wasn't just no sign of Sam; it was strangely still and eerily quiet. She sat in the Rover for a while longer before stepping out and closing the door. Her eyes ceaselessly searched the misty area. Something didn't feel right. Tenuous, drifting mist swirled around her, driven by cool air that sent shivers down her spine. Mary pulled at the lapels of her jacket, closing them around her throat. She turned and walked away along the road towards Chingleton, her heels clicking on the road surface. Gradually, almost unintentionally, her pace increased to a trot.

Why was she running? she wondered, but she could find no reason to it. *And why had other thoughts begun pushing their way into her mind?* Thoughts she didn't want there - thoughts that only heightened her fear - mental images of the deformed murderer who had once stalked this road still grasping a young man's severed head by its blood-soaked hair.

Stop it she chided herself. Her own fear was making her irrational. No one was following her, especially not a lunatic who had been institutionalised ten years ago.

But what if he's escaped?

'Get grip,' she cried out, breathing heavily.

From somewhere nearby she heard an odd, semi-audible sound; what might have been a muffled cry.

Oh God! She hurried on, unable and unwilling to look over her shoulder.

Imagination, she reassured herself. But it didn't stop the hairs on the back of her neck stiffening.

There it was again … a scream. Suddenly stifled, as though by a smothering hand.

Curiosity almost made her turn around, but she refused herself permission. If there was something going on back there, it was best to get away as quickly as possible. She pushed herself forward, pretending there was nothing at her rear even though a few yards behind something was now audibly moving … *coming closer…*

'No, nooo,' she whined.

She heard what sounded like the scuffing of feet.

Headlights then cut through the darkness ahead, startling her for a moment. She raised a hand across her eyes as the vehicle came to a screeching halt.

A grey-haired man in a heavy coat exited the vehicle.

'Walk towards me,' he called out.

Smack . . . smack …

Mary partly turned towards the dull sound that now resonated behind her.

'Don't do that!' he shouted.

She turned back to the man.

'That's it. Look at me and keep walking.'

Smack … smack … smack …

What the hell *was* that? But she followed the man's advice, advancing tensely.

'Keep to a steady pace,' he instructed.

Smack … smack … The sounds continued. A repeated fleshy impact, as of something striking the road.

Again, she felt compelled to take a quick look.

'Run!' he screamed.

She needed little persuasion as she bolted forward. In her mind's eye she could see the thing that stalked her, a grotesque caricature of the human form, its hairless head fused onto a monstrous hunched back, shadowed eyes, a dark slash of a demented grin.

She tripped but the man caught her. He rushed her to the passenger side.

'Get in quickly,' he said.

Mary threw herself into the vehicle and closed the door as her saviour ran back around the front of the car.

Hurry! her mind screamed.

The door opened and he jumped in, slamming it shut. He reversed the car and sped off in the opposite direction.

'What the hell were you doing out here on your own?' he stuttered.

'My car ran out of petrol,' she replied almost sobbing.

'Haven't you been listening to the news? An inmate's escaped from Chingleton Hospital. He's a real nutter.'

He turned the radio on, and she caught the tail-end of a broadcast.

'... contact the police and do not approach under any circumstances ...'

She shook her head. 'I can't believe this is happening.'

'You're safe now.'

She looked out of the passenger window, shaking all the way through *Hold Me Close.* Somehow David Essex's voice helped soothe her; it brought normality to an insane situation.

Another news bulletin followed: *'Police have confirmed that one inmate from Chingleton asylum is still on the loose and another murdered ...'*

She turned to the driver, more thankful than she could say for his intervention. God only knew what might have happened if he hadn't turned up.

'Did you get a good look at him?' she asked, glancing over her shoulder into the back of the car. It was cluttered with books and empty beer cans.

'Who?' he replied as the news continued.

'The dead inmate was found mutilated and repeatedly bitten around the face and head, but is thought to be Hugh Loomis, better known as Old Huey, responsible for a spate of murders in the mid-1960s.'

She looked back to the driver. 'The man behind me ... making that noise.'

'Police reassert that escapee Victor Craven should not be

approached. He is considered extremely dangerous.'

'There was no one behind you ... but an old plastic supermarket bag was caught on some thorns, and it kept bellying in the breeze.' He stopped the car and tugged on the handbrake. They were still in the mist, but now seemed to be in a layby somewhere.

'Lucky for me, eh?' he added.

Mary stared dully at him – in particular at the blood-stained hospital gown under his coat.

'Not so lucky for you.' He treated her to a broad, jagged-toothed smile.

She didn't have a chance to scream.

A VISION OF HIS OWN DESTRUCTION

The folk-histories of Britain are filled with prophecies and wise old sayings as allegedly uttered by wandering fortune-tellers and village sages. It seems that almost every part of the country, at some time or other, played host to a tavern seer or hermitage mystic, who, despite a lack of formal education and often with no real knowledge of the wider world, would claim second sight to foretell doom and disaster, not just for the local community but maybe for the kingdom at large – sometimes to a degree where even the great men of state would pay attention to their warnings.

Whether the famous 'Prophet of the Northwest', Robert Nixon, had dreams, fits or trances, is unrecorded, though some visions were said to have come to him while he was engaged in everyday procedures such as ploughing or milking. However, the one thing that marks Nixon out from so many others of this ilk is that his ability to predict disaster was more or less proved – and in a rather terrible and personal way.

Nixon, who was regarded locally as a kind of village idiot – 'a drooling, goggle-eyed lackwit,' as one contemporary wrote – was born in Cheshire in 1467. There is dispute as to where exactly he lived. Some claim the parish of Over, which is now part of Winsford in the very heart of the county; others say Delamere Forest, which is further west. One thing is certain; during the course of his relatively short life he made a number of complex Nostradamus-type predictions, which, somehow or other, were recorded for posterity. As is so often the case with these things, some were so vague and tenuous as to be almost meaningless both then and now, but one or two others would go on to have an eerie resonance in later ages.

For example, he appeared to predict the defeat of Richard III at the battle of Bosworth in 1485, the dissolution of Vale Royal Abbey in 1538, the imprisonment of Napoleon on St Helena in 1815, and even the arrival in Britain of cigarettes, this latter perhaps the least imprecise of all his many forecasts – 'all sorts will have chimneys in their mouths'. Before he was even 20 years old, word of Nixon's talent had reached the royal court, where Richard III, who was not yet aware that his own destruction had been foretold (fortunately for Nixon), and hoping to gain an advantage in his struggles with the remnants of his Lancastrian opponents, issued a summons to the young countryman.

Strangely, Nixon was terrified by the prospect. As far as he knew, he had nothing to fear from the ruthless new king, but it seemed that his most recent vision concerned his own fate. When friends advised him that one simply didn't refuse an order issued by Richard III, Nixon told them that if he went down to London he would starve to death. At length, this message was delivered to the king, who reissued his command, but advised Nixon that should he attend the royal court, he could sleep in the kitchens, where he would eat whenever and as often as he wished.

Somewhat reassured, Nixon made the journey from Cheshire to the Tower of London, and he did indeed take up residence in the royal kitchen – in fact, he rarely strayed out of it. How often he counselled the king is unspecified, though it seems that Richard spoke with him at least once, and was particularly interested in one new prophecy, which from his own perspective looked fairly promising:

Then rise up Richard son of Richard,
Blessed be his happy reign;
Thrice happy he who sees this time to come
When England shall know rest and peace again …

Ironically, this was one prediction that would prove itself badly wrong, Richard dying the following year – as Nixon had earlier warned – at the battle of Bosworth, and the House of York falling from power. But Nixon would never see this. Unluckily for him, another of his forecasts was more accurate. His occupation of the Tower kitchen proved a great nuisance to the cooks, who one day locked him in a closet. While he was so imprisoned, news arrived that the court was to leave London. In their haste to obey, the cooks forgot about Nixon – and when he was finally discovered many weeks later, he had indeed starved to death.

THE UPPER TIER
Paul Finch

A big, old house - once the scene of gaiety and laughter, now dark and empty. Where crystal chandeliers hung, canopies of cobweb rustle in undetectable breezes. Where corridors and stairs rang to voice and song, now there is silence.

And dust.

Dust is everywhere in this place. It particularly shrouds the upper tier, a boarded-off jumble of gutted rooms and desolate passages where the smell of decay and the blackness of night seem ever to linger. And yet this upper tier is not untenanted - for, as you watch, something stirs in its depths. The next thing you know, this something is approaching through the gloom and the slanting blades of moonlight.

From a distance it has the appearance of a person.

But perhaps not quite.

No person ever walked like this: lurching, seesawing. No human face ever resembled this face: raddled, twisted, hanging loose in empty folds ...

'Oh my God!' Brenda shouted, her eyes snapping open.

'Dear Lord!' Max replied, almost swerving the car. 'What's the matter?'

Brenda felt at her throat. 'Bad dream.'

'You've been asleep long enough,' he said. 'Good couple of hours, I'd say.'

She glanced from the window, trying to recall the horrible vision, though it was fading with astonishing speed. As such, she didn't immediately notice how dramatically the landscape had changed. The green woods and flat fields of Cheshire were now replaced by a rolling georama of slag-heaps and mill chimneys. The pebble-blue sky of late April was smeared with smoke.

'Is this it, then ... Wigan?'

Max nodded. 'Wouldn't believe it boasted a haunted manor house, would you?'

'What's it like, this Haigh Hall?'

'According to Harry's notes, quite something. The "Borley Rectory of the North".'

'We'd be so lucky,' Brenda said.

When they entered the town, it was as grimy and smoky as the wasteland surrounding it. The houses were of basic redbrick stock and stood in terraced rows. The town centre was crowded; there was an ongoing clangour of bells and factory whistles. Narrow streets wound between tall, dark buildings of Victorian origin, and thronged with vehicles: wagons, vans, even horses and carts.

'Is that bomb damage?' Brenda asked, spying a rubble-filled gap between two shops.

'Could be.' Max tried to negotiate the busy streets and at the same time wave to a group of pavement urchins entranced by the sight of his cream-and-red 1934 Humber Tourer. 'The *Luftwaffe* dropped a few of their payloads around here. Trying to kill off the nation's industry.'

'No-one escaped, did they?' Brenda said distantly.

'Course, it could also be coal-mining subsidence.'

Again, she wondered what she'd been dreaming about. 'No-one *ever* escapes.'

When they arrived on the cobbled forecourt of the London & Northwestern Railway Station, they found Guy waiting in his duffle-coat. He was smoking a cigarette; two sports bags were dumped alongside him.

'Rum old place, Wigan,' he said, climbing in. 'Seemed to take an age getting here.'

'You've never been to Lancashire before?' Max asked.

'Can't say I have. Knew a few Lancashire lads in the forces, of course. First rate fellas. Never knew it'd be as dingy as this, though.'

'I think we've seen worse.'

'Speaking of which ...' Guy leaned forward until he was almost between them. 'What about Haigh Hall then? Still amazed you got permission.'

Max nosed his way back into the traffic. 'It wasn't as tough as I expected. The Corporation have only just taken possession – and already they don't know what to do with it. We've got the complete run of the place, so long as we report to them first.'

'Hoping for a clean bill of health, are they?'

'Something like that.'

Guy sat back, produced a hipflask and took a sip. 'The chat is there are ghosts coming out of every wall. Especially on the top floor.'

'I'm taking that with a pinch of salt.'

'Either way, are we going to enjoy ourselves this week, or what?'

'We're going to be working, old bean.' Max eyed him through the rearview mirror. 'And you can knock *that* on the head, if you don't mind. It's only lunchtime.'

Guy grinned, re-screwed the cap and shoved the flask into his pocket. When Brenda glanced around at him, he winked. She pointedly looked away.

They drove through the town via the aptly named 'Wigan Lane' – though the traffic made progress slow. At one point, a police constable on points-duty looked twice at the big touring car and promptly stopped all other vehicles to let it through. The constable touched the brim of his helmet as they passed.

'Salt of the Earth, these people,' Max muttered.

Guy chuckled.

Gradually, the cluttered shops and smoke-pouring chimneys fell behind, and they found themselves among trees and open fields, with only occasional rows of houses. They passed a memorial to an ancient battle-site, and then the walled grounds of a hospital. According to the directions Max had been given, the Haigh estate's southwest entrance was the closest to the town centre, and when they reached it, it was unmistakable. There was a towering stone arch, maybe fifteen feet tall, with neo-classical wrought-iron gates underneath it, now rusted and covered by vegetation. Two empty lodge houses stood to either side. Planks had been fixed over their doors and windows. Everything was suddenly a lot quieter.

'Certainly looks the part,' Guy said.

'Isn't it supposed to be open for us?' Brenda asked.

Guy climbed out and pushed against the gates. With a metallic groan, they began to shift. At last he'd made sufficient room for them to drive through. They proceeded downhill along a metalled track which passed through a canyon partly formed by manmade walls, crossed a narrow wooden bridge over a river, and then followed a winding route surrounded by lush woodland.

'Could be back in the jolly old southeast,' Guy commented.

'Not quite,' Max said. 'There was once mining in these woods, but since the estate went to rack and ruin, nature has reclaimed everything.'

'I can see,' Brenda said, spotting yet more neo-classic architecture: the balustrade of a bridge spanning a deep cutting through which a railway line ran. The balustrade was green with age, broken in many places.

As they pressed on, the woods grew denser. Though it was only spring, the canopy blotted out most of the natural light. But then, after several minutes - rather suddenly - they came in sight of Haigh Hall itself, and Brenda felt her heart skip a beat.

It stood at the far end of a long, broad lawn, though this was more like a meadow it was so deep in grass and dandelions. The road ran straight up to its front door.

At first glance it was rather drab: a single central building, square and squat by country manse standards, though it stood three stories in height. It was flat-roofed with several chimneys, and built from sombre, yellow-grey stone now coated with moss. There were numerous windows - tall rectangles of multi-paned glass, though those on the upper tier were smashed or boarded or covered on the inside by stained sheets. Those lower down were simply curtained. The front door was a massive slab of oak studded with nail-heads, nestling beneath a porch formed by mock-Grecian pillars and a horizontal stone awning. There was a graveled parking area at the front, currently empty.

They climbed from the car and stretched. Brenda fancied they were being watched - though this wasn't an uncommon sensation on first approaching these derelict edifices. At times like this she wondered why she supported Max in his curious hobby. Not, she had to admit, that many of the places they'd been to had genuinely frightened her. Of course, she hadn't been part of the team at Borley Rectory. There were many curious incidents recorded during *that* expedition, though Max had been less impressed than others. Since then, he'd made no effort to co-investigate with his former associate, Harry Price. There'd been mumblings that the odd things going on at Borley had had nothing to do with the supernatural, though that hadn't stopped Harry making a killing out of it.

Still, that was in the past. Borley was burned and gone. Haigh Hall was the new target, and now that she was here, gazing up at its scabrous façade and the blank eyes of its windows, Brenda felt she could understand why.

Very slowly, the Hall's front door creaked open. They regarded it, saying nothing.

A man appeared in grubby overalls; he was late middle-aged, with a stooped posture and pale, wizened skin.

'Been expecting you,' he said. 'Name's Jowett. Fred Jowett.'

He was clearly a local man, but, perhaps knowing they were Home Counties folk, had made some effort to moderate his accent. 'Am th'caretaker here. Which is Mr Rawlins?'

Max, short and stocky, and with his matching tweeds and thick salt-and-pepper moustache, was perhaps the obvious suspect, though Guy, tall, fair-haired and handsome, had a commanding aura of his own.

'I'm Rawlins,' Max said. 'This is my wife, Brenda, and my associate, Guy Denton. You're aware we have permission to stay here for the week?'

'Your funeral,' Jowett replied.

'I'm sorry?'

'Better come in.' Jowett turned and ambled into the darkness.

They glanced at each other, and Guy had to suppress a laugh.

They entered a lobby area, notable for a colossal wood-burning hearth, now filled with cinders and what looked like charred feathers, and, high on the wall, an ornate brass compass with odd astrological symbols inscribed around it. Beyond the lobby lay a grand hallway, the central staircase of which divided half way up and ran in parallel flights to an overhead balcony. Carpets were still laid, but there was an aura of mould. Beyond the hallway lay other large rooms. The light filtering around their curtains played dimly over objects shrouded by sheets. Strips of damp paper hung from the walls.

'Such a shame,' Brenda said, recognising what had once been a fine residence.

Jowett led them through to the next room, which was long and wood-paneled. Its floor was smoothly boarded, and on its facing wall there was a row of tall casements, all curtained. 'Ballroom,' he said simply.

'We need somewhere to bivouac,' Max replied. 'And I think this looks promising. Once settled, we'll commence the baseline tests; work out where the cold-water pipes are and so on.' He turned to Guy. 'Shall we get the stuff?'

Guy nodded. While he and Max traipsed out to the car, Brenda wandered the ballroom. A number of paintings adorned its walls. They were portraits mostly, done in dark oils, but now old and cracked. Faces gazed from past centuries; the men under long wigs woven into ringlets, the women in high 'Fontage' headdresses made from linen and lace. All wore that strange, enigmatic half-smile so favoured by artists of distant ages. At the room's eastern end, three paintings occupied space beneath a trio of timber arches. In the first and third, the gentlemen wore shorter wigs, powdered grey. In the second there was a black woman - very handsome, wearing a frilled cap tied under her chin.

'This one's unusual,' Brenda remarked. 'A negress ... in an English country house?'

'Servant,' Jowett said. 'Least that's the story. No-one really knows.'

'Why have these pictures been left?'

'Lindsay family returned to Balcarres – that's their ancestral home up in Scotland. Suppose they run out of money. Left a lot behind in th'end.'

'How sad. You know, Jowett, this house gave me a start when I first saw it, but now that I'm inside … there's an air of melancholy rather than fear.'

He shrugged, as if this was to be expected.

'You work here,' Brenda added, 'and obviously *you're* not frightened.'

'When you spent your first wedding anniversary on the Somme, miss, and the next thirty years underground, there's nowt much can frighten you.'

'But there is something here that's supposed to be frightening? At least that's what we were told.'

'Aye. But th'only uns I've ever known be exposed to its power are those it don't want here.'

'And who would they be?'

'Whoever they are, miss, they're usually t'first to know.'

On the first floor they found more reception areas than bedrooms. All were in a state of elegant decay. Ceilings once intricate with plaster-work were peeling. Panels in some of the connecting passages had come loose or were warped by damp. Having explored a number of rooms and galleries, they finally returned to the balcony overlooking the hallway. Jowett made to descend, but Max stopped him, mentioning that there was still the top floor.

Jowett shook his head. 'Pardon sir, but I don't go t'th top floor.'

'You don't?'

'It's blocked off. No-one goes there.'

'That's bally inconvenient,' Guy said. 'We were told the top floor is where it all happens.'

'Can't help you, sir.'

'You're the caretaker,' Max reminded him. 'And you have no

access at all?'

'No-one has. Door were locked up there a long time ago, and th'key thrown away. We don't know why, and we don't ask.'

'I think we'll at least have a look,' Max said. 'The upper tier is reputedly the most active part of this house. But even if it wasn't, no-one said anything about my only having half the place to investigate, and I came a long way for this. At no small expense. Someone will need to know.'

Jowett regarded him steadily, his doleful expression implying contempt for a class of people who had nothing to do with their time and money but pursue hobbies. If Max's oblique threat about reporting him for being obstructive was a concern, he didn't show it. But eventually he sighed and led them along a dark access-passage at the end of which a shaft of grimy light spilled down from a circular skylight.

'Back stair,' Jowett said. 'Were another stair at one time, but that's gone. This is the only way up, and the only way down.'

The steep, narrow stair's enclosing walls had formerly been papered, but huge sections of this appeared to have been clawed away from the plaster beneath. The treads were loose, so Max ascended warily. At the top, there was a single door made from solid black wood with a handle of tarnished brass. When Max got up there, he was surprised to find the palms of his hands greasy with sweat. He rubbed them on his trousers and tried the handle. It turned, but the door would not open. He glanced behind. To his surprise, none of the others had followed him up.

'Got the jitters already?' he laughed.

Then a rustling sound distracted him. Had it come from the other side of the door?

'Isn't much room up there for all of us,' Guy called.

But Max wasn't listening. 'Jowett, you sure you haven't got a key?'

'Never been a key to that, door, sir.'

Max came down again, stopping once to glance back up. 'This place is rotting, Jowett. That's plain to anyone. But if it's rotting from the top down, the Corporation aren't doing themselves any favours ignoring it. You should send some chaps up there to see what's what, or this stately home will finish up an empty shell.'

'Might be for the best,' Jowett said, his stooped back receding through the shadows.

Again, Guy had to suppress a snigger, which irritated Brenda. His attitude implied that the caretaker was a credulous old fool, but *she* didn't get that feeling. There was something stoic and honest about Jowett, even if he was a rather taciturn chap. Perhaps he was uneducated; but he didn't give the impression that he was the sort to believe in gibberish.

'Have we seen everything?' Max asked, as they re-emerged onto the balcony.

'Excepting the cellar, sir,' Jowett said. 'Full of rubbish though, so you'll need to watch your step.'

From a chamber adjoining the ballroom, they descended a short stair to a small, pokey landing with walls of bare brick. Jowett lit an oil lamp, and passed through another door, beyond which lay a second stairwell, utterly black. Max went next; it was a tight fit even for someone of his relatively small stature – he had to duck, and the width of the passage was barely larger than the breadth of his shoulders. Brenda, being slimmer, had less trouble, but Guy, who brought up the rear, had to bend painfully. Not that this prevented him fooling around; as they descended, he squeezed Brenda's right buttock. She just managed to suppress a yelp.

According to Jowett, the cellar was the only part of the property remaining from the manor house that had stood here in the Middle Ages. It was a series of connecting tunnels, arched and built from dripping black stone. It resembled a dungeon but was used mainly for storage. They navigated narrow paths between stacks of furniture slathered with dust-webs, and crates overflowing with bric-a-brac.

'Were once a priest's hole down here,' Jowett said, speaking so quietly that Brenda wondered if he was being reverential. Perhaps he was Catholic, and this place had meaning for him? 'No-one knows where. Story is, passage may lead as far as th'town centre.'

'That's quite a hike,' Max said, sounding doubtful. 'They wouldn't go to all that trouble just to build a priest's get-away, would they?'

'Didn't spare much effort in them bad old days, sir. When Queen Bess's priest-hunters were knocking around.'

That settled it, Brenda decided. Jowett *was* Catholic.

He ambled on, taking his light with him. They scrambled to keep up, though Brenda caught her sleeve on a nail protruding from a shelf and found herself at the rear.

'Ill feeling dies hard in Wigan,' Guy mumbled.

'Sectarianism was rife in the Northwest until relatively recently,' Max replied.

Already he and Guy were several yards ahead. The light faded fast. Brenda tried to disentangle herself gently, not wishing to damage her fashionable 'box jacket'. But opaque blackness rose steadily, as did an eerie sensation that there was someone else behind her. She stiffened when she felt what might be a chill breath on the back of her neck. Only slowly did she pluck up the courage to glance around.

But she saw nothing.

'The families occupying Haigh Hall after the Reformation were Protestant,' Max added, his voice already a distant echo. 'But they held sympathies for local Catholics ...'

Whimpering, Brenda yanked her arm hard, the material ripping, and then heard a splintering *crack* as a higher shelf, attached by struts to the lower one, broke loose. Several dust-caked books descended, one striking her shoulder, the other landing on the shelf in front of her, open on its title page.

Brenda stared at it, shocked. For a bewildering moment she felt as if it had fallen that way on purpose. It had been inscribed with handwriting, though this was illegible in the darkness.

Something touched her shoulder.

Startled, she spun around.

The blackness behind her was so black it was almost solid, but she could still feel whatever had touched her. And then she realised what it was, and almost laughed. The book she thought had struck her shoulder had not been a book at all, but a glove. And it was still lying there, limp and muddy-gray, two of its fingers caressing the skin of her neck.

Except that – no, it wasn't a glove.

It was a spider.

Brenda screeched and flicked the enormous creature away. She tried to stumble off, only to collide with Max, who had come back looking for her.

'What's got into you?' he asked testily.

'I'm … I'm alright,' she said. 'Let's just get out of here.'

Guy had come back as well, but Jowett was pressing on speedily. As they forged after him, he disappeared around a corner – and the minuscule light remaining was swallowed. Brenda grasped her husband's arm; the ensuing darkness was black as treacle.

'Jowett!' Guy shouted. 'Hold up, man!'

When they finally tottered around the corner, having blundered into all sorts of sharp-edged objects, Jowett was making his way back towards them.

'What the deuce is the matter with you?' Guy demanded.

'Apologies, sir. Hearing's not what it were.'

'Hearing be damned! You must've known we weren't with you.'

'I was on my own back there, Mr Jowett!' Brenda complained. 'Anything could have happened.'

'There's no danger down here, miss,' Jowett said.

'I'm not sure you'd know, you were in such a rush to get out,' Guy retorted.

Jowett continued to focus on Brenda, or rather on the scruffy book that she still clutched in her hand. 'There're only memories in this part of th'house.'

As if that was all that needed to be said, he moved on towards the foot of the staircase.

'What's this?' Max asked, noticing what his wife was carrying.

'A book I found. I didn't mean to bring it with me.'

'Perhaps you'd better put it back?'

'I'm not going back down there on my own.'

'Well, bring it with you then,' Max snapped. 'I'm sure I don't care.'

They followed Jowett in single file to the surface. Brenda knew why Max was so vexed. Always on these expeditions he was concerned that she might become afraid – and that would distract him from the work, as he'd feel he'd have to look out for her. Of course, interrupting *this* investigation, when he was hoping to use it to launch himself as a serious rival to Harry Price, would be tantamount to treason.

The curtained gloom of the ground-floor seemed dazzling after the cloying blackness of the cellar. Once back in the ballroom, Brenda examined the book more carefully. It seemed to be a diary, though it was so encrusted with grime that it was difficult to read. She thought the name 'Adela' was visible on the title page.

'Gooin' now,' Jowett said, pulling on a cap and patched up jacket. 'Be back in a couple of days to make sure everything's fettled.'

'Thank you,' Max replied tersely.

'One more thing, Mr Rawlins. You're aware there's gents from th'press comin' this afternoon?'

'What's that?'

'I'm told they're very keen to speak to you.'

Max glowered. 'Blast it! Should've known we couldn't trust everyone in the Corporation to keep their mouths shut.'

Guy waved it away. 'It'll just be the local boys.'

'*Manchester Guardian,* I understand,' Jowett said.

Now even Guy looked surprised. '*The Guardian* ... interested in a ghost hunt?'

'Our war records will have added spice,' Max grunted. 'All right, thank you, Jowett. Look, before you go, there are one or two things ...'

He walked out of the ballroom in company with the caretaker.

Guy looked puzzled. 'Thought that's what Maxie wanted – the world to know who he is?'

'Only for the right reasons,' Brenda replied. 'He doesn't want to see the press 'til he's got something to show them.'

She knew that after the Borley Rectory controversy, her husband was determined to prove that not all psychic investigators lacked integrity. In fact, he'd become a little obsessive about this, which had mildly worried her. For some reason, that old saying kept creeping into her head: *be wary of looking too hard for something – you may actually find it.* Almost on cue, she thought she heard something upstairs: a dull *thud.* Initially it made her jump, but experience had proved that this was the sort of mundane thing you could actually hear anywhere at any time – so she put it from her mind.

The press arrived late that afternoon in a shabby old Plymouth. There was a photographer and a reporter. As it was now almost five o'clock, and the light was fading, they held the interview outside, just beyond the ballroom windows. Brenda stayed indoors. A couple of times now she'd tried to read the diary. But it was so old, its pages so brittle with age and dirt that it was almost indecipherable. While the men talked outside, she again leafed into it.

'So, Wing-Commander,' came the reporter's half-muffled voice, 'you and Mr Denton only met when you were in Colditz together?'

'Yes,' Max replied. 'We weren't imprisoned at the same time, but we got to know each other while we were in there …'

Brenda tried to concentrate on the book. About half way through, the pages became more legible. On these, it could be seen that the handwriting was actually quite elegant:

April 18, 1746
Clemmy is increasingly nervous as news filters back about the battle in Scotland. I tried to explain that this is no concern. We are a respected family and are in no danger. However, since she learned to read, she has become absorbed in history books, and has now discovered that on the day of Princess Clementina's marriage to the Old Pretender, in whose name the Jacobites first rose, His Holiness the Pope proclaimed her 'Queen of Great Britain'. When I tried to reassure Clemmy that a coincidence of names is nothing to worry about, and that no-one will associate her with treasonous acts purely on this basis, she declared that everything happens for a purpose. She now talks as if her arrival here predestined disaster for us. I reminded her sternly that she is in England, not on the

plantations in Jamaica, and that the mob rule of which she lives in dread has no place in this society. Clemmy is a very superstitious girl, which is understandable given her upbringing. However, she has been made irrational by fear, and it would help me enormously if Jack were here to calm her. His gambling debts are proving more than just an inconvenience, but alone I cannot raise the funds to have him released. If only his father were alive.

Brenda glanced down the ballroom towards the portrait of the black lady. Hadn't Jowett said something about the subject of that painting being a servant here? Could this 'Clemmy' – from Jamaica – be the same person?

Outside, the men were still talking, describing how Guy, after being shot down in December '43, was hunted for several days across the frozen German landscape, before being captured and handed to the Gestapo.

'I was given a pretty rough time of it before I was sent to Colditz,' he said.

Max then explained how he took the emotionally exhausted young pilot under his wing and involved him in ghost-hunting activities initially as a distraction.

'And the German guards tolerated this?' the reporter asked skeptically.

'They tolerated a lot so long as it kept us out of mischief,' Max laughed.

Brenda tried to concentrate on the next diary entry:

April 24, 1746
The positive news received yesterday – that one of Jack's former shipmates has made good his debt, and that he is to be released from the Marshalsea – was tempered today by disturbing developments in Wigan. Joseph, one of the under-footmen, returned from market this morning, and reported that several town-houses have been set on fire. As we feared, these houses belong to prominent local 'Papists'. The families concerned have gone into hiding, but gangs of ruffians are running around, seeking them out. It makes no sense to me.

The Highland army that passed through the outskirts of Wigan last year was little more than a colourful parade. Their pipers played a succession of reels and jigs. 'Bonnie Prince Charlie', as the Scots call him, cut a gallant figure in his tartan trews and cloak, waving his French cocked hat to the girls in the crowd. Almost the entire populace, not just the town's Catholics, flocked to the roadside to watch. There was no animosity. I can only assume that, with the Jacobites now destroyed, people are fearful of retribution and are trying to show that they have always been loyal to the king.

Brenda heard another dull *thud* overhead.

She'd dismissed the one she'd heard earlier, but on this occasion, it was more distinct - it reverberated through the entire building as if something had banged heavily against a door. She placed the diary down and walked from the ballroom.

'Hello?' she called up the stairs. There was no response, so she ascended to the first floor. 'Hello?'

The landing was deserted. The little light the curtains admitted was noticeably dwindling, only faint gleams visible along the lengthier corridors. In various rooms, 'trigger objects' - mainly crucifixes - had been positioned by the investigators on top of pieces of paper, with pencil lines drawn around them. Max and Guy had also set up cameras, which could be activated by tripwires. A reel-to-reel tape recorder had been fixed in the east wing. There was a thermographic gauge on the main landing. Brenda wondered if one of these might have fallen over - though, when she checked, all were as they should be. Which didn't totally surprise her. For some reason, it seemed more likely that what she'd heard had not been on this first floor, but on the top floor - in the upper tier.

What was it Jowett had said?

'Th'only uns exposed to its power are those it don't want here. And whoever they are, they're usually th'first to know.'

Was it trying to let them know now?

Had it realised they were here, and was it trying to come

down from its place of confinement?

Unsure why she was having such thoughts, Brenda processed along the access-passage to the foot of the upper stair. The skylight there shed little light as it was, but now, in late afternoon, its single shaft was paler than a moonbeam. With trepidation, she glanced upward.

The door at the top was open.

Brenda's breath caught in her throat.

Then she sensed a presence directly behind her. She squeaked and whipped around, tripping backwards and landing on her bottom.

'What the devil's the matter now?' Max asked, sounding cross again.

'I ... you ...?' she stuttered, wide-eyed. 'The door to the upper tier ...'

Words failed her when she saw that the door above was closed - as it presumably had been all along. Only a trick of the failing light had made it appear open.

'Yes?' Max said impatiently.

'Nothing. I made a mistake.'

'There's a surprise. Look ... we need you outside for a photo.'

'Why do you need me?'

'Because you're part of the team, and you look good on camera. Come on.'

Before following him down the passage, Brenda glanced one more time at the upper door, now veiled by shadow. She wondered if it was her imagination that she could hear a light *clicking* - as if its handle was being furtively tested.

Brenda was innocent.

She'd proclaimed it over and over. She'd wept it until there was insufficient moisture left in her body to provide further tears. But it had made no difference - and it would make none now. The road was a muddy track, and there were crowds of people gathered along it, who threw stones and rotten vegetables. Their jeers were hate-filled, but she felt too weary to be frightened – even when the gallows came in sight. It was about twelve feet tall: a single sturdy post with a braced crossbar. Its timbers were darkened by age, but the rope looked new.

The crowd surged forward when the cart halted, though a small troop of red-coated militiamen formed a tight cordon – trying to protect her, she realised. If she hadn't been so tired and cold, she'd have laughed at the absurdity. The roars of the mob reached a new crescendo as the cart driver turned to face her. The eyes behind the slits in his hood glinted like coins. He checked that the leather cord binding her hands was secure, then fitted the noose around her neck and drew it tight. Across the market square, a portly, bewigged official wearing a tricorne and a blue satin coat was seated on a horse. He sniffed into a lace handkerchief, looking bored by the whole affair, and, almost as an afterthought, made a vague signal.

'I'm innocent,' Brenda tried to say one final time. 'Innocent as a lamb.'

But the mob began baying again, drowning her half-choked words. She still insisted to herself that she wasn't afraid – though it was difficult to ignore the warm fluid gushing down her legs. As the executioner lashed his reins, she closed her eyes. The cart was hauled away, and Brenda fell ...

She sat up abruptly, her breath coming in short, ragged gasps.

At first, she didn't remember where she was, but then the ballroom swam back into view, noon sunlight shafting through its tall casements. The two other truckle beds, one to either side of her, were unmade but empty.

She glanced at her watch. It was well past midday. The previous night they'd stayed up late holding a vigil. Remaining awake until the small hours and sleeping in long after the sun had risen wasn't good for the body-clock, but it was the only way in this business.

'Max!' she called, slotting her feet into her heeled, ankle-strapped shoes and pulling on her cardigan. When she entered the hallway, she called again. 'Max! Guy!'

The echo of her voice resounded from distant corners of the

building. Otherwise, the silence was quite profound – as if she was the only person here.

Last night's vigil had been disappointing. It had been spooky of course; they always were, but with every room lit by candles, and the aura of scientific enquiry that Max brought to these occasions – they'd spent more time checking gauges and making notes than sitting and listening – the old building had felt more like a laboratory than a haunted house. There hadn't been so much as a cold spot.

When she walked into the lobby, she found the front door open, but there was no sign of anybody outside. The car was absent from the parking area.

'Anyone here at all?' Brenda called, walking to the edge of the lawn.

The sun was out. Birds twittered. Yet she felt strangely vulnerable. A flicker of movement drew her attention to the nearest clump of shadow-filled foliage. She strolled cautiously towards it. 'Hello?'

The foliage mainly comprised rhododendrons – dense wads of heavy, hanging evergreens. It would be easy for someone to conceal themselves in there. Brenda's hair began to prickle. She suddenly knew that she was being watched. But not from among the bushes, from behind. She spun around, half expecting to see someone framed in the Hall's front door – but there was nobody. Her vision roved across the rest of the dilapidated exterior. For a spilt-second she thought she spied movement in a top floor window – and then a hand slapped over her mouth, and an arm hooked around her waist.

With muffled squeals she was dragged back through the undergrowth into the dim-lit space beyond. Frantic, she sank her teeth into the fat, fleshy palm. There was a squawk, and she was released. She stumbled away and turned, gasping – to find Guy rubbing at the base of his thumb.

'What got into you?' he said indignantly.

'What's got into *you*?' she retorted. 'Of all the stupid tricks ...'

'Hey ... it was just a joke. I think you really hurt me.'

'That's what you deserve.'

'Come and kiss it better.'

Brenda shook her head. 'You've got to stop this playing around. If Max finds out ...'

'He won't. He doesn't notice what goes on under his nose.'

'Don't be too sure.' Brenda peeked back out through the foliage. 'Where is he anyway?'

'Well, he was pretty irritated about last night's poor show. So, he's driven to the town library. Feels it's time we learned a bit more about the place. In particular, why the famous top floor has been locked for so long.'

Brenda glanced again towards the silent Hall; especially at the upper tier, with its moss-covered stonework and the threads of old sheets dangling from its casements. 'I can't help thinking there's a rather awful reason for that.'

'I'm sure the only things up there are rats. Maybe an owl or two.'

'I hope not for Max's sake.'

'He's really thrown all his eggs into this basket, hasn't he?'

'He wants his research to be taken seriously. Harry didn't do the industry any favours.'

'Ah, so it's that old rivalry thing again.'

'Max's civilian life has been dedicated to this field. You know that, Guy.'

'Gracious, Bren. You almost sound like a loyal wife.'

Brenda looked away. 'I feel terrible about this.'

Guy approached from behind and slid his arms around her. 'Hey, we all get pangs of conscience now and then. But I don't mind. Anything that raises the tempo ...'

She pointedly disentangled herself. 'Don't tell me *this* is why you've been lurking around out here?'

'Actually, I've been exploring.' He grinned like a cat. 'But while you mention it ... we *are* alone.'

'You seriously want to make love now? In a wood?'

'If it was good enough for Robin and Marion ...'

'They weren't already married to other people.'

'Look, we go at it indoors, and that old codger - what's his name, Jowett! - might walk in on us.'

'You really are the last of the romantics, aren't you?'

'Come on, Bren. When did we last see each other? It's been over a month.'

She moved away, out of his reach. 'Not long enough, in my opinion.'

'What do you mean?'

'Well, it's not like there's any future in it. We've neither of us got many prospects.'

Frustrated, Guy shook a cigarette from its packet and slipped it between his lips. 'I wasn't aware you had plans to take it that far.'

'I don't.' She glanced shyly round at him. 'How can I?'

He regarded her carefully as he lit up. It was such an awkward moment that she blushed. Both had known when they'd first entered this affair that it had the potential to cause problems. At first it had been purely sexual. Brenda was a bright young thing - pretty, petite, always fashionably dressed. Guy was tall and athletic, roguishly handsome, much closer to her age than Max was, and yet in some ways less robust. When she'd first met him, she'd been attracted to him because for all his manly looks, he was so damaged, so in need of love and tenderness. Of course, as he'd recovered, all that had changed. Gradually, as the war faded into the past, he'd reverted to his old cavalier self, the carefree young scoundrel who'd joined the RAF as a fighter pilot - and, yet ironically, the increased edge of danger this had brought to their arrangement had excited her all the more. It did now, if she was honest.

'Why don't you put that cigarette out?' she said. 'And get over here.'

Wigan Library was well stocked with worthy literature, but there was surprisingly little relating to the esoteric history of Haigh Hall.

Max found a couple of volumes, but overall these were dry and factual. If anything, they made the Hall's life-story seem almost benign. Originally the possession of Hugh le Norreys, a

Norman noble who settled after the Conquest, the estate passed to the Bradshaigh family in 1295 and to the Lindsays in 1785. There'd been the occasional incident - the penance of Lady Mabel, the beheading of the Earl of Derby - but there was nothing hugely exciting. Max spent the afternoon gleaning what he could from these sketchy details, but in the end none of them made reference to the mysterious upper tier. He packed his satchel and was about to leave, when, as an afterthought, he crossed to the librarian's desk and asked her if she had anything concerning crimes and atrocities in Wigan. The librarian, a stiff, prim lady, raised an imperious eyebrow. But eventually, after rooting along the shelves, she found a small, cloth-covered book entitled:

Murders and Mayhem in Old Lancashire

Four chapters in was the subtitle:

1746 - frightful scene at Haigh Hall

Max read avidly for the next twenty minutes.

On completion, he'd generated more information from that one tome than all the others put together. He wasn't completely satisfied, but here at last there was something to work with. He left, heading uphill towards Wigan's Central Post Office, where he'd made an arrangement to have his mail collected. He hadn't expected there'd be much - but to his surprise a telegram was already waiting. When he tore it open, its message was stark and simple:

Ring me. Harry.

There was a telephone kiosk outside, where Max dialed his old friend's number. The call was answered with almost indecent haste.

'Harry Price.'

'It's me,' Max said.

'Maxie!' Despite the manner of their last parting, Harry was his usual jovial self. 'Good of you to call so quickly.'

'I'm going to make this whole thing quick, Harry. If we hadn't been friends for so long, I wouldn't have bothered at all. And before you even ask, no, there's no possibility of your joining this investigation.'

'Wouldn't dream of crashing your party, Maxie. In fact, I'm only contacting you because, as you say, we once were friends.'

'Stop flannelling me, Harry.'

'This fellow you've got with you, this Guy Denton. How are you finding him?'

Max was more than a little surprised by that question. 'He's a slow-learner, but that hardly matters to you, does it?'

'Well ... sorry to say this, old boy, but he's not so slow in other departments. About six weeks ago I saw him in the West End, having dinner with a young lady.'

'And?'

'What's that pretty wife of yours called again?'

'Brenda, of course ... wait a minute. *What the devil are you driving at, Price?'*

'I'm sorry to break it to you like this, old boy. But I waited until Brenda had gone off to powder her nose, then I introduced myself to this Denton chap. Said I was an old associate of yours. He was cool as a cucumber. Told me he was Brenda's brother, over from America.'

'Brenda doesn't have a brother,' Max stammered.

'I didn't realise that at the time. But only this morning I saw you all together in *The Guardian.* The caption said exactly who you all were.'

'Harry, if this is some ridiculous attempt to ...'

'Fabricate? Hmmm ...' Harry's tone cooled. 'You accused me of fabrication once before, as I recall. But I didn't then. And I haven't now. You may not believe this, Maxie, but I always liked you. You were a knowledgeable and thorough researcher. I don't enjoy seeing chaps of your calibre made fools of. Especially not by some callow young oaf ...'

Max slammed the receiver onto its cradle.

He didn't believe it. He didn't need to believe it. It was simply untrue. It had to be. And yet, for all that he and Harry Price hadn't seen eye-to-eye for some time, there was absolutely nothing for his former colleague to gain from telling such a lie.

It was several minutes before Max left that kiosk, but when he did, he was so angry that he could barely walk straight.

It was mid-evening, but it was spring, and the sun was setting over the verdant woods of the Haigh estate. In a leafy dell near the Hall, Brenda climbed hurriedly into her slacks.

'Conscience again?' Guy asked, reclining lazily.

'It's getting cold and we ought to be getting back.' Her tone was brusque, clipped.

He too began to dress. 'You must admit … *that* was fun?'

'Why don't we just keep things platonic for the rest of the time we're here? We've got a job to do, after all.'

He stood up and buckled his trousers. 'You may call it a job. Others would call it ballyhoo nonsense.'

Brenda glanced at him, surprised. 'You don't believe anymore?'

'Did I ever?' He stuck a fresh cigarette into his mouth. 'Tell the truth, I don't know.' He lit up. 'I know I was in a state and grabbed hold of anything I could. Some of the chaps in Colditz threw themselves into making escape plans. I couldn't face that. My nerves were gone. So, I did the next best thing - I looked beyond the misery of this mortal coil into a completely different world. But that's in the past now.' Guy almost seemed embarrassed by these admissions. 'Would it be too much of an exaggeration to say that I'm only here today because you are?'

Brenda pulled her shoes on. 'You don't have *any* interest anymore?'

'It's not intentional … it's just, well, after some of the things I've experienced, I'm pretty indifferent when it comes to spooks. They might be real, they might not be. But I've got to the stage where I don't care two hoots. I mean, take you … you're a woman of the world. You don't think it's all a bit childish?'

'Not the way Max does it,' she said. 'He's trying to understand these phenomena.'

'Good on him.'

'Do you have to sound so scornful?'

'Come on, Bren ... let's be honest, what's he doing now? Scuttling around Wigan town centre trying to find evidence there's something on that no doubt dusty, deserted upper floor. And why? Just to get one over on his ex-pal.'

'The upper tier is supposed to be the evil heart of Haigh Hall.'

'Evil heart?' Guy snorted. 'I've told you ... rats and owls.'

'Well *I've* sensed something up there.'

He smirked. 'All of a sudden you're a sensitive?'

'Well why is it closed off?'

'Probably because it's dangerous.'

'Hmmm.' She buttoned up her cardigan. 'Pity you can't prove that.'

'You think I can't?' Guy flirted his cigarette to the ground and, with a burst of energy, thrust his way out onto the lawn. 'Well, let's see ...'

'Guy, don't do anything silly.'

'It's only a locked door, Bren. It won't take much to force it.'

Brenda followed. 'Look ... they said we shouldn't damage anything.'

'We're here all week. I can put it back before we leave.'

She peered along the drive, then followed Guy inside the Hall, ensuring to brush the bits of grass and leaf from her clothes.

'Good job I played a bit of rugger,' he said, heading up the staircase. 'Doubt there's a lock in Blighty can stand up to my shoulder-charge.'

Brenda wanted to go up with him, but things suddenly seemed very muddled. Though she'd enjoyed the affair with Guy, part of her had kept on hoping that soon he'd get itchy feet and move abroad or something. On one hand it was a good thing that he was starting to find Max's ghost-hunting exploits a bore, but if he'd now developed such feelings for her that he'd go along with them anyway, that was less encouraging.

She walked disconsolately into the ballroom.

Guy made one good point: Haigh Hall was an eerie old pile, but so far there wasn't much sign of – what was it they'd been told, 'spooks coming out of the walls'? She picked up the diary, flicking through until she found the woman called Adela's next legible entry. Somewhere overhead, she heard a succession of heavy impacts.

She tried to ignore them as she read.

April 25, 1746
Talk is rife among the servants about the Jacobite rising in 1715, when an armed mob descended on the Hall because a number of Catholic spokesmen had taken refuge here. Despite Sir Roger's protestations, some thirty men were forcibly taken from the estate. Then, as now, those victimised had nothing to do with the Jacobite movement. Several were not even known to be Catholic but merely suspected of such, though this suspicion was enough to seal their doom. I have tried to reassure the servants that three decades have passed since then and that we are now in the Age of Enlightenment. But they are alarmed. And as for Clemmy – she has taken to inhabiting the upper tier, that old, disused portion of the house, and will not come down …

Brenda jumped to her feet. 'Guy … I think I'm onto something here!'

She twirled around, only to find that she was alone in the ballroom – of course she was, though for a second, she'd had an idea that she wasn't. The house was now filled with deepening shadow. Fading streaks of reddish sunlight showed on the wall.

Adela's narrative continued:

To reassure everyone, I found an old military uniform. We stuffed it with sticks to give it a firm skeleton, and then padded it with discarded clothes. We even tied bundles of rags together so that it had a head on which it could wear its mitre cap. Armed with a sabre and a broom-handle with a rusty bayonet on the end, we set it in a window on the upper tier, so that any would-be transgressors will think we have military protection. But

Clemmy fears it won't be enough. All she does is cling to the dummy-soldier and mutter in that childlike way of hers: 'I won't be taken. I won't. I'm innocent. Innocent as a lamb.'

Brenda almost dropped the book.

It was impossible not to associate what she'd just read with that vivid dream. Then she noticed how silent everything was – upstairs, the blows to the door had ceased. It was also much darker, which was making it difficult to continue reading. She lit the candles on the shelves. As she did, the glow of two headlamps trailed past outside. There was a grinding of gravel.

Brenda grabbed the diary and raced out into the lobby – just as the front door swung open. Max stood there, though he was only distinguished by his silhouette. He said nothing, but Brenda was so excited that she didn't notice anything strange about him.

'Max, I think I've learned something about the upper tier. This diary was written by a woman called Adela ...'

'Lady Adela Bradshaigh,' he interrupted huskily.

'Oh ... yes.' Brenda was surprised. 'Well, apparently she had a black servant ...'

'Clementina St Clair. Who was terrified of mobs. Men carrying torches, aggressive men, that sort of thing. In her youth in Jamaica, she and her brother were runaway slaves. Their owner sent the "Maroons" in pursuit. The Maroons were ex-slaves too, but they'd formed their own lawless society – and they played it rough, hunting with torches and dogs. When they recaptured Clementina and her brother, they beat them savagely. Clementina was repeatedly raped.'

'You know about this?' Brenda couldn't help feeling a little deflated.

'I've done my research.' He pushed past her towards the candle-lit ballroom, where he dumped his satchel.

Brenda followed him in. 'Then you know that this poor girl, Clementina ... when she came here, she was hanged by an anti-Jacobite mob. And I think there were prominent townsfolk among them, and after they realised what they'd done, they closed the upstairs. Maybe there was evidence up there that would implicate them. I mean, it's supposition, but ...'

'Clementina St Claire was not a servant in this house,' Max replied, wheeling to face her. Brenda was stunned by how pale and hollow-eyed he looked. 'She was a guest here. And she was hanged lawfully – for the murder of her common-law husband, a disreputable sea-captain called Jack Bradshaigh.'

'What?'

'She hacked him to death with a sabre. A crime which Adela, his mother, was witness to – and as such went mad and was confined in the local asylum.'

Brenda glanced into the diary, trying to make sense of what he'd just told her. Surprisingly, there was only one more entry, and it was written in a frenzied scribble rather than that familiar stylish hand. Beyond it, all the other pages were blank.

'But ... she was innocent,' Brenda said to herself. 'I felt it in my dream ...'

'Women protesting their innocence when they're guilty is nothing new,' Max said tersely. 'But that's something we'll discuss later.'

Brenda glanced at him, distracted. 'I'm sorry, what?'

He regarded her coolly. 'Where's Guy?'

'He's ... he's gone to the upper tier.'

'How appropriate.'

Without another word, Max turned and strode away. Brenda would have gone with him, but she knew she had to read more. There was a mystery here, and maybe Adela Bradshaigh herself could explain it. As such, Brenda didn't notice when her husband stopped by the fireplace to pick up a heavy poker, or how, before he left the ballroom, he drew from a pocket his old Webley revolver.

April 26, 1746
This has been a dreadful day. The danger is now passed, though it was a great ordeal. Just as it turned dark, the anti-Catholic mob arrived, armed with cudgels and firebrands. Thankfully I had already bidden the servants lock our doors. But before I describe what happened next, I must mention the strange

madness that took possession of Clementina.

All through today she has remained in the upper tier, performing strange rituals which she learned as a child on the plantations. At first, we found this a mere diversion, but it became steadily more unnerving. We heard her dancing and chanting. We even heard music – the sound of drums and pipes, though there are no instruments on that top floor. With an increased sense of dread, those remaining servants took refuge in the cellar. Joseph, who, as former man-servant to Jack, accompanied him on many voyages, in particular to the Indies where Jack first met his dusky-skinned beauty, describes ungodly rites practiced by the slaves on those lonely isles … rites which supposedly can make soldiers out of the dead. Joseph is a sturdy fellow but, at these memories, even he hid himself below.

Shortly before nightfall, Clemmy ceased her caterwaul, but by then the mob had come. I shouted through the barred door that there were no rebels here. They responded with oaths, but no violence. I wondered at first if they refrained from this in respect of my person, but then I learned the truth. A clash of hooves and a barrage of angry shouts signalled that Jack had returned. When I glanced through the glass, I saw him riding around, whipping those hooligans. They don't share the stuff of their forefathers, for they fled. Once they had gone, I opened the door and flung myself into his arms.

Jack is much changed since his incarceration. Many have called him 'black sheep' and 'ne'er-do-well', and his appearance matches this. He has lost weight and vigour, but in my eyes he is still my sea-faring son: a tall, bold adventurer. I assured him the villainous band had not hurt me, and when he asked if they had dared hurt Clementina, I sent him to the top floor to find her.

I write this entry in joy, for Jack has gone to reunite with his beloved. I can't help wondering if it was Clementina's magic that brought him home in such timely fashion, though I know in my heart that this could never be. I don't hold with pagan foolery. In any case, as Joseph said, the ritual we heard was designed to animate that which is not living. And my son is very much alive, for he calls lustily as he ascends ...

Overhead, Brenda now heard Max shouting, though her thoughts were elsewhere – on the events in this place two centuries ago. On how Captain Jack Bradshaigh was slain when he mounted that top floor. But if Clementina St Claire wasn't responsible – as Brenda knew she wasn't – who was?

Scarcely believing what she was thinking, Brenda began to flick backwards through the diary. Individual quotes hit her like pellets of ice:

... we stuffed it with sticks to give it a firm skeleton, and then padded it with discarded clothes. We even tied bundles of rags together so that it had a head ...

... the ritual we heard was designed to animate that which is not living ...

Upstairs, Max was still shouting, demanding that Guy show himself.

What was it he'd said earlier – about Clementina being terrified of 'aggressive men?'

'Max, stop shouting,' Brenda said quietly. But then louder, more urgently: 'Max, for God's sake, don't go up there shouting!'

She dashed into the hallway. His voice boomed down.

'Denton ... you wretch! Get out here now!'

Brenda hared up the main stairway, calling: 'Max, I know what happened. Adela Bradshaigh was put in the madhouse because she saw something she couldn't comprehend ...'

'Denton, I'm going to kill you!'

'Max!' Brenda reached the first floor, only to find herself in total blackness, knocking one of their fixed cameras from its tripod.

'I'm going to kill you stone dead!'

'Max, don't say that!' She stumbled to the access-passage, focusing on the pall of dim moonlight at its end.

'After everything I did for you!' Max roared. *'You pay me back*

by messing with my wife ... you bloody hound!'

Brenda was half way up the upper stair, but now stopped rigid. From overhead there came a furious smashing of wood.

The rage still pounded inside Max's skull. He'd managed to suppress it during his journey back from Wigan, but now, as he entered the black hole of the upper tier, it exploded. He went dizzy with it. So fogged was his vision that he could barely fix on the rotted doorways that gaped around him, or the sheets of fluttering web draped over them. He blundered through one after another, barking the name of his enemy. Some rooms were latticed with spectral moonlight, others black and fetid as tombs. Lumpen shadows rose – ancient furnishings furred with dust. He struck with his poker, reducing them all to splinters. Just ahead, a low, curved stairway became visible. Max stalked up it. At the top, a door stood ajar, silver moonbeams filling the space beyond. It had the aura of a final refuge.

'Denton? This is your last chance. Don't make me come in there and get you.' There was no response. '*Damn you!*

The door was stiff and unwieldy, so Max had to fight his way around it – at which point he halted, confused.

The room, which he could see clearly thanks to moonlight shimmering through an open window, was spacious and weirdly shaped – almost octagonal. But this upper tier had evidently *not* been sealed off for too long – because a football sat in the middle of its floor. Had local children been up here? Or had they just kicked their ball through the window? Either way, it was an almost comically mundane thing to discover in a place like this.

Not that it mattered.

Max breathed hard and slow as his gaze shifted from one empty corner to the next, finally fastening on the window – which Denton might have used to escape. Swearing, he started across the room, but halted midway to gaze again at the football.

At what he'd *thought* was the football.

Closer up, it was nothing of the sort.

What he'd taken for alternating patches of black and white

leather was an intricate pattern of fresh bruising. Two larger patches were the yawning sockets where a pair of eyes had been gouged from their orbits. An even larger patch was the rent crevasse where a human mouth had been; it was now glutted with blood and pulped tongue-flesh.

Even Wing-Commander Max Rawlins, who'd seen every kind of horror that could be wrought on the human body, stumbled backwards - until he collided with the door, and a bulky object jammed on top of it was dislodged. Its weight almost knocked him to the floor, but it was his identification of it - as Guy Denton's beheaded corpse - that drew a hoarse shriek from his lips.

On the stair, Brenda was still frozen with shock.

Surely Max had been surmising? It wasn't possible that he could actually *know*.

They'd been so discreet. But no ... Guy hadn't been discreet. Not recently. Suddenly she had to get away from this place. She made a stumbling descent, her mind a whirlwind of doubts and terrors. At the bottom she veered into the access-passage, but here she stopped again, every muscle in her body stiffening.

A figure was standing at the far end.

Her eyes had now attuned to the dark a little, and could see enough to ascertain that, whoever he was, he wore a reddish coat and trousers, and an odd mitre-shaped cap. He also had a weapon, for she glimpsed curved steel. But it was only when the figure began lurching along the passage towards her - with a crazy, twisty-turning, puppet-like gait - that she went scampering back the way she had come. She ascended the stair blindly. When the broken-open door to the upper tier appeared in front of her, she didn't hesitate but flung herself through into pitch darkness, her incoherent gibbers rising to hysterical screeches when two strong hands suddenly reached from the shadow, took her by the cardigan and flung her back against a wall.

Max's gaze burned into her. His eyes bulged, sweat drenched his pallid features. She didn't need to explain, merely to point at the rectangle of dimness at the top of the stair. As they looked, a ghastly shadow appeared there.

'Into that room!' Max growled, shoving her towards the nearest doorway.

The distorted figure had now emerged into plain sight. With bizarre, uncoordinated steps, it lumbered towards them. Max shouted a warning, but when he saw the cavalry sabre he opened fire, flashes of light interspersed with echoing reports. The figure advanced regardless. Brenda caught fleeting glimpses of an old bandolier belt, of ragged, mismatched limbs, of that hideous blade – dabbled with fresh blood.

Max emptied all six chambers before blundering after his wife into a room stacked with ancient, rickety furniture. Desperately, they tried to battle their way through it. When the shadowy form followed them in, Max hurled his pistol. It struck home, but to no effect. They reached another door, though this one was closed. Max beat on it and tore his hands to shreds wrestling with its bolt. All the while, trudging footsteps encroached from behind; furniture crashed as it was flung aside. The thing was less than a yard away when the door burst open and Max hauled his wife through.

They were back in the central passage, and the way to the stair was clear. Frantic, they tottered down, but it was steep and narrow, and the treads were loose, and when Brenda's left foot twisted on its slender three-inch heel, she fell screaming, turning over and over, all the way to the bottom.

Stunned by the impact, she still tried to get to her feet, only for pain to lance up from an ankle that now ground like broken glass.

Max had reached the end of the access-passage before he realised with chilling horror that his wife wasn't with him anymore. His initial thought was that only a lunatic would go back and face the abomination he'd glimpsed through the flashes of gunfire. But then he recalled his days in Fighter Command, and those fearless battles over the Channel – and his old warrior spirit was reignited.

Brenda's leg hurt so much that she couldn't crawl along the passage; she had to worm her way, and ungainly as her pursuer was, it didn't take long for it to catch her. It stumped down to the foot of the stairs, turned into the passage and a second later was standing astride her. She flattened herself on the floor, hands clamped over her head. But a moment passed, and when no blade bit down she dared glance up. Even the agony of her ankle faded in the presence of such a moon-lit monstrosity. Once again, she saw a dusty red tunic, a bandolier belt, a row of tarnished silver buttons. But worst of all was that face - oh God, that mildewed canvas face, baggy, shapeless, with sticks and soggy cloth poking out where its eyes and nose should be.

No further screams were possible. All words perished in Brenda's throat.

'You Hun bastard!' came an enraged shout.

Dazed, Brenda looked to her front and saw Max advancing like a swordsman, only instead of a sword he had a fire-poker. It was almost absurd, but the horror stepped over her to meet him, slashing down hard with its sabre.

Max met the stroke full on.

There was a resounding *clang* as the much older sword-blade broke.

Max roared with triumph, and smashed his second blow onto the mitered head, which seemed to implode. And yet the thing remained upright. With one gauntleted claw, it snatched Max by the throat and pushed him back against the wall. Eyes goggling, Max attempted to grapple with it. He never saw his assailant's other claw steal beneath its tunic, and draw out a second blade, this one with the tapered outline of a bayonet.

Brenda tried to speak, but it came out a strangled choke.

She gagged as the bayonet was thrust back and forth, repeatedly puncturing her husband's torso. Max's response was a series of guttural gurgles, followed by a faint slushy sigh - before he slumped down.

Brenda stared dumbly at his crumpled form, but she found her voice again when the monster turned and lurched back towards her. Timorous whimpers rose rapidly into prolonged, hysterical shrieks.

Only after it had passed her by and its footfalls had dwindled up the narrow staircase, did this hysteria dissipate. By the time she heard the upper door being wrestled back into its fractured frame, her cries had become mewling moans, which went on for the rest of that night.

'Can you tell me … is this Adela's room?'

'What's that?' the big man asked.

'Is this the room Lady Adela used?'

The big man scratched his head. 'Don't know anything about that, miss. We keep records of former occupants of course, but I ain't got permission to look 'em up.'

'You know I'm innocent,' she said coyly. 'Innocent as a lamb.'

'Just relax now, miss. It's for the best.'

'How did a harmless creature like that come to commit such deeds?' the smaller man wondered.

The big man, who was the senior of the two orderlies, shrugged. 'Love-triangle, apparently. That sort of stuff's enough to drive anyone potty.'

'Even so, they've been strung up for less.'

'They certainly have,' Brenda tittered from the steel-framed bed in the corner.

'Now then, miss,' the smaller man said, going back over there to check the secure straps that held her down. 'You try to sleep. It's never a good thing to get over-excited.'

'Much less,' she giggled. 'Much, much less.'

SOURCES

All the stories in *Terror Tales of Northwest England* are original to this publication, with the exceptions of *Writer's Cramp* by David A Riley, which first appeared in 'Fantasy Tales 10' (1988), *The Drain* by Stephen Gallagher, which first appeared in 'Fantasy Tales 4' (1990), *Only Sleeping* by Peter Bell, which first appeared in 'Acquainted with the Night' (2004), and *Root Cause* by Ramsey Campbell, which first appeared in 'Night Visions' (1986).

The Upper Tier by Paul Finch is published for the first time here but was originally performed live, narrated by the author in front of an audience at a special ghost story night at Haigh Hall, Wigan, in 2011. (Though many of the geographical and historic details mentioned in the story are accurate, the supernatural elements are entirely fictional).

OTHER TELOS TITLES YOU MAY LIKE

PAUL FINCH

CAPE WRATH AND THE HELLION

Horror Novella

TERROR TALES OF CORNWALL Ed. Paul Finch

RAVEN DANE

THE MISADVENTURES OF CYRUS DARIAN

Steampunk Adventure Series

1: Cyrus Darian And The Technomicron

2: Cyrus Darian And The Ghastly Horde

3: Cyrus Darian And The Wicked Wraith

DEATH'S DARK WINGS

Standalone alternative history novel

ABSINTHE AND ARSENIC

13 Horror and Fantasy Short Story Collection

HELEN MCCABE

THE PIPER TRILOGY

1: Piper

2: The Piercing

3: The Codex

GRAHAM MASTERTON

THE DJINN

THE WELLS OF HELL

RULES OF DUEL (with WILLIAM S BURROUGHS)

THE HELL CANDIDATE

TANITH LEE
BLOOD 20
20 Vampire Stories through the ages

DEATH OF THE DAY
Standalone crime novel

TANITH LEE A-Z
An A-Z collection of Short Fiction by renowned writer Tanith Lee

SIMON CLARK
HUMPTY'S BONES
THE FALL

FREDA WARRINGTON
NIGHTS OF BLOOD WINE
Vampire Horror Short Story Collection

PAUL LEWIS
SMALL GHOSTS
Horror novella

STEPHEN LAWS
SPECTRE

RHYS HUGHES
CAPTAINS STUPENDOUS

DAVID J HOWE
TALESPINNING
Horror Collection of Stories, Novels and more

SOLOMON STRANGE
THE HAUNTING OF GOSPALL

DAWN G HARRIS

DIVINER

SAM STONE

KAT LIGHTFOOT MYSTERIES

Steampunk Adventure Series

1: Zombies At Tiffany's

2: Kat on a Hot Tin Airship

3: What's Dead PussyKat

4: Kat of Green Tentacles

5: Kat and the Pendulum

6: Ten Little Demons

THE COMPLETE LIGHTFOOT

Hardback limited-edition compendium of all Kat Lightfoot books with bonus extras.

THE JINX CHRONICLES

Dark Science Fiction and Fantasy, dystopian future

1: Jinx Town

2: Jinx Magic

3: Jinx Bound

THE VAMPIRE GENE SERIES

Vampire, Historical and Time Travel Series

1: Killing Kiss

2: Futile Flame

3: Demon Dance

4: Hateful Heart

5: Silent Sand

6: Jaded Jewel

ZOMBIES IN NEW YORK AND OTHER BLOODY JOTTINGS

Horror Story Collection